D1010566

OUT OF
THE BLUES

OUT OF THE BLUES

TRUDY NAN BOYCE

G. P. PUTNAM'S SONS
NEW YORK

PUTNAM

G. P. PUTNAM'S SONS
Publishers Since 1838
An imprint of Penguin Random House LLC
375 Hudson Street
New York, New York 10014

Library of Congress Cataloging-in-Publication Data

Boyce, Trudy Nan.
Out of the blues / Trudy Nan Boyce.
  p.   cm.
ISBN 978-0-399-16726-3
I. Title.
PS3602.O927O77   2016   2015015991
813'.6—dc23

Printed in the United States of America
1   3   5   7   9   10   8   6   4   2

BOOK DESIGN BY MEIGHAN CAVANAUGH

For my father, Reverend James H. Boyce

And the days keeps on worryin' me,
there's a hellhound on my trail,
Hellhound on my trail.

—Robert Johnson

OUT OF
THE BLUES

UNCOVERING

The girl climbed the tree so she could sit in her spot, look out through the limbs and leaves, and pretend about an imaginary dog. When she patted the pecan leaves, they gave off a green, peppery smell. It was like breathing the breath of the tree. The jaggedy streaks of gray bark where she sat were like the tree's hard fur.

Wearing conspiratorial smiles, her mother and brother had waved from the car windows, knowing that she had been headed to the tree as they started out the long driveway around the house. Later she realized, when she saw the note on the table, that he must have thought she'd gone with them, because it wasn't long after the dust from the car settled that the gunshot sounded from the house and she dropped from the tree, forgetting almost forever the longed-for dog.

Frantic, she couldn't think how to clear his eyes of the blood. She couldn't leave him to get a cloth. Her shirt? She used her fingers to try to wipe the sticky globs from her father's eyes. His head in her lap, she cried for him to help her know what to do. He was a cop. He should know how to handle this emergency. The gun, black and heavy, lay next to the *dusty-rose bed skirt. She thought if he could somehow just see, he'd be able to help her, but he quit moving, his groans stopped, and she held his head, blood seeping through her red shorts and into the ruby dahlias and violet peonies embroidered in the rug.*

And then their return. Their faces as they held the balloons at the door of the room. Their fallen faces. And the note left beside the cake for her tenth birthday.

NO ONE in her family ever claimed to know where the old steamer trunk had come from. The trunk had been painted over in a flat country blue that had faded to gray, the original color revealed beneath the leather clasps that were now brittle, one completely worn through. Smudged and blurred, some brushstrokes had come through the top layer of paint, "ST . . . ," but the rest was faded. She'd moved the trunk out of the upstairs closet when the carpenters were doing renovations and had been using it as a nightstand beside the downstairs bedroom window. Sometimes thinking right before she fell asleep that she would get around to opening it, she'd go over the items she remembered might still be in it.

Removing the lamp and embroidered runner and letting the metal lock fall, she was eager about the coat. Beneath some quilts and baby clothes it was there in its original Rich's box, wrapped in fragile, yellowing tissue. The Atlanta department store had been gone a long time, bought out by Macy's, but the coat still had the tag attached to the sleeve with thread.

Looking at herself in the age-flecked floor mirror, Sarah Alt thought that even though she wasn't as tall as her dad, it was still a good fit. Twenty-five years after it was purchased, the tan trench coat now fit her, falling to calf length on her slim five-foot-nine frame— her father's coat, one he'd never worn.

WELCOME TO HOMICIDE

Known throughout the department as "Rosie," the large man in transition with red-polished nails and long, blond, waved hair and wearing a ruffled white blouse sat at the receptionist's desk and buzzed her in. "The code is number 1524," she said without looking up from the paperback she was reading.

"Thanks." Salt held her father's coat as she punched the numbers on the keypad and turned the handle of the inner door to the Homicide Unit.

Rosie mumbled, "Keep your chin up."

During the ten years Salt had been in uniform, a beat cop, she'd been to the Unit many times, making statements as the first uniform on murder and assault scenes, providing information from the streets to detectives. But this, *this* was her first day, first shift as a newly sworn detective. A shiny gold-tone badge clipped to the belt on her slacks had replaced her old silver-finish shield, the one she'd worn for ten years of uniform patrol, most of them spent in The Homes, the most densely populated housing project in Atlanta. She'd worked there so long that it had felt at times more like home than her own. Now she heard talk that the city was making plans to tear down all the projects, including The Homes.

Two detectives, one white, one black, both on the small end of medium in height, wearing short-sleeved shirts and bright ties, were standing at the front cubicles in the rows of workspaces. "Well, well, well," exclaimed the black guy she knew as Daniels. "Lookee what the dog done dragged in."

"Yes in-deed-dee," the other guy said. "Got us a brand-new big-city detective."

"I got your big city," she shifted the coat to shake hands. "They told me to report to Sergeant Huff."

There were caricatures of the Three Stooges on Daniels' tie and Barney Fife's face on the other guy's. "He's around here somewhere." Daniels motioned toward the back of the big office space.

"I think I saw him go in the break room," said the guy with the Barney tie, pointing to the back right.

The Homicide room was huge and smelled of burned coffee and mildewed paper. Thirty or so gray cubicles filled the center space, less than a quarter occupied most of the time; only the detectives from the on-duty shift were working, and some of them were taking their weekend days off or were out in the streets. The walls were lined with supervisors' offices, interview rooms, and rows of five-drawer file cabinets in mismatched grays, tan, and military-green colors. Salt wound her way through the aisles past the attached desks stacked with murder books and decorated with personal touches: framed photos, patriotic posters, military memorabilia, and action heroes. She walked past Wills' desk, noting with a smile the "Dog Is My Copilot" bumper sticker on his file bin and photos of Violet and Pansy, his Rottweilers. She and Bernard Wills had begun a relationship the year before, and while he'd encouraged her to test for detective, neither of them had anticipated working the same unit, or "squad," as Homicide was called, much less the same shift. Wills' partner, Gardner, ever optimistic, ever ready with a look-on-the-bright-side comment, had the cubicle across from his. A photo of his garden hung on the gray-fabric cubicle wall.

She found Sergeant Huff, whom she knew from having talked to him on a couple of cases, in the unfortunately bright break room peering into a humming microwave. She whisked her fingers through her dark hair, which she wore short with a messy part on the left, a part made permanent by a bullet scar through her scalp.

"Sergeant Huff," she announced herself.

The microwave pinged and the heavyset sergeant took out a plastic bowl with a blue lid. "You're taller in clothes." He sat down at one of the metal and veneer tables and took a plastic spoon from his shirt pocket.

"Yes, sir, five nine in shoes." She pulled at her new cream-colored linen jacket and navy slacks. "In case . . ." Her voice trailed off as she realized she was standing at attention like she was back at roll call in the precinct. She tried to cover by slumping.

"My goddamn wife is starving me here. I'm forty-five years old and she's feeding me New Age hippie mush."

"I called Lieutenant Pierce yesterday to ask about my assignment and he told me to report to you today at four p.m." Salt sat down at the table, draping the coat across her lap.

Head lowered to the bowl, Huff shoveled the food into his mouth with the little spoon as he talked. "Doctor says I've got to lower my cholesterol, lose weight, quit smoking, 'limit my alcohol intake'"—he made air quotes—"reduce stress, exercise." His close-cut brown hair had receded to the middle of his scalp. The bowl held something that looked like beef stew but with no aroma. "So the missus," shovel, "packed my lunch bag with an apple, which I ate on my way to work thirty minutes ago, and this fuckin' tofu stew," shovel, shovel. He tossed the spoon into the empty bowl—it hopped. "I just finished my lunch and I got eight hours left in the shift. Now that's stress."

"Sarge . . ." began Salt.

"'Sarge,' don't call me Sarge. I hate being called Sarge. Sounds like some fuckin' war movie. Call me Huff or Charlie or Shithead but don't call me Sarge. Nobody calls me Sarge." His belly popped from behind a large Harley-Davidson belt buckle as he pushed back from the table.

"Hey, Sarge." Daniels stuck his head in the door. "We got incoming."

Sergeant Huff leaned back, belched loudly, then stood and threw his plastic bowl into the sink. "I'll show you your desk. You'll get the same one as the only other woman who ever worked Homicide nights in this city." He led her through the cubicle farm. "She worked kids' murders, something wrong with her head. She was nuts, totally, but for some reason they let her stay till she retired. She only got one or two cases a year. Went out on all the dead babies."

"Sar—" Salt stopped at a barren desk across from one festooned with a rainbow flag and a purple flag. "Can I have this desk?" She pointed to the empty spot.

"If you're thinking you might want to partner with Felton, our gay caballero there"—he pointed to a photo of two men in a frame on the desk with the flags—"forget it. Every man here wants him, as a detective partner, that is. You probably already heard he's the best homicide dick in the city, state, and a contender for best in the nation, maybe the world. But he won't partner."

"Can I have the desk?"

"No."

At a cubicle far from the entrance and far from the center of the room, Huff stopped and unclipped the radio from his belt. "Go ahead for Homicide," he spoke into the handheld.

"Zone Three is requesting Homicide to 441 Brown Avenue on a body found in a warehouse." Homicide dispatch sounded less urgent than Salt was used to from the beat dispatches.

Salt positioned herself in the sarge's sight and pointed to herself, requesting "Me?"

Sarge shook his head at her. "Homicide units 4125 and 4126 will be responding," he advised dispatch. "Daniels, Barney," he shouted across the room. Turned out the guy with the Barney Fife tie was named Barney.

"4125 and -26 copy," the detectives acknowledged the call.

Daniels' and Barney's heads bobbed across the tops of the cubicles as they walked toward the door.

"This was the chick's desk," Huff said. "Now it's yours."

Other than the desk, a stained chair, and an old tower PC and monitor, the workspace was empty, except for a manila file lying on the desk. Huff picked up the file. "This is also yours. Wasn't a murder and now it might be. You'll start with that. Welcome to Homicide." He dropped the file on the desk, turned his back to her, and walked away.

Before she could hang up her coat, fat fingers were on her wrist, soft, strong, and insistent. Salt turned as Detective Hamm from day watch grabbed her and began pulling her toward the exit. "You're coming with me. We've got another one."

"But Sar . . . Huff said—"

"Fuck Sarge. My regular partner is off today, so I get to pick. Even if he was here, I'd make sure you went with us. These guys are going to put you through the wringer, but I'm going to give you some starch first."

Salt followed the lumbering detective, whose wide buttocks shifted and quivered up and down and side to side, to the elevators.

"How's the head?" Hamm asked as she hit the call button. Hamm and her partner, who matched her in girth, had been the responding investigators to the incident last year when Salt had been shot. Charissa Hamm was the only woman, until today, currently working Homicide, also known as the Hat Squad. Hamm worked days. Salt, as a rookie detective, would work nights, four p.m. to midnight, but often the three shifts worked scenes together if a case was close to one of the shift changes or was a "red ball," as the high-profile cases were known. An Atlanta native, Hamm had solid ties to her black working-class community, church, and high school friends—connections that had proved helpful to her both in her career and in solving cases.

"Fuck." Hamm cursed the malfunctioning elevators and headed to the stairwell. Then the elevator pinged and the overhead panel lit up. They turned back but the elevator doors didn't open and it scrolled up to the next floor. "Double fuck." She slapped the wall beside the call button. "Your head?" Hamm repeated, her voice competing with their footsteps echoing in the concrete and steel stairwell, each floor marked with conflicting floor numbers, the "4" in red and "5" in black on the same door.

"Better," answered Salt, lifting a lock of hair that covered the scar that began at her hairline.

THE NEIGHBORHOOD was a mixture of middle-class homes, a few houses falling to lower-middle, and seventies-built apartment complexes, some designated as government assists. A dog barked continuously, its howling seeming to come from differing directions. The residences backed onto a wooded area, bisected by a ravine that was owned by the city's watershed management. Salt cocked her ear, listening to the dog.

"And the chick detectives aren't ever fat." Hamm was sitting in the driver's seat, legs out the open door, pulling on old-fashioned rubbers over black loafers that were sprung at the sides, her brown, wide foot overrunning the leather. She zipped up a gear bag, tossed it in the backseat, and grabbed the Handie-Talkie off the console. "Fuckin' TV makes juries expect a detective to look like—well, like you, Blue Eyes. You're gonna ruin those new shoes." She tipped her head toward Salt's spotless navy athletic shoes.

"I bought a couple of pairs in different colors. They can be thrown in the washer," Salt said.

"Smart girl. Just the same, get a pair of these." Hamm pointed to the overshoes. "They're cheap and will save having to clean shit, piss, and other body fluids off your shoes."

"I love it. Just us girls talking about shoes," Salt said as they walked toward the crime scene.

They followed the uniform who'd told them that the body, that of a young boy, was in the nearby ravine. Spring rains had come almost daily and made the ground soft and covered with dark, steaming layers of composting leaves and newly green tangles of briars and vines.

"Careful," warned the officer as he led them to a part of the gully where the decline was less treacherous. In spite of her heft, Hamm's step was sure as she gracefully navigated the roots and muck going down the bank. Once on the bottom they could see north up the ravine to where other uniforms had begun to string the yellow tape, marking off the scene at the tops of the banks and on both sides. People, including more than a few children, were starting to gather along the tape on the side where the woods met the backyards. A dirty blanket had been hoisted between two trees as a makeshift curtain so the spectators could not see the body.

Uniform supervisors and the rest of the two shifts from Homicide began arriving. Salt spotted Sergeant Huff and the crime scene techs. More people milled behind the tape. "Where's my baby?" One woman ran from the group as word spread that it was the body of a child. Another uniform stood to one side with an elderly can man and his industrial-sized plastic bags of recyclables. "Grunge found the victim and started yelling," said the first officer, nodding at the old man.

Salt and Hamm stood at the blanket, which smelled of old garbage. The dog's barking kept up, coming from somewhere north of them. "Ivory need to shut up," someone said from above. Overhead, the limbs of a massive pecan tree spread up and out, shading thirty yards in both directions. The ravine bed was dark with past years' slough and brackish puddles. The banks became increasingly dry closer to the top and were covered with tiny green sprigs, the fallen flowers of pollen from the big tree overhead. The woman who was looking for her child screamed from the street, "I can't find him. Help me, somebody!"

"This is going to get bad. I'm going to go set up a command post in the parking lot," Huff said, and pointed above. Hamm nodded and went around the blanket. "I want you to come with me," he told Salt, "but go take a look first." He nodded to the other side of the blanket. The dog's bark was more insistent. Salt's shoe made a sucking sound as she turned.

The light-skinned boy was facedown on his right cheek, hunched with his buttocks bare, tan shorts around his calves. His hands were positioned as if he were going to push up. Except for some rust-colored smears on his backside, there was no obvious trauma. "You didn't have to see this," Hamm said in a low voice, not looking up from her note taking.

"I know." Salt left her and followed Huff up and out of the ravine. "Merrily We Roll Along" played over and over from an ice cream truck's plinky speaker. The sun shone through the canopy of mostly water oaks, their small leaves whirl-a-jigging in the bright breeze. Huff assigned the six investigators and five uniforms to a grid search for evidence and witnesses. They were to interview anyone and everyone and make notes.

No one had to say it, but the Atlanta Child Murders were on everyone's mind. From 1979 to 1981 more than twenty black boys and girls were killed, and their deaths still haunted the city, especially the APD. Atlanta had been forced into a conversation about race then while the city's police tried to avoid distraction from the work. They finally broke the case when Wayne Williams, a young black man, was arrested. He had lured the children with the promise of a music audition. Even though the murders had stopped after he was arrested, and physical evidence solidified his guilt, some people weren't convinced the murderers hadn't been the KKK or other racist crazies.

Salt was assigned to search the ravine north of the scene. The leather shoulder holster crisscrossed her new shirt—she'd left her jacket in the car and hadn't thought to remind anyone that she'd not been issued a Handie-Talkie with a detective frequency. She began her part of the search, looking back once to see Hamm kneeling next to the dead child. She realized that she'd been assigned an area where she'd be least likely to encounter any witnesses or evidence, but it felt right to her to head in the direction of the barking that had been distracting her since their arrival. Reminding herself to stay focused on the terrain, to look for anything that could be significant, even if it just looked like trash or newly turned leaves, she slowed her quickened step toward the dog, his bark becoming raspy.

The murdered children had begun turning up right after her father died. Scared, she'd gotten the idea that the children wouldn't have been killed if he'd still been alive and on the job. Her brother, who was only seven at the time, talked about the murders constantly and wouldn't go to sleep in his own bed.

She came to a place where the ravine rim was about eight feet above and found freshly turned marks in the red clay bank. The dog's barks were closer and coming from directly above. Pulling herself up by tree roots, she climbed out into a backyard Bible grotto. There were home-made signs everywhere warning of the coming Rapture, of hellfire, of the opportunity for salvation and predictions of doom. A white dog barked at the bottom of wooden steps that led to the back of a house. He turned his head, almost as if he were expecting her, wondering what took her so long, then turned back to bark at a screen door at the top of the steps. He was a large dog, uncommonly clean, more cream than white, some shepherd mix with a plumy tail held high.

"Ivory," she called, remembering the comment from the crowd. A doll's head was nailed to a tree trunk on her right. "Truly I tell you, whatever you did for one of the least of these brothers and sisters of mine, you did for me" read a framed hand-lettered message, dangling from a tree limb by a sash.

"Here, Ivory."

The dog barked up the steps.

At a bricked-off blueberry bush there was a stake in the form of a cross, draped with a necklace of baby pacifiers. "Jesus wept" was painted in red on a flat stone. The sides of the yard were enclosed by pines bent inward, heavy with kudzu so thick the sounds from the neighborhood were muffled, almost shut out.

"Ivory." She lowered her voice.

Through more signs, some hanging from tree branches, there was a path of sorts, bordered by toy parts, broken trucks, pieces of balls, plastic blocks, a pink doll's bed.

Ivory held his tail high, his front paws on the second step. The back of the house had been covered with chicken wire through which had been braided what looked like old clothes. It gave the appearance of quilting. Ivory was well groomed, his coat smooth and lush, but his tail had picked up some catkins that clung to the long, feathery fur. She approached him, patting her leg, which he sniffed, and he ceased barking. He allowed her to rub his ears and pat down his back. She was careful at his tail, pulling at one of the sprigs caught in his fur, examining it in the palm of her hand.

The door above opened. An elderly man wearing a brown pin-striped suit and red tie stood holding a worn Bible. He began to laugh. He was small and stiff in his composure, his skin the same color as his suit. He bent to his knees laughing, and as he did, an enormous presence came from behind him, rushing past and launching from the porch toward Salt.

She managed a break fall onto her back and tried to use the momentum to continue into a backward roll, but it was all she could do to get her knees between herself and the huge man before he was on her, one of his hands at her throat and the other clawing toward the gun beneath her arm. She became aware of the sound of her own breath and his heavy grunt, both amplified and muffled like the roar from inside a seashell. One of his exhalations filled her nose and mouth with the taste and smell of sour milk. She felt the thick cotton threads of his shirt fabric as she grabbed his collar for leverage. She pushed the soles of her feet against his stomach, pulling his chest down and pushing up, and used his weight to propel him over and away as she rolled up into a ready combat stance.

"Fuck," she said when she realized that on her first day as a detective she'd made a mistake worse than the stupidest rookie. She'd failed to check out a radio. "Call 911," she implored the old man, while she tried to catch a breath and crouched in anticipation of the man now rising from the ground. If she'd just told Hamm to wait for her to grab a radio, she could be calling for help. She scanned the yard and sides of the house for a way out as he got up, his eyes searching the sky, unfocused like he was blind, yet he aimed himself at her. The dog was quiet now, but the old man threw back his head and either laughed or howled as she sidestepped and her assailant stumbled past, turned, and rushed her again. Salt pivoted, looking for some advantage as the big man came at her. But her left foot caught on Christmas lights strung at knee level between two bushes. Before she could untangle, he wrapped his meaty arms around her shoulders and chest and was falling to the ground on top of her. As they accelerated downward, the man drew back the fist of his other hand while she fumbled to get ahold of the fat fingers holding her neck. The blow glanced off her left cheek just as she turned her head and leveraged her weight against his fingers and wrist. He grunted and tried to jerk away at an angle that caused him even more pain. She swiveled from under him and into another ready stance.

There was no exit she could see and she was backed against the rim of the ravine, breathing hard, balancing each foot as she moved backward and closer to the edge. If she pulled her weapon she knew he'd go for it, and then she'd have to use it or he'd take it. He ran at her, and at the last instant, when he towered over her, his sweat flying into her eyes, she reached out and pulled his arm straight and used it as a fulcrum to throw him over and into the ravine below. Momentum took her with him in as controlled a fall as she could manage, knowing that if she was lucky and quick, she'd have half a chance. As they dropped she pulled at the cuff pouch on her left shoulder strap. Air whooshed from his lungs as they thudded onto the ground. Her fingers found the bracelets as she landed on his back, and before he could inhale she had one cuff around his right wrist. Using the cuff against his wrist bone for pain compliance, she jerked his forearm, bent it back, and snapped the second cuff around his other wrist.

She rolled off him, sat up, and looked at the rim of the bank some eight feet above where the old man, laughing still, stood beside the dog. She touched her stinging cheek with a dirt-streaked hand. Her new pants were torn at one knee, the linen shirt gaped where the buttons had been torn off, but she wasn't bleeding. She couldn't see any bloody injury on her assailant, who was rapidly gaining consciousness. She pulled him to a sitting position. His head was shaved to stubble, his face round, pink, and greasy with oily sweat. He had on matching workmen's tan shirt and pants, new-looking and freshly dirtied from their fight. And there were smears of some unidentifiable substance on the front around his zipper.

"Alone," he said breathless. "Why they send you alone?"

"What's your name?" She stood up, trying to control her now trembling arms and legs.

"I am The Baby, Jesus."

She pushed at his back and pulled him to standing. "What's his name?" She yelled to the man above, who only put his hand to his waist, now bent with maniacal laughter that echoed down the bank.

THE MAN sang Stevie Wonder's "Ebony and Ivory" as they walked back down the ravine. He insisted he be identified as "The Baby, Jesus," not "Baby Jesus" or "The Baby Jesus" but—and he was adamant—it was "The Baby, Jesus." Fine, Salt just needed his compliance as they trudged to the scene. "Ivory white like me," he substituted some of the lyrics. His accent was stone black projects, missing verbs and mangling tenses. "You should shoot me."

She didn't want to expose TBJ to the crowd and therefore wanted to bring him out north of the scene. When she could see the light color of the blanket curtain in the distance, she veered toward the ravine bank. It was rough going to get the large handcuffed man enough momentum to reach the random footholds. "Left foot," she said pointing to an exposed root and hefting his arm as he planted his boot. At the top the crowd was thirty yards or so south of where she brought him out, and they weren't noticed. But they'd come up and

out in the common area of the apartments where the command post
had now been established.

It shouldn't have come as a surprise, given the city's still painful
memories of the Child Murders, that quite a few city politicians and
the chief of the department would, along with most of his command
staff, converge on the scene, if only to assure the media and community that every resource would be made available to find the culprit.
So it was just as the chief exited his car, camera people on his heels
getting footage for the evening news, that Salt, abraded and covered
in filth, emerged with The Baby, Jesus from between two apartment
buildings. "Who's this, Salt?" Chief asked. When he'd come to her
hospital room last year after she'd been shot, he'd already known her
street name, a contraction of Sarah Alt as it appeared on her first uniform name tag, "S.Alt."

"The Baby, Jesus," answered the suspect for himself.

"Of course, Baby, I thought that was you." The chief raised his
eyebrows at her.

"You need any assistance?" He turned to his driver and motioned
for him to attend to Salt.

"Sorry, sir," she said. "This is my first day in Homicide and I
hadn't gotten a radio yet. If you could ask someone to radio for Sergeant Huff, I believe The Baby, Jesus is our suspect."

"Yes, I killed, murdered, homicided that baby boy there in the
gully in the ditch. I choked and crushed the baby right out of his air."

"Shit," said the chief.

"Film at six," said some wiseass from the media scrum as they
turned in unison and ran toward their trucks.

"I HAD TO look it up, too," she told them. "They're called 'catkins,'
those little dangles that fall from the pecan trees. It's why some people

don't want pecan trees—they're messy in spring. I have pecan trees at my place, so I noticed. The tree where the boy was found was the only pecan along the ravine."

"Catkins in the dog's tail," repeated Huff.

"But why did you go to that house?" Hamm asked. "Not that I'm in any way complaining. Thank you, Rookie Detective, for clearing this certain-it-was-going-to-be-a-red-ball-on-my-head case, not to mention he'd probably be a serial kind of guy as well."

"The dog," Salt said. "The dog kept barking. I heard someone in the crowd say, 'What's Ivory barking at?'"

"Did you go in the house?"

"No, Sar—sir. He came out after me."

"We tried to interview the old man who lives there," Hamm said. "He's way, way off his rocker and supposed to be monitored by some home health-care company. I think the house is a group home."

"Well, I don't know how you're going to write this up. Don't get me wrong, I'm as relieved as Hamm to have this guy in the Gray Bar, but we're counting on those blood smears on his pants to come back a match for the kid, 'cause flowers in a mutt's fur ain't exactly what juries expect in these days of 'Atlanta CSI.'" He made air quotes again and tipped his chair forward. "Thank God for his spontaneous admission to the chief, crazy as that was." He shook his head and stood. "I leave the articulation to you ladies." He tapped the thickening blue file on the conference room table and left the room.

"You're a mess." Hamm smiled at her. "A fine mess, and I need to get some photos of you before you even wash your face." She used her Handie-Talkie to call for a tech to take the photos. "But while we wait, Salt, here's some more advice you didn't ask for. You and I work different shifts, so I can't help you much. You might hope this gets you off on the right foot here, solving this case on your first day."

"I don't—"

"Let me finish. It won't. These guys are all all right, but they, most of them, have been burned by the Homicide fires too many times to appreciate any gift horse. You get what I'm saying?"

"All I did—"

"Salt, I don't care. They don't care. They'll be lookin' all up in your mouth and hoping that the next dog you hear barkin' will be at a wrong tree. They want you burned and scarred, tattooed and branded to their brotherhood. Do not be talking about how you knew how to find this guy by the burrs in a barking dog's tail." Hamm lowered her head. "And, I'm sorry. I didn't check to find out if you'd had time to get a radio. My bad. And yours. You got to stand up for yourself, even with me. And thanks for being stand-up and not mentioning it."

SALT HUNG her father's coat on a plastic peg beside the desk and sat down in the chair, which dropped suddenly to one side due to a missing wheel. She opened the gray metal bin above the desk and the drawers below, all empty except for some brittle rubber bands and bent paper clips. She picked up the thin file labeled "Michael Richard Anderson—861430587," her first assigned case. Other than the autopsy report, which listed the cause and manner of death as "Accidental drug overdose," the initial uniform reporting form, a short investigative report by the responding detective, and an envelope of scene photos, there wasn't much to the file except for the new information that had prompted the follow-up Huff was assigning to her. The recent documents were first in the file and described the circumstances under which a new statement had been obtained from Curtis Dwayne Stone, who was doing time in federal custody. Salt looked up from the document and said the name out loud, "Stone." She'd left The Homes, but it seemed The Homes would not leave her. She had been the one who'd arrested Curtis Stone.

Under federal sentencing guidelines, those convicted of federal crimes were eligible to have their time reduced if they gave reliable information about other criminals and crimes.

"So, my man Stone, you're snitching now," she said, turning to the next document, Stone's signed statement.

She pushed a switch over the cubicle desk and a fluorescent light flickered across the transcribed pages.

> Q: *For the record, my name is Lawrence Jones, Special Agent with the Federal Bureau of Investigation. I am recording this interview. Please state your name.*
>
> A: Stone.
>
> Q: *Curtis Dwayne Stone?*

Salt lifted her gaze from the page, closing her eyes, her memory reigniting the odor of gunpowder, replaying the bleating of a sheep. Stone had been The Homes gang member who was feared most. In her rookie days she'd witnessed the destitution of his childhood, and then it seemed he had determined it would be better for her to fear rather than pity him. Over the years he'd found opportunities to try to threaten her—finally last year assaulting her in her home. "Stone," she said, and returned to the page.

> Q: *Do you have knowledge of illegal drug sales, prostitution, and child exploitation by the individual who owned Sam's Chicken Shack and a strip club, Toy Dolls?*

A: I don't know about no child exploitation, but, yeah, I know about drugs and hoes.

Q: *Mr. Stone, please describe what you know. What is the name of the man who you knew to be running those businesses?*

A: John.

Q: *Last name?*

A: That's all his name I know. They call him "Tall John." I can't remember if I heard any other name he was called.

Q: *Please describe the man you know as John.*

A: White, tall.

Q: *Any marks or scars?*

A: He look just like anybody.

Q: *How did you come to know John?*

A: I was hungry. He got me in back of Sam's trying to get some bags of peanuts off a truck.

Q: *How old were you then?*

A: I guess about twelve.

It would have been right around the time she'd first encountered him, when she was a rookie. Christmas, him in his thin sweatshirt, his shoulders like the unfolding wings of a vulture. She'd tried to find his guardian instead of taking him to Juvenile and found only a dreadful, sad apartment where he and other children were neglected. Salt pressed the length of her palm to the scar.

Q: *Who did you live with?*

A: I stayed with lots of people.

Q: *What did he do when he caught you?*

A: He said I had to work to pay for stealing.

Q: *What kind of work did you do for John?*

A: Work around the bars.

Q: *Did you go to school?*

A: Sometimes.

Q: *What work did John have you doing?*

A: Whatever he tell me to do.

Q: *What did he tell you to do?*

A: Clean the bathrooms, sweep, pick up trash.

Q: *What else?*

A: Go with men.

Q: *Do you mean you had sex with men for money?*

A: I didn't have no sex with them.

Q: *What did you do when you went with the men?*

A: They gave me blowjobs.

Q: *Are you saying that they performed oral sex on you?*

A: Yeah.

Q: *Did you do oral sex on them?*

A: If I had to.

Q: *What about anal sex?*

A: What about it?

Q: *Did John send you with men that wanted anal sex?*

A: I'm not that way.

Q: *Did some men put their penis in your anus when you were twelve years old?*

A: Yeah.

Salt looked away from the file again, stood, and strode to the back wall that was lined with file cabinets labeled by year. "Damn." She drew a breath, looked down the long wall of file cabinets, then turned back to the flickering cubicle.

Q: *Did John have other people who exchanged sex for money?*

A: He had hoes, some of the dancers.

Q: *How long did you work for John?*

A: Until Man let me stay with him.

Q: *By Man you mean James Simmons?*

A: Yeah, he hid me from John. He looked out for me and had his boys look out if John came around.

In The Homes the gang was headed by charismatic, handsome Man and included his brother and others, mostly young men who'd grown up together in The Homes. Some were now dead and some, like Stone, were in prison, put there by her. Man had always kept a safe distance from direct contact with the drugs and guns. Man, with his wide smile, and Lil D, with a birthmark the shape of a continent on his neck. Lil D, whose mother's murder had, in part, led to Salt's assignment to Homicide.

Q: *Did John sell drugs?*

A: Yes.

Q: *Did you see drugs?*

A: Yes. He the head junk man in this city then.

Q: *By junk you mean heroin?*

A: Yeah, H.

Q: *Do you know if he still deals?*

A: Word that he don't have no direct connection after them
Black Mafia brothers moved in. But back then he deal some
H. He still run hoes, but he big money now, runnin'
high-dolla bitches out his clubs.

Q: *What other businesses is he involved with?*

A: Now he got dealing with Sam's and the Blue Room, Magic
Girls, and maybe some white club somewhere.

Q: *What do you know about the death of Mike Anderson, the singer
and guitar player?*

A: I know Tall John give that blues boy a hot pop.

Q: *How do you know that?*

A: 'Cause he told me. He said that's what he do when people that
work for him don't do what he say.

Q: *Did you see him give heroin to Mike Anderson? How did he
know Mike?*

A: That blues boy worked in one of the clubs, singing and
playing the guitar. Got his H that way. I didn't ever see John

changing junk for cash personally. Just saw the product in his office.

Q: *When was the last time you had contact with or saw John?*

A: Right before I was locked up last year. He pass by me all the time in the street.

Q: *You said you hid from him.*

A: Not after I got grown.

Q: *Is there anything more you can tell me about illegal activity?*

A: That's all I've got to say.

Before closing the file, she turned to the back and Stone's booking photo. In The Homes the faces of young men grew hard and sharp, calcified, their bones fixed like knives, a fearful hardening with things you could never know, things they didn't even tell themselves. The scowly surfaces glistening in sunlight or streetlight. No bit of softness.

Salt closed the file, stood, and put on the coat over her torn clothes.

HEAD LOWERED to the phone that he held in his left hand, Huff raised his eyes when Salt appeared in his office doorway. "Yes, I realize the pressure you must be facing, Councilwoman," he said, swiping his free hand over his scalp and rolling his eyes up toward the ceiling.

"The press has been all over us, too." He leaned his head back on his shoulders and closed his eyes, listening. "Detective Wills *is* one of our best . . .

"No, we are certain this case is not related to the Solquist murders. I realize they were your constituents . . .

"Of course the neighborhood is upset. When a crime like this occurs, everyone wants to know it was not random . . .

"No, we don't give out the detectives' phone numbers to anyone. The chief is your best bet." He held the handset away from his ear as an indistinguishable but loud woman's voice emanated from the earpiece. He put the phone back to his ear. "I probably will enjoy walking a beat again."

Huff spoke to the loudly buzzing dial tone, "Thank you, Councilwoman Mars," dropped the phone into its cradle, and looked up at Salt while slamming a desk drawer shut. The room smelled suspiciously of microwave popcorn. "Now, what can I do for you? I just love me some women in my business." Most of the files stacked on his desk were bright green, while purple, blue, and yellow ones were piled on the floor, cabinets, and chair. There was no place to sit.

"I guess you finished reading the file? You cold?" He pointed at her coat.

"You gave me a very cold case." She stood in the doorway.

"You arrested Stone. You know The Homes. Your reputation preceded you, and around here no good deed goes unpunished." Huff grinned.

"The limitations of any statute that could apply are up on everything but murder, so the feds don't care about the rest, the child prostitution, the drugs?"

"You got it. They took the statement and handed it to us. They got bigger fish to fry."

"Did anyone even bother to find out who 'John' is?"

"The Shack is owned by an LLC—I don't remember what name, but if you find the company it's not likely you'll find John's name on the license. That's why they now call you detective, Detective."

"You also know Stone tried to kill me."

"And now you'll be helping him by verifying the information he gave in the statement. You're right. None of the accusations, except the murder, mean anything."

"How much of his time will get cut if I can corroborate his information?"

"Oh, about the amount he'd do for assaulting a police officer. Interesting dilemma. I like a sense of humor in a detective."

"Which of the other comedians will I be working with?"

Huff stood up and stretched with his hands on his lower back. "You mean for a partner? Let's see how you do alone first. Think of it as another chance to prove yourself. See if that dog luck holds."

Salt turned from the door just as a previously teetering stack of green files on his desk began a slow-motion slide to the floor.

As Salt came out, Rosie hung up the phone, the paperback she'd been reading spread facedown on the desk. The cover illustration depicted a bare-chested man with flowing blond hair clutching a buxom brunette.

Salt pointed to the book. "Good read?"

Rosie swept her hair to one side of her heavily made-up face—pancake foundation, blue eye shadow, red, glossy lipstick. "I'm a romantic. What can I say?" Rosie, legally Roger Polk, had claimed her new name and transgender status two years previously, and was in the process—counseling, hormones—of completing the transition.

"I think I'm going to need some help," Salt told her. "My computer isn't hooked up. I don't know where the supplies and forms are kept. Apparently Sarge wants me to learn the ropes on my own."

Rosie leaned back in the chair, eyes resting on the book, sighed, then waved an imaginary wand. "Actually, feng shui is my specialty. Just leave it to me. Did they give you Rita's desk? I thought so. By tomorrow it will be like a fairy godfather-soon-to-be-mother has come to your rescue. Oh, and don't mind Sarge; by the way, don't call him Sarge. He's just a sweetie. I have such a crush on him. Well, that's another story. You just go do your girl detective thing. And I'm sure you get this all the time, but you have the most unusual blue eyes. I love what you're doing with your hair."

Salt made a note to herself to cut some of the flowers that grew close to the sheep paddock. She was almost certain Rosie would love the big pink camellias.

HANDCUFFED and ankle-shackled, Stone shuffled into view on the other side of the heavy clear-plastic partition. The red jumpsuit, the prison uniform that signifies the wearer is mentally ill, hung loosely on his frame. His hair, intricately done in cornrows, formed a galaxy pattern. He sat down and propped his manacled arms on the steel counter. In the center of the partition was a five-by-five-inch square stippled with nail-sized holes. The air smelled of iron, of flesh-piercing slivers, of tears in the universe.

Stone kept his head turned to the graffiti scratched into the paint on the side wall of their divided booth.

"I've read the statement you gave to the FBI agent."

Stone continued his perusal of the scratchings.

"If I can find somebody else who knows that John meant to kill the bluesman, and if your information leads me to an arrest, you're eligible to get your time cut."

"Ain't no 'eligible' about it," he replied. His voice sounded strangled. "So what you got to do with what I'm telling the FBI guy?" Before she could answer, he turned and faced her. She'd thought it was because of the barrier that separated them that his voice sounded different, but it wasn't the Plexiglas or the holes. His mouth had a caved-in look and was ringed with teeth-sized scars. His lips folded inward until he opened his mouth as wide as seemed possible, showing off his teeth, all of which were gone or broken off. He turned his loose lips up in a horrible grin, then flapped them together, making a wet, smacking sound. The shouts of men accompanied by the sounds of metal striking metal came from the hallway behind Stone.

"I've been assigned to investigate the death of Mike Anderson, the bluesman."

Stone went back to examining the wall hieroglyphics. He brought up his shackled hands to touch a finger to a piece of a word. His eyes slid to her in a sideways stare. "That's funny. You end up workin' to get me free."

"You are the second person to see humor in this," Salt told him, "but the first wasn't me."

There was a sudden moldy refrigerant odor, and the close air turned quickly cold.

"So the white bitch cop put me in here now gonna help get me out." He made a click with his cheek.

"It's been given to me. It's my job." Her hand rested on the shield at her waist.

"Oh, and I do know you do your job," he said, then seemed to draw back, realizing what he said and what it might mean for him.

Salt forced herself to lean forward, close to the dirty hard plastic. "There's that," she said, "and also that I may be able to arrest John."

"How you gonna prove what happened ten years ago?" Stone's voice growled from his battered mouth.

"I don't know. That's why I'm here, to ask you."

"All I know is what John tell me. He said he gave the bluesman bad junk 'cause he tried to get out of a deal. I thought it was about singing and playing in the club." Stone brought up his clenched, manacled fists. "Is that enough?"

"Who cut John's dope for him?"

"Back then it was Man."

"You ever know John's last name?"

"Don't nobody have no real last name 'round The Homes."

"Was anyone else involved in John's dealings with Anderson?"

Stone stretched back, his long body in a straight line, his bound arms above his head. "Maybe somebody the bluesman played with. I can't remember all from back then."

Down the long hall behind Stone, at the far end, an inmate made wide swipes with a mop, accompanied by a faint but distinct tap each time the mop end hit the bottom of the wall. His rhythm was constant and steady. He faced the other direction but was backing closer and closer.

A sudden clank from the door behind Salt startled her as it began its motorized draw back into the metal wall frame. "Time's up," said the gray-shirted officer waiting on the other side of the door. Another guard appeared behind Stone. Salt stood. "Can you give him my card?" She pulled a generic blue card, on which she'd written her mobile number, from her jacket pocket and held it out. The officer took it and unlocked a tray to the other side where his counterpart retrieved it.

Stone had stayed seated, the fingers of both his hands again touching the letters and crude drawings on the sides of the space, like a blind man reading Braille. The guard behind him gave him a tap. "Time's up." Stone stuck out his long, thick tongue and licked the scratched steel wall.

THE HEART OF HOME

Salt peered into the lighted kitchen through the twelve small windowpanes of the back door. Wonder, her Border collie mix, kept his sit ten feet from the door while she turned the keys in the locks and let herself in. On the blue table beside the dog was an old amber ice tea pitcher filled with wild poppies and dogwood. The dog sat waving his tail as if he were responsible for and proud of the flowers on the table beside him. He was her dog all right. Five years since she'd found him, emaciated and flea-bitten, five years and he was still a wonder, how he'd taken to the sheep, patrolling the house and grove, and only occasionally investigating the neighbor's cows.

"Good boy." She stroked his fur, setting him off, scurrying, bumping, and turning for his greeting scratches. "Good boy," she repeated, smoothing his silky flanks and scratching his ears.

"Poppies for you and dogwood for Wonder. Love, Wills." The note was written on a page torn from the small Homicide notebook he kept in his shirt pocket, its pages often damp and curling. She lifted a poppy to her nose, inhaling the fragrance of a new spring, of green and white blossoms and leaves.

Wills was practically working twenty-four hours a day on one of the highest-profile cases the city had ever seen, the who-done-it murders of Laura Solquist, a beautiful mother and wife of a prominent up-and-coming real estate lawyer, and her two young daughters, Juliet and Megan. He caught naps at the office and stumbled in at all hours to his house in an old in-town neighborhood, close to the job, where he would have just enough time to get some sleep and walk his dogs in the nearby park. Huff had been trying to run interference for Wills with the politicians, press, and brass.

Neither she nor Wills were phone people. But he left evidence, a covered dish in the fridge or fruit fresh from the market, that he'd been to her old Victorian house in rural Cloud, a one-light town forty or so minutes south of the city. He made the drive down so his dogs could run with Wonder and so he could use her washer and dryer. His laundry capabilities were off-and-on depending on the status of the renovations on his old bungalow.

Wonder was sniffing all around, up and down her new slacks. "I have not been unfaithful with another dog, if that's what you're trying to say," she told him, holding up his snout to her own nose. He flicked his tongue at her mouth.

"Come on, one run to the back forty for you and then bed." She opened the door and followed the dog out. They'd penned the sheep before she'd left but still the dog ran to the enclosure, assuring himself they were grouped up. The five woolies gathered closer in the pen and gave off sleepy, halfhearted bleats. Wonder left off and took his business into the pecan grove. He'd been a stray on her old beat. She'd given him a job, herding the small flock.

The trees were still wet from another spring rain and it was beginning to mist again, drops gathering on the branches and new leaves, reflecting light from the porch like dripping jewels, then falling. With the moon and stars behind the cloud cover, the all-black dog was invisible until he was about two yards away.

"Come on." Salt patted her leg.

It felt like she and Wonder were beginning to occupy the house rather than it occupying her. Fifteen or so years ago the big nine-room Victorian had been left in her care when her mother had remarried and she and her new husband, along with Salt's brother, went to live in North Carolina. Getting shot last year had dredged up all sorts of ghosts, a few of whom had resided in the old home.

After Stone's assault, Wills and other friends had plastered and painted over bullet holes in the walls and ceiling. And she was in other ways trying to make it feel like a safe home again. She slept in the downstairs bedroom. Upstairs she'd ripped out the wall between her parents' old bedroom and another bedroom to build a dojo, a place of serenity and combat, where she practiced aikido, the martial art that emphasized peaceseeking.

Pepper would be in early the next day for their workout. It would be a comfort to see him. They'd been academy mates and worked the same precinct on adjoining beats for all their uniform time. Both had put in for and made detective the year before, Pepper drawing an assignment in Narcotics. She missed his hundred-watt smile, framed on the left side of his face by a long scar that ran from his forehead to his lower jaw. Over the years they'd tell each other's stories. Even though he had been the star of the Salt and Pepper Show, he was more Sancho Panza than Don Quixote, comic relief for their adventures. And he'd been the one who'd noticed her name as it appeared on her first uniform name tag, "S.Alt." Wesley Greer had given her the street name "Salt" and himself the street name "Pepper," bantering with their friends on the shift about his "hotness" as a law enforcement hero and male.

She shed her dirty, torn clothes and showered, finding little more damage on her body than from a workout. In front of the bathroom mirror she dabbed witch hazel on the abrasions on her face, then padded back to the kitchen.

From the window Salt watched the wind pick up, whirling tree limbs in the old orchard. A white poppy dropped from Wills' bouquet on the table. She picked up the bloom and stripped a stamen from the throat of the flower, drops of milky liquid clinging to the delicate stem. Like she did with honeysuckle when she was a kid, she touched her tongue to the sweet fluid.

The dog waited by the bedroom door. Her status as a new detective lay heavy. No Pepper partner; no credibility, again; no other woman on her shift; and assigned an old, cold case. *"Hellhound on my trail."* Some old piece of the song was earworming her. At the bed she knelt down. While she was neither a believer nor a nonbeliever, she prayed to the mysterious, to the force blowing outside, that Wills would be safe, that she'd do some good, that she'd speak for the dead. In bed Wonder circled around on the quilt, then curled against her leg.

SHE LIFTED *a rusted iron latch on a gray board door and stepped across the threshold into the dim interior of a one-room shanty. The only light in the room came from the daylight she'd just let in. The room was bare except for a brown medium-sized dog sitting on top of an old cast-iron stove that spilled cold ashes onto a dirt floor.*

The dog talked without moving his mouth, "mouf" he called it. He had an old Southern street way of talking. He rolled his eyes, twitched his ears, and moved his head around while he stayed absolutely in place, never moving the rest of his body at all, staying in the same sit.

She got very close to the dog's face and looked into his yellow eyes.

WONDER WAS standing over her, watching, when she opened her eyes. As soon as she did, he bowed with his front legs and jumped off the bed, his nails clicking on the floor toward the kitchen. Trying to hold on to threads of the dream, Salt moved slowly, sitting up and lowering her legs over the side of the bed, but the dog's words were lost.

She made strong Cuban coffee and took her heavy, white diner cup outside to let Wonder gently herd the sheep to graze at the back of the pecan orchard. Afterward, she showered and dressed in a clean white gi and went into the dojo, sitting a few feet from a small shelf that was close to the floor and on which there were a sprig of the poppy in a small green glass vase, a burning red candle in a votive bowl, and the photograph of the sensei.

Although she knew they'd arrived, having heard Pepper's car coming up the gravel drive from the blacktop to the house, she widened her eyes pretending to be startled and reared back when the kids slid to their knees beside her on the mat. Pepper's boys, Theo and Miles, seven and nine years old, liked to sneak up the stairs of the old house to try to catch her by surprise. But of course not only had she heard the car, but she'd heard the creaks of certain boards beneath their small, bare toes. Pepper joined them, bowing to the room, then going to his knees and touching the mat in front of the altar with his forehead, the place where the knife-wound scar began in his smooth, otherwise flawless skin. There was just a hint of East India in his African-heritage features and six-foot-two athletic build. He stood, adjusted his gi, and bowed to his sons and Salt. "Namaste," they replied, their hands in prayer pose, nodding in unison.

The dojo room was an extravagant and sensuous joy. The floors had been reinforced and raised to allow the surface to bend and give. A large single piece of white matting covered the floor, wall to wall. The walls were finished in old wood and bamboo, the windows shortened and raised to shoulder height. Mirrored walls on either side of the door reflected the room's earth shades: Pepper's and the boys' brown skin, the white gis, the dried-grass colors of the bamboo, and the weathered gray wood. Pepper began to lead them in stretches, rolls, falls, and then designating uke and nage, the routines of their aikido practice.

The altar was positioned parallel to the place in the middle of the room where she'd cradled her father's head, wiping thickening blood from his eyes, as he was dying.

Pepper effected a hip throw, connecting and levering her into a roll. Without speaking, he led the boys in some elbow-control moves. The only sounds in the room were the whipping of Pepper's hakama, the air as it whooshed from their chests, and their bodies as they tumbled, fell, and rolled to the mat. After an hour Pepper sat down in front of the altar. Sweat ran down their faces as they joined in bowing their thanks.

"IT'S ALL OVER the department—Baby Jesus, the chief. You certainly started your new assignment in style." Pepper high-fived her. They sat next to each other drinking ice tea on the back porch steps. Wonder sat at the paddock gate watching the boys trot around after the sheep.

"Yeah, well, I'm just lucky no one made a big deal out of my not having a radio with me," Salt said.

Dust clouds hung around the boys' knees as they stirred the sheep, running after them and patting their dirty wool.

"Ever heard of Mike Anderson?" she asked.

"The bluesman? Don't tell me they got you workin' that old thing?

I thought it was an overdose." Pepper pinched some mint leaves from beside the steps. "Already hazing you." He shook his head. "Those homicide guys are the worst. Who did they partner you with?" He handed her some mint.

"According to Sergeant Huff—'don't call him Sarge'—my reputation has preceded me and therefore, at least for this old cold case, I don't need a partner." She crushed the leaves against her tea glass.

"What?" Pepper turned to her, scowling.

"Also, I went and saw Stone."

"What?"

"He made a statement for the record that Anderson was intentionally given a hot pop."

"Un-fucking-believable. He wants his sentence reduced. What does Wills say about all this?"

"He's all tied up in the Solquist case. I haven't had a chance to talk to him about it. I don't think he knows."

"God, he must be getting killed with pressure from that one."

The boys had the sheep running the perimeter of the paddock. Wonder fairly vibrated watching the activity.

"What about you, Pep? This has been your first week, too. How is Narcotics?"

"Well, Ann hates it. She's worried to death and really that's the worst. I know when shit's getting hairy, but she's holding her breath the whole time I'm at work." Pepper stood and called to the boys to tell them they could throw the Frisbee for Wonder but that they had to go in a few minutes. "I don't like it that you're working alone again, Salt." His scar lengthened as he clenched his jaw.

"Narcotics as hinky scary as I've heard? Does Ann have reason to worry?"

He stretched his back, bending out from his waist, and grinned as he put on an affected street patois. "What? Now I've got two womens worryin' 'bout my black ass?" His parents being middle-class and teachers, he'd grown up in a home where standard grammar was mandatory. "Actually, my folks used to go to the same church as Mike Anderson's parents, long time ago. That church got to be huge and they didn't really know the Andersons well. I just remember them saying something about his death before they left that mega scam. You know that church, Midas Prince's church. They left there and never looked back.

"Come on, Theo, Miles. Time to get this show on the road." He stood and strode off toward his sons, giving her the "come-back smile" that worked like a magnet and made people want to hang with him. Salt resisted an unfamiliar urge to run and hug him good-bye. They didn't hug.

THERE WAS little furniture left after her mother and brother moved out, just enough to do: a bed in the downstairs bedroom, a dresser, the kitchen table, an old sofa and chair in the living room. The library was empty except for a worn wine-colored Oriental rug and the books. The cassette tapes were in a battered, brownish pasteboard suitcase the size that a man might have carried on an overnight business trip in the '60s. Salt slid the case from the shelf, sat down beside it on the carpet, and pried the tarnished latches open, releasing a faint muddy odor as she lifted the top.

There were a hundred or more tapes in hard plastic cases. Some had factory labels on the spines and others were hand-labeled, her father's long, loopy writing sliding off the edges. "I can't read my own writing," he'd say. "Blind Will" read the label on one tape. Other tapes were blank on the spines, and Salt slid them out in order to see what was written on the tape face. Like the rest of the library, the tapes seemed to be in no particular order, unless, like the library, it was a system peculiar to her father.

The red cedar shelves were full of books belonging to multiple generations of her father's family, though most were her dad's. They were in the order he had read them, with the books about depression on the far wall opposite of where Salt now sat. There was a ledger of his reading on one of the shelves beside the pocket doors.

She let her fingers rove at random through the tapes and by feel slid a tape from the collection. On the shelf beside the case was a tape recorder of the type that used to be used in offices for recording work to be transcribed. The police department had only within the last few years quit using them to record statements of witnesses and victims.

Salt plugged the recorder in an outlet, inserted the tape labeled "Pretty Pearl at the Blue Room," and pushed play. As she adjusted the volume knob on the side of the recorder, a woman's voice, accompanied by a lone piano, broke soulfully through the scratches and drags of both the tape and machine.

Spread your wings and fly
Lil gal, you gonna spread
your wings and fly.

Salt leaned back into the corner. Her father'd had lots of good days. With the grass prickly on her legs and the ground smelling of green onions, he'd be bent over something in the black-dirt yard, weeding, planting seedlings, or sometimes just touching leaves, petals, and stems. Stretching his back as he stood, he'd call her "Angel." She'd run and jump into his arms, his shirtsleeves warm from the sun. He'd lift her to his knees, holding her out, stiff-legged, arms spread wide and facing the world. "Flying angel, spread your wings."

She began to remove each tape and stack them according to genre. About half the tapes were blues and the other half jazz and gospel. One tape, its case less worn and scratched, plastic hinges intact, was labeled "Mike Anderson and the Old Smoke Band."

I dreamed I heard the Marion whistle blow,
And it blew just like my baby gettin' on board.
I'm goin' where the Southern cross the Dog.

The familiar sadness settled like a heavy, old quilt. She worked, ran, worked out in the dojo, took care of the sheep with Wonder. But it would settle nevertheless, as she tried to hold together the pieces of her ten-year-old self. "The blues, eh, Pops?" The spines of the books across from her told part of his story: *Depression and Other Major Psychological Disorders, Dealing with Depression, Living with Mental Illness.*

Salt pressed the stop button.

ROSIE'S MAGIC

On a rusted iron panel of the railroad trestle that ran alongside the mammoth brick Sears, Roebuck building, a graffiti portrait of Blind Willie McTell stared out at the city. The police department leased parts of the old building to temporarily house some of its units, which were now, unit by unit, being moved into the new headquarters building downtown. Homicide was scheduled to be one of the last to leave, so the massive structure was almost empty. At over two million square feet, the building was one of the largest in the Southeast, now only echoing the glory days of catalog commerce, when the rails received goods and then sent them out again, destined for little towns throughout the region. Those rails had delivered, made real, what the treasured catalog had brought into the realm of possibility. Aunt Fanny got the Sunday corset that made her look and feel like a movie star. Great-uncle Jim got heavy overalls—the good ones for town—and a pipe. Cousin Hazel ordered flower seeds, almost any kind—just looking at the packets could make her dream.

Salt parked, gathered a considerable bouquet of flowers from the backseat, and walked from the oil-stained parking lot onto the receiving dock and into the cavernous superstructure. The high ceilings would have accommodated tons of merchandise and all those boxes, stacked, waiting on pallets to be shipped. An ancient elevator with a filigree brass door lifted her slowly past the smoky windows of the empty floors until the bounce stop at the eighth floor where she got out and rolled the elevator panels closed. She walked through to the front side of the building where the windows faced Ponce de Leon Avenue and looked across to what should be hallowed ground, the place where Jackie Robinson broke the color line in 1949 by playing the all-white Atlanta Crackers in old Ponce de Leon Park. Now it was a parking lot for some big-box stores. The old stadium was built in 1907 and torn down in 1966 when Atlanta joined the major leagues with the acquisition of the Braves, along with a new facility built closer to the center of the city and expressways. Atlanta was derelict in honoring its past. A massive magnolia tree that had marked center field and fair ball territory still stood high on the hill above the retail strip, while all that was left of the old green-painted wood bleachers and green-and-yellow dirt playing field were old photos that hung in a restroom corridor of one of the food markets. Atlanta's black fans had been segregated to an area under the railroad trestle that ran above and alongside right field. Jackie had stolen home in the third game of the exhibition series with the Brooklyn Dodgers.

At the door to the Homicide offices, Salt switched the bundled camellias to her left arm, swiped her card, and waited for the green light on the panel.

"Look at you, Girl Detective," Rosie said standing from behind the receptionist's desk. She was six foot seven in heels and wore an electric-blue sheath dress. "That pink matches your lip color so perfectly."

"They will look even more perfect on your desk. For you, Rosie."

Salt handed her the bouquet. "These will have to do till the roses come in."

"Oh, my God." Rosie looked down into the pink and green in her arms. She had been, before beginning the transition, a beat cop and renowned headbanger. When she looked up, her eyes were brimming. "No one's ever. Oh, shit." She opened a drawer, fumbled, and came up with a handful of tissues. "Go on. Go back there to your cubby and let me get these in a vase."

Salt punched the numbers and pushed through to the inner office. As she made her way to the back, one of the day-watch guys and Barney were the only heads visible over the tops of the partitions. The under-cabinet light was on above her desk and where yesterday there'd been only a few bent paper clips and dust now sat a state-of-the-art computer, flat-screen monitor, and keyboard. She switched on her Handie-Talkie, then touched a key and the monitor lit up with a law enforcement search screen. Radio was quiet. She was still getting used to not being bound to the constant demands to answer calls as she'd been as a beat cop, whose time is owned by radio calls. In Homicide her time was hers when she wasn't on a fresh scene, but she would be owned by the cases and her solve rate.

The broken chair was gone, replaced by one that was ergonomic-looking, blue-cushioned, and turned to welcome her. The cubicle even smelled nice; lavender had been stashed somewhere. The drawers were stocked with tablets, forms, and unopened boxes of other supplies: pens, hand wipes, disposable gloves, crime scene booties, even a couple of juice boxes and power bars.

"You like it?" Rosie came up the aisle smiling and carrying a vase with the flowers.

Salt's head came just below Rosie's chin when they hugged. "Thank you."

"Us girls have to stick together," Rosie said.

"What girls?" Barney stuck his head up over the next-row partition.

Daniels' fingers waggled above the partition close by. "You didn't bring me flowers, honey." Something flew over from Barney's side. "Ow."

"Ignore them," Rosie said. "Around here everyone refers to them as the Wild Things. Daniels, Thing One, and Barney, Thing Two."

GARDNER MOTIONED Salt over, nodding his head toward Wills on the phone across the aisle.

Wills stared straight ahead at the cubicle wall, avoiding eye contact with his partner, who was making exaggerated faces in response to what Wills was saying into the phone. "Yes, ma'am . . .

"Since you were ten years old." He noticed Salt but quickly turned his back on her and Gardner.

"Visions . . .

"I'm sure the Hahira police do appreciate your help . . .

"No, ma'am, we have someone we use here in Atlanta . . .

"An Atlanta psychic. He's very good, very professional . . ."

Gardner covered his mouth and fled toward the break room.

"We'll keep that in mind—a silver key and a swamp . . .

"Bye now."

Wills punched the end-call button on the desk phone and banged the handset against his forehead.

"GOOGLE IS MY FRIEND," Salt said to the screen. For hours she'd played with, practiced on, searched, and learned some of what was available using the law enforcement and public search engines. She'd found nothing about the corporation that owned the Chicken Shack.

"Welcome to Homicide."

She looked up and into the steady, focused eyes of Manfred Felton. He held out his long hand. "I see you and Rosie have hit it off. Lucky you," he said as Salt took his hand and stood.

"So far today has been much better than yesterday," she said.

"I heard. Nice work. Sarge giving you a rough time? And I bet the Wild Things"—he swept his eyes around the room—"haven't been tumbling over themselves to make you feel at home either. It's just as well actually. And if it will help you feel better and put things in perspective, imagine how it was five years ago when I first came to the squad." He leaned against the partition and crossed his arms.

She'd heard. He was a legend now, the first openly gay detective in the department; he'd risen in the mythology and lore of not only their department but homicide units all over. He had endured. Endured, overcome, and solved homicide after homicide—the red balls and easy cases called "bones," as in to have been thrown a bone—all while enduring. His rate was one hundred percent clear-ups, every case cleared—unheard of. Now after five years he no longer had to endure. He had the record. He could even look forward to stone-cold who-done-its because he had the record.

"I don't think I can imagine how it was," she said. "I really can't complain, then, but I would have liked just the possibility of solving my first case."

Felton pointed to the open file on her desk. "I see by the coffee rings that he gave you a cold one."

"Coffee rings. Is that what you call 'a clue'? Detective Felton, behold the Mike Anderson case."

Brow furrowed, he picked up an imaginary magnifying glass and perused the spread file in a Sherlockian manner. "Elementary, my dear Watson. Follow the hound." He winked.

THE ANDERSONS

The pristine, snow-white Doric columns on the small porch of the Andersons' bungalow gave Salt pause. She straightened her shirt collar and jacket. Mike's parents still lived in the house in the West End neighborhood where they had been living when Mike had died.

The West End, like the city that would annex it, began at a crossroads. It had official historic status and was exemplary of many of Atlanta's older neighborhoods. It started as a working-class and racially mixed community, and then became affluent and all white. In the '60s and '70s, rapid white flight caused the neighborhood to become more middle-class and all black. But holes of poverty opened up during the crack epidemic of the '80s and early '90s. Even still, pockets of the neighborhood had remained stable, especially around the University Center, where Mr. Anderson taught mathematics, and recently there had been some signs of gentrification.

Mike's father opened the door wearing leather slippers of the kind rarely seen anymore. "Mr. Anderson, I'm Detective Alt." Salt started to offer her hand, but rather than responding he extended his arm, parting the air to the hall. "Please come in." He guided her into a small formal parlor furnished in faux French Provincial and ceramic pastorals, all cream and gilt. Mrs. Anderson (Salt was somehow sure she'd prefer the Mrs. to the Ms. prefix) stood from a rose-colored chair as they entered and indicated with a nod and an outstretched hand that Salt should sit on a brocade settee. Mr. Anderson continued to stand, his hands folded around a hardbound book. Both Andersons, small in stature, had the same dark walnut hue and both were dressed in what Salt thought of as prayer-meeting clothes, not Sunday dressy but well dressed.

"Mr. and Mrs. Anderson, I hope I'm not reopening old wounds, but as I said when I called, we received new information about your son's death that has to be followed up."

"What information? From whom or where did this information come?" Mrs. Anderson emphasized the word "information," as if it were distasteful.

"There is some reason to doubt the credibility of the source, but I have been assigned to the case, and procedures dictate that there be follow-up."

"'Procedures dictate,'" Mr. Anderson repeated.

"So why are you coming to us?" Mrs. Anderson stiffened against the upright back of her chair. "You have no idea how painful this is. Suicide is the worst tragedy for its survivors. We have all these questions that can probably never be answered. For years we have been trying to let this go. And here you are." A large graduation portrait of Mike hung on the wall behind Mrs. Anderson's chair. He looked like both parents except for a huge smile and a 'fro, mushroom-shaped by the mortarboard. The tassel dangled beside the corner of his right eye, lightly brushing his rounded cheek. There were no other photographs, none marking his successes as a musician, no posters, no framed reviews.

"I thought . . . I was hoping you would be the best source for me to get a general sense of how Mike's life was in the days and months before he died. Or the name of someone who I should talk to about any specific problems he was having."

Mr. Anderson tightened his grip on the book. "Isn't that all still in the records, a file?"

"Honestly, because his death was ruled accidental rather than a homicide, it wasn't given much investigation. Back then drug overdoses were coming in in record numbers."

"Detective, you come here to us because of some procedure. But Michael was our child, our only child. You have no idea how it is to lose someone to suicide. It's a tomb we try to dig ourselves out of every day, trying not to ask questions that we can never get answers for."

Salt looked down at her hands, feeling a quickness in her chest and a flash to the yellow-eyed dog in her dream.

"You see, Detective." Mrs. Anderson was leaning forward. Salt looked up. "We knew we were losing Michael, that he'd chosen the wrong road, long before his death. Oh, they called it 'accidental,' but we knew that was out of consideration for us—because they didn't know if he intended it or not. But we'd tried, as soon as he took up that juke-joint music, to turn him back to the straight path. He chose."

"'Juke-joint,' you mean the blues?" Some lyrics from her dad's tapes ran through her head. *We can't let the blues die, blues don't mean no harm.* "He was so talented. My father had some of his recordings. You must have been proud of him."

"He got taken with trashy music, blues, rap, devil's music, ignorant music. My daddy would forbid that kind of old field noise when I was growing up." Mrs. Anderson sat up straighter and looked away.

"You come here askin' again 'bout our son is like throwin' dirt." Mr. Anderson's other accent was showing.

"I am sorry. If you could suggest someone else I could talk to."

"He had talent, could play the piano beautifully, classical and sacred. But he took up the guitar, started hanging around all kinds of folks. Quit going to church. We tried everything." Mrs. Anderson looked out to the sunset beyond the curtained window. "And at the end, our pastor, Reverend Prince, did his best with our son. We felt blessed that Midas Prince took time—even back then he was a mighty busy man—to try to reclaim Michael."

"So Reverend Prince met with him before he died?"

Mr. Anderson looked over at his wife. "I don't think even you could get in to see the pastor these days. We haven't talked to him personally in, what? Five years or more?"

"He's grown Big Calling into the second largest congregation with the largest church building in this city." Mrs. Anderson looked down and tapped the watch on her wrist. "It's time, dear."

"As we told you, Miss Alt, we have to be at our lodge meeting by seven-thirty."

Salt stood. "I appreciate your seeing me on this short notice."

Mr. Anderson escorted her to the door, looked back into the house, and then came out onto the porch, closing the door behind him. "I don't want you to think we're not appreciative of your efforts, but my wife, especially, cannot seem to lose the doubts about whether we did or did not do enough to try to save our son."

"I am sorry and feel your loss."

"He's buried in Westview." Mr. Anderson abruptly turned, went back inside, and closed the door.

Salt made her way back to the Taurus at the curb and then sat behind the wheel for a while, absorbing the vermillion and gold streaks against the deepening sky.

WESTVIEW

About mid-April, around four in the afternoon, on a sunny day, maybe a Sunday, not every year, just most years, the spring wind might gentle, warm and easy. For an instant the forsythia would still have a few bright yellow blooms left, while the bright pink, white, fuchsia, and pastel azaleas would begin to unfold from their tight buds, and the wisteria vines would be growing heavy with new leaves and lavender and purple blooms. Orange-throated jonquils and buttercups, bright tulips, flourishing phlox, and the trees, the pinks of the apple, sweet peach, weeping cherry, and purple redbud and the whites of the dogwood and Bradford pear, all would coalesce in a grand symphony of color and fragrance. Then the breeze might increase and blow the petals apart, upward, out, and the air would fill with soft, whirling beauty while the old hardwood trees stood stately dressed in their simple, new light green foliage, spreading their limbs over the deepening green of the hills, all against a perfect robin's-egg-blue sky, all a glory of an Atlanta spring day.

But as Salt drove through the main gate of Westview Cemetery, she left most of those busy, pollinating, renewing goings-on, left them all over the rest of the city's avenues, parks, and yards. Westview was nearly bereft of trees, and the flowers there were mostly plastic. Here and there could be seen a lone magnolia or an old oak shading the graves over on a hill, such as were left. The place had long ago been leveled and shorn of greenery. That shearing had begun when cannons blasted earth and men apart in the Civil War battle of Ezra Church, the site on which the vast cemetery now existed.

Other than a solitary figure that appeared and disappeared as she drove up and down the dips and peaks of the drive around the perimeter, Salt was the only visitor. As she grew closer, the lone figure became recognizable, first as a woman and then, as her crown of braids became more distinct, as the woman Salt knew as Sister Connelly. The old woman stood at the foot of a grave facing the headstone. She didn't move an inch and only lifted her head as Salt parked beside the row, got out, and walked over. "Oh, my Lord. Ain't white folks done enough to black folks so's you ain't got to keep on torturing me?" Sister was the folk historian of The Homes, her age indeterminate but her memory sharp. She lived across the street from last year's murder and knew all the players and their stories.

"How would I have even known you were here? I got promoted to detective and assigned a cold case. The young man's grave is somewhere . . ." Salt walked the pea-gravel path between the rows. "Why are you here?"

"At my age most of my friends and family are either already here or we escorting them here." She was looking at each gravestone as she followed Salt along the next row. "You feel that?"

Salt thought she heard faint drums but now wasn't sure. It could have been some nearby construction blasts. There was a slight trembling in the ground about every thirty seconds or so.

"This who you investigating? I hearda this child." Sister stopped and stood beside Salt. "A hellhound on his tail, a black dog."

Standing about two and a half feet tall, a dog, shiny and black, snout raised in what could be a snarl or just sniffing the air, marked the grave of Michael Anderson, born April 3, 1950, died November 17, 2005.

"Is that what the dog means, a hellhound from the blues?"

"Black dogs can means lots of things, hellhound or just black dogs. They lead folks to heaven or hell; dogs sit at crossroads. This whole city got a black dog sittin' right in its middle."

"Sister, sometimes I only half understand what you tell me." Salt knelt beside the funerary canine, felt all around his haunches, and slid her hand along the smooth place between his ears.

"I only half understand what I tell is why."

Salt stood. "You know more than you think you know, is that it?"

"That's right."

"It's always what Pepper and I tell each other. Kept us from getting killed, helped us talk about things we didn't have an understanding of or the words to explain."

"So you detecting killings now? Murder?"

"I was assigned to the Homicide Unit."

"How come you ain't workin' on that one all in the papers and on TV, that rich family? I'da thought they'd have all the detectives on that one. What it bein' white folks on the north side."

Salt stood. "I guess they think I don't know enough to help much."

"That's how it goes all right. They put the little know-nothing detective working a dead junkie, bluesman. Same ol' same ol'. Even dead the rich folks get better attention."

Salt rubbed the scar running through her scalp.

"That still bothering you? Where you got shot?"

Salt lowered her hand. "Not really. It's just a habit."

"You get dreams?"

"Everybody has dreams."

"You know what I mean."

SORTING GOD WITH WILLS

G od, these frogs are loud," Wills said to the dog lying serenely beside the glider. The dog, waiting for the woman, his snout between outstretched paws, moved his eyes in acknowledgment of the man's voice. To the dog the man was a small deity whose words held only a little more significance than the other lively sounds of the night—tree frogs, her car still a ways off on the highway, the sheep in the nearby paddock rustling against each other in sleep, one of the small wood beams in the big house settling, and a night bird.

There were fast, smoke-like clouds flying across a high half-moon. The black dog, barely visible, picked up his ears before the headlights could be seen coming up the long drive. The man and dog rose and walked toward her parking spot under the pecan tree. She switched off the engine. Both wedged themselves into the space of the opened car door. The dog was on her first, licking the air, his front legs across her lap.

"My turn." Wills, only a few inches taller than she and built like a high school football coach, muscular without definition or working at it, reached in, extending his hand to lift her from the driver's seat.

"You guys!" She smiled, moved the dog's paws, accepted his outstretched hand, and stood.

"Tired?"

"Not too bad." She handed him the keys and he went to the trunk for her gear bag.

"I'm anxious to hear how it went, first days as a new detective. I remember how eager and proud I was. Everybody was talking about your first day, the child murderer, Hamm's case, your collar, the chief at the scene. It's already turning into quite the story."

She ruffled Wonder's fur as they walked to the house and up the steps where moths and their silhouettes flew around the back-porch light.

Salt changed into soft jeans and with grateful bare feet joined Wills back outside. The glider made a melodic creak as they sipped a single glass of whiskey between them.

"Who did you get partnered with? I've been out on this case so much I've barely even talked to Gardner, much less anybody else on the squad."

"Huff didn't seem very happy with having me foisted on him."

One of the sheep asserted herself with her own distinctive *"Bleeek."*

"Huff, don't call him Sarge, will come 'round. You earned the assignment. And speaking of calling or not calling names—I have to watch myself. I can't be calling you 'Honey' in front of anyone. The less they suspect, the less attention we'll get." The rules for employees stated that neither spouses nor domestic partners could work on the same shift in the same unit. Although she and Wills weren't married and didn't live together, and it was a "Don't ask, don't tell" policy, supervisors and commanders were reluctant to have to consider romantic attachments in managing their people.

"So who did Huff put you with?"

The night bird called again, some deep-throated animal sounded, and the tree frogs made a chorus.

"Uh-oh, I know that tone of voice," Wills said when she didn't answer.

"Maybe there's a good reason lovers shouldn't work together. This might be harder than we thought." Salt turned and put her back against the glider armrest, knees bent, her feet tucked under Wills' thigh.

"Come on, tell me. My blood pressure is going up. Who is he partnering you with?"

"No one."

"What do you mean 'no one'? Somebody has to show you protocols. You've handled the first responder duties on lots of bodies, but you have to have someone tell you how to put together a murder book, prepare for court, all kinds of documents, go help find witnesses, perps. And since I'm already doggin' you out, what were you doing without a Handie-Talkie in a fight with a monster?"

"I'm not putting together any new cases. He gave me a cold case: Mike Anderson. I had just barely walked in the door when the call came on the child." She let out a long breath. "God, Wills, don't you be raggin' on me already."

He turned to the night, looking away; he clamped his mouth tight and squinted up and out. After a minute he reached and drew her close, massaging the back of her neck. "I'm beginning to wonder about your karma—this 'being alone' business." He stood and pulled her to her feet. "Come on."

WILLS TRACED his finger down her back from her scalp to her tailbone as they lay on the bed facing the open window, the lace curtain flaring slightly at the bottom from an unusually warm April morning breeze. "Don't move, okay?"

She heard his bare feet land, heavy steps on the creaking wood floor. Then he was back on the rumpled bed, at her back, encircling her head, and lowering a chain and pendant around her neck. "Saint Michael," he said.

He was the patron saint of cops, in gold and about an inch in height with his sword raised, on a chain the length of which settled it right at her heart. She turned it between her fingers.

"In honor of your promotion and to match your new gold shield. And, if you're superstitious or religious, for your protection. I know you don't wear jewelry, but he can hide there or not. Say something. Do you like it?"

"Wills, I'm—I love it." She clasped Michael in her palm. "Even with all you've had going on with the case and all, you took time to get this?"

"I got the heavier chain so even with your action-hero ways it'll likely stay with you. Besides, as a detective I was hoping you'd be able to leave some of that kick-ass stuff behind."

She shrugged, holding the pendant.

"Seriously, it's just a little less than a year since you were shot in the head." He tapped at the tip of the scar at her scalp line with his knuckles. "You went off on your own after that, shut out everybody. So it really scares me that Huff didn't give you a partner. You're already too much of an I-can-do-it-by-myself person."

Salt, nude, except now for the gold chain and pendant, lifted herself into Wills' lap. "We'll figure it out, Wills. For now, thank you, thank you, for this gift." She leaned him into the pillows with her kiss.

MASSIVE OLD OAK and spreading pecan trees shaded Wills' street in the historic Grant Park community. There were only one or two surviving antebellums in the neighborhood—most were turn-of-the-twentieth-century or '20s and '30s bungalows, like the one Wills recently purchased. Living in town had made his life easier in that he was only ten minutes from the office and could make short stops while he was on the job to let the dogs out to the backyard or for quick walks to the park a block away.

The Rotties' low barks greeted them as they climbed the steps to the gate in a beautifully weathered fence that separated his place from the street and the houses on either side. Inside the entranceway the big brown-and-black lunky bitches swung their entire bodies in greeting, the foyer becoming a jumble of bumping dogs. Pansy and Violet snuffled Wonder, then Salt and their master. Wills squatted to get licked and handle their ruffs. Wills' girls loved them some Wonder, who was smart and affectionate but wanted to run the show. The Rotties happily let him.

There was plenty of room for the graceful Rotties. Wills had stored most of his furniture while he had been renovating. A big kitchen ran the width of the entire back of the house, walls down to the studs and raw boards, but it was fully functional, and he'd set a beautiful, rough-hewn parson's table in its center, where he quickly went to assembling sandwiches and fruit.

Salt let the dogs out in the backyard, then wandered through the rooms, noting a little progress here and there. While maybe not systematic, Wills was meticulous with his craftsmanship—a thoroughly stripped mantel, smooth as skin, fireplace tiles cleaned to their original shine and stacked ready to be mortared back around reconstructed hearths. "I can see how you love this house," she said, returning to the kitchen. "It's going to be beautiful."

"It may take a lifetime at this rate." Wills poured lemonade with lemon slices into tall glasses.

"When will you be able to take your weekends, both days, again?"

"I don't know. I've got no suspects. The husband, even though I haven't been able to interview him 'cause he's 'under a doctor's care,' according to his lawyer," Wills sighed, "and has an alibi. Even the wife's family confirms he had the fishing trip to Florida planned for weeks."

"Any reason to suspect the marriage was shaky?"

"No. And even if it was, I don't see him, from what I've learned so far, killing his daughters." Wills put the sandwiches and a big ceramic bowl of mixed fruit on the table. "Come on—let's leave all that for a bit."

After eating, they took the dogs for a walk under the trees that lined the neighborhood. They shared the sidewalks with couples pushing strollers, tyke cycles, and baby carriages. On one corner sat an old brick church, its steeple reaching far above the rooftops. Beside the steep steps was a sign advertising the online contact at AirJesus.net. Music jumped from the open doors, a gospel band accompaning a rollicking choir as the congregation flowed out to the sidewalks.

With the music following them down the street, Wills stopped and pointed down a weedy access between two houses. "See down that alley? I worked a murder back there five years ago."

"The neighborhood has changed, huh?"

"Some." He squinted down the shaded lane. "I drive through almost any neighborhood now and I come upon someplace that's been tied with yellow ribbon."

The afternoon began to heat as they headed through the park and up the wide path of the hill to one of the last remnants of the Civil War and the Battle of Atlanta. "Last time I was up here I was chasing perps." She laughed. "Pepper caught them both at the same time on the other side of the park. 'Course we never heard the end of his crowing. Anyway, I'd gone to this side of the park, in case they got this far. When I heard Pepper on the radio saying he had them, I started back to the car. I happened to look down and there was this little basket right in the center of some newly turned dirt. In it were two white feathers and about six or so yellow rose heads. It was sitting on a flat slate stone with four dimes, heads up. I thought it was an animal grave or a voodoo shrine, who knows. Right here beside this tree." She looked at the ground, turning over brown leaves with the toe of her shoe. "Nothing left now."

Only an old historical society stand-alone brass marker on a post testified to the significance of the hill that had been Fort Walker. It was the highest land elevation in the city. Downtown buildings in the distance appeared over the tops of the trees.

"Voodoo. Slaves brought it first from Africa to Haiti and then here." Wills climbed and stood on top of the berm, looking out over the park to the city skyline.

Salt strode up beside him. "A lot of soldiers died here. My father's great-grandfather fought this battle. The family said he was never right afterward."

Wills reached over and smoothed back a damp curl from Salt's forehead. "Do you know the rest of the story about Saint Michael?" He lifted the gold chain and pendant from her shirt.

"Didn't he fight the devil or something?"

"Yep, and won. But what a lot of people and cops don't know is that he's also an angel of death. But in a good way. He's supposed to carry souls to heaven, where they're judged and also given a chance to redeem themselves."

"Busy dude, fighting the devil, delivering souls. Speaking of busy, don't we still need to get to the market? You're back on tomorrow, right?"

"I'm afraid so." He took her hand as they galloped down the hill, allowing gravity and momentum to pull them from the berm.

THEY DROPPED the dogs at Wills' place and drove to the market on the north side of the city to an area that was predominantly Asian and Latino, the main artery giving the area its name, Buford Highway, a Southern road, running now through an international community. It had begun as a path used by farmers north of the city to bring their produce to town. In the seventies, cheap housing along the corridor made the area attractive to new immigrants. Those roots took hold so well that when construction began for the '96 Olympics, the highway drew even more immigrants looking for work. Now marquees in several languages advertised the best food in the Southeast. And for shopping there was no better or fresher fish and produce to be had than from what people called the "Asian Farmer's Market."

Inside the immense converted warehouse, Wills began his systematic shopping through the sections, organized according to ethnicity, and left Salt to her usual wandering. This time it was a display, five shelves, three feet in length, at the end of one of the aisles that caught her eye. Where there would normally be impulse-buy items attracting the attention of people passing in the main corridors, there were dozens of religious figurines for sale—seven- and fifteen-inch Shiva, Ganesha, Buddha, Jesus, and bodhisattvas. They were roughly made and poorly painted, flat white or black, with only slight dabs of color and gilt for the eyes and jewels.

Wills came by with a loaded cart. "What did you find?" He smiled.

"Assorted God," she said, pointing to the label "ASSORTED GOD."

"THEY WEREN'T beautiful or even pretty. But they must be worth having for someone, maybe somebody scared, sentimental, or needing luck or good karma? I imagined a woman standing there and choosing: 'Let's see. I've gotten everything on my list: coriander, dragon fruit, noodles.' Then Shiva catches her eye." Salt and Wills sat on the back porch with all the house and porch lights off. The clouds had disappeared and the moon gleamed off everything. Even Wonder's black fur sparkled in the moonlight.

"A thousand people shop that market in a day. At night some worker mops the aisles, a manager locks the doors, turns out the lights, and sets the alarm, that little blinking red button. And Shiva sits there, extra arms extended, and Ganesha, his trunk lifted." She raised her arm elephant-like.

Inside, the timer on the clothes dryer buzzed. "Your clothes are done, sweetie." Wills put his hands on his thighs to stand. "Back to reality."

The dog stuck his nose in her lap, pushing under her hand, the onyx of his eyes crowding out the amber irises.

WILLS AND WONDER watched from the front room window until the taillights of her car disappeared down the road. There were nights when he slept over at Salt's—better to leave in the early morning after a good night's sleep. "Okay, buddy." Wills rubbed the dog's shiny fur, kneaded the lean flank muscles underneath, and followed him to the couch where they both drew deep breaths and began to nod. Wills was soon asleep on the sofa. The dog lay beside him on the floor, ears twitching up when he heard a car on the road, down when it was not her car, his eyes, blinking reflected moonlight, only partially closed, then open.

CHURCH

Vibrations from the gigantic pipe organ came through the shiny ceramic tile flooring to the soles of her shoes and up to her knees. The auditorium of the colossal Big Calling Church reverberated with bass notes of something in a minor key. Salt began to walk toward the back of the space, looking up in order to locate the position of the organist somewhere high in the sanctuary above. The pews, walls, floors, and even the windows were all finished in shades of beige and pastel pinks. Enormous columns down the sides of the aisles were filigreed with plaster cherubs and doves.

"You're not supposed to be in here."

Salt startled. "Damn."

The two men were sitting together in the otherwise empty nave, less than three feet from where Salt had stopped to look up toward the front. She immediately recognized one of the men as Reverend Midas Prince. His dark features and broad nose were ubiquitous at any and all significant events in the Atlanta public forum—celebrations, televised services, civil rights holidays—wherever the media gathered. He was wearing a suit that perfectly blended with the décor.

"Get Madison," he said to the light-complexioned young man beside him who immediately scurried from the pew.

"I apologize, Reverend Prince. I was startled. I didn't see you there."

"So you don't normally curse? Or just not in the presence of others? Or in God's house?" He stood and buttoned his suit coat over a collarless light pink shirt.

"I'm sorry." Salt retrieved her badge case from a back pocket. "Here's my identification. I'm Detective Alt." She had to raise her voice above a crescendo from the organ.

The preacher took the ID wallet and opened it, and then took his time looking back and forth between her photo on the laminated card and her, his nose and mouth scrunched as if he smelled something bad. "How did you get in? All the doors are supposed to be locked." He leaned toward her so he could hear her answer over the organ, which was rising to a flourish.

Salt waited for the music to finish, but the organist kept building to what now seemed an ever-distant climax.

"Enough, Karl." Prince yelled with all his famous oratorical force.

The silence was immediate, a vacuum in contrast with the previous sonic bombardment.

The young man returned followed by an Atlanta police officer, dressed in the green fatigues of the SWAT team, their footsteps echoing as they came down the aisle. "Hello, hello, hello, little lady," hailed Sandy "True Grit" Madison, a square-jawed walking cliché. Even his fellow team members made fun of him, mocking his affected John Wayne walk anytime they could play it for a laugh either behind his back or to goad him. She knew him mostly by his all-hat-and-no-cattle cowboy reputation. But he'd also been with the SWAT when calls on her beat had escalated and procedure required a SWAT response,

more manpower and equipment than were available to beat officers—
some barricaded gunmen, hostage situations, a couple of suicide and
bomb threats, suspicious packages, and explosive materials. He completed his greeting by wrapping her into his six-foot-five bear hug.

"So you know this woman?" Prince asked him.

"Sure, Reverend. Everybody knows Salt. She's kinda like, uh, Wonder Woman, that's it. Fightin' the bad guys all by herself. She shot
and killed one last year, didn't you, Salt? And you just made detective, right?" He play-punched her on her bicep.

"That's why I'm here, Reverend. I've been assigned a case you may
be able to shed some light on."

"You couldn't call and make an appointment?" said Prince.

"Yeah, Salt," said Madison. "You should come to me first with
anything related to Reverend Prince and law enforcement."

"You're right, Madison, but I was out anyway and just stopped by,
hoping I could get a few minutes with Reverend Prince. You know
how it is." She turned to the preacher. "Mike Anderson's parents said
you were very busy and hard to get an appointment with, but like I
said, I took a chance and now here I am and here you are."

"'Mike Anderson,'" repeated Prince.

"Mike Anderson. I loved his music when I was a kid," said the
young man from behind the preacher and previously excluded from
the conversation.

"You can be excused," Prince said over his shoulder. With a pout,
the young man turned toward the exit.

"Yeah, but Salt, Reverend Prince is a busy—"

"Why would anybody be interested in Mike Anderson after all
these years?" Prince cut Madison off and stepped toward Salt. "He
killed himself on drugs."

"We've gotten new information."

"'New information.' What kind of new information?"

As Prince came closer, Salt realized that he was her same height and remembered that she'd always thought he wore lifts in his shoes or stacked heels. "A witness," she said.

Prince made a dismissive, flapping noise with his lips. "What kind of witness?"

"We're trying to corroborate, or disprove, his allegations, Reverend. I'd like to ask you about your interventions with Mike before he died."

Prince shook back his coat cuff and looked down at the large-faced watch on his wrist. "I have an appointment I need to get to."

Prince was already striding up the center aisle as Madison took a business card from the leg pocket of his fatigue pants and held it out to Salt. It had a camouflage background with black lightning lettering for his name and phone numbers. "I'll walk you out. What door did you come in? I need to check the schedule. Somebody musta screwed up, leaving a door unlocked. I give these guys these cushy extra jobs, and then they do me like this."

"Good EJ?" Salt asked, referring to the off-duty job. Most cops worked some kind of extra job in order to supplement their pay. Their law enforcement and jurisdictional powers were active no matter if they were on or off duty.

"It's real cushy, Salt. Want me to get you on?" He put his arm over her shoulder as they walked toward the door. "Directing traffic on Sunday is the most work we do. Otherwise it's just hangin' around, doing whatever the Rev needs doin'."

"'Fraid I can't. I have all I can do to keep up with the new assignment and my home life." She slipped from under his arm. "Thanks, though."

"Yeah, I know what you mean, pardner." He slapped his leg with a flat palm.

"What other things do you do for him?" she asked.

"What?"

"You said you do whatever the preacher needs. Like what?"

He stood in the doorway with his arms stretched up to the top of the sill, as if in preparation for a pull-up. He squinted at her for a second. "Now you sound like Internal Affairs. I thought you were assigned to Homicide."

"Just askin'. Just askin'." Salt turned and walked out to her unmarked car parked in the vast lot. When she looked back, Madison was still hanging in the doorway.

BLUE REPORT

S alt had laid out the eight-by-ten scene photos sequentially, left to right, spread over her desk, far shots on the left, close-ups on the right. She'd had to take care removing them from the envelope because humidity had crept in, causing some of the photos to adhere to the backs of the others.

Mike Anderson's car had been found parked in the wide intersection of Elizabeth Street and Waverly Way facing the wrong way with the left front wheel in a street grate. It was an old 1950s Pontiac wagon, green and cream, funny, funky. According to the reporting party, the friend who found him, Anderson was supposed to have come by his girlfriend's the night before. When he hadn't shown up by the next morning, the girlfriend, Melissa Primrose, called the friend, Dan Pyne. There were no statements from either Pyne or Primrose transcribed for the record. After the medical examiner ruled the death "accidental," no investigation would have been required, and there was no documentation in the file that any had been done.

Salt picked up one of the medium-range photos. Michael was leaning from the middle of the front seat and slumped against the passenger window, left foot turned, heel up against the carpeting of the drive shaft hump. One bedroom slipper, mate to the other on his right foot, had come off and was on the driver's floorboard. He was wearing a navy-and-gray-striped terry-cloth robe, open, the belt missing. He didn't have on any jewelry. His hair was cut in a medium 'fro, slightly uneven at the left back and with what looked to be a small sprinkling of pink glitter where his hair was flattened. Both hands were in his lap, palms up, fingers slightly curled, a receiving gesture. Below his left eye was a spot of whitish dust, maybe salt from dried tears.

"Sad." Picking up one of the close-up photos, Felton sat down across from Salt's desk in the chair from the empty cubicle. "Handsome, vulnerable-looking."

"Do you by any chance have a connection in the city's business licensing department? I'm trying to find out who the individuals are that own a couple of businesses."

"Good luck with that. The bureaucrats are plentiful there and all knee-deep in pissed-off."

"Any advice?" Salt asked. "I don't want to impose. I'm sure you're constantly asked for help."

"You might be surprised." Felton drew the photo closer to his right eye. "Prophet in your own land and all that."

"Oh, come on, with your clear-up rate they must come to you for help."

Felton handed the photo to her. "You'll find that each of us has our strong suits in how we work a murder, Salt. Take the Wild Things, for instance, please." He smiled at his own punch line. "They're terrible with paperwork and documentation. The DA hates to get their cases. But together they work the streets like geniuses and put the cases down."

"You're not going to tell me your secrets, are you?" She leaned back and smiled at him.

"My dear." He bent over and looked up from under his brows. "If my instincts are still intact, they're telling me that you are probably best left alone with no one to get in the way." He touched her shoulder as he stood and left.

Salt gathered the photos, slid them back into the envelope, and turned to the inventory of the car and Mike's effects. Other than the bathrobe and slippers, he'd been wearing only a pair of blue plaid boxer shorts.

As she ran her finger down the inventory sheets, she became aware that she was humming. The report of the first uniform officer was brief and perfunctory, listing the reporting person and the responding homicide detective, followed by the detective's very brief supplementary report.

Dan Pyne's and Melissa Primrose's contact information was included on the now ten-year-old preliminary report. Salt hummed "Step Into the Light," a Mavis Staples song, as she began entering names into the various Internet and law enforcement search engines.

"Hello," she said in response to one return.

AN AWAKENING
IN THE LIBRARY

Cedar. Salt drew in another breath, confirming what her nose told her: she'd fallen asleep reading on the library floor. She peeled her cheek from a page of the open book, a Sherlock Holmes that had served as a pillow, and briefly scanned the paragraphs, searching as if she could get a clue there to the origin or impetus of a dream that was quickly evaporating but leaving her with rapid, shallow breaths and a fluttery anxiety.

Felton's advice aside, she wished she could make better use of the scientific method, be more Holmes-like rather than having the dreams, dreams that produced flashbacks and mixed with reality. Sometimes it was music or just being in a particular place, like at Westview or Fort Walker, some vision would worry its way to her consciousness. Last year after recovering from the shooting, she'd expected the dreams and intrusive images that came afterward to stop. Instead, the dreams continued but had also given her insight that helped her solve the case that led to her promotion. She looked over at the shelves that held the books on mental illness, their titles unreadable in the low light.

The heavy navy brocade drapes were pulled tight and no light shone from behind the panels or up at the top. The overhead fixture surrounded by its crumbling plaster medallion hadn't worked since Salt could remember; she was reminded to worry about the wiring in the whole house. A floor lamp was her only light source, its weak cone doing little to displace the dark, casting just enough light to throw shadows on the shelved walls.

She pushed up, her palms to the prickly wool and worn, bare spots of the patterned rug, some of its fringed trim missing. The green indicator light on the recorder was on. The tape could have played out an hour ago or three. She touched the crease on her cheek left by the book and judged her nap to have been a longer one. She hit the eject button and the lid flipped up with the cassette tape that had accompanied her into the dream. "Mike Anderson and the Old Smoke Band, featuring—" She turned the plastic casing over. On the other side, her father had used a heavy-point felt-tip pen, the words and letters blurred. But the first letters of the two words looked like P's and the words were the right shape and length to be "Pretty Pearl."

"Put the boogie on, Daddy," she'd beg. "Put on the boogie-woogie. Put it on, please," jumping in a circle around him, hopping and wiggling her bony pelvis. She loved it best when he'd boogie—his goofy, hilarious dance—flinging his limbs like a cartoon goon.

"Leave it alone. Do not touch the radio without asking," his other voice said. She didn't want to listen, didn't want him to hear the wailing voices as he drove. It scared her and she couldn't think of how to get him to not listen. The singer sounded like he was crying. Her throat tightened so she wouldn't cry. The guitar strings strained like the singer, like her throat; she tightened and tightened and squeezed her eyes shut but she

couldn't squeeze her ears shut and didn't want to cover them or he would know. She couldn't let him see her sad or scared.

"Play the boogie, Daddy."

She slipped the tape back into its case, closed the lid of the recorder, and put the tape back with the others in the box. The recorder was still warm. As she turned it between her hands, the cheap plastic parts made little loose clicking sounds. Grime dimmed the indicator lights. There were nicks and dings in the silver-tone finish.

With her adult knowledge she understood that her father must have struggled with and tried to understand his mental illness—the books spoke to his attempts at self-treatment. But why did he feel he had to do it alone? Why didn't he get help? And why commit suicide— on her birthday?

She put the recorder away, then fished the Anderson/Pearl blues back out of the box and put it in her shirt pocket.

DESTINATION—DAWN

Salt averted her face and put a hand up to shield her eyes from the headlights of the bus belching gray fumes as it made the turn and pulled up to the curb alongside the downtown Homefront Hotel. She held on to the hem of her coat as the wind picked up and the rain turned to a full downpour. She left the Taurus on a yellow curb and went to wait under the hotel's overhead marquee that advertised in large black plastic letters the "MIDNIGHT SPECIAL."

The bus came to a stop and lights came on inside, revealing a pale, lanky-tall man framed by the large front side window, standing and looking out in Salt's direction. The rest of the passengers stood and began reaching for the overhead storage bins. The accordion doors opened. She recognized Bailey Brown's deep voice. "It's a rainy night in Georgia." A taller dark-skinned man was the first down the steps and out the door. "I feel like it's raining all over the world," he harmonized. The musicians stretched and yawned as they stumbled out and into the hotel. The only white guy, the one who'd been looking out the window, walked from the front of the bus through its lit interior looking side to side at the vacant seats. He bent over one of the seats, picked up something palm-sized, stuffed it in his jeans, made his way back to the front of the bus, and pushed out the door as the youngest-looking of the band called to him from the hotel entrance. "You got the dog?" The guy hitched his jeans beneath a "DUDE" T-shirt and gave the kid a thumbs-up as he came under the marquee, watching a scruffy bellman push a flat dolly toward the luggage compartment on the underside of the bus.

"Where's the dog?" Salt asked, stepping toward him.

Dan Pyne turned to face her. "What? Oh, just a joke." He gave her a friendly but quick smile, shrugged, and turned his attention back to the bellman, who was hurriedly loading the instruments and cases onto the dolly. Pyne fast-stepped over to steady one precariously perched guitar case. As he escorted the bellman and dolly toward the door, Salt intercepted him again. "Dan Pyne?"

Pyne turned, tucking shoulder-length hair behind his ears.

She slung a few drops of rain from her fingers and offered her hand. "Detective Alt, Atlanta Police."

"Detective?" Pyne touched his left palm to his jeans as he took her hand.

"I'm a homicide detective," she said, attempting to be reassuring— that he didn't have to worry about the perhaps illegal herb in his pocket.

Pyne glanced at her, his eyes lingering just a half second longer on the scar that ran through her hair, now wet and flattened by the soaking rain. "Homicide," he repeated.

"Mike Anderson," she said.

He looked out at the night and the rain. "My God."

"Can I buy you coffee?" she asked.

"Since you've tracked me down you must know I play guitar with this bunch, but I also do the road managing, so I have to get us checked in."

She ran a hand through her hair, slinging off some of the water. "There's a bar inside. How about if you meet me there in fifteen minutes?"

"Mike." He shook his head. "My God," he repeated.

"Fifteen minutes?" she said.

He held the door for the waiting bellman and the gear, "Yeah," he said, managing to also hold the door for her. She paused, just for a second, walked through the door into the dim lobby and down a hall where she knew the ladies' room to be.

THE HOMEFRONT was a sad substitute for a home. Not quite a fleabag place, but probably better than sleeping on the bus, although not by much. A cloying, deodorizer smell emanated from the carpet, intensifying when stepped on.

By this time of night the hotel bar patrons had thinned to a couple of sad hookers in a corner. Salt sat facing the entrance at a small table against the wall. Pyne wound his way over. "How'd you get your hair dry?" He pulled out the leatherette chair.

"Restroom hand dryer." She tugged at the one curl that covered the scar.

"I've used them a time or two for that." He ran a hand through his still-damp hair. "Life on the road and all."

"In the street, on the road," she said.

A bleary-eyed waitress in all black left a barstool and came to their table.

"Coffee for me," said Salt.

"How long will this take?" Dan asked Salt.

"Depends. I don't know how much you can tell me."

"I'm too tired for coffee and I don't like to drink alone." He looked up at the waitress. "I'll just have water."

"One coffee and one water," repeated the waitress, dropping her arms. "Will that be on the rocks or straight up? With or without lemon?" She turned to begin her slow trek to the bar, clearly not very excited about the late-night big spenders.

"Wait," Salt said to the waitress. "How 'bout a brandy?" she asked Dan.

He nodded.

"Two brandies."

The waitress clicked her pen and stepped toward the bar with just a bit more energy.

Salt shrugged off the coat and pulled her damp shirt collar out from the black linen jacket that concealed the leather shoulder holster and .38. "Where's the dog?"

Dan gave her a quizzical grin, eyebrows raised, his mouth in a twist. "I left him with Mustafa."

"Funny, you seem slimmer without him." She kept a sense of humor about weed.

The waitress set the drinks on napkins in front of them.

Dan patted around for the cigarettes in his jeans pocket, pulled one out, lit it, and then looked up. "Do you mind?" he asked, sliding the ashtray from the center of the table, ready to put it out.

"I've got my own." She went into a pocket of the coat. "I carry them mostly to give away. Makes talking easier for some folks. I don't smoke, but I don't mind if you do."

She put her giveaway smokes on the table next to his. "About Mike," she said.

"Of course. It was me that found him, his body. That's why you're here, that and Melissa." Dan took a draw on the cigarette. "Do you listen to the music, the blues?"

"Some." The light in the bar was low. As he talked, she leaned forward.

"He was the best, could have been the best-known bluesman of our time, bigger than Hendrix even. When I met him, I was living with friends in Inman Park, near Little Five. Were you around then? It was alive. Not all the rich, phony kids that come there now pretending they're somehow living on the edge. One day I was at that old laundromat on Moreland. I guess it's something else now. Mike came in wearing a bathrobe, that bathrobe, I swear." The smoke from his cigarette curled into the air above the table candle, and he looked up as it projected the past.

"I knew who he was right off." Dan sat back up, returning his focus. "And me, I'm not shy, California boy originally. I went over while he was putting his clothes in the machine. I just wanted to tell him how much I admired his playing. He was so warm, shook my hand, said thanks, and asked if I had any quarters for the wash. We started talking about the blues. Turned out he was living about a block from where I did. After that we started hanging out. We both just loved the music." The corners of his mouth drew up a fraction to an almost smile.

"I'd been listening to the blues since I was nine or ten. I was twenty-five when I met Mike, playing guitar and doing the sound setups for a couple of local clubs." Dan blew out a long breath, then took a sip of brandy.

"Why after all these years is a homicide detective interested? I thought the cause of his death was officially an accidental drug overdose." He leaned over the candle in the middle of the sticky table.

"Officially, it still is. But a con, who's in the federal prison system and trying to make a deal to cut his time, gave us information that Mike Anderson's death may not have been accidental or a suicide."

Dan shook his head. "I thought at the time that things didn't add up."

"What things?" Salt picked up her pack of cigarettes.

"He cared about the music but he didn't care about performing.

I think he felt bad about getting so much attention when so many of the old bluesmen were practically starving. He did use, heroin, sometimes other stuff. He'd drink and do drugs. But he loved, loved, loved the music. He wanted to help the old blues musicians, wanted them to get the respect they deserved. It seemed at times like he was on a mission. He was especially protective of several of the real roots folks. I don't know—maybe the best word to describe him right before he died was focused. I just couldn't imagine that he'd wanted to die, but also I couldn't imagine anybody wanting him dead—everybody loved Mike. Accidental seemed the most reasonable explanation."

"Where did he get his drugs? Did he have someone regular he'd score from?" She shook out a smoke.

"He had some very skeevy people hanging around, people telling him how much he could do for the blues. Also he had some bad guys in his band, talented but bad. There were parts of his life that I didn't know about. Stuff from his old neighborhood, parents, church, and clubs he went to after hours. But here's another thing—when Melissa and I would say something about being scared of heroin, Mike always said that he was careful; that he never bought off the street, only from one guy so he could be sure of the strength of the pop—that it wouldn't be too little or too much."

"Do you know who he bought from?"

"It was a long time ago. I guess I've tried not to think about it."

She lit the cigarette.

"You found out I just happened to be coming through Atlanta with the band?"

Salt inhaled once and put the cigarette in the ashtray. "The Internet is a wonderful thing. Brings the whole world a little closer."

"I thought detectives had partners." He shook out another smoke, turning it over and over through his fingers.

The dim bar was empty now except for the two of them, the

waitress, and the bartender. "I don't have a partner because they assigned me to a cold case." She took off her jacket. "And my sergeant probably doubts there's any truth in what this perp alleges anyway."

"Nice gun. How'd you get the scar?"

"Which one?"

"The only one I can see." He pointed to her scalp.

"I got it when words didn't work. Thanks." She patted the gun, then touched the scar. "Gunshot."

The doors from the lobby swung open, the dark bar briefly brightening and suddenly seeming a lot smaller as the other members of the band ambled in and came over. "Dan, our man," Bailey said as if to claim him.

The big, tall guy put a hand on Dan's shoulder. "You in trouble?" he said, looking at Salt and her gun.

"Detective Alt, these guys are the Old Smoke Band." He pointed to them one by one. "Bailey, Pops, Blackbird, Goldie, and Mustafa." Each offered his hand.

"I'm Sarah. Nice to meet you. I'm a fan," she said with a broad smile, taking each hand in turn.

The men pulled up another tiny table and some chairs, hunkered down, and called to the sad waitress for whiskey.

"Sarah?" Dan looked at her.

Goldie scooted his chair closest to the detective. "What's that you've got there?" He winked at the rest of the guys. "Thirty-eight special?" he pointed his thumb at her chest.

She met him tooth for grinning tooth. "Why, with all your experience, Goldie, I would think your guess would be better than that."

"She got you, Goldie. She got you." Blackbird laughed loud and slapped his knee. "Time out, foul on the play."

"Shut up, Goldie. Mind your manners. Why you think you God's gift to every woman?" Bailey frowned.

"Why, because I could be. There's plenty of me to go 'round."

"Mr. Brown," she said, "I especially like 'Time Is Not on My Side.'"

The heavy man beamed. "Now, that ol' stuff—I didn't think anybody listened to that anymore." He kept on smiling.

Blackbird again cut to the chase. "So what's Dan in trouble for? What do the poleese want with him?" He looked over the room, not at her, as if trouble could come from anywhere.

"I was just explaining to Dan. I'm trying to clear up some loose ends on Mike Anderson's death."

"Now, that's something else that was a long time ago," Bailey Brown said, dragging out the last three words. "I played some of the same gigs Mike played. He made the managers and producers hire the old guys."

"Have things changed much since then?" Salt asked.

"Blues ain't changed in fifty years," Bailey answered. "Not since B.B. came out of Memphis, not since Muddy 'n them, Wolf, out of Chicago. A' course them British guys took it to rock and got it famous thataway, but the actual blues, well, just a few young folks, like Mike, kept to the ol' blues." Bailey sipped some of his whiskey, smacking his lips with an "Ah." "Boy could play the blues, but he had some nasty characters he sometimes played with and some people around him that I wouldn't have trusted. Goldie, didn't you know some of them south side guys?"

Goldie, holding up his glass to get the waitress for a refill, said, "That's a long time ago. I didn't keep up with any of them. But that reminds me." Goldie pulled his phone, started punching at it, then left the bar.

Bailey stared into his glass. "Always been rough in the blues, and now days most of these kids don't realize all that hip-hop and rap come out of the blues. They think they first to invent rough. They tellin' they stories, and them's some scary stories all right. But underneath is the blues. They was rappin' in Africa. James Brown was rappin'. Ain't nothin' new."

"Mustafa, didn't I see you when you played with the Morehouse group at the blues festival last year?" Salt said, turning to the young man.

"What were you doing there? Bustin' guys for smoking ganja?" Mustafa seemed to work at tough.

"Damn, I missed my big chance to arrest some musicians for smoking weed! At the blues festival!" she kidded the drummer.

"So would you lock me up for practicing my religion, smoking the sacred herb?" The young man raised his chin. He was wearing a Che Guevara T-shirt.

"And what religion would that be, Sweet Meat?' Goldie said, arriving back at the table. "You grew up Presbypalian or some shit in a suburb."

"I'm into roots religion, voodoo, from the Islands."

"Don't get him started, Goldie. Leave him alone," Dan mediated.

Bailey began to sag, growing darker circles under his eyes. "Come on, kid. Help me and Pops get tucked in." He threw back the last smack of whiskey and got up from the table. Mustafa rose with the old men. Before following them out of the bar, he pointed at Dan and lifted an eyebrow. "Don't wake the dog when you come in."

Goldie, on his fourth whiskey, barked.

Blackbird stuck out his tongue and panted. After the old men and Mustafa were through the door, he pulled a cigar that matched his size from his jacket and lit it. "I think I'm gonna take this stogie over to the bar and have one more whiskey. Goldie, you might as well come with me. You wearing that waitress out."

The two men moved across the room and left a space of silence between Dan and Salt. "How did you get to be the dog's guardian?" She leaned forward again.

"On every tour the guys find something they keep going, joking around. I like dogs, pet 'em when I see them. I wanted to adopt this old stray that showed up at the bus in Albuquerque. But, well—I'm not home much." Dan looked sideways and lifted his shoulders, resigned.

Then, almost like after she was shot, Salt caught something in her peripheral vision. "I remember an imaginary dog. I hadn't thought of him since . . ."

"Since?"

She turned back to Dan. "Since I lost him," she said, looking down, smoothing the coat across her lap. She cleared her throat. "So the band gave you a dog, of sorts, a dog-away-from-home dog. Home. We were just getting to Melissa when your guys came in. I saw some magazine pieces, some interviews. You and she have been together for a long time."

"Look, I'm dead tired and I've got to make sure these guys turn in, and then I've got to get up tomorrow and oversee the setup for the gig."

"Of course."

He hesitated. "If you want you can come to the gig. We'll be at the Notelling tomorrow and Saturday."

She stood and fished bills from a pocket of the coat. "See you then." She put money under the candle, picked up her jacket, and folded the old coat over her arm.

She thought she heard Dan humming the theme music from an old TV cop show as he followed her out of the bar.

CRIMINAL RECORDS

Criminal Records was an anchor business in Little Five Points, a destination hang for suburban kids looking for edgy. They'd put a blue streak in their hair and come sit on the plaza with other suburban kids with streaks in their hair or a new nose ring or tat, shop at the vintage clothing boutique and the shoe place that carried the most current radical shoe styles. As Salt pushed the door inward, an over-the-door bell jangled but didn't seem to have much significance for the fortyish guy behind the counter, his elbow propped on one of the glass display cases. He was in conversation with his blond counterpart, who was wearing the same plaid knee shorts, except the blond guy's pants were torn at the right hem instead of the left. The store was wall to wall and floor to ceiling with bins of CDs, cassette tapes, and vinyl, and had a pleasant dry-vanilla and old-glue odor.

Eventually, the clerk glanced down the counter at Salt but continued his bent-arm talk with the dude. It seemed a little heavy-handed to have to display her badge just to get sales service. "Excuse me." She held up a finger. The guy said something out of the side of his mouth before he unpropped and ambled over. "I'm looking for some CDs of Mike Anderson."

"Okay," he said.

"Do you have any?"

"Maybe." He nodded at the blond guy who was leaving. "Dude."

"'Maybe,'" she repeated. "Can you show me what you have of his?"

"Tapes, CDs, vinyl?"

"I'd like to take a look at them all."

He motioned for her to follow him to the far-back counter. Along the way he slid out a foot-long box with cassette tapes. At the rear of the store he plopped the tapes down and then reached above his head and grabbed a handful of CDs. "Back in a minute," he said, leaving from behind the counter and heading for the bigger bins: the center of the store. Salt took out her new notepad and began to make a list of the musicians Mike had worked with.

"You going to buy anything or just waste my time?" Record Store Dude was back, two LPs in hand.

"Your tax dollars at work." She opened her badge case.

"Cool," he said, standing up straighter. "CSI shit, right?"

"Right." She slipped the badge back into a pocket. "It has listed on this CD a song with a vocalist, Pretty Pearl. You know anything about her?"

"Sure, she's kind of a Little Five fixture, or was. Homeless. She used to hang out around the benches, asking for handouts from the brats. Nastee, nastee, she hit bottom and was in bad shape last time I saw her."

"What happened? How long has it been since you saw her?"

He tapped his forehead with one finger. "Screw loose. She was mental as far back as I can remember. Most people don't even know she was a singer. Last time I saw her was probably a month or so ago."

Salt handed him two of the CDs. "I'll take these two."

They moved back up to the front and the cash register. While the guy was ringing up her CDs, she studied the photos and illustrations on the covers of the LPs. One front cover had a photo of Mike bent over a guitar, his face hidden. The other cover was a stylized '60s-type black-and-blue silhouette.

"Fourteen dollars and thirty-two cents."

"Anybody around here that might know where I can find Pearl?" She handed him the bills.

"Cops know her better than anybody, those homeless cops."

"The HOPE Team?"

"Yeah, they been dealing with her." Then, flipping a quarter, he said, "Heads or tails?"

"Tails."

He gave her the change. "Tails it is."

A COUPLE OF BLOCKS from Peachtree Street, at the corner of Auburn Avenue and Fort Street, Salt sat down on the curb beside the old blind man in a wheelchair, missing a leg since she'd last seen him.

"Officer Salt, last time I saw you, you know I'm sayin', you were in The Homes."

She told him about being promoted and transferred to Homicide. "Why are you out here and not in The Homes?" she asked. Two ambulances, one with the siren full blast, screamed past over some of the old cobblestones, revealed beneath a torn place in the pavement. Salt leaned in closer to hear him. He smelled of urine and the metallic odor of crack.

"Had to go to the rehab center down there"—he pointed to a yellow brick high-rise a block away—"when they took my leg." Then he grinned. "'Course you know I'm on the street to get my real medicine." Someone had parked him on the sidewalk right across the street from the Fort Street and Auburn Avenue viaduct, a concrete-and-iron structure so massive and thick that the traffic sounds from the fourteen lanes overhead barely registered and were only background for the street life of Sweet Auburn. Dark bundles of homeless men and women lay prone in the shadows against the fencing and pylons.

He planted his dark, gnarled fingers over his stump. "It's just as troublesome as when it was there. What's that you're hummin'? I almost recognize it." His clouded blue-black eyes twitched.

"Something I heard recently," she told him. "I'm looking for Pretty Pearl."

"Yeah, that's 'Hellhound.' Pearl do that song real right."

"It's stuck in my head—an earworm. My dad had the Robert Johnson recording."

"Long as the hellhound ain't stuck on your tail. You know what they say: you see a hellhound three times, you gonna die." He turned his face up, eyes open to the sun. The air smelled of grease and sugar. The big churches, historic Ebenezer and Wheat Street Baptist, were each a block away in opposite directions, but their spires were too tall to be seen from the street where she and the old man were sitting.

THE NOTELLING

Salt was already at the Notelling Tavern sitting at the back bar closest to the rear entranceway. Thunder like a runaway boxcar accompanied Dan and Mustafa through the double doors at the back of the cinder-block building as they pushed the gear on a flat dolly. Lightning cracked just as they got inside.

An albino called Melody met them as they came out of the sparsely lit short hall from the back door. "Oh Danny Boy, the pipes, the pipes are calling."

"Melody, how are you, dude?" Dan grabbed the little man's shoulder. In the humidity Dan's T-shirt stuck to his back and chest.

"From glen to glen and down the mountainside," Melody sang, smiling and holding the doors as they pulled the gear dolly inside.

"Mustafa, this is Melody, the sound man. Melody, meet Mustafa, our new drummer."

Melody cocked his head, taking the measure of Mustafa. "What's your name? What's your name? Young Blood," he sang, arms thrown wide. Mustafa, puzzled, lifted an eyebrow. Dan glanced at Salt then, quickly digging his legs back to get traction for the dolly, stumbling, causing the gear cart to veer off. "Shit." They got it going and carted the load to the stage, where he then stopped and nodded to her from the distance, his hands on his hips.

Salt took a sip from the glass in front of her, set it down, and unhooked her heels from the stool. As she stood, Dan reached down to grab a guitar case and began setting the cases on a foot-high ubiquitous dirty gray-carpeted stage.

"Storm's coming." She came up to his side. "You got here just in time."

Melody floated close, singing Roy Orbison's "Pretty Woman."

"I can't help you," Dan said, aggressively unzipping a gear case.

"No one could look as good as you. Mercy."

"Hey, Melody. How 'bout you help us out here." Dan turned to Salt. "I've got a job to do."

"Mercy," repeated Melody.

"Of course," she said. "When you take a break. I don't mind waiting." She walked back to the bar, where beer signs flickered next to a wall-mounted TV, muted, words scrolling across the bottom of the screen.

The place was dim and had the same stale-beer smell of old bars everywhere. The Notelling was a typical blues bar: dingy, Plexiglas windows, burglar bars, interior supports of paint-chipped concrete. Even still, it was a famous venue for bluesmen. There were twenty or so badly done eighteen-by-twenty-four-inch chalk portraits hanging behind the stage, a who's who of the blues: B.B. King, Lightnin' Hopkins, Blind Willie McTell, Robert Johnson, Howlin' Wolf, Muddy Waters, T-Bone Walker, and so on. A scratchy recording of Albert Collins on guitar, accompanied by a squawky sax, played through the ceiling speakers while Dan and Mustafa set up guitar stands, attached cymbals to drums, and tested the hookups and sound system.

Except for a couple of bartenders, one waitress, and Melody, this time of day the place was otherwise empty, at least that's what Salt thought until a man's voice came from the far back of the room. "Shh-up," a guy, working on an early drunk or possibly a late one, slurred at the woman in the shadows beside him, who was leaning away from the light over their table in an otherwise dark corner.

Salt turned in the couple's direction.

"Ask me that one more time, bitch." The man's voice got louder.

Dan was keeping busy hooking up the gear, doing what everyone else in the place was doing, averting their eyes and likely hoping they weren't going to hear what they were about to hear. Salt put her glass down on the bar and watched the room reflected in the bar mirror.

The woman stood up, but the drunk grabbed her by the arm and pulled her into the light. "You sit your ass down." Her face was almost totally hidden by straight, thin hair that fell to her shoulders.

Salt got to her feet and turned again in their direction.

"I told you." His hand cracked across the woman's face, whipping her hair around her head.

Salt moved quickly toward them.

"Oh no." Dan dropped a cable and caught up to Salt. The bartender came from behind the bar. As she walked, Salt moved her jacket to expose the badge on her belt and pulled an ID case from a pocket.

At the table the tobacco-tan man looked at them with fuzzy eyes. "This ain't your business," he said, stroking his mangy beard.

"Sir," said Salt, "you are under arrest." Blood dripped from the woman's mouth. "Ma'am, if you'll go to the bar I'm sure they'll give you some ice to keep that from swelling. Please go now."

"Arrest? Just who you think's gonna arrest me?" He focused on Salt while the bartender moved toward the woman.

Salt opened the ID case. "I'm Detective Alt with the Atlanta Police

Department." She held it up to the drunk and to the bartender. "Please help the lady to the bar." She kept her eyes on the guy at the table but turned her face slightly to Dan. "You can help by calling 911 and telling them that an officer needs assistance, and make sure they have the right address."

"I'm not leaving you to deal with this asshole by yourself," he said.

"Cunt cop, you're not arresting me, and *she*"—he pointed to the woman still frozen to the chair—"ain't going nowhere."

Salt slid her ID to a pocket and moved to the woman. "You'll need to stand up." She put her right arm around the woman's shoulders and handed her to the bartender. The man shoved at the table and stumbled up, his chair scraping on the rough concrete floor.

Salt put her hand to her waist. "Sir, turn around, face the wall, and put your hands behind your back."

In the otherwise silent blues club, wind blew through a high transom with a sound like a distant train whistle.

She asked the man again. "Sir, is there anything I can do or say to get you to comply with my lawful order?"

The boxcar thunder rattled the walls.

"You must be feeling lucky. Fuck you." The light caught on a silver-colored chain that hung in a wide U from the drunk's leather belt. As he began to draw back his fist, Salt fluidly slid an expandable baton from her waist. The metal shaft clicked and briefly flashed overhead just before the thud that dropped the drunk to one knee, his left shoulder and arm dangling. He vomited on the floor.

"911, an ambulance," she called out over her shoulder. "His collarbone's broken." She pinned the man's good arm behind him, leveraging it with the baton. Dan moved forward. "Dude."

Melody sang in the background, "You ain't goin' nowhere."

"Get the knife off his belt," she said, pulling the man to his back as she reached into his pants pockets and pulled out a leather sap. "Take off his boots." Dan got the knife and pulled at the boots. A small revolver clanked to the floor. Salt scooped it up and tucked it into her jeans

"What else?" she asked the man, who just coughed and then moaned. She patted her palms all along his pant legs, up to his crotch, turning her hands so that she felt his groin with the backs of her hands.

There were distant sirens, then nearer, and then from the parking lot the sound of spraying gravel.

"I'm not going to press charges." The lanky-haired woman was back, tears running down her face, holding ice in a bar towel to her lip. "You can't arrest him," she pleaded.

"Ma'am, he committed an assault in front of me. You'll go to court. The judge will make him go to counseling."

The woman cried louder.

The double entrance doors slammed into the walls as two uniforms rushed through with long strides. They homed in and were at her side in half seconds. "Salt, damn, are you okay?"

Dan expelled a laugh that was close to a yelp or a cry.

"Nice to see you, Sarge," she said.

"Mercy." Melody's voice echoed through the room.

THE HOUSE LIGHTS went down on a full room; patrons of every hue stood against the walls, and every chair and table was taken. A wash of blue lit the stage, empty except for instruments catching the light on their corners and curves, like a promise. The noise in the room lowered as the owner of the Notelling, wearing a tie-dyed jacket, bounded to the stage under a spotlight at the mic, center stage. "True blues lovers, tonight is your night. Put your hands together and welcome to the stage of the Notelling, where there's no telling what will happen and no telling what does, the Old Smoke Band." Applause, whistles, and foot stomping vibrated up through the floor to the tables, where pitchers and glasses of beer splashed.

The crowd quieted as lone Mustafa came onstage, striking a beat hard and sharp with his hickory sticks. He carried the beat to his drum kit and another spotlight came on as he set into a blues shuffle. The audience clapped on his two and four beats. A second light opened to Pops on bass, laying heavy in the groove as Blackbird moved across the stage to the keyboard. The third light bloomed as his hands hit the keys. Women in the audience stood up and started moving their hips. Goldie and Dan came on unnoticed until Goldie blew a first skronky peal from the sax and all the stage lit up.

Dan stepped up to the center mic. "Ladies and gentlemen, we are the Old Smoke Band and here's our Boss of the Blues, Baileee Brown!"

A fifth and last spotlight followed Bailey as he hefted his bulk to the riser, ambled to his chair, and picked up the old Gibson Byrdland. The crowd, already on its feet, screamed when he hit the first fierce squawl. He leaned over the guitar, suit coat open, beads of sweat at his hairline already threatening to become glistening streams.

Young Mustafa's eyes watched Bailey with a reverential focus, barely suppressing his joy, doing better than best to push the band. Dan and Pops built a base with their groove. B-Bird made it full, and when Goldie and Bailey reached out to each other, the band brought both old-time believers and converts to the congregation of "Everyday I Have the Blues."

THE STAGE HAD EMPTIED. Waiting for Dan, Salt swiped one finger down the condensation on the bottle of beer she was nursing.

He came up from behind and leaned close to the silver ring in her right ear. "Are you always this calm after beating the crap out of people?"

"You should see me after I've killed folks." She turned her face up. "Do you have time now?"

"After seeing what you did to that guy, I guess I wouldn't want to obstruct anything you've set your mind to. I've got nothing to hide. Was I imagining things, or did you have some sort of magic wand you waved over that dude?"

She stood and they made their way to the front door. "Retractable baton, regulation issue—good when you don't want to use pepper spray, like in a club."

Outside he said, "Sorry for earlier. It's just that going over this stuff about Mike, bringing it all back up—well, 'Let sleeping dogs lie' has been my motto. I don't like to think about his death. You got any other ninja shit you do?"

"I'm working on my teleporting and time travel." She stiffened her legs and crossed her fists in front of her chest, superhero-style.

A porch with broken-slat rockers and worn, wicker lemonade tables fronted the club. The rain had ended and the lights of the parking lot sparkled off the water beads on the cars.

"I didn't know cops could drink on duty."

"I'm not on the clock. I've got to get something from my car. Be right back." She sat her beer down.

"Again, I apologize for uncovering old wounds," she said, coming up the steps carrying the envelope. She sat down with it in her lap, took up her beer, and rocked. "My dad had a love for the blues," she said.

Dan scratched at his wrists. "This club must have gotten fleas since I was here last."

"When was that?"

"I guess about two years or so ago when we came through Atlanta last. Even though it's on the blues highway, we just had gigs elsewhere. Scene hasn't changed much at all. Always struggling. The blues always struggling."

"Struggling?"

"That's what Mike used to say. 'Blues is like Atlanta,' he'd say, 'struggling.' He loved this city, he said because it got no natural gifts—no coast, no bays or mountains or lakes. Just a crossroads. And he loved the old musicians here. He hated that people wanted to forget them and the hard times they sang about."

"Speaking of hard times, do you remember a singer went by the name of Pretty Pearl?"

"She was terrific. But I lost track of her after Mike died. She was a friend of his."

Bailey began a soft solo, opening the second set alone.

"Isn't that your cue?" She nodded toward the inside.

"Lots of times I sit out on the first numbers of the second set. I recheck the sound. And usually they open with numbers that don't have to have rhythm guitar."

Salt closed her eyes, listening to the music, then asked, "Do you pay attention to your dreams?"

"I'm not sure what you mean."

Her eyes were still closed. "Maybe that dog is talking to you."

"Dog?"

"The one you and the band joke about. Maybe you got a hell-hound on your trail. I think I had a dream about him."

Dan started to scratch his leg but stopped himself.

She slipped eight-by-ten photos from the packet and held them out. "These are of Mike."

"You mean the crime scene?" He shook his head.

She handed him the stack of pictures.

The top photo was a distance shot of the car, the old Pontiac wagon, cream and green. "'Old Ironsides,' we called her." Dan stared at the stark, overexposed picture. "It's his baby all right, but not like I remember. Last time I was in this car was that night. We played The Pub. I remember the chalkboard sandwich board—'Avocado/sprouts sandwich special, $3.19, and a draft Michelob'—beside the open double doors and underneath the name of our band, Leaves of Great Grass. We were pretty good, played everything rock and roll, rhythm and blues, Motown, and, of course, the blues. Mike was like a god to us, our band. He was on the road a lot, but when he was home he hung out with us, me and the guys.

"That last set I was swinging—Bob practically swallowing the mic on vocals, flinging ourselves into James Brown's 'Sex Machine,' everybody dancing with everybody, tables dripping spilled beer and sweating pitchers. Mike ambled in along the wall and stood in back, looking like all he cared about was our music—smiling. He gave me a ride home. And I'll never forget—about three blocks from the house he looked at me. 'Man, you guys were brangin' it tonight, great, really great.' He said it twice, 'Great,' with that quizzy smile he had. I clearly remember looking out at the passing streetlights, trying to memorize how I felt, to hold on to that moment when one of the most admired bluesmen in the world said I played great."

The sole of Bailey's shoe smacked the floor in a chain-gang rhythm.

In the next photo the glare from the camera had made the windows of Mike's car opaque, obscuring the interior. Dan slid it from the top to the bottom and looked at the next photo, which had been taken from the open door on the driver's side. Mike's body leaned, his head against the window. Bathrobe, legs, uneven hair, closed eyes, blue lips in a slack oval. Dan covered the photo with both hands and looked out toward the rows of cars. He handed the photos back to

Salt, got up, and stood at the rail with his back to her. He used his heel to rake his ankle.

She waited again, then said, "God is in the details. I know this is hard, but I would like for you to look at them, at everything, pieces of paper, the folds of his robe, the floorboard, anything that might spark your memory. You've scratched at your ankles several times, you know."

Dan looked down and brushed at the legs of his jeans. "I don't believe in dreams."

"Will you try again?" She held out the awful photographs.

Bailey's voice had trailed off to a lonesome blues moan.

HOPE

————

S alt switched radio channels over to the central city frequency. "4133 raise any HOPE Team unit."

"5582," dispatch called.

"5582."

"Can you name a location?" Salt requested, asking where she could meet the unit.

"Right now we're on the tracks under Piedmont."

"Cross street?" Salt transmitted her willingness to meet them where they were.

"We'll be out at Ansley in about thirty," replied the officer.

"Copy, thirty at Ansley," repeated Salt, confirming the location and her intention to meet there.

"Radio, can you have an ambulance meet us there as well?" continued the HOPE unit. "For an eighteen-year-old white female, mentally ill. And start a sex crimes detective."

———

HOPE, Homeless Outreach and Proactive Enforcement, emerged over the rim of the railroad gulley. They rose from below, heads and chests upright, and, like almost always, together in a pack, rarely less than all four. They patrolled a citywide beat, mostly in places that most folks didn't know existed; wherever *their people* were found that's where they went. Treading the hill, over the rim, with heavy boots and the dark uniforms, they came up to the asphalt of the strip mall lot. An emaciated white girl was supported between them, a small blonde, hoisted by the two female team members, Leeksha Johnson and Joy Adams. Salt had a special regard and fondness for them. They taught classes at the academy on managing people with mental illness, skills for de-escalating those in crisis, often psychotic and off their prescribed medications. The last class she'd taken from them was an advanced, weeklong session led by the two HOPE guys, Swain Blackmon and Jackson Thornton.

Atlanta was an example of the "build it and they will come" consequence as concerned its history with homeless people. The largest city in the Southeast, it also had the largest homeless population in the region. Years ago the city had begun to provide services—shelters, food distribution, hygiene supplies—and the homeless came from all over. Some jurisdictions had finally admitted to dumping their homeless inside the city limits. The HOPE Team had documented and reported people sent from all over the country and the places that had paid people's way to Atlanta just to get rid of them.

Simultaneously with the team's emergence from the tracks behind the businesses, an ambulance and the detective from Special Victims arrived near where Salt had parked.

"We heard you made detective. Congratulations." Leeksha hugged Salt.

"That's great." Swain beamed at her.

"We were so glad to see one of the good guys get the promotion," said Joy.

"This is Jennifer," Blackmon said, touching the girl's shoulder. The girl's eyes were everywhere but on what was in front of her or the cops that led her out. "Come on, child." They continued on over to the paramedics and the female SVU detective. The girl was silently compliant, getting her vital signs taken, blood pressure and heart rate and a preliminary exam for any obvious injuries, all while the detective talked quietly to her. The girl's hair was matted and clumped. She was wearing men's pants and a sweatshirt, so it was hard to determine how thin she might actually be. Her hands were brown from exposure to dirt and the elements, her nails rimmed with grime.

Joy came over to Salt, her back to the ambulance. "One of our regulars called us. Said men were using her down under one of the bridges."

The ambulance stowed the girl on a gurney and took off. The team watched until the ambulance was out of sight, then let their shoulders fall, bowing their heads and giving a collective sigh. "Damn," said Leeksha.

"Damn is right," repeated Jackson.

"Does this ever get any easier for you guys?" Salt asked.

"When it does, we'll know it's time to go," said Joy, all the rest nodding in agreement.

"Got to pay your dues if you wanna sing the blues," added Swain.

"What he means is, like we tell folks in training, 'empathize.' It hurts but it helps, if you know what I mean. If we get in their shoes, get what's going on with them, then we're better able to find a way to help, to make them feel safe."

"And if they feel safe . . ."

"We're safer," Salt finished with the words from the team's training.

"I brought you something." She went to the trunk of her unmarked car, got out a box, and handed it to Leeksha. "It's the cedar stuff I told you about, organic. I buy it by the gallon for using around my place— on the sheep and on the dog. I use it on myself when the horseflies are bad. And it smells good. I put it in some recycled spray bottles."

The team regularly came in contact with body lice, mosquitoes, fleas, red bugs, gnats, stinging insects. They sometimes wore surgical masks and gloves to protect themselves from HIV, hepatitis, TB, scabies, flu, even impetigo. They encountered feral dogs, snakes, rats, opossums, and rabid raccoons, and often were seen painted in calamine after climbing through poison ivy, oak, or sumac in a quest to reach someone, often in bad shape, homeless, mentally ill, addicted, ones who had slipped off society's grid.

And then they were scoffed at, called "social workers" by some officers. Until those officers, like Salt, would witness Leeksha, Joy, Jackson, or Swain manage a crisis where people who, terrified and out of their minds, would otherwise have injured themselves and probably officers. Salt had been there when Joy de-escalated a man who was bare-chested, bleeding from test cuts all over his upper body, holding a large shard of glass to his neck beneath a vein. When a woman blinded by rage, a gun to her elderly mother's head, had been talked into putting the gun down by Swain. There had been many others.

"Follow us back to our cat hole, Salt, so we can clean up a little. We've been out since five this morning, before the sun was up." The team went out early and late, to make contact with the homeless before they left or after they came home to the camps and hidey-holes.

The team had the worst cars, as if working with the homeless warranted shabby vehicles. Salt followed their rattletrap van to a derelict office, a classroom in back of an elementary school that had been closed for years. "Nice digs," Salt said, following them in.

"We don't mind it. Nobody bothers us here and our consumers don't bother anybody when we invite them over."

Mug shots and missing-persons flyers hung from a blackboard and were tacked all around the large classroom. The small hard-plastic desk chairs were still in rows as if the children were expected back.

"I have another one to add to your gallery." Salt motioned to the photos lining the room. She slid out copies of Pearl's mug shot from the envelope she was carrying. Like many of the homeless and mentally ill, Pearl had been arrested multiple times, mostly for petty charges and usually when officers had no other option for her care. In Georgia, if a person wasn't psychotic enough to qualify as being an immediate danger to themselves or others, then the law for involuntary hospitalization did not pertain.

Leeksha recognized her as soon as she had the photo in her hand. "Oh, I know her. She's over in Underground now."

Jackson said, "She used to be around Little Five."

"Yep, that's her," Salt said. "I'm looking for her because she might be able to help me on an old case."

"We'll be doing a detail on Friday with the outreach people from Grady and the railroad police. One of our target locations is the area around Underground, so we very well may run into Pearl. You wanna come along, meet us here at four-thirty a.m."

THE MOBILE MEDICAL BUS from Grady Memorial Hospital, the public hospital known as "The Gradys" from the days of segregation when it was two hospitals, was arriving as Salt pulled up behind the HOPE Team office very, very early on Friday morning. Inside, the team had already distributed maps and water supplies, and the cedar spray was being applied liberally as folks entered, the scent heavy in the room where twelve people were greeting one another and drinking box coffee from paper cups.

"God, Salt, I haven't seen you in too long." Terrance Stewart put his cup down and wrapped his arms around her. Even at the early hour, his dark, pockmarked face was already shimmering with oil and sweat. He was the hospital's coordinator for both mental and physical health outreach services to the city's homeless. He'd started out in a faith-based organization without formal medical or psychological training and had become invaluable to all of the service agencies because of his tenure with and knowledge of the homeless community; he was a crucial instructor for those who had the formal training but lacked experience in the street. Salt knew him from his work on her old beat. He smelled strongly of cedar.

"I see you-all have taken advantage of the spray I brought the team." She sniffed loudly at his shirt, pulled back, and then hugged him again. "I can never thank you enough, Terry, for all you and your group did for my people."

"'My people,' that's just like you. You're the only cop I know who called homeless folks on their beat 'my people.' Worried me some but no doubt about it you knew that beat. What will they do without you?"

"Like they say, 'The beat goes on.'"

"People, listen up." Leeksha was at the front of the room with a clipboard. "Most of you guys know the drill, but for a couple of you new to these details, I'll go over the plan and give you your team and area assignments."

Salt was going with Terrance's team, Jackson Thornton from HOPE, and a sergeant from the railroad police. Everyone in the room began to gather in their assigned groups, coordinating transportation and logistics according to the area they would be searching. A commonality among all the participants was that while they were different shapes, sizes, colors, and ethnicities and from various agencies, they were all fit, some obviously more so than others, and able to stride the awkward crossties, trample through kudzu, and climb up and down the hard terrain of the hilly city. In the high humidity and in all kinds of weather they did their work; especially when it was very hot or very cold, their services were needed more than ever.

The team rode in the medical bus to the heart of downtown and into one of the city university's parking lots that abutted the rails. The attendant waved them through, and they parked under a viaduct where various medical personnel would meet up and man the bus in four-hour shifts. Salt tucked her jeans into the tops of an old pair of uniform boots and retied the laces. Their team of four started down the tracks, heading toward Underground, a mile or so from where they were now.

The Underground area had become a tourist attraction and entertainment district that had come and gone in popularity, and come and gone again. But Underground wasn't underground, it was more like a basement, where you could see the foundations of the city if you cared enough to look past the cheap trappings that were meant to sanitize the past and attract tourists. Attempts had been made to revitalize it, the last effort for the Olympics, but according to some, the place seemed to be snakebit and couldn't maintain.

There were many agencies nearby that served the homeless—Grady's satellite health centers, shelters, churches—and the population to be served camped near the tracks and under the viaducts.

Bessie Smith sang about that part of Atlanta.

Underneath the viaduct ev'ry day
Drinking corn and hollerin' hoo-ray
Pianos playin' till the break of day.

Salt alternated between walking on the rough gravel beside the ties and walking on the ties in an awkward stretch step. The air under the viaducts was damp and still cool from the night. Stained, dripping walls alternated with graffiti, layers of plaster, or brick—a century or more of building, rebuilding, tearing down, reconfiguring, covering up, and uncovering. They were headed in the direction of the government building where the old concrete Zero Milepost, which once designated the end of the Western & Atlantic railroad line, was on display. Atlanta's first name had been "Terminus."

"Hear that?" Salt asked Jackson. She stopped to listen more carefully. Silence, then what sounded like a distant sledgehammer striking the rails with the same rhythm that a man might make driving a spike.

After Sherman burned the original depot during the Civil War, the Union Railroad Depot had been rebuilt during Reconstruction. Other businesses were built in proximity to the depot, through which a hundred trains or more ran: Kenny's Saloon, Gate City Harness Company, Planters Hotel, banks, law offices.

"Hear what?" Jackson answered.

Bridges had been built over the tracks and then joined by a concrete mall. First floors became basements, storage and service entrances, and then speakeasies and juke joints during Prohibition.

There were stretches under the shorter tunnels where light from the streets made its way down the tracks. In other places they had to switch on their heavy flashlights, shining the beams up and down the tracks and walls. In one dark spot they came up to a bundle, and as they approached it they announced themselves in order not to startle anyone who might be easily stressed by contact with people. It was why so many of the homeless with mental illness couldn't stay in the shelters—people.

Jackson stood next to the muddy sleeping bag. "Hey, friend," he said, holding the light at his side pointed down for a less intrusive ambient beam. There was a stirring inside the bag. "Hey, it's the po-leese. We're checking to be sure you're okay. Okay?"

A scaly hand reached from the opening and a crusty-faced white man stuck his head out, blinking, then focused on Jackson as he untangled himself from his cocoon. "Samuels? Is it you, Samuels? Man, I thought you were a goner at Ia Drang."

Terrance stepped up. "Seventh Cav. Right? You're due for your medical. They got your transport waiting."

"Sir, yes, sir."

"We'll be your escort, soldier." Terrance and the railroad police sergeant waited while the man gathered his belongings. They would escort the veteran back to the medical bus and from there would deliver him to the VA.

Jackson and Salt continued down the tracks. "We've always dealt with the Vietnam vets, but now we're beginning to get guys back from Iraq and Afghanistan," he told her. Another set of tracks, its spikes red-brown with rust, merged with the tracks they'd been walking. Horizontal lines on the adjacent brick wall indicated some former use of the structure. "Blest be the tie that binds," Jackson said.

"What?"

"Blest be the tie that binds. You've been humming that hymn 'Blest Be the Tie That Binds.'"

Salt replayed what had unconsciously been going through her head. "You're right. I didn't realize I was doing it."

Down the tracks in front of them was a ledged tunnel, trash-strewn, gang-signed, broken furniture here and there, and people, ten or more, swaddled in blankets and lying on the long, flat concrete shelves. A small drift of smoke wafted from a nearby fire barrel, beside which lay a brown dog of an indeterminate breed. The dog stood and trotted over to one of the blankets.

"Georgia Brown Dog," Jackson said.

"I heard that," Salt said.

"Poleese." Jackson waved his flashlight. "Poleese." They stopped well shy of the mouth of the tunnel while he radioed their location. "5582 to radio, hold myself and 4133 out at the tracks under Marietta and Central."

The shapes began to undulate, then heads and hands emerged. The dog trotted away. The sounds of bottles clanking against concrete echoed through the tunnel.

"HOPE Team checking," Jackson said, moving in. "HOPE Team."

"Fuck you, Jackson" came from one of the sleeping bags, its occupant shifting but not turning out.

"That you, Makepeace? Come on, man." Jackson took Salt's arm and led her to the side of the tunnel. "Makepeace is lots of time really agitated before he gets his coffee. Let's give him a minute."

The rest of the campers were silent as they gradually began to stir, throwing off layers, retrieving toiletries, cans, water, bags, and packets from stashes, packs, and crevices.

"I've got some information, guys," Jackson announced. "The Gateway has gotten more rooms, SROs," he said, referring to the city's center that coordinated services for the homeless.

"Fuck the Gateway." Makepeace stuck his head out, eyes bulging.

"Naw, man. Not *at* the Gateway. Rooms, single-room occupancy, SROs, in apartments or houses, not shelters. Gateway just makes the arrangements."

Two women, both wearing Grady bracelets indicating their recent stay in the hospital, came over. "What we got to do to get them rooms?"

"Just check in at the Gateway. They do the paperwork and you're in," Jackson told them.

Salt unfolded some of the Pearl flyers. "I'm Detective . . ." She stopped and took out one of her new business cards. "They call me

'Salt.' I'm looking for this woman." She handed them both a flyer and a card. Jackson passed Makepeace and went on into the cavernous tunnel, passing out his cards and the Pearl flyers.

The women took their time looking at Pearl's mug shot. "Uh-uh." They shook their heads. "We ain't been out here long. Ain't seen her."

"Goddamn. Goddamn." Makepeace ripped back his wrappings and slung his legs by picking them up at the knees, hurling himself upright. "Give me the goddamn picture." He motioned Salt with his fingers, then snatched the flyer from her hand as soon as she was within his considerable reach. "Pearl. You satisfied now? Her name is Pearl. Used to be Pretty Pearl, a singer, now she Pitiful Pearl. Yeah, I know most every goddamn soul out on these tracks. You'd think they'd hire me for the fucking HOPE Team. HOPE Team. You better hope they leave you the fuck alone."

"Dude, is that any way to talk?" Jackson walked back to them.

"Fuck you, Jackson Thornton. In case you hadn't noticed, this is not the fucking Biltmore."

"Mr. Makepeace—" she began.

Makepeace interrupted. "So Mr. Hope here told you who I am. What's a nice white girl doing out here anyway? Don't you have some doilies to make or some tea to sip?"

"Do you know where Pearl is staying?" Jackson asked him. "Salt is a homicide detective. She's hoping Pearl can help with an old case, Mike Anderson's death."

"What's it worth to you?" Makepeace reached behind him, grabbed aluminum crutches, adjusted the braces, and swung himself to standing. "You got any fucking cash?"

Salt looked to Jackson, who said, "Come on, man. Don't be like that."

Makepeace turned his face away and spit, then turned back. "I saw her 'bout a week ago out on the corner at Spring and Mitchell, in that parking lot where those churches come and let the do-gooders feel they selves all warm all over 'cause they put together some peanut butter sandwiches and went all the way to the jungle of downtown Atlanta to feed some actual black people." He slapped a crutch against the tunnel's concrete support.

"Do you know where she's sleeping?"

"If she's street-feeding could be anywhere, but I'd look for her around that parking lot on the sandwich days." He jerked his head down, then turned his body toward the abutment. Over his shoulder he said, "Now I've got to go attend to my toilet," giving the last word the French pronunciation "twa-let."

Jackson reminded the campers again about the newly available rooms, and he and Salt returned to the tracks. "I thought the Gateway was supposed to be coordinating with the churches so that they wouldn't be doing street feeds anymore," Salt said.

"We met with those churches. Gateway gave them the tour, showed them the facilities where they could serve and prepare meals, the whole spiel. But for some of these churches and organizations it's more about them, their charity, than helping people get off the street. Makepeace in his own way was telling the truth."

"What about Big Calling? Midas Prince seems to have a lot of clout. Can't he get the message to the other churches?"

"Shit, that place is the worst of all. They just warehouse people and collect the grant money. Last week I watched a van pull up in their parking lot and throw a garbage bag of sandwiches at some guys. Reverend Gray? You know him? He quit there."

"Really?"

"He went to the health department, the district attorney, told them the place was infested with body lice and that the drug dealers run the place," Jackson said.

"They hire enough off-duty guys at the church. I ran into Sandy Madison there the other day," said Salt.

"The church is one thing—Reverend Prince has plenty of money to keep things looking good there. But he runs the shelter on grants, very little of the shelter's funding comes from the church. It makes him look like he's the savior of Atlanta's homeless, the go-to expert."

Salt stopped. "Listen."

"What?"

She went over to the rail closest to the wall on their right, the southbound line, knelt, and put her hand to the rail. "Sounds like someone hammering on metal."

"Not on that line. It's been out of use for a long time. The railroad isn't working on them either, not until they decide what they're going to do with the area. It leads to the Gulch," Jackson said.

"I've heard something about them rebuilding the area, a new terminal or something? We've been chasing perps into that place forever," Salt said.

"President Obama's administration is backing the project. They want to turn it into something like what it was in the beginning, a terminal that serves local, state, and interstate lines. Maybe they're excavating or surveying. Maybe that's what you heard." He knelt down and put his hand beside hers on the rail. "Or maybe it's John Henry's ghost." He nudged her with his elbow. "Come on. Let's finish up."

They continued on down the line, Jackson alternately humming and singing, "My daddy was a steel-driving man, Lord, Lord. My daddy was a steel-driving man."

WHISKEY AND WATERMELON

finally take a day to be with my girl and I find her cavorting with not one but three other guys." Wills stood smiling in the entrance of the dojo. He bent down to untie his shoes, came in, and performed a mannerly bow to the sensei altar. Theo and Miles, gis flapping, belts askew, aimed their small bodies toward him as he slouched into an exaggerated protective squat against the wall.

Salt and Pepper caught the boys before they pounced on the detective, forcing them to maintain discipline, a bow to each practitioner and the sensei. "Patience, Grasshoppers, patience," Wills said to them. Then they fell on him, hugging and trying to get him down. Wills tumbled them to the mat, then he and Pepper bowed to one another in collusion against their small opponents. It was all too much for Wonder—even though he was trained not to enter the dojo, he barked in the doorway.

Wills laughed as he pushed each of the boys into showing off the forward rolls they'd been taught. Pepper pushed them back toward Wills as the boys somersaulted into combat stances, back and forth.

Salt bowed to Pepper, to each of the boys, to the sensei, and went over to Wills, bowed and kissed his eyelids. "I have a little patience, only a little," she whispered. They left Pepper sitting seiza with his sons and went downstairs to the kitchen.

"Water, lemonade, juice?" Salt opened the refrigerator.

"Whiskey. My hours are all turned around," Wills answered.

Salt got lemonade from the fridge, opened the cabinet below the butcher-block counter, and took out a bottle of good bourbon. "You're handsome even when you're dragging."

Wills slid his loosened tie from his shirt and leaned on the edge of the kitchen table. "I'm beat. Went by the house just long enough for Pansy and Violet to tell me they hate me."

"Your dogs don't hate you. All your girls go belly-up for you." Salt widened her arms, exposing and wagging her middle, Pansy and Violet–like. "They miss you, just like I do." She went to him and teasingly kissed each side of his lips lightly.

He put his arms around her waist, his face in the V of her gi. "After this case is wrapped, let's go away somewhere, for at least a week."

"Agreed." She held his head for a moment, then was distracted by a whiff of cedar. "I'm sure I don't smell very good. We've been practicing for over an hour. Let me fix you your whiskey." She slipped from his arms. "You want to tell me about how the case is going?"

"The case is all I've been talking about, thinking about, working on, for weeks. I need a break."

The boys, thumping and yelling their way down the stairs and hall, ran into the kitchen with Wonder on their heels. Theo screamed, "Get him, doggie." Both boys jumped on Wills.

"That'll do, Wonder." Salt held her hand for the dog to come to her side. "And you boys, too. I'll get you some lemonade."

"What is all this noise?" Pepper stood in the doorway from the hall.

"Theo was trying to get Wonder to bite me," said Miles.

"Was not."

"Were too."

"Was not. I just told him to get you."

"Okay guys, cool it," Pepper said, offering both forearms for each boy to grab. He swung them up and then to the floor.

"Neat trick." Wills grinned at him. "How's it going, big guy?"

"Goin'." Pepper and Wills clasped hands in a brother shake.

"Who wants lemonade?" Salt reached for glasses from an overhead shelf.

"Nope, not today. I've got to get these guys home and get ready for work."

"Oh, Dad."

"How is Narcotics?" Wills asked.

"Daaad."

"Let's get together and talk sometime when I don't have the monsters with me."

"Aw, Dad."

Woof! Wonder circled the boys, skipping and skidding on the wood floor. He stretched out his front legs, inviting them to play.

"Hey," Salt shushed him.

Pepper had both boys at the back door. He bowed to Salt and pulled the kids outside.

"Whew, kids sure fill up a house," Wills said.

"You must be beat. How 'bout I run us a bath?"

"Us?"

Salt smiled while Wills took a big sip of the whiskey she'd poured.

Wonder groaned and sank to the floor.

"I WISH you could see yourself." Wills leaned toward Salt at the other end of the claw-foot tub. "Your curves shine."

She leaned forward and cupped her hands around him.

"Oh, girl," he groaned.

A PERFECT BREEZE carrying the earthy, lanolin scent of sheep and gardenia cooled them as they lay on top of a faded blue quilt.

"I don't want to talk about the case, but I have to tell you." Wills lifted the Saint Michael from between her breasts. "We're getting a Homes connection."

"The Homes?" she repeated. Man's gang materialized in her mind's eye, standing, propped against the short walls of the housing project walkways. "The Homes is a long way from Buckhead." She lifted her head, mirroring his position. A mockingbird squawked on the limb of the tree nearest the bedroom. Wonder could be heard scratching on the inside porch screen door. Salt sat up. "I want to hear about it. Let me get the beastie." She grabbed a T-shirt and shorts from the chest of drawers.

Wills wrapped a large towel around his waist. "My wardrobe, I fear, is limited. I didn't stop to think about a change of clothes."

"You're fine. Come just as you are, perfect for eating watermelon."

LARGE WEDGES of red melon on grass-green plates sat on the table in front of Wills and Salt. "First good melon of the season." Salt fed Wills a bite. They ate with their fingers, slicing bits with table knives and sharing the saltshaker. Wonder had finished warning the mockingbird and was lapping from his white bowl, lifting a mouthful of water and letting it sluice through his jaws to the floor.

Salt admonished the dog. "Do not slop."

"Snitches are saying that somebody heard somebody, you know how it goes, say that a guy, 'DeWare,' common spelling"—he rolled his eyes—"is the only name we have, supposed to be a crackhead, stays in The Homes, bragged about killing the rich white woman." He dropped his shoulders with an audible sigh, the pressure from the case was growing, accumulating and rolling down on Wills.

In the 1800s, "Buckhead" had been a rowdy trading post distinguished by the deer head and antlers that marked the intersection of what would become two of Atlanta's most prosperous avenues. The north side neighborhood was now Atlanta's well-to-do, mostly white area. A photo of the victims accompanied every media update of the case: Laura Solquist and her two pretty daughters, blond with flawless complexions. They'd been found dead in their upscale home, the mother with arms around both her daughters, all three with entrance wounds to the front of their foreheads.

"To make things even more complicated"—Wills leaned over the melon, juice dripping from his chin—"it's beginning to look like the marriage wasn't all that happy. A dancer from the Gold String came in after having seen the victims' and the husband's photos online. She said he was one of her 'regulars'—that he was at the club a lot and that he paid her for 'extras,' as she put it. Now I'm wondering if his wife knew. But his alibi is still holding. His phone records show him calling from Florida, and his business associate confirms his story." Wills stuck the knife upright in the scooped-out rind. "What about your case? How's it going with the squad?"

"Okay." She shrugged. "I went out with the HOPE Team. I love those guys. I've met some interesting characters, a blues band, their manager–slash–guitar player who knew Mike Anderson," she said, then took a breath. "And I've had a dream about a dog," she added.

Wills cocked his head. "Do not, whatever you do, go telling anybody, especially in the squad, about dreams."

"I wouldn't. But these dreams I have sometimes seem like . . . connections or something. I don't know how to describe them."

Wills leaned forward. "You—your fine mind makes the connections. You pay attention to what might not seem important to others."

Salt got up and took the rinds and plates to the deep sink. "I'm just
sayin'."

Wills followed her, put his arms around her from behind. "Chick
detectives." He nuzzled into the back of her neck.

PEARL

---

know how you feel, girlfriend," said Salt. Pearl's face, drawn and sad, looked up from the stack of flyers on the passenger seat beside her—a Be-On-the-Look-Out, or BOLO, for "Pearl White, aka Pearl Wolf, Pretty Pearl, Black Female, 5'3", 135 lbs., dark skin, and possibly mentally ill." Salt sat behind the wheel of the Taurus parked in a deserted parking lot. Sunday mornings left this part of downtown forlorn, its surfaces bare, the shabbiness exposed.

The Sunday eleven o'clock bells rang out across the city, calling and reminding folks of the morning's services. The harmonizing tolls of the bells from the northeast, the brassy sound of one church bell to the near north, and another farther away chiming a melodic peal accompanied scores of birds winging across the sky. The air above filled while Peachtree Street below was mostly deserted, at least on the south end where Salt sat watching. If there had been any peach trees anywhere around, somebody had probably chopped them down long ago and tried to sell pieces to tourists. "Peachtree" was the name wrongly repeated after people misunderstood "pitch tree," the original name of a Creek Indian settlement called "Standing Pitch Tree" for a large, gangly, lone pine tree that had marked the location. Not that there weren't plenty of pretty peach trees in Georgia. Their blooms sweetened the spring, and the fruit was longed for all year by those who knew where and when to buy. But the pitch tree, pedestrian, unlovely, with prickly cones and needles, a more practical and useful species, had been the original marker.

In the pay lot Salt kept an eye out over three or four other empty lots nearby. The sun had begun to move from behind the pawnshop, bail bondsman, and shoe repair place that lined the sidewalk on the east side of the street, businesses that mostly served people involved with the city court system and jail located two blocks south. Once the sun got directly overhead, without benefit of any shade tree, the lots would begin to heat up. One block over and under a city rail stop, the Greyhound bus station picked up and delivered brave or desperate souls.

The street wasn't completely deserted. It was just that its denizens kept mostly out of sight until desperate and in need of some kind of, usually emergency, help. Within a half-mile radius there were churches, hospital annexes, the Gateway Center—all organizations that were moving away from the shelter business in favor of resolving the causes of a person's homeless status. All except for those like the folks now arriving across the street. A sky-blue passenger van pulled into the middle of the lot and stopped. "Deliverance Church of the Holy Spirit" over a sunburst behind a cross was airbrushed across its sides. Exhaust continued from the rear for a bit before a white male driver in his mid-fifties cut the engine, came around, slid open the door, and held it for three women dressed in slacks and identical blue T-shirts with the cross-and-sunburst logo. All four went to the rear of

the van and began to slide folding tables from the hold. They immediately had help. Two heavyset men appeared from nowhere when
the tables began being unloaded. The church people quickly acqui-
esced to the men's insistent takeover of the table setup. A third citizen
of the street, a skinny young man with baggy britches and a sunk-
cheek hungry look, joined the group and began offering unneeded
help, as there were only two tables to be set up. A lively conversation
ensued between the three street dudes, and although Salt couldn't
hear the words, it was easy to guess the gist by the speakers' animated
gestures. Meanwhile, the multitudes arrived and a line or two lines of
sorts had begun to form.

Bibles and pamphlets were put on display on one of the tables, and
large cardboard boxes that held what Salt's experience told her were
the ubiquitous sack lunches were stacked under the second. Very
quickly it was like Jesus' miracle of the multiplying loaves and fishes,
only in reverse, as the lot began to teem with mostly dark and hungry
faces, far more mouths than was possible for the supply of under-the-
table boxes to satisfy. Pushing and shoving began between the two
lines, and Salt radioed for a beat car, then drove over to the fray. It
took barely a second for the Taurus to be recognized as a city detective car, and some of the combatants broke off from the mostly still-
verbal disturbance. But the pamphlets had begun to litter the asphalt,
and one of the boxes holding the lunches had been pulled from under
the table, its contents on the way to becoming another point of con-
tention. Salt stopped and got out beside the church ladies and gentle-
man. "I have a patrol car on the way," she told them.

The man put his arms over the shoulders of two of the huddled
women and bowed his head. The third woman, taller and larger than
he, kept her head up.

"I'm Detective Alt, Homicide."

"My God! Could we have been killed?" The tiniest of the women squeezed her eyes shut and buried her face in the man's shoulder.

"Coincidence. I was out looking for a witness who's been seen around here. I was across the street." She pointed. Just then her eye was caught by a quick there-and-gone reflection off the window of the shoe repair shop.

The beat cars must have been close because two units arrived within minutes and began further restoring peace. The downtown officers ignored the creative obscenities being lobbed at the church people by the original street helpers, who clearly felt mistreated as they were asked to move on and denied their sack lunch. "Suck on this. Eat shit. Shriveled white pussy. Knobby-kneed bitch."

One of the ladies looked down at her knees as if scrutinizing them for the first time in a new light. The man smoothed his thinning hair with a trembling hand. "This was God's will. God sent you," he told Salt. The small group drew in toward her.

"Have you been saved?" One of the women asked without any sense of irony, and handed her a dusty tract.

Salt took it. "Ma'am, I'm glad I was able to help you out today, but haven't the Gateway folks gotten you the information about how to help out here? Why the city would rather not have street feedings?"

"Yes. But God has laid it upon our hearts that we should give our, His, message to these people personally." The woman looked over her shoulder with wary, wide eyes, took off her glasses, and began wiping the lenses with a tissue from her pocket. Her smaller colleague put her arm around the large woman, patting her back.

The last words from the two slighted heavies came as they turned the corner of a building. "Pussy motherfucker."

The churchman shook his head as if he were taking it personally.

The uniforms enlisted two street guys, who they called with

friendly familiarity "Pimp Daddy" and "FU," to manage an orderly distribution of the bagged sandwiches, as well as the stack of pamphlets. There were a few homeless women pushing shopping carts, some empty and some with cargo, on the periphery of the feeding. Salt unfolded one of the Pearl BOLOs from her jacket pocket. She searched over the heads around her, on the lookout for women of the approximate weight, height, and skin color as Pearl, although the photos often distorted skin tone and people gained and lost weight. So height remained the most reliable search criterion. Unfortunately, Pearl was average to short. Salt pegged a couple of the women as possibilities and tried to get closer to compare them to the mug shot before the distribution ended. After the food was gone, the rush away was like a receding wave; the parking lot and sidewalks in all directions cleared. A few tracts blew about as the Deliverance folks folded and loaded the tables without assistance.

Again, there was a change in the light, a glimmer or glint catching Salt's eye, as a woman walked rapidly by the shoe repair store window. It was hard to judge her height because she was wearing at least three hats: the top one, a navy blue Braves baseball cap, was perched on the dome of an elaborate wide-brimmed lime-green confection of the type referred to in the circles of black church ladies as "crowns," and barely visible underneath was something red and knitted, probably a stocking cap or do-rag.

Salt hurried to her car and grabbed the Handie-Talkie she'd left on the console. By the time she'd locked the car and radioed her status— "on foot and following a subject"—the behatted woman, already a block away, was disappearing in a gap between two storefronts. Salt crossed the street, ran to the alley, and then steadied herself, touching the walls of the buildings as she jogged down the weedy, crumbling concrete and stone steps. At the bottom she faced a brick wall in front of her, and to the left an expanse of space leading to the Gulch, where everything—tracks, weedy fields, and small mounds of rubble—provided limited options for hiding. To the right was a passageway between buildings that seemed to narrow farther down. Salt rushed to get a quick view of as much of the Gulch as she could see. Except for some dark figures across the tracks in the distance, the space looked deserted.

She turned and ran toward the right and narrowing end, finding a human-sized passage the shape of cartoon-like mice holes busted through the wall. On the other side there were no other remains of the structure, only a weedy embankment that led her to more tracks and a tunnel farther down. Stopping to listen, she thought she heard movement coming from the darkened direction to the right, toward the tunnel and Underground. She radioed her position as the cross street under Peachtree, though it was hard for her to determine exactly where under Peachtree she was. The small flashlight on her key ring wasn't going to be of much help, so she kept it off but handy as she walked into the increasingly dim tunnel. Decades of runoff had left an almost black slime on the concrete walls. The smell of creosote and black tar from the track crossties was strong. A pair of broken, rumpled red sneakers hung by their laces from the end of an iron support sticking out of the concrete. A shopping cart missing one of its wheels was turned on its side, rusting against a wall.

In the tunnel the whine of cars passing overhead drowned out sound, but occasionally, when there was a lull in the overhead noise, Salt could hear something—footsteps, shuffling, scampering, some kind of movement down the line. Light at the end of the tunnel flickered as if something or someone was passing back and forth, a silhouette in motion.

She startled slightly when she felt the mobile phone in her pocket vibrate, but when she looked at the screen it registered "no service."

All the metal supports overhead would also make radio reception iffy, but she tried to check in anyway. "4133 to radio."

"Unit calling radio, go ahead," replied dispatch to Salt's relief.

"Continue to hold me out" . . . where? Salt had lost track of the streets she was passing under.

"Radio copy." The dispatcher presumed she was still at her original location.

She came out of the tunnels into an open stretch where the plastic-bag-catching weeds grew tall, where mounds of old tires and other trash had been dumped from the railing above. It was strangely like a meadow, a post-apocalyptic meadow. In contrast to the tunnel, the sun was bright and directly overhead. In waves the hot breeze fanned tall grasses and wildflowers—Queen Anne's lace, yellow ragweed, blue bachelor's button.

Near a waist-high pile of rubble, a movement out of sync with the rhythm of the wind caught Salt's eye.

The lot was a minefield of bottles, cans, and broken glass beneath the overgrowth. "Pearl?" she announced herself. Next to the other side of the stack of tires, a hem of iridescent brown cloth lifted in the breeze. "Pearl?"

"Don't look at me. Don't come around back here," said a woman's voice.

'I'm staying right here." Salt stopped where she was, several yards from the tires. "Pearl?"

The brim of green preceded a dark caramel face as she peeked from behind the mound.

"You are Pearl? Right? Pretty Pearl?"

The green brim fluttered slightly as it caught the wind. "Who aksin'?" The reluctant woman's accent was heavily urban Atlanta, with some rural Southern roots.

"They call me Salt, Detective Salt, with the Atlanta Police. I've been looking for Pretty Pearl—you, I hope. I want to ask you some things about Mike Anderson."

The woman began keening such as Salt had never heard in all her years in the street. It was some kind of lament, like a howl but also like a lullaby, a moaned ululation. "Ah ooh, ah ooh, ah ooh." Loud but not shrill, from some place deep down. "Ah ooh, ha. Ah ooh, ha."

Among the waving weeds, sunlight glinted on long bladed grass, off bottles and broken glass. The cry morphed to indistinguishable sounds, words. "Water—awa, waa . . ." The woman Salt now knew was Pearl moved out from the stack of tires, flinging herself to the ground, her full skirt spreading, the iridescence catching the light. "Gas-o-leen," she sang.

Salt walked closer. This was definitely the voice from her father's tapes. "Pearl, let's talk."

Her age could have been anything between forty and seventy. She put up a hand to stop Salt.

"What can I get for you? Water?"

"I ask you for water, gave me gasoline," Pearl sang.

"I need your help, Pearl. I'm trying to find out what really happened to Mike Anderson. Maybe we can help each other." Certain though she was that this was Pearl, anyone would have been hard-pressed to match her face to the mug shot in the flyer. Expression animated and changed her features. Her color was very different, wrinkled and darker from the sun and elements. Salt searched her pockets and found a business card and some cash. "Here is a little money and my card. How can I find you?"

Pearl sat up, wiping her nose with the back of her hand. Salt walked within reaching distance and squatted down next to Pearl, who leaned back on stiffened arms but inclined forward to accept the offered five and card.

"My phone number is on the card. I'd like to be able to talk when you're ready."

"Church."

"Which one? Where?"

"Red door."

SECOND NIGHT OF THE GIG

AT THE NOTELLING

S miling, she met his eyes from a few yards away.

"You seem in a good mood." Dan greeted Salt as she came up the steps of the Notelling.

"I'm happy to get to listen to your music again, and lucky to get to talk to Melissa. Thanks for calling—letting me know she was going to be here."

"She's backstage. She had a couple of days between gigs, decided to surprise me and do a guest appearance with us."

Smoking a cigarette, Dan leaned against the porch rail. A big, fat moon rose large between two tall buildings in the downtown city skyline, giving the warm night a natural glow. "Atlanta. Mike loved this fucking city, always going to some back street or alley lookin' for the blues." Light streamed on the nearby freeway where a brightly lit green highway sign pointed to the Freedom Parkway and Auburn Avenue exits. Lights: headlights, the bar marquee, parking lot pole lights, streetlights, string lights, and fireflies under the trees. "From the beginning, around the first firelight when someone sat down on a log and turned it into a drum and then somebody blew through a reed, conch shell, or bone, we've been connecting." Dan tossed his cigarette.

Salt cocked her head, listening. "The band's playing. Why aren't you onstage?"

Cars and trucks rolled in, tires crunching in the gravel parking lot in front of the Notelling. People poured into the bar.

"Melissa asks me to lay out sometimes, to watch. On some numbers she'd rather not have a rhythm guitar."

They followed the crowd, singles, couples, men, women, all dressed in good jeans, lucky blouses, or favorite shirts. The people fairly ran up the front steps of the Notelling, rushing into their Saturday night and hurrying to take their place in rituals as old as music.

Mustafa, dreads spinning, bent over the kick drum, laying down a backbeat on the snare, left foot pumping the hi-hat, working the crash cymbal, and sizzling on the ride. Goldie alternated fat honks, sterling squeals, and snake charming. The fingers of Pops' left hand, shiny and gnarly, lifted and pressed over the fret board while his right hand plucked a pulse, digging a deep groove. Blackbird swayed over the keyboard and laid into a boogie-woogie romp. Bailey stood up, signaling for the band to take the volume down. When they got real quiet, the beat low and steady behind him, he began a rumbly growl. "Ah um, ah um, catfish . . . ah um, ah um, honeybee."

They kicked it up again. Melody threw the switch for the rotating pin lights that flew over the crowd, over their bodies and back and forth. The floor of the Notelling bent and gave to the foot pounding, butt bouncing, body rockin' that accompanied the jump blues.

Dan and Salt stood against the wall with another standing-room-only crowd. The music vibrated the room. Salt tapped her toe, recognizing the song as one she'd danced to with her dad. *"Play the boogie, Daddy."*

Dan leaned over so he could be heard above the music and raucous audience. "I can't dance."

She blinked, realizing she'd lost track of the room focusing on the memory. "Oh. Me either."

Bailey went to humming while the band went low again, the jump beat ready, anticipating. "And now, ladies and gentlemen, a real treat for you tonight. Making a surprise guest appearance, all the way from West Texas and her current tour across this great country, Miss Melissa Primrose." Bailey's voice rose in a crescendo.

The band exploded again. The audience clapped, whistled, yelled, stomped, and the band played louder. Then just when it began to feel like she'd missed her intro, Melissa came prancing on—all of about five foot two, in a red dress with a flouncy skirt and high-heeled cowboy boots, her long, wavy red hair flying. She bounded around the stage and presented her pale-white cheek to each band member, then "sashayed"—it was the only word to describe her skip-kicking march— to the center mic and lit into "Jambalaya."

Jambalaya and a crawfish pie and filé gumbo *
'Cause tonight I'm gonna see my ma cher amio
Pick guitar, fill fruit jar and be gay-o.

Salt, applauding along with the crowd, looked at Dan. "Ma cher amio?" she mimed the question, widening her eyes at him.

He shrugged his "I guess."

Melissa danced while she sang. The crowd swayed in front of her and joined in on the chorus.

Cupping her hands to her mouth, Salt said, "She's a wonderful performer."

"How come you never learned to dance?" Dan asked.

"So THIS IS your detective. You old nut." She batted at Dan's shoulder. "You didn't say she was pretty. Now I find you been hanging out with a long, tall beauty." She pecked Dan's cheek and held on to his arm.

Salt put her hand out to the singer. "I really enjoyed your performance," she complimented Melissa, feeling large and awkward, her hand a paw over the singer's small fingers.

"Goodness, I'm all sweaty. Honey"—she pulled some bills out of a skirt pocket—"could you get me a wine spritzer?" She held the money out to Dan, who looked for an uncomfortable moment like he wasn't going to respond.

"Hey, guys, why don't you let me buy," Salt said.

"Detective," Dan drawled, "our drinks are comped. Miss—" He held up his hand for the waitress.

Salt didn't want to let whatever was going on between Dan and Melissa interfere with getting some answers. She turned to Melissa. "Dan has told you that I've been assigned to follow up on some new information we received on Mike's death. Can we talk outside?"

"I can't tell you any more than I told the cops ten years ago. Maybe less. I've tried to forget a lot of the stuff that went on then. He didn't kill himself—that's one thing I can tell you for sure. But, of course, the cops didn't care then. I'm surprised they care now." Melissa turned and walked toward the front doors.

The band hit the final notes of the set. The house lights came up on the dingy room. People milled around and sat down at the worn tables. A little shabbiness seeped into the atmosphere.

Stiffly, Salt and Dan waited for the drinks. "I ordered a whiskey for you." His voice sounded flat.

"That's fine. I'd like to talk to Melissa alone."

"Sure. I'll warn you, though, she's never gotten over it. Mike has become godlike to her. I certainly loved him, but he invited some bad people into his life."

Their drinks came. Salt picked up her whiskey and the spritzer. "You guys hitting the road tomorrow?" She looked away toward the stage when she asked.

"No, Goldie's lined up something off the books for day after tomorrow, some juke joint he says is on the south side."

"Can you ask him the name of the place? There aren't many upright clubs down that way."

"Knowing Goldie, upright wasn't a consideration in his decision to play there."

"Let me know, okay? After I finish talking with Melissa?" She headed toward the porch, threading her way through the people waiting for the music to start back up.

A group of fans, mostly men, was gathered around the singer. Salt lifted the drinks to catch her eye.

"That's it, honey. See that pretty lady," she explained to her admirers. "She's a cop. Wants to talk to me about Mike Anderson's death. After all these years. You come find me later, sweetie, and I'll autograph anything you want." She patted arms as she passed by on her way to Salt. "Whew," she said, taking her spritzer. "Life on the road's not all it's cracked up to be."

"You and Dan ever think about a life without touring?" Salt led them to the far end of the porch.

"Honey, I got a career to think about. Dan isn't exactly getting rich playing rhythm guitar, basically a backup player."

"Was Mike getting rich?"

Melissa took a long pull on the drink. "Nope. He had no sense about money, but he would have been rich someday. Seems like it's my lot in life to hook up with men who don't have money. So here I am, out on the circuit, singin' and shakin' my bootie." She gathered her hair at the back of her neck, let it go, then looked at Salt. "You got a husband or boyfriend? He don't mind you hanging around honky-tonks?"

"Yes. No, he's a cop."

"Well, there you go. You know how it is to have to make a living."

Salt took a sip of her whiskey. "Melissa, did you know who Mike got his drugs from?"

"I told all that to the cops right after he died. Why didn't they do something then?"

"His death was ruled accidental. There was no murder to investigate."

"I told them it was murder." She flung back the hem of her skirt and sat down.

"There were no first-person statements in the file. I need whatever you and Dan can remember. Do you know anyone that might have wanted Mike dead? Why did you think it wasn't accidental?" Salt sat in one of the rocking chairs.

"Look, I was twenty-three years old ten years ago. Mike was thirty-five. He was teaching me about the blues. We all did cocaine back then, but Mike had started using heroin. A lot of the bluesmen had heroin connections. I think that's why he tried it, because the old guys had or did." Melissa looked over the people on the porch, and lowered her voice. "And he said he only got his H from one guy he said was reliable. I didn't know who exactly, but from time to time I saw him with a guy everyone said sold heroin, and I saw him cop from the guy. I only knew his first name: John."

"Did Mike seem worried? Did he say anything about this John? What about the last time you were with Mike?"

"There was an impromptu after-hours party at Mike's the night before he was found. I don't remember if he was worried, and I don't remember much of what went on that night. Some of his band had dropped by, me, a couple of other women, girlfriends of the band were there, somebody's kids. At one point I'd gotten way high. I was drinking and doing cocaine. There was a lot of cocaine. Mike walked me two houses down to Dan's place so that Dan could take me home. I never saw Mike again."

Salt handed Melissa a bar napkin. "Was John there that night? Band members? Names of the girlfriends? What about a singer called Pretty Pearl?"

"I don't know if John was there. I was too fucked-up to know who came and went. I didn't know the women. I'm pretty sure Red Saylor and Tiny Peterson were there. I'm not sure who else." She wiped the corner of her eye and blotted her eyelashes. "Pearl was kind of special to Mike. She'd come out of Mississippi pretty raw, natural, an original. She wouldn't have been at the party. He was very protective, tried to keep the predators off her, maybe because she was somewhat lost in the big city. I don't know what happened to her either."

"Where are Saylor and Peterson now?"

"Saylor went on to play with B.B. King's tour band. I lost track of Tiny."

"What about Mike's life outside of music? Church? His parents?"

Melissa dropped her eyes and bit her lip. When she looked up, it was out into the night, and light reflected off a wet streak on her cheek. "Back then, even just ten years ago, there was the whole black-and-white thing, especially with his folks. I had two strikes against me as far as they were concerned, me being white and a blues singer. He said his mother and father were old-school, wanted him to marry a nice black Spelman girl. I never met them."

"Was he religious? Did he go to church?"

"A couple of times he ranted about some preacher his parents sicced on him, but I don't remember a name." Melissa dabbed at her eyes again with the bar napkin.

Salt gave her a minute and then asked, "Dan didn't take you home that night, did he?"

Melissa stood up with her back to Salt. "No."

The band was back on, starting out the set low and slow.

Melissa turned, patting her face with the napkin. "Mike was the love of my life."

"Dan has been with you for ten years. He seems pretty loyal."

"Loyal—well, I guess. Loyal." She dropped the napkin and walked away back into the bar.

Salt sat there. A train whistle blew in the distance. Atlanta was still a town where a single whistle could sound lonely.

Then Dan was standing beside her. They were both quiet.

Finally he said, "Goldie says the name of the place is Sam's Chicken Shack and Blue Room."

"You've got to be kidding, right?"

"That's the name he gave me."

"Why would Bailey Brown's band play a low-down place like that? It's in one of the worst neighborhoods in the city. It's practically in the projects." Salt knew it well. Sam's was the center of social activity for The Homes, as well as where a lot of drug dealing took place.

"Apparently Goldie has some ties there. It's a one-off for the band— off the books. But the blues has always thrived in tough places."

"You know, when I talked to Mike's parents, they really believed that the blues, 'juke' music they called it, was what caused Mike's downfall."

"People been saying that about all kinds of music."

"Did he ever mention Midas Prince? He was the family's preacher. They asked him to intervene with Mike."

"Hmm?" Dan looked off in the distance. "That I don't remember."

"Was he religious?"

"It's a cliché, but music really was his religion. He'd stopped going to church. His folks had gotten all judgmental." Dan paused. "I did remember, last night, I remembered that Mike's H dealer was a guy named John. White guy, tall. In fact, they called him 'Tall John.'"

"Last name?"

"I don't think I ever knew it."

"Would Bailey, Pops, or Goldie know? Can you get me the names of the guys who were in Mike's own band?"

"I'll ask the guys and I'll get you a list of anybody I can remember who played with Mike then. You gonna hang around till we finish tonight?"

Salt set her glass down. "How about I just see you guys one more time, down on the south side."

"I'd hoped to get to talk to you again." Dan looked at her plainly. "And worried I would." He covered his upper lip with his lower.

"You're a good man, Mr. Pyne."

"And you, Detective Alt, are an interesting woman." Dan reached and touched his index finger to the knuckles of her hand on the porch rail.

WORKOUT

Over the double doors to the church gym was a sign in script bordered by flowers and vines: "Your Body, Your Temple." Little black girls in pink T-shirts and boys in blue leapt from the last step of the church bus onto the parking lot and filed drop-shouldered and slow through the doors. Other kids got out of cars, quite a few of which were older models, some beaters. The kids arriving in the cars were handed T-shirts at the door by an older boy who dipped into a cardboard box for the shirts. Some of the children hadn't had a comb or brush through their hair, or they looked dusty, wearing less-than-clean pants or jeans.

According to the church's website and other sources on the Internet, Midas Prince had come to Big Calling Church more than fifteen years ago when the nondenominational congregation was only three hundred souls. The church had grown into a megachurch of more than ten thousand. Prince had come from nowhere, literally. His hometown was listed as Nowhere, a tiny crossroads in rural South

Carolina. He had degrees from nonaccredited colleges and an honorary doctorate in preaching. Salt had run his name through the department databases and had come up with only a couple of traffic tickets over the ten years that were covered by computerized records. She'd called the church office for an appointment and hadn't received a return call. Madison seemed irritated when she'd pressed him over the phone. "He's a busy man, Salt," he said, his voice rising like he was mad at her for putting him on the spot. "His secretary will call you."

The church website had a schedule that listed something called "Youth Health," led by Reverend and Mrs. Prince for this Saturday afternoon. Salt leaned forward against the steering wheel, slipped her arms out of the shoulder holster, removed the 9mm, and tucked it inside a belt holster at her back. She got out, grabbed her jacket off the backseat, and followed the children through the doors.

Inside, the boys and girls crossed a basketball court, gleaming beams of sunlight crosshatching the out-of-bounds, half-court, and full-court lines on a high-gloss floor. The children broke off by gender, the line of pink going toward a far door and the blues headed to one of the large-windowed rooms that bordered the court. The sound of free weights falling to the floor clamored from the room. The young man Salt had seen previously with Prince was at the door to the boys' room, clipboard in hand, checking the boys' names as they entered. "The girls are in the kitchen—" he said to her, then halted. "Oh, you're that policewoman. Reverend Prince—" he turned, calling across the room.

Midas Prince stood in the center of the room, a semicircle of boys seated on the rubber-matted floor in front of him. His upper body in a tight-fitting red athletic shirt was freakishly muscular and large in relation to his wasp-like waist and short stature. Black stretch shorts showed off his overly developed thighs. He was smiling at the boys and taking selfies with one of them with his phone. He looked up, frowning at being called, as Salt crossed to where he stood, his frown deepening as the floor-to-ceiling mirror reflected Salt next to his own squat bulk.

"I tried to make an appointment," she said.

"Dismissed." Prince clapped his hands at the boys. "Go with D.V." He made a basketball shooting motion to the young man at the door. The boys scrambled to their feet and ran, bumping and tugging one another until stopping at the door, where D.V. reached for the boy Midas had been taking the pictures with. "God doesn't like you." His fingers closed over the boy's shoulder. "Quit shoving."

The preacher once again glanced at the mirror, sat down, picked up some free weights, and began doing alternating bicep curls. "As you can clearly see, Officer, I'm a busy man. I don't know anything about Mike Anderson's death. It was more than ten years ago when his parents asked me to help him."

"Did you know any of his friends? Young people he met here at church?" She glanced toward the boys on the court, nodded in their direction.

Prince let the weights fall from his hands to the rubber mat. "You can't expect me to remember from back then. I've had probably a thousand kids through my groups since." The voices of the boys on the court bounded off the walls along with the sounds of balls bouncing on the floor and against the backboard, and the occasional ringing of the rim and swoosh through the nets was accompanied by excited yelps.

"Did you meet with him? Do you remember counseling him? Did he confide in you?"

"He quit coming to church. That's all I remember. I don't know who he knew."

"Were there others in the church, other young people who might remember him? Was he part of a group? What about your assistant?" She turned her head in the direction of the court. "He said he was a fan of Mike's music."

"D.V. couldn't remember much. He was only ten or so. He wouldn't have known Michael." Midas Prince stood, looked in the mirror, frowned, and then walked to a far corner of the room to a leg-lift machine. Salt followed only to give him her card. Prince let the leg bar fall, ignoring the offered card in her hand, and grabbed a towel and patted his face. "How tall are you, Officer?"

"How tall?" Salt repeated.

"Tall people have an advantage starting out in life, you know." He squinted at her through the sweat dripping into his eyes. "But as you can see, I beat the odds." He kept seated, yelling, "D.V., show this officer the way out."

"My card," she said, placing it on the bench. "I'd appreciate any help, anything that you might remember."

D.V. shifted his weight from one foot to the other as if he might take action but didn't know what course to take. Salt relieved his uncertainty by heading to the door. He followed, jogging behind her, but before she could ask him anything, he ran back when Reverend Prince called.

IT DID SALT no good to come back into The Homes. A teenage girl stood talking to Latonya on the stoop. Parked on Thirkeld half a block from Latonya's apartment, Salt stiffened her leg, pressing her foot against the floorboard of the Taurus as she watched Lil D's eighteen-month-old son toddle toward the brindle pit bull chained to the girl's wrist. Latonya's tall, skinny body in profile looked like a stick figure, while the soft, plump baby, Dantavious, was all roundness, at the bouncing stage, ricocheting from destination to destination.

Finally, the girl with the pit jerked the dog's heavy-gauge chain, wagged her fingers at Latonya, and walked up the sidewalk toward Pryor Road. Salt exhaled and put the Taurus in drive.

FENCING

Before the day began, she knelt beside the dog in the backyard and took in a deep breath, inhaling the fragrances of the clean early morning: sheep lanolin, the peppery smell of the new leaves on the pecan trees, the scent of sun on Wonder's fur as she patted his flanks. She closed her eyes against the unwanted image of the boy The Baby, Jesus had killed beneath another pecan tree. Hearing the sound of Wills' truck, she said to the dog, "They're heeere," and stood to greet Wills and his dogs.

Pansy and Violet fairly bolted out of their crates in the truck bed. Wonder ran and jumped around them in excitement. The three dogs brawled, rolled, and twisted with each other until Wonder broke off and ran to the sheep pens, back and forth. "He's showing them the sheep, 'Look, look, sheep! We have sheep, you guys! Sheep! You wanna catch sheep?'" Salt laughed. "Look at him. He doesn't know what he's more excited about."

"Yeah, and my ladies are all like, 'We'd like to have a go at the sheep, Wonder, but first we'd like to sniff you, please.'" Wills did

Pansy's and Violet's voices in a British falsetto. He kissed Salt's neck before hefting a market bag from the truck bed. "Beans and corn bread, deviled eggs." He grinned, proudly raising the tote bag away from the dog fray.

"Yum." Salt's mouth watered already. "Need help with anything?" she asked.

"I got it," he said, holding the bag up on his way to the kitchen.

"You want coffee? There's some made. Help yourself." She had on old jeans, torn at the knees, a long-sleeved gauze shirt, and work boots. While Wills took the food inside, she began laying out shovels, gloves, insect repellent, and sunscreen in preparation for the day's work, a start to fencing the acre in front of the house. Her dream was to have the property, the five acres, become self-sustaining, beginning with the sheep replacing her mower for the front acre.

"Perfect weather, not too hot, low humidity." Wills came down the steps with his coffee. "Do I hear company?"

The sounds of motors revving and rattling came from the drive as Pepper and his family in their minivan arrived, followed by Mr. Gooden, Salt's neighbor, on his small tractor. Pepper's boys, like Wills' Rotties, flew from the van before it was fully stopped so they could watch the approach of the tractor. Ann, Pepper's wife, was out after them, grabbing their collars as they danced, then dangled, trying to get out of her grasp. "You cannot be jumping out of cars like that. Stay away from any vehicle that's moving. Do you hear me?"

Mr. Gooden, smile set in his sun-weathered face, idled the tractor. "Hello, hello! Now I bet I know some boys who might want a ride on this little bitty tractor." His long legs were bent up around the sides of the motor so that he looked like a praying mantis, his little tight belly pushing against the wide belt of his jeans.

"Me first." Miles strained against his mother's hold.

"Me, me," cried Theo.

Pepper got the van parked under some shade and joined them, carrying a big, flat cardboard box. "Where do you want this?"

Ann tapped the box. "Chicken, ham, and fruit."

"Who's in charge of this operation?" Mr. Gooden pointed at Theo. "You?" He handed his gloves to Miles, who was suddenly shy.

Wonder barked three times at the old farmer.

"Oh, the Border collie's in charge, as usual." Mr. Gooden climbed off the tractor.

Ann shook hands with Mr. Gooden. "I believe we met once, when we brought Salt home from the hospital the last time," she said.

"Yep. You're right. She does have her ways of bringing folks together." Mr. Gooden smiled over at Salt.

Wills and Pepper and Ann all hugged each other. Wills, with mock gravity, shook and held the boys' hands before they broke away toward the sheep in the paddock.

"Oh, God, they're wearing me out before the day's even begun." Ann wiped her brow, her cream-'n'-coffee color already gaining some pink. She was petite and pretty, and her jeans showed her strong thighs to their advantage.

"What is the plan, Salt? You've got a bunch of city slickers out here to build a fence for sheep. What were you thinking?" Pepper hooked his thumbs in his jeans pockets and rocked back on his boot heels. "Pardner?"

"Well, Pilgrim," Salt said in her best John Wayne. "The onliest one of us not a greenhorn is the man with the tractor, and he's agreed to be our boss today. The rest of us, well, just call us 'Pilgrim, Pilgrim.'"

Sweet-smelling white oak posts from a discount lumberyard nearby were in a stack on the south side of the house where Salt and Wills had hauled them. She'd measured and marked every six feet around the perimeter where Mr. Gooden would bore down with his auger attachment for the postholes. The day's task was to get a third of the posts in, with Mr. Gooden doing the digging and the rest of them putting the posts in the ground. There was nothing on the property that could hurt the boys and nothing they could damage, so they were free to roam within calling distance.

"Grab a cup of coffee in the kitchen if you need one. I've got water and ice tea in a cooler," Salt told them, and followed Mr. Gooden on the tractor around to the front acre.

After they were all reassembled and Mr. Gooden had dug the hole, Wills and Salt hefted in the first post. "Let the fencing begin." Wills poured water over the post, anointing it. They paired off, bantering and catching up with one another, carrying the posts and taking turns holding, filling, and tamping the dirt around the righted posts. The boys' shrieks, the dogs' barks, and the sheep's baas and bleats could be heard coming from the back of the house. Every now and then one or both of the boys would run to the front chased by Wonder, followed by either the other brother or the Rotties or all three.

After the first hour and the first four posts, Salt and Ann waited by the cooler while Wills and Pepper wrestled the next post into a hole. There were jugs of water, ice tea, and mismatched glasses on ice in the cooler. "If it had columns and a bigger front porch this place would look like something out of *Gone with the Wind*." Ann looked around at the house, field, and woods, wiping her brow. "I declare, Miss Scarlett, you got some of us darkies workin' back on this heah plantation again."

Salt grinned. "When we get back in the house, I'll just get right to tearing down those drapes to make my dress for the cotillion." She dusted her gloves, hitting them against her leg.

"Seriously, this is an amazing property, Salt. Not many of us belong to a place and history like you have here." Ann filled a glass from the jug of ice water.

Salt wasn't sure which "us" Ann was referring to—"us" as in everyone or "us" as in black people.

"It's a privilege that comes with a price." She paused to regain some of their levity. "I've been mowing this front acre since I was nine years old." They both laughed, then Salt sighed. "It goes back—generations. There's a lot of history. Well, you can imagine."

"Really. Did your family own slaves here?" Ann looked at Salt over the rim of a blue glass.

"Except for the house and the few acres around it, the big farm was sold off. But that doesn't answer your question. My parents and grandparents wouldn't have talked about that, like a lot of families—at least those ashamed enough didn't talk about it. I believe there were slaves. Most of the descendants of slave owners destroyed the documentation, but if you go to the Atlanta History Center library there are records."

"How do you reconcile that? I'm sorry. Maybe not you in particular, but how do people—"

"White Southerners?" Salt bent down to pour herself a glass of tea.

"The owners, their descendants, those who benefited, still benefit by having had advantages." Ann had put her glass down and had her hands on her hips, feet wide. "Not being from the South, I don't know if asking these questions is considered rude." She tipped her head attentively. "People don't seem to want to talk about race here, but it feels like it is always such a presence, the elephant in the room."

"Or like a hellhound?" Salt said. "I don't know, Ann. The South never really recovered, never caught up economically, and in a lot of other ways, with the rest of the country. The South failed its children. Individually, some families thrived, continue to thrive, some lost everything. Most poor people, black and white, were kept or stayed poor. I suspect there's quite a few, like me, with the house, some property, an education, that still don't understand what having those advantages means or has meant. And we're left with a whole lot of, not guilt, but you used the right word, 'reconciliation,' to do. It's a hard, complicated conversation. People get defensive and offensive." Salt looked up at her old house. "I guess we have to find reconciliation individually, personally. Then that gets mixed up with all kinds of stuff like religion and family."

Pepper yelled. "Y'all just gonna stand there girl gabbin' or you gonna do some actual work?"

Ann grabbed a handful of ice and ran after him. Salt admired her forthrightness. Atlanta folks especially seemed to want to tiptoe around their history, like it was a hellhound at the crossroads—always there, ready to bite if it was acknowledged or when folks weren't paying attention.

Mr. Gooden had gotten quite a few holes ahead of them. Wills and Salt carried a post to the next hole. "This work really makes a person appreciate what it must have taken to run a real farm. Helps me understand how people developed such strong ties to the land," he said.

"Yep, it's an investment," she replied, settling the post into the ground as Wills held it upright.

They'd gotten fifteen posts in when Salt waved to Mr. Gooden for a lunch break and they all walked together to the back porch. Wills and Ann came and went from the kitchen, uncovering dishes of deviled eggs, potato salad, sliced ham, and chicken. Salt had set out more of the mismatched china and silver, pieces she'd found at estate sales. She also took charge of keeping everyone refilled on tea and water, then coffee.

They sat around the screened porch, Ann and Pepper in the glider, the boys on the steps just outside. Mr. Gooden leaned back in the wooden straight-back chair next to the door. "This is nice, Sarah. Reminds me of when Peggy and I were young. There used to be parties like this where people, mostly church folks, would come together to help each other out. Don't see too much of that these days."

"Not everybody is so lucky to have a neighbor with a tractor." Salt smiled at him. She and Wills were in wicker armchairs across from him, plates in their laps. She'd relied on the old man over the years, especially the year before after she'd been shot and when she'd needed him to check on Wonder from time to time. He regularly brought her produce from his garden. He and his wife, who died twelve years ago, had known three generations of Salt's family.

Pepper said, "This is good for Theo and Miles, to see how things are built, how hard people have to work to actually make something themselves, to learn where wool comes from, how pecans grow."

"Dad, can we go climb the tree again?" Miles asked.

Salt had nailed small step boards to her tree about every third year, as the tree grew, so that her old perch was still accessible. The boys' legs dangling from the limbs reminded her how much she'd once loved being in that tree.

"Go." Ann shooed them. "Good riddance," she mumbled after they'd raced away. "They're driving me nuts. I think they've picked up on how nervous I am about Pepper's new assignment. I hate it." Ann also called him Pepper when they were around others who used his nickname.

"What is your new assignment?" Mr. Gooden asked.

"Drugs, Narcotics," Pepper answered.

"I know I sound like an old man, but somebody please explain to me how drugs have taken over. I just don't get it." Mr. Gooden shrugged. "'Course, we had moonshine back when lots of folks were poor and that's all they could get. Rich folks drank it, too, but they didn't have to."

Pepper stood up. "And we, Pilgrim, are not going to figure that one out today—got a fence to build." He tugged Ann to her feet.

"Ann and I will put stuff away and be right out." Salt looked over, caught Ann's eye, and motioned with her head. Together they started gathering up the dishes as the men left the porch.

In the kitchen Ann put down the platter she was carrying. "I'm sorry, Salt. I didn't mean to lay that on you guys. It's just that I'm scared for him. And that earlier legacy thing. If it weren't for so much poverty, especially in the city's black communities, narcotics wouldn't even be an assignment and my husband wouldn't be in danger." She turned her back to Salt, who quietly finished putting the dishes in the sink and waited. Ann tore off a paper towel and blew her nose.

"You haven't seen the upstairs yet, have you?" Salt asked.

"The dojo? No."

"Come on." Salt reached for Ann's wrist, escorted her down the hall and up the stairs. At the door of the new room Salt took off her shoes and pointed to Ann's. "Just for a second, I want you to feel what it's like." She went to the shelf, lit the votive candle, came back to Ann, and motioned for her to sit in front of the shelf with the candle and photo. "I'm sure Pepper has told you what happened with my father here. Actually, it was probably right where we're sitting." Salt kept looking at Ann, who lowered her chin and touched her eyes with the wadded paper towel. "Ann." Salt turned to the framed photo on the shelf. "I don't fully understand how the past has affected me— like the Bible says about the sins of the fathers? We work out in this room, struggle, so we can get better at making peace in the street." She bowed her head to the photo of the sensei, her father in his police uniform. "It's a small bit of finding some kind of reconciliation."

The boys' feet were pounding up the stairs, Wonder's nails scurrying on the wood behind them. At the door of the dojo they flung their shoes off and bowed in. "Mom, Mom, Mom, that's the picture of our sensei. Dad says 'sensei' means teacher." They slid to their knees beside their mother.

Ann put her hands in prayer pose and nodded to the photo. "Come on, guys, show me a few of those aikido moves before we go back outside."

After the boys showed off for their mom, they all went down and back out to join the guys on the fence. They worked and the boys played for a few more hours, but it was beginning to heat up. On another break Pepper brought Salt a glass of cold water. "Whatever it was you said to Ann must have been right. She seems to be relaxing, at least for now." They watched Wills and Ann laughing as they carried another post. "By the way," Pepper said, "yesterday I got a phone call from one of the guys I work with at Chastain." One of Pepper's extra jobs was at the Chastain Park outdoor theater.

"You still working all your EJs?"

"Yeah, tryin' to. Anyway, he's on the SWAT team."

"And?"

"He also works an EJ for Sandy Madison at Big Calling. He wanted to know why you were, his words, 'poking around the preacher.'" Pepper kicked at a clump of newly turned red clay.

"'Poking around,' that's good. Poking around. I'll have to use that at the office. Ask the guys what they're poking around on. What's this about, Pepper?"

"I wouldn't have thought anything about his call, wouldn't have even mentioned it to you, except that not thirty minutes after that call one of the narcotics guys, Sam Brocket, came up to me as we were going out and asked me about you, something about if you were 'hard-core.' Then asked if you understood about EJs. He also works at Big Calling, at the shelter. Look, I know how you feel about the extra jobs."

"So you've been given a message for me, haven't you? Interesting. I guess the preacher is used to folks bowing down to him and thinks I didn't show sufficient humility."

"Well, it's hard to be humble when you're perfect." Pepper gave her the grin.

"Here, let me baptize you." She slung a handful of water in his direction, too tired to tackle him any harder.

By mid-afternoon they'd done enough. A third of the posts were in and Mr. Gooden had left with the tractor. The various other vehicles loaded, the boys and dogs worn to a frazzle, Salt waved to Wills' truck, the last out of the drive to the highway.

THERE WAS A PATH. It was pleasant and convenient since neither she nor Mr. Gooden tended to use the phone. Wonder had done his share of wearing down the narrow trail, over the side fence, through the field between Salt's pecan grove and Mr. Gooden's backyard garden, a hundred yards or so.

He came out his back door when he heard the chickens squawking at the dog's approach. "Have you had supper yet?" Salt asked. "I've got lots of leftovers."

"I was just going to fix a sandwich. You talked me into it." He tucked his shirt in. "Just let me grab my boots." He reached back through the door and sat down on the top step, pulling plain Western brown boots over his white socks while Wonder sat waiting, tail swishing the dirt. "Those are good people, Pepper, Ann, and Wills," he said. "Who says young folks don't work hard. Another five days like this and we'll have your fence done."

"We did put in a day's work thanks to you and your fine tractor." They walked beside a row of new lettuce, the delicate green shoots lacy against the dark earth. "Speaking of Ann, she was asking me today about the property, about my family," Salt said.

"Anything in particular?" Mr. Gooden walked with his hands stuck in his jeans pockets.

"Just in general. How long we'd owned the land. That kind of thing."

"Slavery. She ask about that? It'd be natural for her to wonder. But maybe not polite to bring it up."

They got to the fence and she climbed over first. "I don't know why we don't put a gate here. We've been climbing over this fence forever. Maybe Ann feels like she and I are close enough to ask. Or maybe since she's not from the South she doesn't get how we're wary of that conversation—so many folks having weighed in, rightly and wrongly."

In the kitchen they helped themselves to the platters and bowls of leftovers Salt had uncovered and set out on the table. "People my age are still too prickly, embarrassed, or ashamed to talk about it," said Mr. Gooden.

"Anyway, at least for me, I'm glad to have that conversation going, to get it out." Salt said.

Over their supper they planned out the rest of the fencing, what hardware and materials they'd need for the gate, how many more days of work it would take to get the fence completed. When they finished, the old man stood and picked up his plate.

"Leave that. I'll take care of the dishes. Come, come." She motioned him to the hall. At the entrance to the library Salt pushed back the pocket doors while Mr. Gooden closed his eyes. "Hmm, I remember that smell. I can't remember the last time I was in this room, must have been twenty or more years, but I remember that smell."

"Sorry there's no place to sit." Salt saw the room for what it might look like to someone seeing it and its lack of furniture for the first time.

Mr. Gooden walked on in and looked around. "You know, I'm like a lot of old people. I've accumulated too much of just about everything. I'd be pleased if you'd take a chair or two or a settee off my hands. Help me get some room so I'm not stumbling into things."

"Now I'm embarrassed. I didn't bring you in here to get furniture off you. I brought you in here because I wanted to ask you something about my father. See all these books on this shelf?" She showed him the row of ten or more books at eye level, the ones on mental illness.

He pulled out one or two and slid them back, then opened *Living with Depression*. He looked up and his eyes went to the shelf above, the one that held some Southern writers, Eudora Welty, Richard Wright, the organization of the books, again, her father's.

"How much were you around him right before he died?" she asked.

"You know, your mother." He put his arm out to indicate the room and that he recognized her mother's hand in the dearth of furnishings. "I knew she took a lot of what was in the house, but did she have to take all the furniture in this room? Probably some of those were antiques, been in your family forever." He twisted his lips tight, slowly shaking his head. "She had, probably still has, her own way of seeing things, and she kept him away from people or kept them away from him. But she'd need me or Peggy every so often. Maybe once a week or so I'd come over to help with repairs or heavy lifting, and your dad would be here."

"These were mostly his books. Here's how he kept track of what was where." She showed him the ledger and how the books were cataloged by location.

"He had his own way of doing things, too."

"Mr. Gooden, was he seeing or hearing things, hallucinating at the end?"

"Sarah, if he was I wasn't aware of it. He mostly just sat and stared. I'd speak to him, of course, but he'd shut himself down, except for that very last week when he seemed better. I guess I talked to him a couple of days before. He was more engaging than I'd seen him in several years, peaceful, happy even." They walked toward the hallway and stood looking back in at the room. "What I mostly remember, though, was you, always sitting out there in the tree, skinny legs hanging down." He waggled two fingers. "Talkin' about how you were gonna get a dog." He smiled and shook his head.

"Ranger. I hadn't thought about him till just recently."

"That's right. I remember. Ranger."

Arrff! Wonder stood in the hall looking in at them.

"Arrff yourself, Wonder Dog." She went to the entrance and ruffled his fur.

"I need to get going, Sarah. An old man gets tired. But I'll think on your question. If something comes to me—well, I know where to find you."

She and the dog followed him down the hall, through the kitchen, and out to the porch, where they watched him go back over the path by moonlight.

BLUE ROOM

———————————————

Mustafa hopped off the bus on Dan's heels. "Dude, this one funk-lookin' juke joint."

One bottom edge of the corrugated metal door to the Blue Room was rusting away, speckled with slowly enlarging holes. "Yeah, I can't for the life of me understand why Bailey lets Goldie get us into some of these off-gigs." Dan began unloading their gear from underneath the bus.

"Roots," Mustafa mumbled.

"What?"

"You know, back to where the blues come from. This here place is for folks who got the real blues, baby, can't buy no tickets to no up-town club. Goldie probly takin' a piece off the side, but Bailey, he do it 'cause of roots." Mustafa was doing his best impression of Atlanta street slang. He stuck his head in the flaking door and popped back out. "There's not even a stage in there. This looks shaky."

"Well, I've been told this place is all about 'roots,'" Dan said setting gear on the rough-gravel lot.

Twenty or more weathered, gnarly-looking people were milling around under the overhang of the adjacent retail strip, and there was another group standing under two worn-out-looking trees at the far end of the broken pavement parking area. The Blue Room itself seemed like an afterthought, a cinder-block extension attached to the back of the Chicken Shack take-out joint.

Mustafa glanced toward the people. "Voodoo dudes—some of those folks look like zombies, like somebody put the hex on them." In the growing dusk his skin had a copper glow, his dreads highlighted with glints of color from the orange-and-pink sunset.

Dan hitched up his jeans, tucked gear cases under each arm, and picked up two of the drum cases. Mustafa wheeled the keyboard and held the bent-back door.

Inside was one room with a bar; behind it was the kitchen that served both the Shack in front and the Blue Room in back. A large sign announced "Restroom Outside." A big man wearing a stained apron over his stomach came from the kitchen. "Sam." He put out his hand. "I run the Shack and the Room."

"I'm Dan. This is Mustafa." He put the gear on the floor and shook Sam's meaty hand. "We got the bus right outside."

Mustafa offered Sam a fist bump, which the big man ignored, looking at the dreadlocked young guy sideways. "We got one of the old guys lookin' out for you," Sam said. "He'll show you where to park it and look after it."

"Where do we plug in?" Dan scanned the room.

"In the corner there." Sam pointed to the left far end of the schoolroom-sized joint. White plastic chairs were stacked to the ceiling in the corners. Otherwise the room was empty, the only reference to "blue" being the scuffed paint on the walls.

The door opened and a light-skinned man, late twenties, wearing a plain white T-shirt, shorts, and new clean high-tops, came in. "My man," he said, handing Sam a small athletic bag and giving him the grip-and-hug handshake. He sat down on a stool beside the door and lit a cigar that smelled suspiciously un-cigar-like. A thin woman with lip-smacking, lip-puckering tics had followed him through the door, her hair clipped all over with children's plastic barrettes, her walk lop-sided. Dan and Mustafa unpacked the instruments, set up the amps, and duct-taped extension cords to the floor as best they could in order to reach the remote wall sockets. The barretted woman, lips darting in and out, followed them around, fiddling with her hair and watching them work. Early arrivals began to filter in. The guy at the door had propped it open, and people handed him money as they entered. Some didn't, and the why and wherefore of who paid and who didn't was obscure. Young and old, men and women, sharp-dressed, shabby, good-looking, worn-out, they filled the room, and their voices began to blend to an excited din. Some scratchy blues was barely audible from speakers hung from the ceiling corners behind the bar.

Baby, and I'm leaving this town
Say you didn't want me
I'ma quit hanging around.

"What's that you're singing?" Mustafa asked.

Dan pointed up at the speakers.

"I don't know it. Sounds like it goes way back."

Dan screwed on a cymbal. "Blind Willie McTell—played street corners here in Atlanta. Mike used to fool around, playing McTell's stuff. He had recordings, 'Bell Street Blues,' 'B and O Blues.' McTell was the guy that wrote 'Statesboro Blues.'"

By the time Bailey, Goldie, Pops, and Blackbird's cab arrived, the place was packed. The chairs had been unstacked and lined the wall. People held boxes of chicken on their laps, or stood with sweating drinks in plastic cups. Shaking hands, hugging every woman, Bailey, followed by the rest of the band, pushed his bulk through the packed room. "Whew, got a crowd tonight." He mopped his brow, sat, and picked up the old guitar.

Dan had done his best with the setup. He retreated to the bar for water. From there it was possible to get only glimpses of Goldie and Pops over the crowd. Mustafa's drums began to rumble, then Bird and Pops and Goldie joined in. But the night really began with Bailey.

THE BAND BUS stood out in the parking lot like a derailed box-car, made even more noticeable by the emptiness of the surroundings, not that many cars. Most of the people would have walked or taken MARTA to the Blue Room. Someone was smart; they had hired one of the old men who hung around the Shack to watch over the bus. Before Salt was barely out of the car, he'd recognized her and limped over. "Officer Salt, where you been?" He looked down at her jeans, then stepped back and gave her the once-over. "You look good in clothes."

"Be careful who hears you say that." Salt took his offered hand between her own, careful of the swollen, arthritic fingers.

"Aw, you know what I mean. You here on bidness or you come to hear Bailey?"

"Actually I came because of a dog. Always good to see you." Salt headed toward the music spilling from the door of the bootleg club.

SITTING ON A STOOL just inside the door of the Blue Room, Man, head of The Homes gang, apparently acting as doorman to-night, took the cigar from his mouth. Heads turned. Salt came over while Man just sat there giving her a sideways wary smile. Sam stepped back, hands propped on his hips, grinning. A couple more people near the door moved closer, pointing her out to those nearby, grinning and nodding their way. Word passed and some of the folks stuck their heads up over the crowd, watching the meeting at the door.

Man and Salt stepped outside. "I know you're not trying for some undercover gig here in The Homes." Man pointed toward the project buildings across the street catching the last light of the day. They'd long been friendly adversaries. She'd graduated the academy and been assigned The Homes about the time Man had gained control of the narcotics business in the area. From the beginning the two of them had talked, exchanging worldviews and opinions on some issue of the day. He was astute and could nail extraneous bullshit. His cash money, wide smile, and slightly bowed legs made him a target for girls wanting to give him babies.

"I actually came to hear the band," Salt told him.

"So you got promoted to a detective and just left The Homes." He examined the unlit stub between his fingers.

"You miss me, Man?"

"Some ways. This new cop don't get it. He frontin'. But then he don't know shit either." Man's smile widened.

"So how is business? Was that Lil D I saw behind the bar in the kitchen with Sam?"

"Nothin' much changed. Yeah, Lil D learnin'. He already know a little somethin' 'bout cookin'." Then he looked off as if distancing himself from her. "You look a little bit skinny in them jeans."

She wasn't going there either. "I went to see Stone. You visit him?" she asked.

"Enough." Man dropped his cigar and ground it on the curb.

A shiny black sedan caught their attention as it pulled into a far corner of the lot. The driver's-side window slid down and the face of a young dark-skinned boy appeared. Man nodded to the boy.

"He looks young to be driving a car like that, too young to even have a license," Salt said.

"He's just a driver."

Dan stepped out of the club as the back door of the sedan opened and a tall white man, light buzz-cut hair, wearing black over black, unfolded himself from the backseat.

"Who's the dude, Man?" Salt asked. The man, mid-forties, leaned back against the car, his hands clasped together as if waiting for something overdue—waiting, head bowed, making a show of patience but making clear it was for show only, rolling his shoulders and stretching his neck.

Man pushed off the building wall. "He own Toy Dolls and the Shack and Blue Room," he said over his shoulder as he headed toward the man from the sedan.

Dan came up to her. "You seem to have a lot of acquaintances around here." They watched Man cross the lot. "I'd recognize him anywhere, no matter how time has or hasn't taken its toll."

"Who?"

"What do you mean 'Who'? Didn't you set this up? John, the white asshole next to the car over there—the guy who dealt to Mike back then."

Salt turned to Dan, her back to the lot. "The guy leaning against the black sedan is the guy, John, who supplied Mike?"

"How many white dudes do you see in the parking lot? Like I said, I'd know him anywhere. Why is he here if you didn't set it up?"

"You and the band are working for him. Man said he owns the place."

"Man?"

"The guy I was just talking to. You're sure? That's Tall John?"

"The last time I saw him was the last time I saw Mike alive. I had blocked a lot of the bad stuff, the drugs, the party. But when you showed me the photos, Mike's car, I remembered seeing that guy sitting in a car outside Mike's that last night."

Salt reached for Dan, put her arm through his, turning him away from the sedan as it drove past with Man and Tall John in the backseat.

As they came back inside, Bailey was digging down deep with his raspy voice.

Hellhound on my trail,
Hellhound on my trail.

THEY DEFINITELY didn't need another guitar in such a small space. Dan and Salt, sitting close together at the bar so they could hear one another over the music and the crowd noise, could hardly see any of the band; between them and the musicians, the audience jumped as one body. Mustafa's drums called down thunder, conjured a continent, cast a spell of galloping hooves, and slammed on the turnarounds. Streams of condensation from beers and water from melting ice ran together along the counter. People mostly went outside to smoke, but the odor of fried chicken and beer was thick.

Salt caught another quick glimpse of Lil D in the kitchen, with the usual white towel hanging around his neck, covering most of the dark birthmark.

"I'm still trying to piece this together," said Salt, worrying a cup of beer on the bar. "The Tall John you knew to be supplying Mike back then is the same guy that's still running this joint and from what Man says at least one other club. Then he's probably the same John who pimped Stone. Damn," she said.

Dan leaned closer. "Who is Stone?"

Goldie blew red and gold lava notes from the deep bell of his horn. The lights on the band turned the audience into one dark, quaking shape.

"Stone was one of Man's gang. He's the one that gave the new information about Mike's death, but I've known him a long time. Man just now told me Tall John owns this place, too."

"How is it so many folks here know you?"

"This area and its big projects were my beat for more than ten years until a couple of weeks ago when I made detective."

"Your beat, like in a patrol car, blue lights, siren?"

"Yep, uniform, gun, the whole costume."

"The projects?" Dan repeated it as a question. "Don't laugh. I only know about detectives from TV."

"The Homes across the street." Salt tilted her head east toward her old beat.

Pop's bass thump, poof, and bounce built the groove, tying the rhythm to the harmony. The crowd shouted encouragement, call and response.

"Why?" he asked.

"Why what?" she asked back.

"You're very attractive, obviously smart. You don't seem like a cop."

"You would prefer your cops ugly and dumb?"

"Come on. That's not what I mean and you know it. It's about you. Why?" Dan put his beer down and leaned closer.

"It just fits me—what I was born to, I guess." Salt turned to the crowd and the band, her right leg keeping time, foot on a rung of the barstool, knee up and down with the beat.

Blackbird's hands danced, beating a honky-tonk pattern on the rhythm floor. Dan leaned back. "I'm not trying to pin you down or make you answer if you don't want."

Salt took another long look over the people and nodded her head toward the band. "I police for some of the same reasons Bailey plays the blues. It's what I do, what my father did."

"Your father?"

"Yeah. And by the way, he loved the blues. I found some of Mike's recordings in his collection."

"That's kinda strange, eerie almost."

"It's Atlanta, a city that's really like a small Southern town in some ways. There's all kinds of connections that are hard to see sometimes." Salt looked over the room at many of the people she'd come to know over the past ten years. She thought about her father's connections, about his blues. "There's also the dog I'd forgotten."

"The dog?"

"The day my dad died—I was just a kid—I was playing, pretending, like kids do, with my imaginary friend, a dog." She shrugged. "It's what a lot of kids do. But I'd forgotten until your dog came along."

The band began a slow blues. Bailey gargled some lyrics and barked out words wrapped in cotton.

Dan pulled Salt onto the dance floor where at first they swayed to the blues until the people pushed them together into a kind of dance. Her hand was slender in his long guitar-playing paw.

Bailey sang.

This old night life, this old sportin' life
Is killing me.

"I had a dream about your dog," Salt told Dan. He smelled like a nice combination of smoke and clean fur.

"Ranger," said Dan, inhaling her green fragrance.

"The dog's name is Ranger?"

Most of my friends are dead and gone.

Salt pulled back to look eye to eye with Dan. "Ranger?"

"Yes," Dan pulled her close as Mustafa hit the kick drum. On the front end of two pistol blasts, somebody yelled, "Gun."

Dan thumped into Salt like he'd been kicked in the back. His blue eyes opened in surprise, then folded as he dropped against Salt, heavy, his arms losing hold of her shoulders, sliding down her sides as he crumpled to the floor. Salt reached for the weapon at her waist, scanning the room, kneeling over Dan. She was bumped by people running, pushing toward the door. She didn't see anyone with a gun. Then Bailey was there, on the floor, shielding them. She holstered and turned Dan onto his back. Mustafa, kneeling, punched at his mobile phone. Dan shuddered, made a small yelping sound, and stopped breathing. Salt tipped his head. Blood was pooling on the floor under Dan's back. She covered his mouth with hers, breathed twice, then checked his pulse with two fingers to his wrist and couldn't find one. She pushed back a howl coming up in her throat.

Mustafa was saying into the phone, "He's shot. Somebody shot him. I didn't see."

Salt pressed the heel of her hand in the middle of Dan's chest and started compressions, lost count, then estimated and went back to Dan's mouth. His breath tasted metallic. Back to his chest. "Tell 911 to start Fire Rescue and Homicide and that a detective needs assistance." Twenty-five, twenty-six, twenty-seven, twenty-eight, twenty-nine, thirty. Two more breaths. "Does anyone else know CPR?" she asked, starting back on the compressions. "Three, four, five, six." Bailey was down on his knees beside her. Pops, Goldie, and Bird stood over them. Mustafa was still on the phone. "A detective, Alt. She's not injured, she's doing CPR."

"Twenty-one, twenty-two," she counted again to thirty. "Breathe, breathe, breathe." Her arms were getting tired, and her ears longed for the sound of sirens. They came, faintly, then louder. Bird ran for the door. "A fire truck is here."

Salt breathed twice again into Dan's mouth as a firefighter medic came in, knelt down beside her, and took over the chest compressions while other fire rescue guys broke open medical gear: oxygen, breathing bags, defibrillators. Salt moved back and pushed away, still on her knees, shaky, covered with Dan's blood. The door filled with uniforms. She stood up, found one of the white plastic chairs, and sat down, her body buzzing like electricity was running through her veins. Her hand smeared blood on one of the armrests as the Blue Room evaporated, replaced by a dream-like image of the upstairs bedroom at home, her father's head in her lap, so heavy, his blood thickening. "Breathe on me, breath of God," she repeated the right words to the old hymn. "Breathe."

Then Sergeant Huff and two of her new colleagues were there. Dan was shifted from the floor to a gurney and wheeled out. Focusing, she asked Huff, "What do they say?"

"He's low," he answered.

DAN'S CHEST rose and fell with the rhythm of the air as it was forced into his lungs—*whoosh, whomp, whoosh, whomp.* He tried to open his eyes, to move his hands but couldn't. Then he was sitting at a table on which there was a green bowl with oatmeal and a silver spoon. A whirlwind began to blow the room from around him, board by board. Log drums beaten with sticks echoed through his body— *whomp, whoosh, whomp, whoosh.* He opened his eyes to a vast plain on which a dog appeared, then unfolded, falling from its own mouth, a paw, leg, flank, disappearing. The view was as if through a blue lens overlaid with dust whipped by the wind. He felt the sticks beating the drum of his own body.

The detective, naked, her breasts iconic, conical, grew up out of the earth, her hair in black twists. She was covered with dried red mud and white tribal markings. Beside her, Ranger lifted his snout to the sky and howled.

Lights filtered through his slit lids, but then the drums rumbled into thunder and there was lightning, a laser of gold, filling the dusty air. Black beetles swarmed the table but left an ace of spades turned up in a scattering of red-and-white playing cards. Dan picked up the ace, knowing he would need it later as a ticket for a ride. He lost sight of Salt and Ranger among the rust-colored rocky hills. He listened carefully for the dog's long yowl and kept watching for the black twists of Salt's hair—a hound and a woman he somehow now realized he'd been searching for.

"BREATHE," SALT SAID to herself as she stood against the wall of the Homicide conference room while a police photographer took distance and close-up shots of her and her clothes. She was still wearing the white blood-smeared blouse. Her mouth still tasted of Dan. Sergeant Huff, Wills, and several other detectives sat at the polished table waiting for the photographer to finish.

When she sat down, from across the table Wills handed her a bottled water. He kept his eyes on hers with no hint of expression. As she twisted the top, the thin plastic bottle crackled in her grip. "How is he?" she asked, gulping from the bottle.

"In surgery. They aren't saying one way or the other. Critical." Wills had just come from the hospital.

Sergeant Huff, seated at the head of the table, had a yellow pad and pen in front of him, as did Wills and the others. Salt took another swig of the water. As she took the bottle from her lips, a rusty red residue filtered down through the water in a swirl.

"Now, Alt, what is it everyone calls you?—Salt?" Huff leaned forward. "I'm gonna try to be sensitive to what all you've just been through, but still, you're a cop and a witness to a possible homicide, and I'll be goddamned if I can figure out how in the hell you have managed to get from working an old, cold, suspicious death case to now being mixed up with the Solquist case and with a man who is shot while you are dancing with him—in the Blue Room, of all places. Were you the intended target?"

"What? What does this have to do with Solquist?" She sat up, focusing on Wills.

"Solquist's alibi—John Spangler, the guy he was with on the fishing trip?"

Salt looked at Wills. "Wait. Tall John, John Spangler?"

Wills nodded. "He owns the Blue Room, Toy Dolls, and has some kind of interest in both Magic Girls and the Gold String."

"All I had was a first name, 'John.' Wills had mentioned the name 'Spangler' to me in connection with the Solquist case but didn't say his first name, and even if he had, I couldn't have connected John Spangler to the John I was trying to identify." Salt took another gulp of the water.

"What does Spangler have to do with your case?" Wills uncapped his pen and wrote something without looking at her.

She felt the muscles across her chest tightening. "Both Dan Pyne and Curtis Stone told me that a man they only knew as 'John' was Mike Anderson's supplier. Neither of them remembered or knew his last name. Stone said John owned and ran drugs and prostitutes out of Sam's and the Toy Dolls Club."

"Wait," Huff said. "I know who Stone is. I read his statement about Anderson's death, but how is the guy that was shot—what's his name? Dan?—how is he connected and how did it happen that you were dancing with him?" Huff pronounced dancing like an accusation and a statement of incredulity. "I'll ask you again—was the shooter aiming at you?"

Salt licked her lips. "Are you interrogating me? I don't know if Dan Pyne took a bullet meant for me. I don't know."

Wills began making slashing marks with his pen on the yellow lined paper.

DAN CRAWLED UP a red, crumbling, flaking hill, climbing until his hands were abraded. The thunder had ceased, never having produced rain. The wind seemed to have settled in a steady *whoosh*. The harder he tried, the more his legs and arms turned to sludge. He lifted his head again to search for Salt and to listen for Ranger's call. All he saw was blowing dust. All he heard was *whoosh, whoosh, whoosh*.

REPERCUSSIONS

One of the little dams was penned against the fence, held there by Wonder's stare and Salt's knee. Salt bore down with the clippers, snipping at a bit of hoof.

"First time I came here you were armed with those." Wills stood at the paddock gate, holding a cup of coffee. He nodded at the clippers in her hand.

"You brought me tiger lilies." She let go of the sheep's spindly leg and called the dog off. The spring afternoon sky was beginning to darken, and the wind had the new green leaves of the trees twirling, loose petals from the dogwoods scattering over the paddock and orchard. She shoved the clippers in a back pocket of her jeans and picked up her cup from the fence post. "Maybe we ought to have breakfast. Looks like we're in for some rain."

As they walked to the house, Wills said, "I called Gardner. Pyne is still critical, on life support. He has spinal cord damage. They still don't know if he'll survive."

Salt sat down on the back porch steps. After a pause she began to loosen the laces of her boots. "We have a lot of work, a lot of follow-up from last night." She jerked at the laces.

"You're off today and tomorrow, your regular off days, remember?"

"I can't just take off now." She tugged at the boots. "I made a mess. Dan Pyne might die."

Wills bent down, lifted her foot by the heel, and grabbed the boot. "Who made you the center of the universe? You think you're the only one who makes shit happen or who can solve these cases? One piece of advice I will give you about working murders," he said as he pulled one boot off and then the other. "You can get to a point where your personal life seems less important than the cases. But if you have no life other than murders, you'll find yourself wrapped around an axle." Wills lifted her with one hand and gave her shoes with the other. "Come on, I'll fix us breakfast. We need to sort through this."

SALT WAS at the old sink washing the dishes and looking out at the rain. Wills sat at the kitchen table feeding Wonder little pieces from his last strip of bacon. "We've just gotten the background on Spangler. He was raised by his grandparents, who lived over on Adair Avenue when the area was mostly working-class whites. Their only heir, he inherited the buildings and properties now occupied by the Shack and Toy Dolls. The actual businesses are licensed as LLCs with generic names: "Freedom First," I think is one of the names; the other is similar. We also think Spangler's branched out and probably has investments in Magic Girls and the Gold String. The feds are helping us with the paper trail to Solquist."

Salt turned and grabbed a dish towel. "I wish the feds had been as helpful when Stone gave them the information he had on John

Spangler. Maybe Dan Pyne wouldn't have taken that bullet. But I guess some victims get more justice than others."

"A part of me understands how you, you being who you are, could come to be dancing with a—I'm not sure what Dan Pyne is. A witness? A suspect? Victim?"

Salt dried her hands and sat down across from him. "And the other part?"

"I worry that you've gotten enmeshed again—that a combination of the newness of being a detective, the mystery and romance of the blues, your father, and the Michael Anderson case has you entranced. You've always worked, in my opinion, way too close. You were too close to the gang on your old beat. It scares me because it's dangerous, both to you and maybe to us."

"I don't see it that way. I don't think of it like that."

"How do you think about Dan Pyne?"

The chair scraped as Salt pushed back from the table and went back to the window. "Wills, I'm working this case the way I do. Dan is part of the case. There was this dream I had. I can't ignore the connections."

"My God. Do you know how crazy that sounds?"

She jerked open a drawer, pulled out a tablet and pen, slapped them on the table in front of Wills, and sat back down. "Just the facts, ma'am. Ask me your fucking questions now, Detective."

"You're not right," he said.

"One, Dan Pyne knew and was close to Mike Anderson in the months, weeks, and days before he died. Two, Dan Pyne manages and plays with musicians who knew the scene back then, who played with Mike and knew the business and, therefore, maybe John Spangler. Three, he saw Mike with John Spangler the night before Mike was found dead. Four, Dan's current live-in girlfriend was Mike's girlfriend at the time he died." She pushed the pad toward Wills. "You're not writing, Detective."

Arrff, arrff! Wonder's barks were loud, directed at Salt, responding to her harsh tone.

Wills stood. "I think I'll take the dog for a walk. The rain has stopped. Maybe you can take the time to catch your breath, get yourself under control." The screen door sounded like a slap behind them. Salt stood at the window and watched them walking away, Wills with his hands in his pockets. Wonder, at his side, had on his bent ears.

She went straight to the bedroom, put on her gi, trying to begin the breath practice while tying the belt. Barefoot, she took the steps to the upstairs dojo two at a time. At the door to the white room she took another deep breath and bowed, knelt, and placed herself in seiza on the spot where she always guessed her father's bloodstains to be beneath the mat. She tried breathing exercises but started to choke, gave up, and lay facedown on the white mat. "Crazy. Crazy."

"It was a poor choice of words, a figure of speech." Wills stood in the dojo doorway. "I'm sorry."

Salt, silent, bowed to him.

He took off his wet shoes, socks, jeans, shirt, and underwear. The rain must have started again. Stripped naked, he entered the room. "I knew from the beginning that you'd always be only yourself. What draws me to you is also what scares me. I accept it. I'll find a way to trust that you can do the job your way. Now, tell me the dream." He sat cross-legged beside her.

Salt brought herself to sitting, wrapped her arms around her knees. "The night I met the bus when Dan's band got to town, the band was joking with Dan about an imaginary dog."

Wills leaned forward so that his waist hung a little over his shy genitals, in a way Salt found sweet and erotic. "What are you looking at, girl?"

Salt smiled.

Wills laughed. "Stop it." He covered himself with his hands. "The dream?"

She looked off. "In my dream the dog was in an old gray board house, not much more than a shack, one room. I let light into the room when I opened the door. There was an old wood-burning stove, unlit, cold. The dog was sitting perfectly still on top of it. Only his head moved as he talked. He was talking, but I can't remember what he said. That was all there was to the dream, but my strongest feeling in the dream was that the dog had been alive once, and its words were ones I needed to hear."

"A talking-dog story, hmm?" Wills pulled Salt into his lap and wrapped his arms around her. "So what does the dog have to do with the case and dancing with Dan Pyne? It scares me that maybe you were the intended target." Wills turned her so that she sat almost cradled in his arms.

"I keep trying to recall what the dog was saying." She laid her head on his shoulder. "Then just the other day Mr. Gooden reminded me that before my dad died I used to talk all the time about wanting a dog, and I remembered. I wanted one so bad that I invented him and called him 'Ranger.'"

"So, lots of kids have imaginary friends, dogs, fairies, whatever. See, you're making this into some kind of karmic happening."

"Maybe, maybe," Salt said. "Wills, just before Dan was shot he was telling me that he and the band called their imaginary dog 'Ranger.' It just seems like too much coming together. My dad's connections with the blues, my first case connected to Stone, the dream, Ranger." Salt shook her head. "And I keep thinking about Stone. He's so sick, crazy and sick. I know he's dangerous, but he never stood a chance. It doesn't seem right. Prison. He's always been in prison."

Will stroked her hair. "You keep nothing at arm's length. I could almost murder Huff for giving you a case that puts you up close again with a guy who almost killed you—to put you in the position of working to get his time cut."

She turned her face to his shoulder and kept talking. "Please don't be mad at me when I tell you this. There's a way in which I owe Stone. He was another child on my beat, from The Homes, and represents for me failure, at every level, everything this city, all of us, have gotten wrong."

"Who failed those children, Salt? Who were the individuals who failed them, almost all of them? Who? Their fathers, that's who." Wills held her tighter. "Like your father failed you. You think you're going to fix the world one sociopath, one case, at a time? I love you, girl, but if you keep giving yourself away there won't be enough of you left for me or anybody. We bleed enough for our own. I'm not going to bleed for the Stones of the world."

"I don't think my father failed me, Wills. That's part of what I keep trying to figure out."

Wonder could be heard running up and down the stairs and through the downstairs hall. "The dog is nuts. He's upset and letting us know," she said, nodding to the sound of the dog's clicking nails on the wood floors.

Salt wiped her eyes with the sleeve of the gi. "You're right." She took his hand and stood, pulling him up with her. Facing him, she said, "I'm not going for self-inflicted wounds. I want you and me."

Holding hands, they walked to the doorway, turned, and bowed to the altar. Salt said, "I didn't start out to dance with Dan Pyne. It was his dog. I was trying to figure out the dog's message."

BAND AT HOMICIDE

Salt hit the buzzer to allow admittance to the Homicide waiting room. Warily eyeing the premises and giving Rosie sideways glances, the band ambled in. "Please, have a seat," Rosie said. Bailey presented himself with a little bow in front of Rosie's desk and shook hands while the others glanced around at the photos of police commanders hanging on one wall and the large blue-and-gold department logo, a rising phoenix encircled by the words "PRIDE, PROFESSIONALISM, PROGRESS" on the opposite wall. Rosie's red dress was a brilliant contrast to the dull grays and blues of the room.

Salt introduced them. "Rosie, this is the Old Smoke Band, and they're here to give statements in the Pyne case."

"Good afternoon, ma'am. My name is Bailey Brown and these supposed gentlemen"—Bailey swept his arm back toward the men—"are with me."

Instead of picking up the phone, Rosie opted to treat them to a view, all six foot three of herself in the tight dress, as she stood. "I'll go tell Sarge you're here." She turned to go through to the inner office area, providing the men with an unobstructed view of her posterior, greatly enhanced by new butt padding.

As soon as the door closed behind Rosie, Blackbird whistled. "Whew, that is a lot of he/she."

Salt smiled. "It's not your grandfather's police department anymore."

Mustafa sniffed the air. "What is that smell?"

Blackbird inhaled. "Fish sauce. Smells just like Saigon. Smells like a war I was once in."

Goldie cracked his knuckles. "I'm invokin' my right to remain silent. If you-all know what's good for you, you-all will do the same."

"Hear that, Pops?" Bailey laughed. "Pops ain't said five words in three years. Aaw, Goldie, we got nothin' to be silent about. We got nothin' to hide."

"Since when did that matter with black men and the poleese?" answered the sax man, slumping into a battered chair.

Rosie returned. "Sarge is ready. In the conference room."

"Come on back," Salt said to the band, holding the interior door open.

Bailey led the crew. As the band passed, Rosie took out a compact mirror and made a show of touching up her lips. They assembled around Salt on the other side of the door. "Where's the beautiful girl receptionist they got in all the movies?" Mustafa asked, pointing his thumb toward the outer office.

"They wouldn't let us in to see Dan. How is he?" Bailey took out a handkerchief and wiped his forehead.

"Nothing's changed. Still touch and go. This way." Salt led them through the cubicles, past detectives poring over paperwork in their small spaces, past empty desks covered in files, stacked, waiting for the return of their murder men. The band seemed diminished under the office lighting, out of their element, like a song played off-key, wrong. "In here, guys." Salt showed the way into the conference room, where Sergeant Huff, Wills, and several other detectives sat waiting with pens and notebooks ready.

"Please have a seat, gentlemen," Wills said. "Make yourselves comfortable. Does anyone need water, coffee, or a soda?" He addressed the room, but his eyes stopped for a half second longer, smiling, on Salt.

Huff had a carton of Asian carryout in front of him, chopsticks clicking as he cleaned out the bottom of the box.

The band went to the far end of the table. Thing One, wearing a tie-dyed tie, picked up and relocated to sit beside Goldie. "You the sax player, right?"

"Yeah, how'd you know?" Goldie stretched back and straightened his suit jacket.

"Google. Listen"—the detective leaned in close to Goldie—"I played sax back in high school. Been thinking about taking it up again. I still got my horn. You guys gonna be around for a while, maybe I can sit in with you some."

Goldie looked away, turned toward Bailey. "See what I tell you. Man says we gonna be here awhile."

Sergeant Huff pushed the empty carton to the center of the table and looked around for something to wipe his greasy fingers on. "Okay, people, let's get this show on the road." Finding nothing, he rubbed his hands together. "My name is Sergeant Huff and I'm in charge of this case. We got a man shot a couple of nights ago, your guitar player. Man comes all the way across the country, stopping in lots of cities and towns, and then gets shot in my town, and I wanna know why. So the way this works is my fine detectives here are gonna take a sworn statement from each of you. And if I understand right, you-all have to leave in a few days?"

Bailey, at the opposite end of the table, leaned forward, his big arms stretched out, hands open. "Sergeant, my name is Bailey Brown.

I guess you'd say I'm the leader of this group. Right now we're all pretty torn up about Dan, but they won't let us in to see him at the hospital. His girlfriend is flying in tonight. Nothing much for us to do except make our engagements. We all got mouths to feed, and if Dan's gonna get paid, we have to make money for us and for him. So other than that, the best way we can help Dan is to give you every bit of information we can. We've talked and we can't come up with any reason for Dan being a target. But we'll leave that to you to figure out and help you any way we can."

"Good enough," Sergeant Huff said as he stood. "It doesn't matter to me who interviews who. You guys pair off any way you want. I'll be in my office if you need anything."

Thing One slapped Goldie on the back. "As one sax man to another—let's blow."

Goldie rolled his eyes.

"Mr. Brown?" Salt said, standing up.

"Of course, Detective," Bailey stood.

Wills and the other detectives paired up with Blackbird, Pops, and Mustafa, each person differently prepared to hear or tell of events relevant to the shooting of Dan Pyne.

THE DOOR to the Blue Room was closed. Salt pulled at the corrugated metal and found it unlocked. Inside, Man sat reading at a small round table in the far corner facing the door. As Salt approached, he looked up and with one hand closed a worn Quran.

"I didn't know you were religious," Salt said, pointing at the red cover.

"Naw, just trying to figure out what all the fuss is about. Some brothers in the West End all up in this shit. Don't make any more sense to me than the Bible."

"Rules to live by."

"Ain't all about no shall and shall nots. I can tell you that for sure."

Salt pulled up a chair and sat down a few feet to the left of Man so she could see the door. "What about rules for your boys? Can they lie to you, steal from you? What about murder?"

"Rules never kept anybody doin' what they supposed to do anyway. Police got rules; churches, banks, all kinds of business got rules. I don't see rules keepin' folks from doin' what they want." Man tapped the Quran. "Just words. My boys loyal. They won't lie to me or steal from me 'cause they loyal."

Salt leaned toward him. "And if they aren't?"

He shrugged.

"What about you being loyal to your boys, say, Stone? You took him in when he was young, to get him away from Tall John. You might be the closest he's ever had to family."

Man looked out into the room. "That was a long time ago."

"I'm sure Stone could give the feds something more, something on you to help get his time cut."

"That's what I'm talking about. Stone loyal."

"The other night, right before the shooting, you met up with Tall John. Someone else books the music, runs the Shack and the Blue Room, but you're the moneyman here, aren't you? You're the contact with John Spangler."

Man leaned back and put his feet on the table, close to the Quran. "Me and John is just business. I'm going to go legit in the club business."

"With John Spangler? Legitimate? You're fooling yourself, Man."

"How else I'm going to go legit? You know how it is. How else I'm going to go straight?" Man let his chair fall back to the floor with a thud.

"Here's the truth. Stone gave a sworn statement that John Spangler, ten years ago, gave an intentionally hot dose to the bluesman Mike Anderson. Stone can get his time cut if I can verify that information. The statute has run out on Spangler's abuse of Stone and the drug dealing. But the statute hasn't run out on murder."

"You doin' it again. Why you bringin' this shit to me? Puttin' me in the middle?"

"You're already in the middle."

"And why you trying to help Stone? He got convicted of trying to kill you."

"We're both in this, Man. I didn't choose it either. But you're right. It's not about rules. The other night—" Salt stood up and walked to the spot on the floor, the sealed cement, still stained with Dan's blood. "The other night, right here, Dan Pyne was shot. I'm loyal, like you. I'm loyal to doing my job. Just like you know everything about what happens in and around The Homes, I know you know, or can find out, who shot Pyne, and I'm going to count on your loyalty to Stone to find corroboration for his information on Spangler."

Man stood. "I'm sick a' you always comin' to me with shit. Last time you was all on me about who killed Lil D's mama. You put my boys in jail. Why you all on me? I'm tryin' to break out of this shit."

Salt turned toward the door, then stopped. "One thing." She went back to the table and picked up the Quran. "Something you said, Man—it's not about the rules, it's about finding the truth. That's what I'm after." She respectfully put the book on the table and left the Blue Room.

PEOPLE ON their lunch hours hurried past the downtown hotel where Melissa was staying. Only the top third of their bodies was visible above the café curtain rail. Salt alternated watching people outside and glancing at the entrance to the café. Melissa had agreed to meet her at noon. It was twenty after.

"Are you sure I can't get you anything?" the waiter asked again.

Melissa appeared behind him. "I'll have a Bloody Mary," she said, sliding into the booth. "Your dime, right?" She looked at Salt.

"Sure. Would you also like something to eat?"

"If ever there was an occasion to drink my lunch, this is it, don't you think?" The singer's face was made up with eye shadow and lipstick, more hard-looking than Salt remembered from the Notelling. Melissa glanced briefly at the waiter. "Just the Bloody drink."

Salt's stomach growled. "I'd better eat. The breakfast special, if it's still available."

"One Bloody Mary and one special." The waiter left them.

"Melissa, I'm sorry about Dan. Thank you for meeting with me today."

"Did I have a choice?" She picked up the stiff napkin and patted her nose. "You were with him when he was shot. Right?"

"Yes, at the Blue Room," Salt answered, her blood sugar dropping, hoping the breakfast would come soon. Her patience grew thin when she was hungry.

An old man wearing a dirty jacket peered in the window right next to the booth, his hand held over his eyes to cut the glare. Melissa picked up a knife and struck the window with the handle, startling both the man and Salt. "Bum," Melissa said.

Salt shook out her napkin and placed it in her lap. "He's probably just hungry."

"Look, Detective," Melissa said, pointing the business end of the knife at Salt. "Can we get on with this. For God's sake, tell me how someone could shoot Dan right in front of a cop and still get away." She threw the knife on the table just as the waiter arrived with her drink, which she picked up as soon as his hand left it. "Why don't you go ahead and get me another one," she said to the waiter while facing Salt. "Hotels are stingy with their alcohol."

Salt brought the water glass to her lips, giving the waiter time to leave. "I didn't see who shot Dan. The room was crowded, and after he was shot I was doing CPR, trying to keep Dan alive."

Melissa emptied her drink. "CPR, the last kiss. Kind of romantic, in the broader sense. Poetic actually. How was it for you?"

Salt folded the napkin and said, "Excuse me. I need to find the restroom." She slid from the booth just as the waiter was returning with Melissa's second drink.

In the ladies' room Salt splashed her face with cold water. Her skin looked pale. She lifted the coil of hair that covered the scar at her hairline. Today the scar was red-looking. "She might have something you need," she reminded herself.

The breakfast was there when she returned to the table. She was so hungry she nearly choked on the first bit of eggs, barely tasting them. She tore the toasted bagel into bite-sized pieces.

Melissa drained the tomato juice–stained glass. "I'd weigh a ton if I ate like that."

"Are you sure you don't want to eat?"

"I'm still thirsty," she said, looking for the waiter.

"Melissa, do you, did you know John Spangler?" Salt began.

Melissa slumped down in the booth. "That was a long time ago."

"But you knew who he was? Dan and I saw him outside the Blue Room right before Dan was shot."

"I knew Spangler. Okay. He was Mike's dealer." Melissa tipped her glass to Salt. "Happy?" she said, and then lowered it to the table with a thunk. "I was a dumb kid back then."

A siren made its way through the city toward the hotel. "You were already performing?"

"Yeah, I was sitting in with different bands when I could. I'm a singer. I don't like the way you say 'performer.'"

"Was Mike encouraging? Did he help you get gigs?"

"Most of the time I wasn't even sure if he knew I was there. It was like he'd look around and say, 'Hey, Melissa's here.' He got more sex from the guitar than me. And if one of his blues buddies came around, I ceased to exist. And then there was the coke and heroin."

Salt saw lights from an ambulance reflecting off the building across the street before the ambulance actually arrived. "Did you and Dan score from Spangler?"

"I didn't use. Dan would only snort occasionally if there was free stuff, like at a party. It's never really been his thing."

"Did either Mike or Dan say anything about Spangler being angry with Mike around the time of Mike's death?" The ambulance pulled up right next to the café window.

"Look, Mike didn't talk to me about his using and I didn't ask. After he died, Dan and I didn't talk about Mike or anything to do with Mike. We wanted to forget."

Salt pushed back the café curtain. The paramedics were strapping the old man who'd been at the window onto a gurney. She let the curtain drop. "I know this is a bad time for you. But I'm getting the sense that you either don't want to answer or genuinely don't know much about the two men who have been the primary love interests of your life. Of course, I'm presuming you were in love with them."

"They were there when I needed them. Love to me is like Santa Claus, Detective. I stopped believing in that shit long before I met either Mike or Dan." Melissa slightly slurred her *s*'s. "But I can fake it like a mother." She stood up and was stumbling, trying to get out of the booth. "Adios, Detective. I hope you catch the son of a bitch." Melissa swayed toward the hotel lobby.

"Will there be anything else?" the waiter asked, putting the check on the table.

"Did you see the ambulance?" she asked while she got out her wallet.

"Yeah, it's sad really," said the young man. "That old guy comes around all the time. Homeless. I think he has heart problems."

"Not as bad as some folks," Salt said. She could still see Melissa's red hair as she made her way up the lobby escalator.

DAN SLOWLY curved the fingers of his left hand to form chords on the edge of the sheet. The fingers of his right hand strummed an imagined Gibson, E minor 7, A minor 7, B 7. Something was wrong with his throat. He reached for the A minor again and his fingers wouldn't remember. When he woke again, he thought of nothing but the chord changes. He tried to open his eyes the next time, but the lights from the machine in the dim room hurt.

He came to again and realized there was a tube in his throat. "There's no safe life," he thought. "No need to hedge your bets." E minor 7, A minor 7, B 7. The hospital room with no window was in perpetual timelessness. Then Melissa was there, her red hair backlit by the bright lights outside the room. He tried to catch her scent but couldn't due to some kind of disinfectant and a plastic odor from the tube. Melissa was there and then she wasn't.

This time he could smell the green of the detective's fragrance, mixed with a furry scent. "How had she gotten that dog in here?" He thought he said things out loud but then realized he hadn't. "Muddy, Bailey, Howlin' Wolf, Mike. Never played it safe. I won't sleep again." He nodded off.

He moved, feeling the catheter against his legs. "I'm all in. It's not worth it unless you're all in. It's all good, Ranger. This just something to get through. I'll play this song for sure." E minor 7, A minor 7, B 7.

DAN BLINKED, opening his eyes wide, then squeezing them tight, as though he was trying to see through a blur. "Da," it sounded like he said.

Salt leaned closer. "You're not going to die. The doctor says you'll make it." She felt some relief now that he was no longer intubated.

Dan moved his head slowly from left to right. "Do-og" came out in two long syllables.

Salt looked down at his hands moving on the sheet, at the wired patches on his chest, then up at the blue numbers on the monitor above. "Dog?" she repeated, while a red line on the black screen rippled with a blip sound. "I just wanted to say I'm sorry, Dan. You stopped a bullet that may have been meant for me. I hope—" She turned her head away from him, looked around at the small bedside table, the empty portable tray against the wall. "Water. I'll get you some water. Be right back," she said, barely escaping, just to the wall outside the ICU room, leaning there with her face in her hands. "Damnit. Pull it together." She pinched her fists against her cheeks. "What do you hope? It is crazy. He's still talking about that dog." She realized she'd said the last words out loud.

A passing nurse asked if she needed something. Salt checked with her to be sure Dan could have ice and water. She returned to the room with both and put them on the tray.

Dan opened his eyes and shook his head. Salt put the straw to his cracked lips. When he had sipped, he tilted his chin up, asking her to lean down. "Dance," he repeated. Then in a hoarse voice, he said slowly, "Save another dance for me."

———

SALT WAS back at her desk sorting out copies of the band's statements, as well as those of other witnesses, all of whom seemed to have
seen nothing of the shooter at the Blue Room. She looked up to find
Wills standing there wearing his jacket, having just come in.

She put down the paper.

"Sarah," Wills said. "I'm sorry."

Salt stood up to look across the cubicles to make sure there was no
one to overhear. "We're fine, Wills. We'll work it out." She touched
his elbow. "We'll be fine," she reassured him.

Wills closed his eyes for a half second. "Sarah." He looked at her.
"Dan Pyne went into cardiac arrest. He died about a half hour ago."

MAGIC GIRLS

Smoking the once-in-a-blue-moon cigarette, with the metal grate of the fire escape landing growing hard and cold on her rear, Salt lifted herself on her haunches and pulled her jacket against the cool damp air. The street below was a noir avenue, not much bigger than an alley, four-story brick buildings enclosing a narrow, undivided, unmarked two-way. The building she was using was vacant. Decrepit fire escape landings at each level were joined with black metal ladders that only went close enough to the sidewalk to satisfy old safety codes.

Less and less frequently the double doors of Magic Girls, the high rollers' strip club across the street, would unseal and a din of noise accompanied by a dominant bass rhythm would erupt from the pink-lit interior, drowning out the rest of the dying sounds of the city and the drifting notes from a street saxophonist whose solo echoed for blocks.

Three in the morning now. Rain fell sporadically, splattering in standing water and causing ripples to shine with streetlight reflections.

The view from her perch seemed intimate. The shimmering dark, a black-blue diamond light, was unpolluted by traffic exhaust, noise, or hurrying people. The only sounds were water notes, drips and splashes against the white noise and muted chords of the city that began somewhere down the street. Music could bend around blocks, and the sax man had a wail with a will, even when he'd walked farther downtown; as long as the doors to the club stayed shut, Salt could catch bits of his brass notes against the muffled sounds of Atlanta pulling up her covers.

She stepped back through the large wood-frame window just as moonlight broke through the clouds over the buildings across to the northwest. An old, large mottled mirror between the windows caught the reflection of her eyes, wide-open, dilated, moonshine-flecked, and unblinking.

Salt thought how it might have been for Pearl; how hard it had been for women in the blues, the prostitutes, the dancers, the singers, those who performed double duties in order to survive and to keep on with their blues. She knew a stripper who called herself "Miss Atlanta," good name for a stripper. Some of the young girls that she'd watched grow up in The Homes, only a few miles to the south, had gone in the front doors of these clubs as dancers and come out the back broken and full of dope. Women and the blues had a history.

Magic Girls' pink-and-gold neon marquee poked up into the night sky, letters almost as tall as the building. Catering to an almost exclusively black clientele, it was the flashiest, biggest money club in the city. The parking lot was full of flash: Hummers, Jags, tricked-out vintage sedans, some with rims costing more than the cars, pimped-out SUVs, all of which shone under the lights as they arrived. But while parked they lost the shine to the dust kicked up from the cheap, gravel-covered lot.

She focused her binoculars to pull into view the faces of people leaving the club, not that she'd likely miss the white face she was looking for. In this town people tended toward separate but equal in looking for God and sex.

Atlanta had billed itself as "The City Too Busy to Hate" during the civil rights movement of the '60s. Salt thought that was close to right; closer might have been to reveal what folks were doing that kept them so busy—lots of backslapping and hand-holding, under tables and behind doors, doors not unlike the one she was surveilling across the street.

The street was still beautiful, even with the colors of Magic Girls' neon bleeding into the reflections. All around, like a Romare Bearden collage, in every direction, around the Zero Milepost, where things came together at the end of the line, the churches that Sherman had spared, incongruously close to the titty bars and jail down the street.

There were only a few cars left in the parking lot when the marquee shut off, leaving only the light above the front door of the club illuminating a small space underneath and the street right in front. The door opened with a split of pink from inside and two men appeared, Spangler and Sandy Madison.

Madison, smoking a cigarette, was wearing fatigue pants and a pistol strapped to his thigh. A sweatshirt covered his uniform insignia and badge. He looked up and down the street, then up at the light overhead. Salt blew out a long breath. Madison's face looked greasy, Spangler's chalky white. They spoke, but their voices drifted up in muted monosyllables that she strained to catch. The two men, walking close and side by side, moved to the darkened parking lot on the side of the building.

She'd dressed in a dark T-shirt and black jeans. But now she sensed she'd let herself get careless, carried away with the night. She shouldn't have smoked the cigarette on the landing. Something in the way

Madison didn't look up her way made her think he'd already seen her. She had dismissed him, underestimated his connections: Madison. Reverend Midas Prince. Spangler. And he might be a fool in many ways, but as far as surveillance, he was sure to know his stuff.

There was enough street light coming in the old windows for her to make her way through the vacant rooms and down the hall to the stairwell. She winced at the sound of the rusty door opening to the pitch-black hollowness of the stairs and switched on the penlight from her key ring. All she could do now was to focus on the steps in front of her.

Opening the side exterior door from the building, she stood flush against the brick wall that still held warmth from the day and allowed her breath to even out. She considered the best route to get to her car, parked a block over in a spot where she'd doubted anyone would notice the beat-up Honda, a more covert vehicle than the tip-off Taurus. The side of the building was dark, but there was a bit of ambient light from the moon and a few made-to-look-old gas streetlights. Hugging the wall, she made her way to the back corner of the building, quick-peeked to be sure it was clear, then lengthened her stride as she crossed the narrow strip of broken asphalt to a retaining wall above the adjacent lot. Five or so junk trees, mimosas in varying heights, had grown up in the margin of dirt between the cracked pavement and the brick barrier. Salt sat down, swung her legs over the wall, lowered herself, and dropped to the open alleyway below.

"Pretty girl like you—why doncha just call for backup?" Madison was leaning against a corner of a building ten yards away. He was picking his nails with the tip end of a matte-black buck knife. There was another drop-off in front of Salt and a dead end to her left. "I see you got your radio on your belt, but I doubt you have it on. Word is you're a loner; you go after them bad guys all by yourself—a tough girl. Anybody know you're up there spyin' on me?" He straightened out of his lean. "Bet not."

"Madison, I had no idea you worked this EJ. I'm investigating ties between the club scene now and people who knew Mike Anderson from the clubs back then. It's none of my business if you work strip clubs on your own time." She caught a glimpse of her lone car across the lot below and estimated the drop.

"You come after me, snooping 'round my EJs, you likely to get a whole lot of guys out of their jobs, too. They work for me, talk to me. I'd be doin' all them a favor by discouraging you, tough girl. Besides, I think you ain't so tough." Madison sheathed the knife and stuck it inside his right waistband. "You think you're tough, huh? Let's see."

He started coming toward her, doing the swagger for which he was mocked. "I wouldn't go to no titty bars if I had somebody like you to wrestle me. You like to wrestle? I heard you and that black guy, Pepper? I heard you wrestle with him." He stopped and stood looking down at her. "What kind of white girl goes with black guys?" He reached out and levered his right arm around her neck, pulling her into his chest and locking her into a hold with his left arm. She felt his chest rise as he drew in a deep breath. "But you shore do smell good."

Salt put her arms around his middle, as if appreciating his girth, and moved her palms back to his sides and under the sweatshirt. "Aikido," she whispered, turning her mouth up to his ear.

"What's that?" He tipped his chin down and back, still tugging her in with his arms locked.

The back of her hand touched the handle of the knife and he reacted, pitching his pelvis backward. But Salt was already drawing it out and lowering herself into a squat while flinging the knife away barely an instant before he was on her. Using his own momentum, Salt lifted him, keeping him in motion as he continued over her back.

She heard only his heavy scrambling as she sprinted down the alley, around the corner, and to her car, where she found the passenger-side window smashed. The glove box had been rifled, though there had been nothing in it but some of the cassette tapes. They were all still there.

"Mothafuck," she said. "That'll teach me." She slammed the door, threw the Honda in gear, and tore out of the city's metered parking space.

WONDER AND WILLS

As was often the case when Salt woke, Wonder was asleep with his back to her, lengthwise facing the open window. Early-morning light played with the breeze on the hydrangea bush outside. She lay still for a bit watching the tips of the dog's ears quiver and the embroidered half curtains flutter in the breeze. She reached with her index finger and touched the knob at the top of Wonder's head, his cue to roll on his back. He splayed his hind legs and folded his front legs in total acquiescence. This early-morning ritual was the only time or place he was off duty enough to bare his belly. "Breathe on me, breath of dog."

He cut his eyes as if to say, "That's not what you usually say."

She ran her finger through the spot at the bottom of each ear where his fur sometimes tangled. She rubbed the nicks, scratched his scars, and then buried her face in the soft fur under his chin, inhaling his light musky realness. "Dog breath." She ruffled his fur and rolled him over, and he bowed his down-dog stretch and hopped from the bed, waving his tail in anticipation as she got into running shorts and sneakers.

To cool down from the three-mile run Salt walked the last fifty yards from the county road in front of her property and up the gravel drive, appreciating the beginnings of the new fence. She visualized how it might look once completed and painted white and began to think about all the trees, shrubs, bushes, and flowers and the vegetable garden that she might plant once she had the sheep taking care of the mowing. In the back at the chest-high paddock she slid back the bolt to let the sheep into the orchard. where they kept the grasses and weeds under control while enjoying the pecans when they fell in season. She barely had to supplement their feed.

The tree was twenty or so yards back, one of the more than thirty pecan trees on the property. The only thing that distinguished it now was the footboards she'd nailed to the trunk. Winding down from the run, she broke into a sweat that gathered and ran down her legs, painting muddy tracks along her dusty calves. Still breathing hard, hands on her hips, Wonder panting at her side, she walked to the tree and looked up the trunk to where the footboards ended at the branch. Without stopping to think, she took hold of one of the head-high boards and stepped up on the bottom rung. Hand over hand she climbed to the last rung and with an easy motion swung her arms around the branch above, settling her rear on the smooth scoop of her old childhood haunt. The warm wind tousled the limbs, branches, and leaves, waving them in the morning sun, scattering the light and bouncing it all around her. "Ranger. I remember. Ranger."

She sighed and lowered her chin to her chest. *"Breathe."* She had watched her father's breath leave, had not thought anything about giving him her breath. *"Breathe." Where did it go?* she'd wondered in that moment when his breath was gone. That precise moment of her ten-year-old life when she realized her father was dead and she should have tried to give him her breath. "If I could find your breath—"

Breathe on me, breath of God
Fill me with life.

She imagined hearing the choir sing. "What could I have done to get you to stay in this life? I didn't think to give you my breath. If I had done enough, been enough, could you have stayed? I did not give you breath." The thoughts came in the same old pattern.

Wonder stared up from below, happily swishing his tail. "Breathe on me, breath of dog." *Ranger. Dan. Breath of dog.*

THE ROTTIES and the warm aroma of just-baked biscuits met her when she let herself in Wills' place. "Honey, I'm home," Salt called, walking down the hall while scratching the dogs' ears, their nails tapping and sliding on the polished wood floor. The fragrance became increasingly delicious as she neared the kitchen and her appetite was further enhanced by the sound of perking burbles from the coffee brewing on the counter.

She'd called Wills after coming down from the tree. He suggested breakfast before they went in to work.

He stood next to the stove pushing soy patties around a small pan. "I could get used to hearing that," he said, smiling at her. He was wearing his standard work clothes—a short-sleeved dress shirt and khaki pants, covered with a white half apron tied under his chest. A day-of-the-dead skull tie was slung over his leather carryall on a chair by the wall.

"Oh, yeah. Wait till I've told you my latest adventure. I need some advice, dude. I'm actually asking for help." Her phone rang. "Hi, Chuck. Hold on." She motioned to Wills. "I actually need to take this one." She put the phone back to her ear. "Yep. Honda Accord. Yep. You got it. Passenger front window. Anytime today. It'll be in the parking lot. Blue. Yep. BIF2988. Thanks, Chuck." She turned the phone off, tucked it in her bag, and looked up at Wills waiting. "Sorry, but Chuck's fixing my window today."

"Your window?" Wills piled the biscuits in a red ceramic bowl lined with a green kitchen cloth.

"Wills, I'm telling you right away. I'm going to tell you all of it. I want to be better with you, to not be so, so . . ."

"Hungry?" he asked.

"I'm starved," she said as she sat down and began giving him the details about the surveillance. "Don't dog me out. I'm doing this. Okay? I didn't have any clear idea what I was looking for or who I might see, but I set up across from Magic Girls."

"Magic Girls—thug central." He turned with his hands on his hips.

"Wills. Mostly I wanted to get a sense of Spangler, who he hangs with, bodyguards, posse pals, associates, the usual suspects, who I might need to go around to interview him."

"Did you stop to think that since he's connected to my case that you might talk this over with me?" He stirred eggs with his back to her.

"You've got your hands full and we're not officially assigned partners. What would you have said if I told you I would be doing the surveillance? I can't check in with you asking about every move I make. If I've got an opportunity, I need to be able to take it. Same as if I were a guy. So I set up in the vacant building across from the club."

"God, God, God. This is going to be the death of me. And to think I was the one encouraging you to go for detective."

"Wills, you are going to have to trust that I can handle myself.

And I am going to promise to try to ask for help when I need it. Like now."

"Salt, even a guy would make a phone call, pull out with radio."

"But wouldn't you just have worried if I called first and then had my phone off? And okay, so maybe I'm sensitive about being treated different, but it's sometimes hard to know when someone's safety concerns are a disguise for paternalism and thinking that a woman's not up to the job."

She told him the rest—about Spangler and Madison, and Madison's assault. Then finding the window busted.

They sat with mugs of rich Cuban coffee, real butter, watermelon-rind preserves, free-range organic eggs, and soy sausage. "Have you noticed I'm not even ranting about your run-in with Madison?" said Wills.

"No, you're not. Why?"

"I'm also going to try to do this better. I'm not going to go flay the skin from his body inch by inch. I'm not going to go remove his eyes from his head or his teeth with a tire iron. I'm not even going to say a fucking word to him. In fact, I'm going to seriously avoid him or any place he might be." Wills put his mug down on the table and started clearing the dishes.

"Uh-oh."

"No. You're right, honey. As things stand it would be just your word against his. But I know how to get more. This needs, we need, help and I have friends. You have friends. We can do this." He refilled her cup.

"What about his connection with Midas Prince and now Spangler? What about all the cops who work EJs for him? I don't know who we can trust. Do you?"

"The EJ thing is a problem. Right now I don't know who all works for him either." Wills sat back down with his own fresh cup of coffee.

"I've had EJ discussions with Pepper several times. I think he's even worked some jobs for Madison," she said. "Ann called me and she and I are going to go to lunch tomorrow. I think she's worried. She and Pepper are having a hard time with the new assignment."

"Understandable. Narcotics is the most dangerous job in the PD for lots of reasons. And it can change people if they start to identify with the dark side."

"I'm assuming you mean that metaphorically?" Salt widened her eyes.

"God, you Southerners are so sensitive—Atlantans especially." He shook his head. "Everything has a subtext about race. It's tiresome."

"Sister says the city has a black dog hanging around."

"Black dog?"

"A hellhound." She looked down into her cup. "Wills, one of the reasons I wanted to see you is because I was thinking about my dad this morning and I realized that I might be, I don't know, for lack of a better word, haunted by his death, by having found him after he shot himself. This case of the blues, Michael Anderson's death, my father's blues collection, Dan Pyne bleeding out while I tried to give him CPR—it's all brought up some things I'd forgotten."

He laughed. "Shazam! Well, aren't you the smart shrink. You think? A little girl finds her father bleeding to death from a self-inflicted gunshot to the head and he dies in her arms. Yeah, that might put a crinkle in your gray matter."

"The dog in my dream . . ."

He looked at her from under raised brows.

"Don't give me that look. Besides, no one, no cop, is a blank slate. We all have scars, even you." She reached across the table for his hand.

Wills got up, came around behind her, and encircled her in his arms. "Remember when we first came together, I told you I wanted you, in part, because of your history. I do have broken places myself, and you wouldn't be you without the history."

"This stuff blindsides me sometimes. It comes up and I want to remember and I don't."

"Well, Detective, we've got a lifetime to figure it out."

SISTER'S HOME

I knew I'd be seein' you soon." The hinges of the screen door made a salutatory rasp as Sister Connelly, wearing one of her immaculate, albeit worn, old-fashioned housedresses and flat sandals, opened it wider. With her halo braid, tight and neat, adding inches to her already impressive height, she narrowly missed the doorframe as she motioned to Salt. "I've got a fresh pitcher of tea. Come on back to the kitchen."

Passing the small parlor as they went down the hall, Salt said, "This is a treat. I feel like I've graduated—getting invited to your kitchen."

"Might as well, you keep comin' 'round anyway."

"I come because you know The Homes. You've been living here forever and you know almost everybody and who's kin to who."

Sister's house was a small hundred-year-old cottage near The Homes and across the street from the apartment that had been the scene of the murder a year ago.

"Sit." Sister motioned her to one of two red vinyl chairs at an aluminum-rimmed Formica table in the middle of the tiny kitchen. She took a large pitcher out of the refrigerator, removed its plastic cover, poured two glasses, and added ice from the freezer. A bouquet of collard greens lay on the counter by the sink. Salt began to get the same feeling she'd had before at Sister's, of shape-changing, of growing larger, like Alice in Wonderland, the already small kitchen growing smaller. Sister was so tall the two of them filled the room.

"I meant to tell you at the cemetery, I went to see Stone." Salt took a slow sip of the tea, remembering how sweet Sister made it.

"How's he doin'?"

"Terrible." The tea slid down Salt's throat like syrup. She didn't usually drink her tea sweetened, but Sister's was old-fashioned sweet, the sugar added when the tea was hot.

"He was never going to make it," Sister said. "Just too messed-up from the git."

"What do you hear about Lil D?"

"Latonya don't put much in the street, so he probably takin' care of her and that baby." Sister nodded her head to Salt, as if she were affirming something.

"Dantavious." Salt said the baby's name. Sister's back door was half pane glass. A wood-line barrier behind the house separated her quiet residential street from the parallel, more heavily traveled city street on the other side. But the trees grew up close, leaving her just a small backyard. Birds flitted back and forth across the view from the door's glass panels. An open worn Bible lay on the table at Sister's elbow. A black cat clock on the wall ticked with a switching tail.

"Is it Lil D or the new job brought you 'round again?" Sister asked.

"In a way both, I guess. I found a recording that belonged to my dad of Mike Anderson with Pretty Pearl. I think I told you I'd been assigned to look into some new information about his death."

"So that's it—your daddy."

Salt stood up, went to the back door, and looked out. "Can we go sit on your front porch? It's too pretty to be inside."

"I got your glass. Come on." Sister was halfway down the hall by the time Salt turned around.

The old woman sat down on a hard-back wood chair and waved Salt to the two-seater swing. "I'd like to just sit on the steps here if you don't mind—better view of your yard," said Salt.

There were flowers blooming everywhere in the crowded yard and along the wood fence. And everywhere there were starter containers: coffee cans, plastic tubs, anything that could be used to hold seedling plants. A climbing rose had grown up and into the trim on one of the corner supports. Flowering vines had begun sprouting on the fence posts. It all blended in an impressionist blur around the paint-peeling, weathered-wood house, patched in places with faded-tin advertising signs. "Atlanta's prettiest, best time of year," Salt said.

"Your father loved this city, too—one of the reasons he was a good policeman. He'd come by sometimes, even if he didn't have no real reason or police business."

"I just have these little pieces of him that I remember, since I was only ten when he died. But sometimes something will happen, like last year when I was shot, and I am able to grab at another piece." Salt put her nose to the fragrant jasmine that twined around the post beside her.

Sister had been rubbing the smooth, shiny skin that stretched over her big knuckles, then she looked up sideways, narrowing her eyes at Salt. "You think maybe you took this job so's you can make a whole out of them pieces? You chasin' a ghost?"

"That's funny—chasing ghosts. It's what homicide detectives do, in a way. It's my job. You have the best memory of anyone I've ever known and you knew my dad."

"Lord, chile. You can't expect me to remember much from maybe ten conversations that he and I had twenty or more years ago."

"No, but you might have noticed something, remember some impression."

"What kind of impression? What are you looking for?"

Salt felt a constriction in her throat, a hardening under her breastbone. She held her fist there. "Do I remind you of him?" She closed her eyes when her view of Sister's yard blurred.

"You mean are you like him?"

Salt nodded.

"You worried you are or are not like him?" Sister leaned toward Salt with her elbows on her knees and hands folded together. "Do you want to be like him or are you worried you messed-up from the git?"

"Both probably. Did he ever say anything, like he saw or heard things?"

"Not that I remember. Mostly my recollection of him, and I'll tell you straight, when I think back on him, it's how he saw connections, how things come together, crossroads, where the black dog sits. There's the song goes, 'None of us are free 'long as one of us is chained, none of us are free.' He understood how we all tied together. As much as anybody I ever knew. I used to think it was because he was a policeman. But it's come to me, since I met you, that it was just his way. He paid attention and got the connections."

The building across the street, where last year a twelve-year-old girl with tight braids had led Salt to her mother's body, was now stripped and gutted. "At first I thought maybe you were here about that killin' that's so much in the news these days. The rich lawyer's wife and her girls that were shot."

"Solquist?"

"Yeah, folks 'round here been talkin' about the detectives, all kinds of police, looking for DeWare. What kind of connection he have with killin' rich white people on the north side?"

"Good question," Salt said. Only the brick façade of last year's murder scene remained.

"You thinking about Stone again, and last year?" Sister asked.

"Should I?"

"Who else?" Sister said.

BREATH OF DOG

There were two dead and five wounded at The Manor (otherwise known to cops as the Razor Wire Arms) on Fort Street just off Auburn Avenue. The Homicide office was in official post-murder chaos: uniform cops escorting all manner of citizenry, witnesses tromping back and forth between cubicle rows, their kids playing games on the vending machines in the break room, detectives reporting in with each other and with supervisors, and supervisors fielding phone calls from command staff and the press. "Where the fuck are my lead detectives? I can't raise them on radio. One of you squirts call them on their bat phones, please," Huff yelled across the room. Then when he saw the chaplain standing beside Salt's desk, "Sorry, Chap."

"They're still out there, Sarge," Wills shouted.

"Do not the fuck call me Sarge, and where 'there'? Why?"

"Still at The Manor, interviewing the lords and ladies."

"This isn't a good time, Chaplain," Salt said.

"Is there ever a good time in Homicide?" The rotund cleric took in the room. There were even fewer white tufts on his pink head than this time last year when he'd first tried to counsel Salt after she'd been shot.

Thing One escorted a slouching woman wearing a large red T-shirt that said simply "Jesus" to Salt's cubicle. The woman was wearing only the T-shirt apparently, no pants were evident beneath the hem, and she had no shoes. "You can't smoke in here." Thing One removed the unlit cigarette from her lips. "She's a witness. Sarge wants you to do the interview, take her statement." He pulled a rolling chair from the nearby desk, pushed the woman into it. "Sit," he said, and walked away.

"Young lady, you need some more clothes on," the chaplain said, starting to take Salt's coat from the hook.

"Not that." Salt stood abruptly, startling the already disconcerted cleric.

"I like that jacket you wearing better anyway," the woman said to him.

He looked down at his coat, then enthusiastically came out of it and handed it to the woman, who used it to cover her bare thighs.

"Salt, I brought you some books that I thought you might be interested in." The chaplain dipped down, lifted two books from the market bag at his feet, and put them on the desk.

"I've read that one." The lady from The Manor tapped the cover of *Herding Dogs of America.*

"I saw it at a yard sale," the chaplain said.

"I love yard sales," said the woman, picking up the dog book.

Huff and Wills were walking together down the aisle and passed the chaplain, the books, and the lady at Salt's desk. Huff stopped beside them. "Is it just me? It is. I blame myself," he said to Wills and picked up the other book the chaplain had brought. "*What to Say*

After You've Said I'm Sorry," he read, wiping mock tears from his eyes and sniffing loudly.

"Oprah had that one on her show," said the lady. She swung one bare leg from under the Chaplain's jacket.

"Really?" said Sarge, dropping the book on the table, turning his back and striding off.

"How 'bout if I get coffee in the break room. I don't mind waiting." The chaplain picked up the bag.

Wills lingered. "Problem?" He nodded in the chaplain's direction.

"No, he's kinda, well, he thinks of me as a project—from last year—you know." She tapped the tip of the scar with her trigger finger.

He nodded. "I'm on my way to the hospital," and made the phone sign with his fingers for her to call him as he walked away.

"Your boyfriend?" the witness said as soon as he was gone.

"Let's talk about you." Salt pulled up to the keyboard and began getting the woman's information, typing her statement and asking questions for clarification as "Theresa" gave her version of the gun battle at The Manor. She'd seen what she believed to be the first gun drawn before she ducked into a doorway. In between giving details, she asked Salt about Wills and the chaplain. She seemed to be getting more and more comfortable in the Homicide office, in spite of having on only the Jesus shirt. Salt printed the statement and asked her to sign at the bottom. Theresa took her time reading and rereading the two pages. "Is my testimony good?" she asked.

"The truth is always good."

"But I mean will it help you? Also, I hope you don't mind my saying this, but I was watching your fingers typing. You should get some nail extensions. You've got long, pretty fingers." She took the pen Salt was holding out to her. "I used to do nails. I could do yours sometime if you had some acrylics."

"Thanks, Theresa. Did you work in a salon?" Salt stood up to take her to the waiting room.

"I worked in a couple of places." She dropped the chaplain's jacket over the arm of the chair and tugged the hem of her shirt.

The chaplain had been watching from the door to the break room and was back at Salt's desk when she returned. "They can't teach that, you know," he said.

"What?"

He held a child's pink sippy cup, minus its lid. "It's all that was left to drink from." He lifted the cup in a toast and took a sip. "Tell me about this coat." He pointed at Salt's trench coat, picked up his jacket, and sat down in the chair vacated by Theresa.

She took the coat off the hook and folded it.

"It's a nice coat, old-fashioned but new," he said.

"Hey, Chap, back off." She swiveled her chair around so her back was to him, but then felt hemmed in by the small cubicle space.

After an awkward minute, he said, "That's a great-looking pooch."

He pointed to the small framed photo of Wonder, the photo she used to carry in her uniform cap where other cops carried their family pics. She looked down at the coat in her lap and smoothed its folds. "It was his coat, my father's. Sorry, I didn't mean to snap."

"It's all right. I brought you the books but I also wanted you to know that my office is moving next week, not that you've ever come there, but, you know." He shrugged. "We have a history."

"Thanks, Chap. I appreciate you more than it seems. And by the way, Theresa, who was just here? She might be ready to do something better with her life. Here's her address." Salt wrote Theresa's information and handed it to him on an orange sticky note. "She's likable but she does live in the Razor Wire—The Manor."

"It's always a challenge and a pleasure, Salt." He stood, and again lifted the pink plastic cup to her and set it on her desk. One tuft of his hair was visible floating above the dividers as he made his way to the lobby.

Salt relocated the coat hook to a corner of her workspace, holding one of the sleeves, the lyrics to the old hymn came back again. "Breathe on me, breath of—" She hummed the last word, remembering back then she'd change it from "breath of God" to "breath of dog."

ANN

The café was on a corner of the intersection of Wylie and Krog, streets that ran alongside the rail yards above and that connected two historical neighborhoods, Cabbagetown, dominated by a huge former mill, and Reynoldstown, founded by freed slaves in the 1800s. "Who or what is 'Krog' anyway?" Ann asked.

They were having their first lunch, just the two of them. "I've read about these neighborhoods and driven through the underpass so many times and always wanted to explore them." Ann looked out the wide storefront window beside their booth.

"I have no idea about Krog," Salt said. "As tunnels go it's not much lengthwise, but they pack enough graffiti onto it for a small city." The window had a view of the south end of the underpass. "The railroads shaped how our city developed. I'm sure the mill site was chosen because of proximity to the rail lines."

"Do you know about the neighborhoods?" Ann asked. "Since I'm not from Atlanta and we do a fifth-grade module on Atlanta history, I've done some reading. I'm always surprised when I find out I know more than the natives, not that there are many of those." Ann's black hair was smoothed back into a tight French bun, not a hair out of place. Her skin always had a fresh shimmer.

"What's up, Ann? You took the day off from school. It must be important." Salt recognized a change when she saw it.

Ann sat back against the booth seat. "I can't take a half day from work to have lunch and go shopping?"

Their waitress, a dwarf, appeared at the table. "You want something besides water to drink?" She handed their menus up.

"What's a Krog?" Ann asked, grabbing a menu.

"Just your average, white robber-baron railroad-capitalist motherfucker," replied the girl, who hadn't an inch of visible skin that wasn't tattooed. "I'll be right back with your water."

Ann rubbed her eyebrows and propped her face between her hands. "Well, that was special."

"Pepper's new assignment still getting to you?" Salt asked.

"Okay, you got me. I guess they made you detective for a reason. It's not just the narc thing, although the competition to see who can get most in character for the street is bringing out the juvenile in all of them. They're like a bunch of ten-year-olds playing dress-up with beards and dirty shirts. The real problem for me is that he's kept the extra jobs and I'm sick of it. Sick of his working all the time and not spending time with the boys, me. I thought when he got this promotion and the little pay raise that he could drop some of the other work."

"You ready to order?" A thin guy with earlobe plugs held a pen to an order pad.

"What happened to our waitress?"

"A little dispute. She quit. You guys know what you want?"

"Bean burger," said Salt.

"I'll have the chicken. I hope we weren't the cause of her quitting. How long had she been working here?"

"Second day. Things are a bit transitional. I'll be right back with your order."

"Transitional." They shrugged at each other after he left.

"The EJ problem is as old as the job, Ann."

"It's gotten very old for me. How come you don't work them?"

"Lots of reasons. Maybe I'd feel different if I had kids." Most cops couldn't afford to live in the city's safe neighborhoods with the good schools. And most couldn't afford the private schools. So they lived in the burbs and that meant cars and commute time, gas expenses on top of a mortgage.

"All the more reason you could work the jobs. You don't have kids. I'm really most upset with Pepper because he's rarely with the boys. About the only time he spends with them these days is when they work out at your place."

"What does he say when you talk to him about it?"

"He says he's afraid if he quits the EJs now he won't be able to get them back, not the good ones."

"Can you afford to lose the money?"

"With my salary and watching our pennies we could make it. But since he's gone a lot he tries to make it up by buying the boys stuff. He bought me a new car. All of which just keeps him having to work the jobs. I'm also really scared that he's wearing himself out, and being in Narcotics he needs to be on his toes. I'm not one of those worrywart wives. I knew what I was getting into when he, make that we, decided that he'd join the PD. I'm also not fooling myself. I know how dangerous the drug world can be. He needs to be rested."

A third waiter brought their sandwiches.

"I feel bad now that you guys worked a whole day on my fence."

"No, no, Salt. That's one of the best days we've had in a long time—working together, all of us out—the boys love your place. It's a huge treat for them, a big deal. What's not for boys to like—dogs, sheep, trees to climb, running, and then there was Mr. Gooden and his tractor."

Across the street an old man wearing what looked like a monkey suit began setting up paints and a ladder in front of the sidewall to the tunnel where there was already a plethora of slogans and paintings. A large mandala in purples and greens dominated the wall.

"This place isn't bad. Actually the food is good once you get it ordered. The neighborhoods are quirky, charming." Ann was watching the monkey man.

"Actually there was another mill that burned prior to the cotton mill, a mill that refurbished the track rails and for a while also made cannons. We used to get calls where somebody would find old munitions of some sort and we'd have to get the bomb guys to recover them," Salt told her.

"I read several theories about the name 'Cabbagetown': that it was from hillbillies who came down from Appalachia and grew cabbage, the smell of cooking cabbage coming from their kitchens, and there was an overturned cabbage truck story," Ann added.

"On the other side, Reynoldstown was one of the first communities founded by freed slaves. They rebuilt the rail lines, some hired to do it and some arrested on trumped-up charges and conscripted into forced labor in the mills and on the railroads."

"We've got some history—this city—selling souls for pieces of silver," Salt said.

"Which brings me back to my husband. I also worry that Pepper's allegiance could become compromised with the EJs. It seems at times like he feels more loyalty to whoever has the jobs than to the city or the laws he's sworn to uphold. Maybe that worries me most—it can be a slippery slope, trying to serve two masters." Ann stared out to the raised tracks.

"You've hit the nail on the head as the main reason I don't work the extra jobs. I don't like feeling I owe anyone a break when it comes to the law. Everyone should be treated the same, nobody should be able to buy extra consideration from cops."

"I tell Pepper that. The EJ traffic cops give preferential treatment to drivers leaving or coming to the corporations, drivers who might otherwise vote to fund better public transportation if it was harder to get to and from their jobs. We have some energetic discussions at our house sometimes." Ann laughed, then sobered and looked out at the intersection again. The monkey man had outlined lettering across the top of the wall just below a notice in blue about an upcoming "Blues and Bluegrass" event. "Bluegrass and blues side by side, beside the railroad," said Ann.

"Back then I think they just called them both 'country.' Black and white both listened to the same radio stations. Big Mama Thornton wrote 'Hound Dog,' the Elvis tune. What EJs is Pepper working?"

"One traffic a couple of mornings a week and one after-hours at the Gold String."

"Does Sandy Madison run that one?"

"Yeah. Why? It's the one I really hate, and not just because it's a titty club. I just wonder how much Pepper has to look the other way there."

"The lines are sometimes fine. I think it can get confusing, especially if people feel they need the money. The jobs begin to stake their claim," Salt said.

"If the city paid right, cops could afford to live in the city, protect the neighborhoods they live in 24/7. If the citizens insisted that all the schools be excellent, and funded that excellence, cops would stay in town and help improve neighborhoods. Now you've got me going." Ann pushed back from the table and stood up.

"Hey, you're preaching to the choir," said Salt.

They went to the register to pay, then walked out to the parking lot. The mill towers loomed over the neighborhood, the red brick-work in strong contrast with the cloudless blue sky.

Salt hugged Ann, finishing their conversation. "You guys could come live at my place." She grinned at the fantasy.

"On the Plantation?" Ann laughed.

"Yeah, that'd be some karma, right?"

"Bye, Scarlett." Ann made a mock curtsy.

BACK TO STONE

S alt needed names, the men to whom Tall John pimped Stone, street names, other victims, descriptions, anything. She came prepared, wearing her coat for the chill inside the prison walls. Behind the pockmarked, scratched, and dirty Plexiglas partition of the entrance station, the corrections officers went about answering phones and filling out paperwork with seemingly practiced indifference to the people, including Salt, who appeared on the other side of the barrier. She put her weapon in the retractable receiving tray and pushed it through, then waited for someone to acknowledge her. An officer finally came over, asked for her ID, and tossed the chit for her weapon into the tray. A second officer said something to him, cutting his eyes at her, before coming to the intercom to tell her someone would escort her back. Their uniforms, light gray shirts over dark gray pants, blended with the walls and office furniture. On the other side of the station opposite Salt, inmates stood or sat waiting to be processed.

As always, there was a continuous cacophony of banging steel and iron, clasping, clicking and clanking, hollow hard noises from throughout the jail. Over the metallic din another clank sounded as a female officer with an upswept hairdo that looked glued into place activated the door down the hall, called Salt's name, and motioned for her. As Salt went through the door, propped open by the officer's significant hip, the woman offered no response to her greeting, no nod of the head, nothing, maintaining a look of annoyance, eyes narrowed, mouth squeezed to one side. Salt followed in the draft of the guard's rolling ass cheeks as they made their way through the prison labyrinth.

While they waited for an elevator, Salt tried again—asked if the corrections personnel had been given better working conditions since a federal overseer had been ordered by the court because of a class action suit. "No." The woman looked up at the ceiling without elaboration. The elevator arrived and they stepped in without further conversation. In the elevator the officer kept her eyes on the floor numbers scrolling above the doors. They got off on the same floor as the last time Salt had been to see Stone, but this time the officer led her to the right instead of the left. Down another long hall they stopped at a door marked "Private." "Wait here," said the officer as she went in and closed the door behind her.

The door was marked "OFFICE" but was secured with a high-tech lock and had no window. When it opened, the woman who'd brought her was gone and another officer was there with Stone, having made their entrance from an interior door opposite the one Salt now entered. Stone was again in the red jumpsuit that was issued to inmates with mental illness. The room was bare, no tables or chairs. Before Salt realized what was happening, the officer accompanying Stone had gone back out the entrance he'd come from and closed the door, the locking mechanism making a resounding *thunk* as it took hold, leaving her alone with Stone. He was without either ankle restraints or handcuffs.

Stone leaned his back against the wall and looked down at his fingernails. He curved his long fingers inward and brought them up to his face. "They screwed up." He looked up from his nails and seemed to be trying to smile while keeping his ruined mouth shut. "We ain't supposed to be alone and me with no bracelets." He held up his arms as if they were bound together, the cuffs of his prison uniform slipping back to reveal his bare wrists. "Are you scared?" he said.

"I don't think it was a mistake. I think someone hopes the worst for both of us." She considered her options and drew in a breath. There was something different in him this time. His face seemed flat, his eyes dull, more stoned than Stone.

"You the reason I'm in here to begin with." He raised himself off the wall, jangling his arms at his sides. "You don't have good sense."

"Are the meds working, Stone? You feel any different?" She tested the knob on the door behind her to the outer hall. It was, as she guessed it would be, locked. She moved over to the inner door, finding it to be locked as well. As Stone moved to the center of the room, she knocked, knowing there'd be no response. She faced Stone ten feet away. Of course he could kill her. It was like a cage. "They let you work out here? Lift weights, run?" she asked him.

He moved a few feet toward her, smacking his lips over his broken teeth, then went over to the wall opposite her and leaned against it as his eyes briefly rolled back in his head. "What difference it make to you if they give me drugs or I work out?" He slumped and seemed to lose consciousness still on his feet.

She debated trying to get the attention of some passing guard by banging on one of the doors, but at the risk of rousing Stone. His eyes opened but were hooded, his face remaining dull and expressionless.

He blinked and slowly swiveled his head as if trying to stretch out some kink. "What?" His eyes clouded again.

She went to the inner door and kicked it hard. Stone straightened against the wall. She crossed the room quickly to the other door, knocked, and called, "Officer!" She turned and faced Stone, who was now back in the middle of the room. "How are they treating you? Any problems with anyone? The guards? Other inmates?"

He looked at her as if seeing her for the first time. "Man got my back, even in here. You arrest Tall John? Man always got my back."

"Stone, I need names, more information, anything you can remember." But she realized that now, under whatever medications they were feeding him here, it was unlikely he'd ever remember much.

"Didn't nobody tell me no names." He slid down the wall to a squat, his arms at his sides, head hanging between his bent knees.

"What about people around John, people who worked for him?" Then she remembered he'd said previously that Man had been Tall John's partner back then. "Would Man know?" But Stone seemed back in his stupor.

She called out again at the inner door, "Officer?" Stone began stripping the jumpsuit from his chest and arms as he came toward her. "Think, Stone. Think. Someone wanted, someone put us together in this room so one or both of us would get hurt, hurt each other. Like killing two birds . . . well, you know. You'll never get out if you don't back off. Now."

He pushed the suit to his ankles and stood there naked, fingers flailing with energy. He sprang just as the outer door rattled and then opened. Before the officer could react, Stone wrapped his arms around Salt, and covered her lower face with his horrible mouth, broken teeth and flaccid lips. "That's for Man," he whispered, wincing at the first blow from the guard's baton.

———

SHE REPORTED the incident to Sergeant Huff, filled out the forms, made the institution's report, but held little hope of anyone finding out who'd allowed the "mix-up," as they were calling it, that had put her alone with a mentally disturbed, unshackled inmate.

She'd called Wills and he was on his way to meet her at her place. "They wanted to get Stone and me at the same time." She made the drive home in record time, not caring about speed limits or the possibility of getting stopped. She made it to the driveway, held herself together till she got the car switched off, and went up to the back door to let Wonder out. She got as far with him as the paddock fence before she leaned against the rails and began retching. Squeezing back tears, she attempted to catch her breath, but it sounded to her like she was sobbing. Wonder ran to her, then ran around her barking, as if she were a stranger. "It's all right." She reached and held out her unsteady hand. He waited in a sit in front of her until her knees began to register the rough ground and she sat back against the fence, brushing pieces of dirt from her palms. Wonder then lowered himself beside her, where he remained until Wills' headlights washed over them as he came up the gravel driveway.

MAN

————

Salt waited in the lot across from Sam's and the Blue Room. Beyond a weary water oak on the nearby rise, the downtown buildings were dark silhouettes against a dusty-rose sunset. Not much ever changed around Sam's and its strip mall neighbors, just gradual decay. The large billboard frame overhead was empty. Someone had finally torn down the beeper business sign over one of the storefronts. The amateurishly painted globe on the window of God's World Ministries looked a little dirtier. Taggers had scrawled obscenities on the posters for a gym advertising cage fights.

Salt tried to forget the stench of Stone's saliva. She had her own message for Man. People traversing the lot cut their eyes in her direction, some made a detour when they recognized the Taurus and recognized who or what she was. Others went ahead with purchases at Sam's window and left with Styrofoam boxes or canned sodas, but most didn't bother. They made their transactions with the drug boys leaning on the wall beside the take-out window. They knew murder police from narcs.

Streetlights and building security lights came on at the corner, deepening the dark outside the immediate area of the dope hole. She rolled her shoulders and adjusted the straps of the shoulder holster that crisscrossed her back. The old man again approached to see what she was up to. Before he could offer his usual greeting, Salt cut him off. "Tell Man I'm waiting for him. Won't take long, and then I'll be out of here and quit making folks nervous."

"Oh, I ain't spyin' for them. You my friend." But he stepped back away from her car window, his diseased hands drawn farther inward, like claws.

"I know—it's all right. Just get word to Man. Now."

His face stayed low as he crossed back to the business. In minutes the SUV, gleaming black, jacked high and decked out with rotating rims and running lights, rolled to a gravel-crunching stop in front of where she was parked, back end to the side of the building. Behind the wheel, looking out with a skeptical eye and a clenched jaw, was a young man with a port-wine birthmark on his neck: Lil D. It saddened Salt to see Lil D with Man. Over the years she'd been working The Homes she'd come to know most of Lil D's family, and had hoped that of all Man's gang he might be the one to find his way out of the thug life. Lil D reached with his right arm and the truck responded, audibly switching gears to park. Man waited for the dust to settle before getting out from the other side. Pedestrians stopped to appreciate Man's entrance. In the few cars that were in the lot, people's faces turned in his direction.

Man raised his head as he came around the front bumper, as if he'd been troubled but was ready to be friendly, arms wide, a smile growing on his lips but vacant from his eyes. Light from the street caught some sparkle off a fat gold watch at his wrist and rings on each hand. Lil D turned on the headlights, which gave their spot a stage-like feel. "Detective." He smiled, and a glimmer from one diamond tooth caught the light.

Salt got out of her car. "Oh, look, and here I am in jeans. I didn't realize it was a dress-up occasion." She waved at his ensemble. She'd never seen him or anyone from The Homes wearing such a suit, black with a gleaming white shirt and silver tie. His hair was tightly done in small horizontal cornrows; his light skin had a silk-like shimmer.

"Naw, I'm on my way. Wass up?" He held the smile a little longer.

Salt nodded in Lil D's direction. "You trust him with all your business?"

"Go 'head. You ain't know nothin' Lil D cain't hear."

"You are dressed for success, Man."

"Like I was telling you, I got plans. You was always telling me I could do something else. Well, I'm doin' it."

"What? You giving up the streets?"

"Might. I'm gettin' connected, club bidness, and music. I got some rappers want me to produce them." He grinned and nodded.

"Music, huh," she said. "You make anything off the old guys that played here the night the guitar player was shot? He died, you know."

"I mighta made a minute, but I ain't into that old shit. The blues ain't where the money is. Big money in rappers and video, and getting play in clubs."

"You'll have to somehow lose your past to go legit, Man. How are you going to do that? And speaking of the past—I saw Stone again."

Man shifted his posture; muscles tensed or loosened, some of both. He briefly closed his eyes, and then drew a resolving breath. "He taken care of."

"I can see how it would be no trouble for you to have one of your boys or connections watch out for him with the inmates. But what about the guards, the corrections people, the institution? You don't have that kind of pull. This city and who controls it do not bend to your wants."

"Who controls you, Miss Dee Tec Tive?"

"I've got a couple of murders and I'm looking for answers—for who killed Dan Pyne and who might have given Mike Anderson a hot dose years ago. Both of the victims bluesmen. The connection could be your associate Spangler."

"Spangler. And here I thought you might be lookin' for DeWare."

"DeWare?"

"Yeah. Ain't he the one they got word on for killin' that rich woman and her kids?"

"Do you know where DeWare is?"

"I hear the manager of Toy Dolls be runnin' snow out his crib. Top of the club. Might be where you find DeWare, too."

"Hold on. Why are you telling me this?"

Man straightened the cuffs of his shirt.

"I get it. Toy Dolls. You moving up."

"So what? It all works out for everybody, doncha know. The narcs get some blow, you get DeWare, and I get in the club business. No harm, no foul, as they say."

"What about your friend Spangler? Won't he be unhappy that his manager is in trouble? If his club comes under investigation?"

"How he gone know I told you 'bout DeWare? This between you and me, right? I got reason to trust you and you said you needed my word. 'Sides, I think you got some mojo, somebody"—he pointed at the sky—"on you side, lookin' out for you. DeWare aimin' at you that night, you know. You keep gettin' outta messes woulda got other folks killed. Like I say, you got some powerful root workin' for you. And Spangler ain't my friend. He bidness."

"What about his business? What he did to Stone back then? I still

need names. Names of other boys, girls he pimped, customers he supplied with kids. Is he still in that business?"

Man turned his head, then looked down at his beautiful white
shirtfront and dusted some imaginary particle. "Why don't you ask
that cop he got on his pay?"

"Who, Spangler? Are you talking about Madison?"

"That SWAT cop. He go back and forth between Spangler and
the biggest customer for baby bootie in the city."

"What are you saying, Man?"

"The preacher, Prince, he the one hurt Stone." Man walked to the
other side of his ride and got in. Lil D spun the wheels, leaving a wake
of dust that swept over everything.

POST–MAGIC GIRLS

With a view of the church doors, Salt sat in the Taurus, waiting in the parking lot. She counted at least four elected officials, a PD deputy chief, and one aspiring mayor, all paying homage to Reverend Midas Prince and courting his patronage as they shook his hand exiting after the Sunday morning service. Prince and his wife were in matching white suits, his wife balancing a tall, sequined crown atop her elaborately coiffed and lacquered-looking hair.

As the last of the service-goers made their way to their cars, she timed her arrival at the reverend's white Lexus. "It's a beautiful day," she said.

Without acknowledging her, he waved as one of the officials' sedans passed. "What did you think of the service, Officer?" he said, reaching for the door of the sedan.

"I'm sure it was impressive, Reverend Prince, but I only just got here. I have just one question I'd like to ask you."

He took a pair of sunglasses from his pocket and put them on.

"Ask," he said. "My wife is waiting." He opened the door and stood in the wedge between the door and the car.

"What do you know, or did you know, about a man named John Spangler?"

"No," he said too quickly. "I mean, I don't recall the name." He dropped into the leather seat.

"He's also known as 'Tall John,' white guy, controls some of the clubs around town? Officer Madison might have mentioned him. Madison works another after-hours job for Spangler." Salt moved to block him from closing the door.

"You'll have to take that up with Officer Madison, now won't you? Good day, Officer Salt." She moved away as he pulled the door closed, concealing himself behind the window glass, tinted, she was certain, to an illegal opaque.

AT CHURCH WITH PEARL

Near the gold-domed capitol and state government buildings, the church was one of three that Sherman had spared when he'd burned the rest of the city. In response to a plea from the priest of the Catholic church, instead of torching them, the general put the churches to use as billeting and storage and as slaughterhouses to feed the soldiers.

Salt was sorting the connection between Midas Prince, Madison, and Spangler when she drove past the Methodist church, as she'd been doing, on the off chance of seeing Pearl. And this time Pearl was sitting right where she'd said, on the front steps that led up to the red door, her belongings in two shopping bags on either side of her spread skirts. Salt stopped at the curb and got out. She offered Salt a seat, brushing a place beside her with a yellow towel from one of her bags. There was a cloud of cologne surrounding Pearl that at first was overwhelming, but gradually Salt grew accustomed to it. The scent was some strange blend, orange, lavender? Mixed with something dark, coffee?

"I come from where the Southern cross the Dog and my daddy

was a wolf," Pearl said, using an old-time South rhythm to introduce a story. Pearl began to rock back and forth, humming. "My Mama told us she got to Mississippi by a straight dirt road that stretched out for more than a lifetime. She said that she was almost dead, starving right on that road, a road lit all red, yellow, orange. And beyond that was a dark cloud that colored the long, open road blue. It started to rain and at her feet the first drops smelled sweet and damped the hot silt road." Pearl's hands moved like she could have been telling the story in sign language or painting it on an imaginary canvas, and she told it with a cadence that was close to singing.

Salt stared through the blur of passing traffic as she listened.

"On either side there was nothing but mown scratch hay. She said she saw her feet below the hem of her brown dress and they were the same color as the dirt. There weren't nowhere but the ditches to take cover, and the coming cloud was lightning full. She said it was so hot she fanned her skirt, bringing storm air to her thighs and privates. Seemed like a little to be happy for. She was like that. It somehow made it easier, owning only the dress on her shoulders and the horn under her arm, she said. Searching for Louis Armstrong was enough. She didn't need a case for the horn or underclothes to bind her up." Pearl's telling had a mesmerizing, rhythmic quality, like a poem she'd memorized.

"When she found the struck crow on the side of the road, its heart was still beating, so she broke open its feathered chest, scooped out the heart, still fluttering, only about the size of a quarter, and popped it right in her mouth." Pearl mimed the motion, throwing her hand toward her own mouth. "Then she lay in the ditch face upward to the pounding storm and drank lightning-flavored rain. She said the white streaks across the sky reminded her of Louie's shimmering smile, and she slept with notes of laughter in her dreams.

"When she woke up, it was a new day broke and a large black dog was sniffing her. He seemed friendly enough, his large paws were gentle on her shoulders. He panted awhile in the ditch beside her until some sound, unheard by her, called him off. 'Well, thass all right, dog. I hear a high horn myself.' She'd say it like that. Then she'd smile and pick up the horn. That's where she say I come from. She kept a handbill in the horn's bell that said Louie'd be playin' in Tupelo.

"She would tell other dreams of cows, spiders, and plants growing in 'fast time' she called it. Cows that had winter wavy fur that felt soft between her fingers. Spiders with eyes that beamed out shiny and brilliant. A Bonnie Brae tomato vine forwarded from seed to shoot to a yellow-blossomed scrub in seconds.

"But that's the one 'bout who was my daddy. She say later she learn that he was a wolf from around there. She never found Louie, just the folks in that part of Mississippi who took her in, and there I was born where them railroads come together. She would never talk about before that road or her people, nothin' but that wolf, that road where the blues come from, where the Southern cross the Dog."

Pearl tapped her on the shoulder. "Wake up. You the poleese."

"My eyes are open, Pearl. I was listening."

"You look like you in a spell," Pearl said

"I came looking for you because I—"

"You got questions 'bout Mike. Hum hum." Pearl nodded. "I was young when I was Mike frien'. But he knowed I come from the Delta, hearin' my mama an' them all my life. He try to help all us who knowed the real ol' blues. And we teached him some stuff, and it was still 'fore I got sick in my head that I helped him with some devilment of his own."

"The heroin?"

"No. He just played with that stuff, he mostly into blow. Mike's folks tried to get him what they call 'saved' by Midas Prince. That's how I met Mike, 'cause he help me after he heared me sing in church and knowed that I was out of the blues. Mike wouldn't go with the preacher, and he want Mike dead 'cause he wouldn't go with him, and Mike know some more in that church that did go with him. We was gonna get some of the others to report on Midas Prince and all report together, but then Mike was dead and I was sick."

"Wait a minute, Pearl. You know something about Reverend Midas Prince?" She put her hand on Pearl's shoulder, turning her toward her.

Pearl stopped and looked at Salt. "I see you got Legba 'round your neck."

"Legba?"

"There." She pointed to the Saint Michael pendant that had made its way to the outside of Salt's shirt.

Salt held the medallion out, shifting it in her palm for Pearl to see. "This is Saint Michael, patron saint of police and soldiers."

"He play Legba in church. See that stick in his hand. My mama, she know 'bout that ol' voodoo. She don't say how, but she know."

"Legba, the voodoo guy?"

"He go back and forth at the crossroad between the folks living and them that's dead. Good man, but he's tricky." Pearl twitched her head for emphasis. "He gots to be, communicating from one world to the other. He the spirit in voodoo church that gets called first and last. He opens and closes the door to the other world." Pearl sniffed. "And he got a dog with him. Maybe a hellhound."

"I wish he would get me a message from Mike. I wish he could tell me if Mike wanted to die, or if somebody killed him, who. If there were other boys, who they were." Salt held the medallion in the cup of her palms.

"The preacher didn't just get boys. He got girls, too." Pearl looked down at her lap.

Cars were stopped at the traffic light, close by at the end of the block. The breeze blew, then stalled. There was a sudden lack of motion around Salt and Pearl. The sun bounced off the shiny surfaces of the cars. Then the church bell above began to clang and the light at the corner changed. Salt waited through the chiming, then said quietly, after the bells stopped, "I need your help, Pearl. I don't think I can do this without you. You'd have to come off the street and let me get you a place to live, and to a doctor."

Pearl kept her eyes down. Her hands pulled at the edges of her sleeves.

"When was the last time you saw a doctor?"

"I got sick from the pills."

"When, Pearl? How long ago?"

"You ever fight a shape-shifter?" Pearl leaned back on her arms against the top step.

"I'm not sure, Pearl. I got shot last year. My head was messed-up for a while, and I wasn't sure about some things I was seeing."

"I don't have no sure thing to hold on to. I see things that one side of me knows ain't real, but the other side say is real." Pearl looked at Salt.

"With me," Salt said, "I know which is which—like the difference between dreams and being awake. But after I got shot, some barrier between awake and dreams seemed gone. And now, sometimes, the dreams make me pay attention to things I missed when I was awake or that happened in the past. It's troublesome since it's hard to explain to other people."

Pearl nodded. "That's what it's like for me a lot. I'm scared but don't know what's what or who to trust."

"God, Pearl, that's true whether or not your head is messed-up or not."

"Poleese scares me, but you don't."

"I know some police that you can trust and some other people, doctors and some social workers, that I trust who can help you."

"You trust them?"

"I do. They aren't always perfect and sometimes they make mistakes or can't make things right like they'd want to. But they're always trying to do right by folks."

Pearl looked back behind her at the red doors of the church. "This church do okay, but Reverend Prince church got some evil in it. He evil, and he everywhere. Lot of folks in this city on his side."

"Maybe we can change that."

MAKING THE TEAM

The young woman on her knees in the reception area beside Rosie's desk was pretty, with long white-blond hair curtaining the sides of her pale face. As Salt came in, the woman lifted her eyes heavenward, her hands beneath her chin in prayer. "Jesus, we know the end times are on us."

Rosie looked up at Salt from beneath her bowed head.

"Lord, we pray for these policemen that they will find the devil who killed Laura Solquist and Juliet and Megan." The woman's voice rose to a revival-tent rhythm.

"Tell Sarge Mrs. Christian is here," Rosie said to Salt in a low voice while maintaining her reverential pose.

Mrs. Christian rearranged her knees, walking on them a few inches, and continued her prayer. "God, we implore your guidance. Forgive their sins." There was a wheeled carry-on bag parked beside her.

Salt punched the entry code into the door.

THE PINK SIPPY CUP that had appeared during the interviews for the Razor Wire Manor shootings was on Sergeant Huff's desk beside the phone. As usual the rest of the desk, and the shelves and chairs, held murder files of all the years' colors. It looked as though a rainbow had exploded. But the dominant color, the color of the files on top, was bright green. Huff took a sip from the plastic cup. "As if I didn't have enough shit to deal with, now I'm getting calls from cops asking me if you're trying to make an issue about extra jobs. Sandy Madison seems to be the source of their information. And I'm getting calls from 'well-connected'"—more finger quotes—"members of Midas Prince's congregation asking me why you got to be bothering the good reverend."

Salt stood in the corner, hands clasped together, shoulders hunched, taking up as little space as possible in the small office. They were waiting for Wills, the two of them having been summoned to update Huff on the progress of the Solquist/Spangler/Pyne/Anderson cases.

"This is not rocket surgery," Huff said.

"Sir?"

"Rocket surgery. It isn't hard, doesn't have to be hard," he said.

Appearing at the door, Wills walked in, picked up a pile of folders from the edge of Huff's desk, and sat down on the corner. "Like the pink cup, Sarge. It suits you."

Huff looked at the cup in his hand as if noticing it for the first time. "Fuck. I'm changing the name of the unit. 'Homocide. The 'Homocide Unit.' Everything about this bunch is gay, pink, purple, whatever. Used to be detectives were called 'dicks.' You know why? 'Cause they were all men. All men in every sense of the word."

"What's up, Sarge? You wanted to see us." Wills winked at her.

"I was just explaining to the rookie here"—he nodded up at Salt—"that I don't like people calling me complaining about my detectives. There's ways of getting information without making a lot of noise, and now this." He pulled a copy of the city weekly from a top drawer. The headline was printed over a forties-style lurid graphic of a woman, breasts spilling, holding a bloodied man: "'Musician Shot, Dies in Beautiful Cop's Arms.'" Huff read with dramatic intonation.

"Well, for once that fish wrapper got something right. Salt is a good-looking dame." Wills leered and gave a wolf whistle.

She crossed her arms over her chest and leaned back against the glass partition. "How 'bout fuck y'all and the horse you rode in on."

Huff sighed. "Okay, enough fun. Where are you on Spangler and the Pyne case?"

Salt took a breath. "I don't get the motive yet, but DeWare, one of Wills' suspects in the Solquist murders, may also be the shooter at the Blue Room. Before you ask, the ballistics don't match, but that just tells us different guns were used. I have a Homes informant telling me DeWare is hiding out at Toy Dolls and that they regularly sell drugs to their customers. Narcotics might be able to help us find him with a search warrant on the drugs."

"Really?" Wills asked, chin drawn back, a slight grin on his lips, eyebrows raised. He sounded a little incredulous but pleased.

"Also, I need help from Special Victims," Salt added.

"Shoot," Huff said, holding his hands up. "Not really. Please continue." He lowered his hands. "What do we need Special Victims for?"

"Those calls you've been getting on Reverend Prince's behalf—seems like too much pushback for an innocent preacher. I've now heard allegations from three sources that say Midas Prince likes his sex partners very young, and I'd like to know if there have been others. Maybe kids' parents paid off?"

"What's wrong with the three you've got? Why aren't they enough?" Huff asked, dropping his arms to the desktop.

"One victim is dead—Mike Anderson. One is mentally ill, schizophrenic. I'm trying to get her into treatment. One's in prison *and* crazy—Curtis Stone."

"So let me just review for my benefit." He leaned forward, the wheels on his chair clacking. "You now want me to formally open an investigation of child molestation against one of the most powerful—shut that door, Wills—one of the most powerful men in this city and you're just now, because I asked, telling me about it? Did you know about this, Wills?"

Wills squared with Huff. "Look, Sarge. Salt is new. She's a great and going to be a greater detective, but she hasn't had time to get the politics of things. After all, you're the one who sent her out without a partner. Just sayin'." Wills shrugged his shoulders and held his hands beseechingly.

"What politics?" Salt jumped in. "Commit a crime and go to jail. Hurt a child and go to jail. What's the question?"

"Well, I could name several potential issues that could arise," said Huff, folding his arms on his desk and bending toward her. "But let's just imagine one." He pulled out a bag of potato chips and stabbed it with a knife he grabbed from somewhere under the desk. "Look around this room. Give me a brief description of the three of us. Brief. The basics."

"Sarge—" Wills tried to interject.

"Don't fucking call me Sarge."

Wills said, "What Sergeant Huff is trying to point out, Salt, is that race haunts this city at every turn. Every case, especially high-profile ones, which many murders are, has the potential to fetch ghosts, and not just of the victim under consideration." Wills put his hand out for Huff's bag of chips.

Huff pointed his finger in assent to Wills' explanation. "And poking around Midas Prince is like messin' with the King family, or Creflo Dollar or Eddie Long," Huff said, listing some of the biggest personalities in the metro Atlanta megachurch industry. "You can't get near them. Those churches are so powerful and have so many members that they significantly influence elections. And you know how that goes."

"Midas Prince could be victimizing another kid while we sit around worrying about stepping on toes." The air in the small office was being used up, and Salt was finding it hard to breathe.

"We'll get on it, Salt. I'll get on it, but it has to be quiet. By the way, your Baby Jesus, aka Charles Post." Huff tapped the top of a file. "He also came through one of Prince's programs. He was fostered out through the shelter to that old man he lived with."

"*The* Baby Jesus, Sarge." She glanced away, remembering the thud of Baby landing in the ravine. Outside Huff's office, on the other side of the glass partition, two uniform guys filed in across the room from the waiting area, two buddies from her former precinct.

Huff, mouth turned down, eyes hangdog, and hands together in exaggerated pleading, said, "I'll get with someone in Special Victims. You two work out the Narcotics deal. Keep me advised. Pretty please."

"Those uniforms"—Salt pointed across the room—"are probably here to see me. Wills, can we work out the drug angle over dinner? I'd like to say hi to these guys." Salt opened the door. "You clear for a sit-down meal?" she asked.

"Sure. Take your time." He gave the chip bag back to Huff and reached for the sippy cup. "Want a refill, Sarge?"

She'd barely cleared Huff's door when Fuzzy bellowed, "There's my girl!" He strode down the aisle and swung her off her feet. Everything about him was over the top, from his spiky blond hair to the volume of the radio on his shoulder. She'd long suspected he was hiding some hearing loss.

Blessing was his shadow opposite, dark skin, short, shaved head. He peeled Fuzzy's arms off Salt. "We miss you," Blessing said.

Fuzzy leaned down to whisper as best he could. "Is there somewhere we can talk?"

Gardner looked up from his desk.

"Private?" asked Fuzz. "I don't know how you stand working in this rabbit warren."

"Come on." She motioned them to follow and led them through the office to the back, where there was a set of double doors with a hazard sign, "NO PERSONNEL BEYOND THIS POINT," and through the doors to part of the unconverted, cavernous space of the old building. The city had needed only about twenty-five percent of the building, and the PD occupied only about half of that. Disconnected wires protruded from the walls and long rectangular tin ductwork ran the length and breadth of the high ceilings. Someone had upended a construction-sized wooden cable spool on which were overflowing ashtrays. "SMOKING STRICTLY PROHIBITED" read the sign on the wall. Broken and stained chairs were scattered around the table and beneath the levered-open windows nearby.

"Wow! All the glamour that I expected in the Homicide office and more," Blessing said, spreading his arms to take in the area.

"Homeland Security be damned. The entire Taliban could be hiding in parts of this building and we'd never know." Salt laughed. "What's up, guys? I am glad to see you. I miss you, too."

Fuzz and Blessing had been part of the crew who'd been determined to help her the year before after the shooting.

"Salt, one of our new guys, just out of the academy, is close friends with one of his classmates assigned to Zone Four." Fuzzy looked over at the door to the inner office. "He asked me if I knew you and what your deal was. He still doesn't know I'd sell my firstborn for you." Fuzz kissed her forehead.

"Nancy might not like that." Salt smiled back at him.

"My wife knows." Blessing shoved Fuzz away and put his arm around her shoulders.

"Anyway, this rookie who doesn't know nothin' but hears stuff said that some of the Zone Four guys were talking about how to burn you."

"What?"

"That's what I said. The rookie said he didn't know more but thought it was something about extra jobs."

"Shit." Salt sat down in a metal chair, its legs wobbling on the concrete floor. "Sandy Madison." She steadied her seat.

"What's that John Wayne–wannabe got to do with you?"

"He somehow got it in his head that I have it in for extra jobs. That I'm investigating his EJs."

"Look, we all know you don't like the EJ thing, but you know we have to work 'em." Blessing had a big family, four boys, and helped with finances for his extended family.

"Guys, Sandy Madison works for some bad people. I don't care about the jobs, the hours, just who he works for and what he might overlook to do the job."

"Just watch your back, girl. He runs a lot of EJs."

Salt stood and gave each of them a hug. "Thanks. I know I can count on you always. And you need anything, *anything*, let me know." They walked back through the warning doors. "Let's get the shift down to my place again soon."

"Wills cookin'?" Fuzzy boomed.

"Shhh." She held her finger to her lips and checked to see if anyone was around.

Fuzz hunched his shoulders and put his finger to his lips. "See you soon." He parodied trying to tiptoe stealthily, leaving the room.

"Quite the devoted posse."

"Oh!" Salt's hand flew to her chest. She turned to find Felton sitting at one of the nearby cubicles in an otherwise unoccupied aisle. "You startled me."

"Sorry, I didn't want you to think I was eavesdropping." Spread across the empty desk were the photos from The Manor shooting; the razor wire in the background made the location obvious.

"You piece together how that went down?" Salt asked as she looked over his shoulder.

Felton bent one hand back at the wrist and rolled his eyes up and sideways. "Oh, darling, this lovely property is now for sale and the fellows suggested that I could have a second career if I took charge of staging it for prospective buyers," he camped.

"Did they really? Don't you get tired of being the subject of all that little-boy humor? I'm afraid Huff might be pissed because I just told him and Wills to fuck themselves."

Felton laughed. "Good for you. I wouldn't worry about offending Huff. Most of the BS is just guys trying to push you, to see what you're about. It's when they don't talk about you to your face that you should worry. By the way," he flipped through the pages of the file, "this interview you did with Theresa Smith is really good. It may not be the most important, but it's clear you got the significant bits of what she was able to see."

"Thanks."

"Now, go have dinner with your guy." Felton glanced up, smiling enigmatically, and then turned his attention to the photos.

Two aisles over Salt found Wills at his desk directly across from Gardner. Both detectives were leaning back, hands behind their heads, feet propped on their desks, eyes closed.

"Should I let sleeping dogs lie?" Salt stood between the two reclining men.

Without moving so much as an eyelid, Wills responded, "Ah, but you're mistaken, Grasshopper. We're ninja warriors in meditation, connecting with the cosmic forces." He opened his eyes. Gardner started to snore. "Okay, one of us is a ninja. You ready to go?"

HAVING AGREED on Cuban, they were headed up "The River Ponce," as the street that fronted their office was known to some, highlighting the divergence of cultures between the more affluent and sedate communities on the north side of the avenue and the club scene, edgy art, drugs, and prostitution on the south side. Businesses and residences differed significantly from one side of the street to the other. New upscale condos on the north side of the street overlooked the "Murder Market" grocery and the Clermont Lounge, where aging strippers were known for crushing beer cans between their breasts; the Majestic Diner, serving breakfast at all hours of the day and night since 1929, majestic in a weirdly beautiful way—neon flickering, never completely out; and the pimps, cops, derelicts, drunks, geeks, creeps, and weirdos of all stripes on the south side.

It had started to rain, spattering the reflections of streetlights, equally glittering on a bank building, the old library, fast-food joints, the garbage bags worn by committed-to-the-street people, and gathering in holes and torn places in the asphalt. Everything shone in the iridescent rain. Salt and Wills parked on a side street and ran for the café's awning. They shook off their coats beneath the rain pattering on the stretched canvas above, the sound making the space below seem intimate, a small protective hollow. "Nights like this— crossing the River—it feels like my city." Salt looked across the six-lane street at a hilly rise to a small park where the street citizens had parked purloined grocery carts.

"You know that back in the 1800s there were actual springs here and a beech grove, where people used to come from downtown, what was considered the city back then, to commune with nature. It wasn't a river, but they'd have picnics beside the streams. That's where Ponce got its name. The springs were named for the explorer searching for the fountain of youth, if you remember your fourth-grade history." Wills opened the door for her and they entered the warm, sweet-smelling café.

A white-shirted waiter showed them to a window seat and left them with menus. "It occurred to me today that it's probably not often that a detective meets and gets to know a soon-to-be victim and ends up investigating his death. How are you doing with that?" Wills asked.

"I don't think I know yet, but I'll feel a lot better if we catch the shooter." Salt looked down at the menu. "Remember, I knew Lil D's mom, had known her and her family for years. I don't know that I'll ever feel unaffected by her death. I'm starting to wonder if there isn't something that gets to us, for better or worse, about every death investigation. You've got a red ball on your hands, a mother and her two children." Salt resisted the urge to reach across the table to Wills.

"Yeah, but I've been doing this for a while. I just put one foot in front of the other, follow the leads, document for court, and overall do the best I can. I love the work—putting the pieces together. Can't let the tragedy derail you." Cars on the avenue sprayed through the rain, flinging prisms of water. "I can't have a black dog on my shoulder while I work." Wills leaned back as the waiter came back for their orders.

The waiter had barely left when Salt leaned forward. "What did you say—about a black dog?"

"Winston Churchill. That's what he called his depression. You never heard that?"

"No, I hadn't heard that one." She shook her head. "I sometimes worry I might have inherited the black dog from my dad." Rivulets narrowed to heavy streams and slid down the window beside them. "A box of blues—connections. I hope it's a good thing. Felton said each of you brings something different." She shrugged.

Wills brought out a spiral notepad that he opened and flipped to a blank page. "One thing for sure you're bringing to the table"—he tapped the linen-covered surface—"is your connection to The Homes, Man, and the gang. It might be just what we need. What did he tell you?"

"That DeWare is at Toy Dolls and that the way in is with a drug warrant." She and Wills leaned back to make room for the paella pans brought by the waiter.

"You think he's reliable?" Wills asked as soon as they were alone again and he had cleared his first mouthful. "Umm, I was starving."

"Yes, but not legal reliable. We can't use him as an informant for the warrant—first, he wouldn't do it by the book and we'd never be able to establish his reliability. He'd never do what the law requires. But yes, he's got his own reasons for offering up DeWare. I think he wants Spangler out, wants to take control of the clubs, and believes DeWare could lead to Spangler's downfall."

"So we ask Narcotics to help us with a buyout of the club." Wills jotted on the pad. "DeWare's photo." He made another note. "He won't go down easy, I'm sure."

"According to Man, he's probably good for both the Solquist murders and Dan Pyne." The window beside her warmly reflected the lights and activity in the café.

"Why does Man suspect him for Pyne?" Wills held up a finger to order coffee.

"He as much as said that DeWare was aiming for me. At this point DeWare may be a loose cannon, like Stone. Their fuses were lit a long time ago and there's no predicting how or when they'll go off. But you know all that." She shrugged. "Why was Stone put in that room with me without handcuffs? We may be missing a piece, something that links DeWare and Stone—I don't know. But if Dan hadn't asked me to dance . . ." Salt looked past the reflections of herself and the café, out to the night and the rain.

Wills shut the notebook as their coffee came. "Come on, girl. We've got this working now. I put a bug in someone's ear in Internal Affairs, the corruption supersecret group. They'll work Sandy Madison. We'll get with the narcotics folks, maybe tonight. Sarge'll get the Special Victims' history. How was your paella?"

"Good."

NARCOTICS

———————

Salt drove while Wills called Sergeant Huff so he could set up a meeting for them with a Narcotics supervisor. She headed in the direction of the Old Fourth Ward, where the Narcotics Unit had taken offices in another closed school. An eight-foot-high controlled-access fence protected the lot where the detectives parked their personal vehicles, indistinguishable from the undercover cars, some of which had been confiscated in drug busts. Wills gave her the keypad code and the gate slid back to admit them.

The rain had stopped and clouds were parting around the kind of close-up moon Salt thought of as a howling-wolf moon, when the sky was very dark and the light from the moon bright, silhouetting the fleeing clouds. She drew her coat around her as she followed Wills along the portico that led to the side entrance.

Fluorescent tube lights lined the hall and room ceilings, giving everything a bluish glow. The entrance double doors clanked shut behind them and one of the narcs stuck his head out of a classroom midway down the hall. Smiling broadly, he said, "Welcome to the war," motioning them forward to the room. "L.T., the reinforcements have arrived," he said over his shoulder. He kept the smile up, grabbing Wills, hugging Salt. "Wills, Salt, it's good to see you. You make a good-looking crime-fighting duo."

Salt and Wills stepped back and gave each other exaggerated scrutiny, scanning each other up and down. "Too bad we're just partnered for this one case." Wills wiggled his eyebrows at her.

The "L.T.," Lieutenant Mary Shepherd, sat at the teacher's desk at the front of the room. Pepper sat in front of her on an aqua-colored hard plastic kid's chair. "Hey, girl," he said, his hands in an almost undetectable prayer bow as she came over.

"Namaste," she replied, sitting down next to him. The room's light called attention to the glassy-looking skin on his long scar. "I thought you'd be out there mixing it up with the boys in the hood," she said, remembering Ann's anxiety and hoping that he wouldn't be a part of this detail, something she'd initiated.

"L.T." Salt held up her hand in greeting. Wills and the narcotics guy who greeted them pulled up desks to close the circle.

Lieutenant Shepherd had a reputation as a tough, street-hardened veteran. She came across as wary, but was known to support and defend her colleagues, especially other women on the PD. "Tell us what you've got, guys, and how my team can help. You both probably know these two. We got our veteran." She nodded her appreciation to her detective. "And our man Pepper is, as you know, new, but has great promise—if we can keep his ass alive long enough to get him past the hand-to-hands." She referred to the street-level buys that the new detectives, their faces unknown to the drug dealers, tried to transact.

But nothing about Pepper looked rookie, from his height to the scar to the baggy street attire he was wearing. Affecting an admiring glance at his outstretched fingers, nails polished to a high shine, he said, "I clean up nice, don't you think?" She thought of their day putting the rough fence posts in the ground. He poked her in the ribs and laughed.

"God, you scared me for a minute." Salt shook her head but wasn't relieved of the anxiety that had set in when she realized Pepper might be in on this.

"Salt has come up with a location where DeWare, our suspect in the Solquist murders, might be hiding." Wills took out the notepad. "We've identified him as DeWare Lovelace, DOB 8/22/75, black male, five eleven and one hundred eighty pounds. Not only is he suspected in the Solquist case, but he might be the doer at the Blue Room last week."

"So he likes to shoot." Lieutenant Shepherd made notes of her own on a yellow legal pad.

"I'd say," Wills nodded. "And he has the usual record a mile long that includes gun arrests."

"But you don't have good probable cause to get a warrant for his hidey-hole, right?" the narcotics guy said.

"Did Man give you this?" Pepper knew The Homes almost as well as Salt did.

"He's always been reliable in my dealings with him for over ten years. He admits his own agenda. Says we can get in with a buy. I've never known him to steer me wrong. I did push him, though."

"Where does he say DeWare is?" Lieutenant Shepherd asked.

"Toy Dolls," Wills answered.

The lieutenant had been relaxed in her chair listening but now sat up, leaning in at a sharp angle. "Could be a cluster fuck to serve that place."

The city's Narcotics Unit had a recent history of botched raids and

bad warrants based on dubious information or outright lies. Undercover work lent itself to eagerness that had to be tempered by someone with a long view. The unit had been cleared of miscreants, some
of whom had completed their careers with the justice system behind
bars. Lieutenant Shepherd had been one of the house cleaners.

"Who will they sell to? Anybody? Everybody? Who's their main
market?" asked the lieutenant.

"They'd recognize Pep at Toy Dolls," Salt said, eager to protect
him, especially in light of her conversation with Ann. There was no
way she wanted him endangered because of a lead she'd initiated.

Pepper frowned at her, lifting his eyebrows in puzzlement, twisting his mouth down.

"Don't look at me. It's close to our old beats," she said.

"I don't know that we'd have to use him for the buy, but he needs
to get the warrant service, as well as the tactical experience. Will they
sell to white dudes there?" The lieutenant looked at her veteran, who
shrugged his gameness.

"Actually, L.T., you fit the perfect buyer at the Dolls," Salt said.
"Black lesbian friendly there."

"My husband, four children, and minister would all take offense
at that," she said, laughing. "'Course my girlfriend would be pleased."

There was a sudden silence in the room. Nobody moved.

"Kidding. Jeez, lighten up."

"Whew," Pepper exhaled. Wills leaned back. They stretched their
legs and waited for the lieutenant's word. "Let me give this some
thought, come up with a plan and think of who to make the buy. I'd
be game to do it myself, actually. I've been off and out of the action
long enough so I wouldn't be made," said the lieutenant.

"L.T., I didn't—"

"I know you didn't, Salt. But if I'm best, I'm best, and I can't think
of any of our folks right now that fit the profile as well, like you say.

I know there's a sense of urgency because of the Solquist murders and now the Blue Room shooting."

"I can deal with the push, L.T. No way do we want to put anyone at unnecessary risk." Wills sat up straight.

"Let me get a plan—two days, at the most next week depending. Okay?" Shepherd put her pen down and stood up, stretching her back, dismissing them.

Wills walked out with the narcotics guy talking about their Rottweilers, leaving Pepper to escort Salt down the hall. "How are the boys and Ann? I enjoyed having lunch with her." Salt stopped halfway to where Wills stood talking, scrolling and showing his phone.

"We're in a bad patch—too little time for each other. The boys take up so much energy—sports, school, extra activities—and then her job, my extra jobs, and the new assignment. It's a lot." Pepper looked away from her, cleared his throat, and adjusted his shoulders.

"It's probably a lot more fun to come here and slip into pretend world, where you can become Mr. Street Cool, no ties, no responsibilities, no one relying on you. I know I'd rather play cops and robbers than . . ."

"What? Figure out that old family crap that causes you to put yourself too close to the edge?" Pepper gave her a playful punch, but it landed on her collarbone and hurt.

She winced and they looked away from each other. They were out of sync, missing their usual cues. "Seems like we're both a little on edge," she said.

"Namaste," he said, stopping and bowing as she continued on out to join Wills.

HOPE FOR PEARL

"You look good," Salt said when Pearl got in the passenger seat. Pearl had shed some layers.

"You look good,"

"I smell better, too. Don't have to try to cover up my stink. I got a shower at the Gateway." The scent cloud that usually followed her had been reduced to a slight mist, a welcome change especially in the close confines of the Taurus. They were meeting Leeksha Johnson at the Martin Luther King Jr. Center. The HOPE Team had found a placement in a group home near there where Pearl could live and receive treatment. Pearl was jittery, turning her head looking at things they drove past, then jerking her head to catch something else, as if she might miss something important.

The morning was fresh from the night before's deluge. Pearl held Salt's hand as they walked from the parking lot past the statue of Gandhi and a civil rights mural in primary colors. Spring field trips for schoolkids had begun and there were lines of kids, some holding ropes to keep them in together, some in uniforms. One elementary class wearing khaki pants and skirts and yellow and blue uniform shirts, quiet, eyes wide open and curious, held hands while they waited to go in the King Center. Abruptly, Pearl dropped Salt's hand and darted in through the entranceway past the groups of children, their chaperones lecturing them on respect and silence.

Pearl grabbed Salt's arm, pulling her through one of the travel-back-in-time exhibits of iconic people and places of the struggle—Selma, Birmingham, Washington, D.C., Atlanta, and Memphis. The life-sized figures had been depicted mid-stride on an uphill path through which visitors were encouraged to walk—alongside Rosa Parks, John Lewis, Medgar Evers, Dr. King, and others on the road to justice.

At the south end of the room where, in the far corner, behind velvet ropes, was the antique wagon that had been pulled by two mules carrying Dr. King's coffin through the streets of Atlanta. Its green-gray weathered boards were loosely fastened with thin, vertical wood strips halfway down the sides of the wagon bed. Three-foot-high wheels were connected by heavy axles underneath. The end of the wagon was open, a spray of white roses where Dr. King's coffin had lain on the bed of the simple farm wagon. Salt could almost smell the soapy-hide sweat off the mules, hear the jangle of the harnesses and the sound of Dr. King's coffin as it slid into the wagon amid silent mourners. Pearl touched her arm. "See?"

Throughout the exhibition, overhead speakers projected Dr. King's voice, recordings of the most famous passages from his sermons and speeches. "Everything that we see is a shadow cast by that which we do not see." Pearl pointed up at the ceiling, cupping her hand to one ear below her Braves cap.

Pearl put her hands out, hovering them along the sides of the caisson. She lifted her eyes toward the ceiling and started to hum, then quietly sang,

I went to the crossroads, fell down on my knees.
I went to the crossroads, fell down on my knees.

Teachers touched their students' shoulders, the children in their lines turned toward Pearl. Other visitors stopped where they were and turned.

Standin' at the crossroad, risin' sun goin' down.

Pearl lowered her head, silence all around. Dr. King's voice came from overhead. "Discrimination is a hellhound that . . ."

"Pearl." Salt leaned down and whispered. "Pearl, our meeting, across the street."

Pearl scooped up the hem of her skirt and stood, straightening the Christmas vest she wore over a sweater and blouse.

"That was beautiful," Salt said.

"Your voice sounds funny," Pearl said, and took Salt's hand again as they walked out to the sidewalk to cross Auburn.

Pearl glanced at the eternal flame and the crypts of Martin and Coretta, surrounded by a reflecting pool, but didn't stop until they entered the museum, climbed the stairs, and turned left into one of the rooms filled with tall, lighted, glass-enclosed cabinets. Behind the glass, on shelves or attached to the sides and top, were items that had belonged to Dr. King: awards, mementos, photographs, honorary degrees. Pearl stopped at one and stood looking at it.

Inside the cabinet was a small pasteboard overnight suitcase that a placard identified as the one Dr. King carried on all his trips, the bag he had taken to Memphis. It was open and packed, as if waiting for him to close the cover—a pair of light blue pajamas with dark blue piping, a white dress shirt, an alarm clock, a shaving kit, and a Bible.

Salt quickly turned around, went out to the hall, and found the nearby restroom.

"You the police." Pearl peered up at her from under the stall door.

Salt laughed and tried to blow into the balled-up tissues in her fist. "Damn, Pearl! Come on, let me open the door. The boys won't let me stay in the club if I cry."

"I won't tell," Pearl said, waiting while Salt washed the pieces of tissue off at the sink. "The wagon and his suitcase always get me, too. But I have to see them."

"There you are." Leeksha came around the corner from the restroom door. "I thought I saw you. I'm Leeksha Johnson with the HOPE Team. You must be Pearl. Salt told me you sing."

"Sometimes," said Pearl. "Sometimes."

ON HER WAY HOME, on the last stretch of highway, the trees grew closer to the ditches and the texture of the road changed, creating a whine-and-thump rhythm as the wheels met each patched concrete section, *ka plump, ka plump, ka plump*. The beat slowed as she got near her drive. Like a scene in a child's picture book, across the front acre, light from behind the white curtain of the front room glowed and light from a high half-moon sparked off the nicks of mica in the gravel of the long drive. Salt parked in the usual place under the trees in back beside the paddock fence. As soon as she got out of the car, she heard him and looked up. Wonder's bright beady eyes glowed down on her, his tail thumping as loud as a drum as it hit on either side of the gable where he straddled the peak over the second-floor sleeping porch.

"Stay," Salt ordered, giving him the hand signal as she hurried to the porch, fumbling the key in the kitchen door lock, at the same time registering a new pile of branches beside the porch steps. Inside the door she dropped her bag, grabbed Wonder's leash from the hook beside the door, made it through the hall in yard-long strides, and took the stairs two at a time to the second floor. She had no idea how Wonder had gotten up on the roof. It wasn't his first time. He seemed to be forever discovering things about the old house—crawl spaces, hollow walls—that she'd never known about. Her only immediate access to the gable was through the attic. Little bits of gray insulation spilled down when she tugged at a cord for the pull-down door on the upstairs hall ceiling and unfolded the ladder. Salt climbed the ladder stairs into the still-warm attic, getting sweatier at every rung. She tugged the string pull for the overhead light. Balancing on the beams, she crossed the unfinished space, made her way to the latticed dormer, and carefully unlatched and pushed on the hinged shutter. Wonder looked back over his shoulder up at her and gave one of his quick barks that meant "Let's play!"

"No, sir," she admonished him. "Stay." She stepped out and put the leash over his head. With the leash wrapped around her wrist she pulled the dog by his haunches and lifted him up through the dormer to the safety of the attic and hoisted herself back inside. "How in the world do you do that?" she said to the dog as she scooped him up under his front and back legs and carried him over the beams, an awkward load but mostly because of his gangly physique rather than his weight. He knew to be compliant when she held him totally off his feet.

The open-space attic began under the eaves, angling in over most of the third level. There was only one bare, hanging bulb for the entire floor, and its dim light allowed only partial visibility of a portion of the south side of the space. Salt sat with Wonder on her lap at the top of the ladder. He was docile and easy to hold until he tried to lift his hind leg to get at a flea. It had been a while since Salt had been up there—the last time the dog had gone up to the roof. It was empty except for a few boxes pushed back to the dark corners that contained old books and family ledgers, things she'd been meaning to sort. There were also some battered trunks that she remembered as being empty and a rolling hanger rack with old formal clothes that were misshapen, faded, and drab.

Salt turned to face the ladder. With Wonder between herself and the rungs, she brought him down step by step. When they got to the bottom and she put him down, he looked back up as if to say "What next? Up?"

"No." She held up one finger to him, then lifted the ladder back to the ceiling, the door folding as the ladder retracted. Amid a scattering of insulation that lay on the floral hall rug was a small jagged piece of lead, a spent armor-piercing slug. She picked up the deadly, heavy-lead mushroom that still gave off heat from the attic, held it in the soft center of her palm, then pocketed it. She let Wonder off the leash and they went downstairs.

After changing into jeans and work boots, Salt went out to tend the sheep with the miscreant dog. After they had corralled the flock, fed and watered them, she and Wonder went to the pile of branches, black walnut, new leaves beginning to fold inward from having been cut. They had to be another gift from Mr. Gooden. She'd briefly mentioned to him that Wonder had brought a few fleas into the house, and he'd recommended the walnut branches as a natural insecticide. Wonder "helped" her by tugging at the ends of the branches as she stood them in the corners of all the downstairs rooms. She got four more for upstairs, their slightly lemony smell beginning to override the cedar that gave most of the house its characteristic scent.

The dojo was the last room to get the walnut treatment. Leaving her shoes at the entrance, she arranged some small branches in a woven-grass basket and placed it beside the altar. She lit the candle and put the spent slug she'd found between the candle and the picture of her father.

Outside, the wind picked up, limbs and branches scratching against the sides of the house. Pepper and Ann were on her mind—Pearl, Dr. King's packed bag, the caisson, Wonder on the roof, sheep chores. Salt transitioned from seiza to child's pose, touching her forehead to the mat, arms lengthened toward the altar. Maybe Wonder, who lay in the doorway behind her, was scratching himself again, or sometimes the house trembled in a strong wind. She was too tired.

"That's armor-piercing," said her father, who sat beside her wearing a black gi.

She sat up. "I know, Pops."

"I didn't have the blues, Sarah. The blues had me rather than me having The Blues. Ain't nothing but a hound dog."

"Wonder?" she asked.

"The hound, you and the hound. The hound and the hounded. You're hounding and hounded." The black gi grew fur. His voice grew growly. "Voodoo, woo oo. Woo oo. Woo oo. From The Bluesman." Her father took a knife and cut off his pointer finger, placed it on the altar as it turned to gold.

It was somewhat disconcerting to keep waking in various locations in the house, almost like she was trying on each of the rooms. But she never seemed any worse or better for having slept in places other than her bed. Actually, waking on the dojo mat felt fine, allowing her to move through various stretches and poses to begin the day.

Somewhere downstairs her mobile phone began ringing. She went down, found Wonder lazing against the bottom step, and called Wills back while she dripped a cup of coffee.

"Huff wants you to call him. Get a good night's sleep?" Wills sounded like he was moving around, walking.

"Where are you? I'm just getting going—had a strange dream." She rubbed at her forehead where it had been touching the mat and tried to pull back the pieces of the dream.

"Salt?"

"I can't remember much of it."

"Oh no. Not dreams. Please. Nooooo, noooo." He made ghost-like sounds.

"Funny, Wills, very funny. So what? I do it like I do." She sniffed the lemony air. Down the hall toward the front rooms Wonder's nails clicked on the hardwood floors along with a rattling sound. "This dog is driving me nuts," she said to Wills. "I came home last night and found him on the gable above the back porch."

"What?"

"He's done it a couple of times, and I have no idea how he gets there or why he does it." She looked out back and saw Wonder at his usual spot at the paddock fence and remembered she'd already let him out—the sounds weren't coming from him. "I've got to go, Wills. I'll call you back." She punched the off key and quietly put the phone on the kitchen counter. Still barefoot, she turned toward the hall, listening hard. Now it sounded like a marble rolling on the floor. The sun shone in a gleam down the hall from the transom above the front door. Except for a dust ball or two there was nothing in the hallway. Past the dining room and bedroom Salt went, not quite in tactical mode, but cautious. It was too strange to go all stealth due to the sound of rolling marbles. The old house was like most old places, floors sometimes uneven from one side to the other and from room to room. Salt listened, standing in the hall between the library and living room. As she shifted her weight on one of the wide floor planks, a black walnut that she presumed had loosened from a branch rolled from the living room at the bottom of the stairs across the hall into the library, stopping at the edge of the woven rug. "Ah-ha." She bent down, picked it up, then saw that the shell was polished, not newly shed of its green husk. "What in the world?" She rolled the nut in her palm.

"Ghosts on the move. I'm remembering more, Pops." The books, the case of blues tapes, the carpet, the drapes, one light, and the ledger. She turned it to the year of her father's death. Beginning in January he'd listed one or two books a week. By May he'd begun to list the books on mental illnesses, depression, along with classics and the Bible. By June it was only "THE BIBLE," in tall, hard lettering. Until recently Salt hadn't looked at the ledger in years. Now she picked up the eleven-by-seventeen gray-covered accounting book and shook it. Nothing. She put it back on the shelf, letting it fall open, and began thumbing through the decades. He'd been an omnivorous reader: contemporary fiction, history, philosophy, Georgia politics, photography books of Atlanta, anything on blues music, jazz, and gospel, psychology, and one on raising a "well-adjusted child."

The Bible, the blues. Salt palmed the walnut and turned to get ready for work.

LAURA'S SISTER

The Metro section of the *Atlanta Journal-Constitution*, the city's daily paper, was faceup on one of the break room tables. "One Month Later, No Arrests in Buckhead Murders," read the headline. Salt sat down with her empty coffee cup and picked up the paper.

> One month after Laura Solquist and her daughters, Juliet and Megan, were shot to death in the family's Buckhead home, detectives still have made no arrests in the case and haven't named any suspects or persons of interest.
>
> The victims, mother and daughters, each shot once in the head, were found March 16 by the family's housekeeper. The victims' husband and father, prominent real estate attorney Arthur Solquist, was on a fishing trip with business associates when the murders are believed to have been committed. He has been in seclusion and reportedly under a doctor's care since the incident.
>
> Laura Solquist was a native of Atlanta, her father . . .

The lengthy piece ended on an inside page with the last line *"The initial police report indicates there were no signs of forced entry."*

It was almost certain that Wills had seen the piece, but just in case he might have missed it, she folded the paper and stuffed it in the trash.

"YOU GOT something pressing right now?" Wills leaned against the cubicle support of Salt's desk, slightly slanting its partition and shelving.

"Hey, big guy, you look beat."

He looked over the room, then turned back to her, lowering his voice. "Can you stay over at my place tonight? Get Mr. Gooden to let Wonder out to do his business? I could really use some TLC."

"I'll call him right now. Something else up?"

"Gardner is leaving early and I need someone to sit in on an interview with Patricia Morehead, one of Laura's sisters."

"LAURA WASN'T the type to complain. We were raised like that—growing up with a certain amount of privilege, our parents made sure we knew it and knew what it was like for people who had to earn their way. We weren't allowed to complain." Patricia's resemblance to her sister was unsettling: fine, straight blond hair, olive skin with blue eyes . . . an attractive combination. She turned as Salt lowered her eyes. "Don't worry. I'm used to it. People get over the similarity after the first time."

They were sitting in the living room of Patricia's condo near one of the newly constructed parks along the BeltLine. The furnishings were comfortable rather than heirloom or chichi contemporary— a bright fabric sofa and matching chairs slightly shredded with picks and pulls from the two tabby cats that wandered through their legs. Family portraits and arty photos of the cats and the city lined the walls. Patricia was single and worked for a local nonprofit.

"But I'm not nearly as easygoing or uncomplaining as Laura," Patricia said, picking up one of the cats. She laughed. "This one"— she patted the cat—"his name is Cliché. You know, single girl, cat." She widened her eyes and screwed up her mouth, mocking herself. "Yeah, we were taught to give back. It's one of the reasons I work where I do. I also love the job and this city."

"Your father asked me to talk to you," Wills prompted.

"About six months ago Laura and I managed a rare girls' night out." She loosed Cliché to the back of the sofa. "Neither of us is a big drinker, but she'd had a couple of glasses of wine, and when I drove her home, before she got out of the car, she asked me if I kept up with Sherman Overmeyer. Sherman's family lived next door to us growing up and he'd gone to school with us. He went to law school at Emory and we see him at church sometimes.

"I didn't think anything of it and told her I'd e-mail Sherm's contact information." Patricia untucked an embroidered handkerchief from her sleeve. "Looking back on that night, I remembered she'd made a few comments about Arthur—his being gone so much. She was worried about some of the people he had dealings with. She might have been trying to confide in me, and I didn't pick up on how bad things were for her." Patricia looked over to the portraits on the wall, then hung her head. "Truth is, I doubted that things could really be that bad. You know, prominent husband, beautiful home, two absolutely precious daughters. I think I wasn't paying attention." She swiped at the corners of her Laura-like eyes.

"But now—Arthur's behavior toward us is just bizarre. It's like we've become his persecutors. He won't take our phone calls. It's hard to know what to think."

Wills nodded. "I'm having the same problem with him. Do you know if Laura ever talked to your friend? What's his name again?" Wills took out his notepad.

"Sherman Overmeyer." Patricia picked up a sheet of paper from the lamp table beside her. "I've written out all of his contact details—mail, phone numbers, addresses. I don't know if she talked to him or not."

"YOU'RE DEAD TIRED and still you want to cook?"

Wills stood at the stove, a glass of red wine on the counter beside him. "Cooking is therapeutic for me. Besides, we like to eat. Right?" The aroma of garlic and onions simmering filled the kitchen.

"Your case seems to be gaining complications, too much for one detective to try to follow up on each thread. You've got leads on her husband's business dealings; information from cops, informants, and people from the projects on a shooter; the family's suspicions; and now working with the feds." Salt simultaneously rubbed Pansy and Violet, who were parked on either side of her feet.

Wills stirred eggs into the pan. "Yeah, but if one person is the repository for all the information, then there's a better chance of fitting the pieces together. The picture that's coming together for me right now is that Arthur Solquist's wife found out something about his business, something either he or his associates may not have felt comfortable with her knowing, especially if she was becoming unhappy in the marriage." Wills flipped the omelet, then slid it onto a plate. "I think it's ready."

IT TAKES A TEAM

The tall, square-jawed, evenly featured officer from the department's Public Affairs Unit stood halfway out the door of Huff's office. "Sergeant Huff, I don't think you really want me to tell them that," he was saying as Salt passed on her way to the conference room. Wills had asked the feds for help in following Arthur Solquist's financial dealings, and for the entire unit's benefit they'd offered to do a day's training on money laundering and financial fraud crime.

"The press is hounding us for updates on the Solquist case . . . No, sir," the PA guy said. "We don't suck media dick."

Huff brushed past him in the doorway.

SALT WAS in her cubicle going back through the physical evidence lists in the Michael Anderson file, hoping that something from the scant documents would connect with the little she felt she had learned, when her phone rang. "It's Shepherd," said the voice. "I already talked to your sergeant and lieutenant. I took your suggestion and made the first buy myself."

Absorbed in the file, it took her a minute to switch gears. "I appreciate that. I can't think of any supervisors who'd do that. You've done your time. You didn't need to put yourself out there anymore," Salt said. "Thank you."

"Really, it went fine. Just like you said—they sold to me mostly because I looked the part. Stripper came from the back when I asked for snow and sold to me. Easy. Your Man was right on that count. I'll make one more buy before the end of the week and we'll be set for our probable cause."

"It's nice of you to call me. You didn't have to, just like you didn't have to do the buy." Salt tucked her chin to the phone.

"Yes, I did, Salt. You know, I have to admit I do have a special place in my heart for women in the PD trying to do a good job. I guess it's a combination of identifying with them and wanting them—us—to succeed. It was really hard when I first came on. But also, your dad was kind to me once when I was a rookie and really needed someone in my corner."

"My dad?" Salt sat up and leaned over the phone. "I didn't know that there was anybody left who knew him. You're the only person on the job who's ever talked to me about having worked with him."

"Could be they don't know how to bring it up, uncomfortable with suicide, you know. And I didn't really know him. But on the night I'm talking about I was driving the wagon on morning watch, hauling the drunks to jail from the clubs in Buckhead, and I sideswiped a college kid's Beamer. There were drunks coming out of the bars, cursing me, having fun at my expense. And I was scared, thought they'd fire me because I was still on probation. Then your dad pulled up. He had someone come and take over the wagon, got me to a diner around the corner away from the crowd of drunks, bought me coffee, and somehow made it all go away. I never heard from court, a supervisor, nothing. 'Course that was back when things like that could be made to go away. But my point is, he did it for me—a black chick, a rookie he didn't know from Adam. I never got the chance to thank him. I was so shook up. I've always been sorry I didn't seek him out to say that. You there?" asked Lieutenant Shepherd.

Salt nodded at the phone.

"Salt?"

"Thanks," she whispered.

"Okay. I'll see you at the planning meeting." The lieutenant hung up.

Salt was glad now that Huff had stuck her in a cubicle in the back corner, grateful when Thing One and Two glanced at her and kept on walking.

THE LEAST OF THESE

The upper and lower lots across from the shelter were half-block slabs of broken concrete where businesses had once thrived but then struggled and given up after Haven House took over the building next door and the area had become the nexus for so many desperate, homeless people. It had become a regular stop for the beat officers, a checkpoint for keeping up with the street. So Salt wasn't surprised when a patrol car pulled into the lower lot just in front of her Taurus and stopped across from the wall that divided the upper lot from the lower. The wall would have brought a kind of liveliness to the grimy spot, with its psychedelic kaleidoscope of bright-colored graffiti, except that taggers had marred the mural with amateur single-line scribblings. Pieces of the wall were coming loose, exposing the red clay and the roots of junk trees that were causing the concrete to buckle.

From the other side of the lot a white female sergeant about Salt's age got out of the patrol car and stood leaning against the car door, checking the area, glancing at Salt. Then the sergeant raised her hand in recognition of Salt's unmarked. She walked down the wall, stopping to make notes on a pocket notepad, and then came over. "Salt, right?" She stepped back so Salt could open the door. "I've seen you a few times in court, but we've not really met. I'm Laurel Fellows." She put out her hand.

"You just made sergeant. I saw your name on the list. Good for you." Salt shook her hand. "I heard some of the guys saying you deserved the promotion."

"And you, congrats as well."

"So why are two nice girls hanging around this urban art installation?" Salt swept her arm toward the wall.

Fellows grinned. "I don't know. Why are we?" The creases were still sharp along the front of her newly striped uniform slacks. She shifted and adjusted the gear belt with its new brass-studded belt keepers. The shiny finish on the sergeant's badge caught the light.

"Last year I came to the shelter looking for a guy from my beat," Salt said.

"The Homes, right? People say you worked it. Props. Not many girls get that kind of respect."

"I know you worked this zone before your promotion. They obviously think you're good since they kept you after you made sergeant."

"I worked FIT, kept my head low." Fellows was referring to the Field Investigative Team, a small, plainclothes, as-needed unit that responded to crime patterns: thefts, burglaries, car break-ins, muggings. "Can I help you with something here?" She nodded toward Haven House.

"I don't know. It keeps coming up in this old case I'm working." Salt was wary of any possible connections to Sandy Madison.

As if reading her mind, Fellows said, "Stay away from True Grit Madison then. He controls the EJs here and at the church, not to mention how many other places. He's gotten in our way so many times, especially on the drug stuff. I don't understand how he stays off Internal Affairs' radar."

Two men crossed the street from the shelter. One carried a white five-gallon bucket, the other carried long- and short-handled paint rollers.

"Whadda ya know," said Fellows as the men opened the bucket and began painting over the wall graffiti with a pea-green color. "I've never seen that before."

The two men got right to work on some large black letters, "D.V. SUCKS," quickly reducing them to "UCKS" as the slight breeze brought whiffs of the paint.

"I'd guess Haven House doesn't usually take much interest in its effect on the quality of life in the neighborhood?" Salt asked.

"They didn't want the addicts arrested when we caught them in buys. They say they just want the dealers arrested. They don't seem to understand that when police witness a transaction that both parties are culpable. We can't pick and choose who gets arrested when we witness crimes. I don't personally think the war on drugs is effective, but I've sworn to uphold the law.

"The neighborhood is swarming with addicts and dealers, but the shelter doesn't have in-patient treatment or wraparound services. We arrest dealers, but because of the huge market—the shelter has five hundred beds, well, mattresses—before the ink is dry on the arrest tickets, other dealers have moved in. It's just too lucrative, too big a demand."

A white limousine pulled alongside the curb on the street above, and the young man Salt had encountered at the church with Midas Prince got out from the passenger compartment. He glanced at Salt and Fellows and at the men painting the wall, lifted his chin, shook out his cuffs like Salt had seen Midas do, and crossed the street to the shelter entrance as the limo pulled away.

"That was the little man himself," said Fellows.

"Who?"

"That slender young guy runs Haven House now. He's Reverend Prince's right-hand man, Brother Twiggs."

"I heard Reverend Gray quit. He helped me last year. Do you know where he went?" Salt asked.

"He was a good guy, but I'm sure he must have burned out. He tried to work with us, but he was limited by lack of funds for treatment and programs, and by whoever controlled the money. I don't know where he's working now, but if anyone would know where the bodies are buried, he would." Fellows leaned her ear toward the mic on her shoulder, tapped the hood of the car, and said, "Gotta run. I hear the call of the wild." She started for her car. "Nice talking to you," she said over her shoulder as she strode to the patrol car.

Salt remembered that Jackson Thornton from the HOPE Team had told her about Gray leaving Haven House. He answered on the first ring, but all she heard was what sounded like breathing. "Hello?" Salt said.

"Hey. Salt. Sorry. Give me a second," said Thornton. More breathing and moving around. "Whew. I was coming from the tracks, up a bank. What's up?"

STAGING

A t the front of the strategic planning room, a blueprint of the Toy Dolls Club was projected onto the pull-down screen. Officers and commanders were arriving, gathering in groups mostly according to assignment: SWAT in their green fatigues, narcs, patrol units from the precincts, homicide detectives, and the white-shirt commanders. Detectives and officers filled in the seats behind their respective supervisors in the front row. One of the admin officers from the Public Affairs Unit went back and forth from the lectern to a computer console, where he changed the contrast on the screen and adjusted the feedback from the overhead speakers. An officer from tech support kept tapping the intermittently working microphone on the lectern.

Most of Salt's shift from Homicide was already there. Wills and Gardner came in and sat down beside her, and some of the day shift, Hamm and her partner, had stayed over to attend the meeting. Hamm tapped Salt's shoulder as they ambled by. In all, there were now about thirty people who'd come to coordinate the execution of the warrant on Toy Dolls. A photo of DeWare alternated with the image of the Toy Dolls' floor plan on the screen, and the flyers with his picture and description were being distributed throughout the room. His dark face loomed—no scars, marks, or tattoos, clean-shaven, but he had a hardened scowl and feral stare.

Pepper came in with one of the other narcotics guys and sat to her left, elbowing her as he settled into the chair. "Another fine mess you've gotten us into, Ollie."

"Oh, God, Pepper, this fuckin' scares me. I'd rather go in alone than have all this drama." She pushed back on the chair, widening her eyes, trying to find an even breath.

"Hey, relax, girl. We're in the big time now, not just hanging our raggedy asses out in patrol cars." He put his arm over her shoulder and punched Wills on her other side. Wills flipped his tie, Oliver Hardy–style, back at Pepper.

"Let's get going, people." The Special Operations commander called them to order. "I'm not gong to waste your time and neither are the rest of the white shirts."

The room erupted in loud applause and approving whistles.

"That means he's got a lunch date," whispered Wills.

"All right, all right." The commander held his hands up to silence the room. "Sergeant Huff will review the cases that got us here. Lieutenant Shepherd will give us the available intelligence on the location, the Toy Dolls Club, and SWAT will detail the tactical plan." The commander moved away from the podium, started to his seat, then came back. "Just one more thing from me. Any of you fuc . . . fellows with EJ ties to this club or any other property owned by the same company should know that as of recently they are under surveillance, and phone records will be subpoenaed if there is even a whiff of a tip-off. You all better pray we find drugs and our suspect."

Wills leaned his head close to her, speaking out of the side of his mouth. "I hear they sent Madison to a week's training on the coast. He thinks he's being groomed to be our poster boy for the film people. He's out there playing golf, schmoozing with honchos on the links."

"I'd be very happy if they hired him," Salt said.

The plan included details about where they'd coordinate—not far from the club at a small commercial area abandoned by its box-store anchor—and the day and time—midnight, a few hours before the club closed, in two days' time. SWAT would make first entry, securing employees and patrons, and search for the suspect. Then Narcotics would search the premises for drugs. Homicide would assist in interviewing employees and any customers that might have information relevant to their investigations. They had two days until execution.

DeWare's photo had been left on the screen. His eyes were deepset. He had a pronounced U-shaped chin and lacked fat and muscle, so his skin adhered closely to the bone. The overall effect was skulllike—probably the last image two little girls and their mother had seen the night they were murdered.

MANUEL'S

M anuel's Tavern was one of the last holdouts for smokers in the city. Long a bastion for an unusual mix of cops, liberal politicians, and newspeople, it was a couple of blocks north of the Jimmy Carter Presidential Library and Museum. But you could still smoke at the bar, and Salt guessed that might be one of the reasons Reverend Gray chose to meet her there. Manuel's was also the PD's bar, every Thursday full of cops, every other Thursday, paydays, full of cops drinking a lot.

The big rooms of the half-block establishment were covered with photos of Manuel, his family, and the staff, with heroes from sports and politics; the Braves and Jimmy Carter were prominently featured. Then there was the table over which hung a sign identifying it as "The Seventh Precinct." Alongside hung an iconic photo of former members of the old Homicide Hat Squad, guns pointing at the camera in a shooting stance, sixties-style cool. Elections at any level of government were followed on overhead TVs, as were significant sports events. Late hours found old print men, newswomen, sportscasters, and local city and state politicians, as well as the occasional congressman, arguing past their cutoff, barely able to mumble at one another.

Manuel, pronounced "Manyule" by locals, had recently died, and the third generation of his Lebanese family was continuing the tradition of banning anyone who carried public tales of what went on in the smoky tavern. The rule was firm. Careers had ended when Manuel's severed connections.

It was after noon and Salt hadn't had breakfast, was just starting what was going to be a long day—the warrant execution was scheduled to convene at eleven p.m. Gray was already there, an empty shot glass beside a smoking cigarette in the cut-glass ashtray at his wrist. When she came up to the bar, he squinted through the smoke from his cigarette. "Ah, it's the Good Detective," he said, smiling and stubbing out the butt. Like the last time she'd seen him, he wore jeans, and ashes littered the top of his T-shirt-covered beer belly like dandruff.

"You make me sound like a character in a parable." She leaned an elbow on the long bar. "I need to eat. Can we go to a booth? Bring the ashtray. I'm okay with smoking. I occasionally light up myself."

"I knew I liked you." He threw back the nonexistent dregs in the shot glass, took two steps, and fell heavily into one of the booths along the bar wall.

Salt slid in across from him. "I heard that you left Haven House. I appreciated the help you gave me with Lil D last year." She looked up as one of the managers tapped her on his way by and congratulated her on the promotion. She nodded thanks.

"You were promoted? What happened to the kid? Both his parents died, right?"

"Yeah, promoted to detective. Lil D's still in the street, but I keep hoping he'll move away from the thug life. Right now I'm working a case that keeps me coming back to Haven House. You want something to eat? My dime."

Reverend Gray said he wanted to taper off with a beer, and Salt ordered a loaded bagel.

"I'd bet you good money that there are few to no degrees of separation between Haven House and many crimes committed in our beloved city," said Gray after the waitress left. "My faith wore out." He shook out another cigarette.

"What about—" Salt nodded at Gray's shirt, on which was printed a large faded Christian cross from neck to navel and across his chest. "You know, the God thing?"

"Oh, that." Gray gave her an ironic grimace. "The Jesus, Son of God, died-for-your-sins thing? You wouldn't know it from looking at me." He brushed some ashes off the crossbeam. "I actually am ordained. Went to a good school, master's from Candler seminary. But somewhere between the thousands and thousands of stinking, lice-ridden, rotting-flesh, crazy-as-a-shithouse-rat men that came through Haven House and Reverend Midas Prince, I lost my religion."

Salt leaned back so the waitress could put down her bagel and Gray's beer. "I can imagine you might."

"Cheers," he said, lifting his glass. "You probably can imagine— the cop thing and all."

"Did you have any dealings with Sandy Madison?"

"I know Madison takes care of security at the shelter and the church, but I was never part of that aspect of the place. I got along with whoever Madison hired. We never had more than one off-duty cop, and that was only part-time."

"How much direct contact does Prince have with Haven House residents? Who organizes his participation?"

"Prince has had a series of coordinators that he claims to be mentoring. Most of them come and go, but D.V. is always at his side."

"D.V.?" Salt had seen those letters recently, seen men painting over the tag on the parking lot wall. "D.V." She remembered the roller passing over the V.

"Devarious Twiggs, slim, light skin?"

"I think I saw him at Big Calling, and then again just yesterday at the shelter," Salt said.

"*Dee*various." Gray emphasized the first syllable, draining his beer glass. "You go to church, Detective?"

"I grew up in the church. Does that count?" she answered. "Actually my grandfather was an old hellfire preacher, a hard man, my dad used to say."

"Oh, yeah. I know the type—some of those guys around here still. Then you've got the prosperity gospel types like Prince, Edith Cents, and Cameron Short. They fleece the sheep."

"There are shepherds, like you, who treat the sheep for hoof rot," she said. "What exactly were your responsibilities at the shelter?"

"My title was services coordinator. I was expected to liaison with whatever community services were available and to match the residents to services, according to their needs—addicts to treatment, veterans to VA, those with housing needs, et cetera. 'Hoof rot'?"

"It's a shepherd thing, a disease sheep get if their hooves aren't treated properly."

"Well, I had more than five hundred 'sheep' coming and going and only part-time volunteer staff that didn't know lice from rice. I couldn't even keep track of who was a resident and who was there just to flop or deal. Fights every fucking night, infestations of bedbugs and lice. Not enough showers, toilets, sanitary sleeping mats. We couldn't meet even the most basic hygiene needs. And don't get me started about mental health issues—that was the worst, watching people self-medicate with street drugs."

"Any treatment programs?" she asked.

"Very little. Midas sponsored some kind of select rehab program that D.V. coordinated. According to him, they were choosing only the very young because they were the most likely to be redeemable and the most at risk. After their initial intake I never saw them again— except maybe they'd be with D.V. and Midas occasionally." Gray took a long drag off his cigarette. "I know how that sounds now. When I first started there ten years ago, I was so invested, so burning with the conviction I could save not only souls but lives." He chuckled bitterly. "And the longer I stayed, the deeper my investment, and I was just not able to face facts about what a failure it all has been."

"That's kind of harsh, don't you think? I'm sure there were salvations."

"Little salvations." He looked into his empty beer glass.

"They add up, don't you think?" Salt asked him.

"Let us hope so." Gray lowered his head.

Salt couldn't tell if he was praying or passing out. "Rev?"

"What? Sorry." He slid out of the booth. "I'm looking for a job, by the way. If you hear of anything, you have my number." The minister trundled down the short hall to the back door of the tavern, backlit by light filtering through one of the faux stained-glass windows.

EXECUTION

On the south side of the city, a mile or so from the Toy Dolls Club, the last full moon of April shone directly over the weedy parking lot behind an abandoned big-box store. Salt leaned back against the sergeant's car trying to loosen her shoulders. More and more of the participants arrived—SWAT, Narcotics and their raid van, uniform officers from the zone, detectives, commanders— everybody geared up. She could feel superfluous with SWAT guys on the scene, all turned out in full gear; enough to intimidate the baddest of the bad, they looked like morphing sci-fi characters, able to transform themselves as needed. SWAT, Special Weapons And Tactics. From head to toe they were prepared and protected: helmets, face shields, body armor, Tasers, gas canisters, batons, guns— sidearms and long guns—and black full-body ballistic shields, knee pads, and arm guards for crawling rough terrain. And it wasn't just gear. They were in top shape, spending portions of most shifts in physical training. They were tested and trained, psychologically and tactically. So when they arrived, fifteen of them from having just completed another course with the Israelis, dismounting from their transport, it was impressive and sobering, if one needed more sobering, which Salt did not. She was feeling the pressure, being new, having been the one to initiate all this, putting officers at risk, including Pepper and Wills. She began the ubiquitous female cop's career-long dance with her bladder—to pee or not to pee, hydrate or not.

"Namaste." Salt turned around to find Pepper, wearing a black face mask, bowing to her. He was in all black: jeans, T-shirt, protective vest, and jacket with "Narcotics" in large reflective letters on both sides of his chest and in larger letters on his back.

"Doing the full ninja, huh? You look like a character in the movies. Actually this whole thing feels surreal," she said. "Oh, God. I think I'm going to be sick," she said, bending from her waist.

"Stick with me, kid," said Pepper, Bogart accent behind the lip holes.

"You know—" she began to say.

The SWAT lieutenant circled his finger above his head and everyone started for the vehicles. Huff and the Things trotted toward the car.

"We're moving." Pepper interrupted, nodding at his team already loading up. He ran toward them.

Pepper was already out of earshot, jumping in with his team. "You know . . . You know more than you think," she said as the door to the van shut. "Namaste, Pepper. Namaste."

The back door of the SWAT transport had barely shut when, led by the commanders in marked cars, they sped out of the lot, the caravan of vehicles tight behind, leaving no room for citizen traffic. She'd no more than sat down in the front passenger seat, door not yet closed, when Huff put the pedal down and tore out behind Wills and Gardner's Taurus.

The inside of Huff's unmarked smelled like stale French fries with a vanilla deodorizer overlay. The Things in the backseat were quiet. Huff was quiet. And then they were there—twenty police vehicles, blue lights splashing against the pinks and purples of the neon sign on the metal derrick above, "Dolls, Dolls, Dolls" flashing over a reclining female silhouette. The glowing full moon shone from between the steel frames. SWAT—rifles and shotguns at port arms, boots thudding, ran along the sides of the building, secured the entrance, and surrounded the flat, big, one-story club. Salt, Huff, and the Things covered the front beside the entrance. Vibrations from the music inside pulsed the concrete bricks at Salt's back. The Narcotics team swarmed the dozen or so cars in the black-surface parking lot, doing tactical quick peeks before clearing each car. Salt lost sight of Wills when his car followed some of the others to the rear of the club.

SWAT was in. There were two or three brief screams followed by sharp commands and muffled yells, and then the team leader came over the dedicated radio frequency to give the signal that the people in the main areas had been detained and that Narcotics could enter to assist and search. The black-clad detectives streamed in, silent, fluid, guns held snug to their legs. Salt couldn't tell Pepper from the others. As they went through the double doors, the pounding music bubbled out. It seemed like it took only seconds to secure patrons and employees and the all clear was given, and then Salt and Huff's team entered.

She rounded the flat-black wall in the alcove that separated the entrance area from the main room and holstered her weapon. One of the SWAT guys yelled, "Somebody find the damn light switch." No one had yet located the house lights, and the stage was bathed in a pink-and-gold swirling disco glow. Multicolored pin lights bounced off the black-tiled drop ceiling. Patrons occupied four or five of the tables: one gray-looking white man sat by himself among the mostly black clientele, two dark-skinned women with shaved heads were at another table, while three older black men sat at a four-top table; there were several younger guys sitting together wearing fake-diamond pendants and shiny athletic jerseys. A dancer in high heels and a G-string sat on the edge of the three-foot-high stage casually swinging her legs to the heavy-on-the-bass music that blared from speakers overhead. She was cuffed in front with plastic flex cuffs, but someone had been chivalrous and thrown a windbreaker over her bare shoulders and pendulous breasts, which were taking a rest on her soft belly, only partially covered by the jacket.

Bumping and scraping, accompanied by barked words, orders, or radio checkpoint queries, came from farther within the club. Two heavyset female employees in Dolls-logoed T-shirts, also in plastic restraints, sat on the floor of the hallway that led toward the back of the club. Strategically positioned SWAT guys stood ready while Lieutenant Shepherd directed her team to begin the search for drugs. "Somebody find the lights," she said. "They can probably use your help backstage." She pointed Salt to the far right of the room. "In the dressing room." Huff nodded, acknowledging Salt's departure while he and the Things sat down at one of the tables and began to interview the occupants of the room, all of whom had their phones facedown on the tables in front of them.

"Can I talk to you?" the gray man asked as Salt passed. "I need to go home—my wife."

"Give us a few," she said, knowing it would be past his bedtime before he made it home. His phone was already lit and vibrating.

Another of the SWAT team officers, a tall woman, stood at the entrance to the backstage area, face shield in the up position. "Salt." She smiled, a giddy gleam in her eye, teeth sparkling in the disco light.

"Girlfriend," she said, walking past and through the beaded curtain and beginning to feel some relief at the initially safe entry.

Two racks of sequined and feathered garments crowded a narrow passage through to a classic noir dressing room—incandescent bulb-lined mirror stations, more costume racks, and a shower-curtained changing room in the rear. There was even a lit cigarette, its plume of smoke drifting up from a glass ashtray on the dressing table beside a very dark-skinned girl with a large yellow butterfly painted around her eyes. She wore only a pair of iridescent wings. "Whatever you find ain't mine," she said, wings fluttering as she gestured to the masked narcotics detective standing over her.

"What might we find, madam?" asked the detective. He grinned and winked at Salt.

"Who you calling 'madam,' Black-face?" Her wings beat faster.

Two more narcotics men, neither of them Pepper, had begun the dressing room search, beginning at the curtained-off area.

Turning to go back to the main room, the answer obvious, Salt asked anyway out of courtesy, "You need me?"

"Thanks, but she ain't concealing," said the detective with Madam Butterfly.

Back in the main room music was still pumping from the ceiling corners. Another SWAT guy occupied a staircase leading up to a low-windowed room overlooking the club, where Lieutenant Shepherd could be seen moving back and forth while one of her team stood on the balcony in front of the window fiddling with an electronics console. Wills and Huff were assisting the two female barkeeps to their feet, bringing them into separate corners to be questioned. Another narcotics detective yelled down from the balcony, "Sarge, ask them where switches for the lights are. We can't get them to come on at the control panel." Huff leaned toward his detainee, then yelled back. "Mop closet"—music cut off abruptly, the room suddenly silent—"second door on the left," Huff yelled, now unnecessarily loud. A glass shelf behind the bar came unhinged and its contents, glasses and bottles, came shattering to the chrome coolers underneath. The nearby detective winced and shrugged.

"I'll get the lights." Salt went to find the light box, breathing better now that the danger had passed. Realizing her shoulders had been hunched, she lowered them and rolled her head, loosening her neck muscles. The door she was looking for was marked "EMPLOYEES ONLY" in black plastic letters. The mop closet and all the other rooms—main room, dressing room, restrooms, and office—had been cleared as SWAT made their way through. But Salt, out of habit, stood to the side of the door as she opened it and did the quick peek, feeling a little self-conscious. A single fluorescent tube lit the closet in which there was a bucket, a mop, cleaning supplies on metal shelving, and the electrical panel. She opened the panel and flipped the lever marked for the house lights. Salt stuck her head out and confirmed the main areas were now lit. The closet stank of sour mop. Dust and pieces of insulation fell from the exposed crawl space above, where there was no finished ceiling, only ductwork, pipes, and wiring. The music blasted back on briefly. More debris drifted from above.

Units were reporting in on the radio. "Clear." "Team One, Clear." "Clear Narcotics, Team Two." "Product, Team Three." Salt listened to the units, allowing herself a second of relief—Team Three was reporting success in locating the stash. She hoped it was indeed a stash, not just a joint in an ashtray.

She looked up at the falling particles, upended the bucket, and stood on top of it in order to grab the top of the attached shelves and pull her head through the ceiling opening. As her eyes adjusted to the unlit space, DeWare's skull-like face came into focus. From a prone position near the edge his eyes glared out of the dark, inches from her face. She let go and dropped back to the closet floor as he came down on top of her, bringing with him part of the metal shelving, one of the brackets slashing her arm and shoulder. DeWare slammed her to the floor and tore the gun from beneath her injured arm. He stomped her shoulder, head, and hand, making an *umphf* sound each time he slammed the heel of his boot into her. She lay there unmoving, waiting for her chance, but he stuck his head out the door, her gun in his hand as he slipped from the closet. She pushed up and staggered out on his heels. Salt instantly, instinctively knew it was Pepper, still wearing his face mask, coming out of the stairwell at the other end of the hall. DeWare with her gun was headed straight at him. She stumbled, grabbing for DeWare, realizing Pepper wouldn't risk a shot if she was in the line of fire. Just as she caught his leg, DeWare fired at Pepper, who ducked into the stairwell. "Hold your positions. Hold your positions," ordered a commander from somewhere below.

DeWare turned, put the gun to her head. "Get the fuck up or I will blow your fucking brains out right here and now." He dragged her past Pepper and the cops stacked behind him in the stairwell, then out the back door to the parking lot. He backed her toward an SUV, her shoulder going numb, blood soaking down the sleeve of her ripped jacket.

"I am going to shoot each one of your feet, your hands, and then your legs if you do not get in the ride and drive exactly how I tell you." DeWare shoved the gun into her right breast, opened the driver's door, and motioned her behind the wheel. As he got in the backseat, he fired twice in Pepper's direction, at the back door of the club. DeWare put the gun beside her cheek and cocked the hammer. "The Homes," he said as she put the vehicle in gear. "And give me your walkie-talkie."

"My hand is fucked-up," she told him, trying to get to the radio on her left side. She drove out to the deserted thoroughfare that fronted the club. At least two of the fingers of her left hand wouldn't work and pain shot up her arm, but she got the radio off her belt. DeWare grabbed it and threw it from the window.

"Move it." They passed a few lone, hollow-eyed pedestrians. "Put the speed on or you will die."

North on Metropolitan, Salt began to feel woozy and dissociated, while her body seemed to buzz. She drove mindlessly, knowing the streets to The Homes; in her sleep she could get there. She tried to interpret the sounds of DeWare's movements in the seat behind her. He smelled of the metallic scent of stale sweat tinged with crack cocaine, rendered by new sweat and adrenaline.

The citizens who traveled these streets by day had good reasons to quit them by this hour. DeWare's dark face, his body in dark shirt and pants, twisting and turning in the backseat, created a shifting black void that blocked her view in the rearview mirror. The street in the rearview appeared deserted, though she felt certain that Pepper and others must be following. They passed a new-looking Taurus, headlights off, parked at a dark, closed gas station pump. A mile later DeWare told her to turn left onto a one-lane street. He reached over her shoulder and turned the headlights off. "Keep driving."

She strained after the sound of a vehicle passing on the road, but once again saw no lights. The white pavement of the deserted street, made fully visible by the moonlight, was ragged with long, jagged cracks.

"Stop," he said. "Stop here."

They were at the bend of a little street, a street that led to nowhere and she knew it. It had been intended as an access to the adjacent low-lying property that developers had failed to develop. High weeds bordered the broken pavement. About a hundred yards away a single streetlight, farther past the bend, was the only sign that the street was still intended for use.

DeWare grabbed her by the throat with his left hand, his fingers closing on the gold chain around her neck, slippery with blood. "Saint Michael," she said.

He jerked the chain and medallion from her neck. "Just the souvenir for Preacher Prince," he said. "He loves him some gold."

"Prince," repeated Salt.

Entering under and emerging from the lone distant circle of light was a beater, a ghetto junker, Oldsmobile or Buick sedan circa 1970s. It slowly rolled toward them, one of its headlights flickering and the other pointed sideways. Unreasonably, Salt thought that on a slow night in a patrol car she'd have stopped it and, if all else was well, given the driver a warning to get the headlights fixed. She was beyond reality. "You were trying to shoot me but instead you shot the bluesman." She could ask DeWare anything now. He was going to kill her and wanted to brag first—to show her he had power.

"You think this little gold man saved you? That man got shot 'cause he turn his back. His bad. And now I get another chance at you. Seem like Preacher right about God want me to be the one kill you. He and my boss say I'm born to be the hand of God, born to be a killer."

"Your boss—Spangler?"

"Yeah . . ." DeWare's voice trailed off as the Buick came alongside them and stopped. He moved to the back passenger side. "Yo, Shawty." The SUV was higher than the beater, so from where she sat neither the car nor its occupants on the other side were visible, although its exhaust, thick and pungent, plumed in the moonlight.

"Man like to know what's happnin' his streets. Know I'm sayin'? Who drivin'?" asked Lil D, whose voice she immediately recognized.

Salt lost awareness of the pains from her injuries. She felt a sense of time condensing. Lil D's and DeWare's voices—inflections, pitches and tones, small words, a hiss, grunts and guttural noises—were amplified by the silence of her other muted sensations.

"Aw, Shawty. This bitch mine. Man don't have no reason . . ." DeWare stopped talking as the beater's door opened and closed.

Lil D appeared in front of the SUV, his long white T-shirt light blue in the full moon, the birthmark on his neck barely visible, and came around to Salt's window. "This that bitch cop and she fucked-up," Lil D said through the open window to DeWare, still on the passenger side in the backseat. Salt tried to open one eye. "You done fucked up bringin' this shit here," he said.

"It ain't like that." The overhead light came on as DeWare opened the back door and got out from the other side of the SUV, his dark shape following Lil D's path around the front of the vehicle.

Salt held up her left index finger and thumb, signaling Lil D that DeWare was armed. Time slowed. Face framed by the SUV's interior light, Lil D closed his eyes and drew a breath. Salt heard his intake of air. He swiveled his neck once as he lowered his hand. DeWare rounded the front bumper and there was a flash from Lil D's waist and three blasts. DeWare folded to the pavement. Salt's ears rang as Lil D went to where DeWare lay. "My name D, motherfucker." His words came to her muffled beneath the roaring in her ears. Then he came back to her. She could not hold her head up but was trying to keep her eyes open, resting her right cheek against the steering wheel. Lil D opened the door of the SUV. "You just witness a murder now, didn't you?"

"No," said Salt. "Defense." She was barely able to stay conscious, just vaguely aware of the arrival of another sound, the distant motorized flapping of a helicopter.

Lil D opened the door. "Get out."

"My shoulder . . ."

"Get out. I'm tryin' my best here to make us even." He pulled her out.

Salt fell onto the weedy stubble beside the street.

"I'm going to give you two presents," said D, "one from me to you." He dropped the gun he'd used to shoot DeWare beside Salt and took another from his camo jacket. "Number one. You found that gun in the car. Didn't you?"

Salt nodded to the lie.

"Number two present is DeWare auntee. She the one hear DeWare making the deal 'bout killin' that white woman and her girls, the deal with Tall John. Tall John the one put DeWare on them."

The whirly sound of the copter was getting closer, missing them by only a couple of miles, its searchlight bouncing off a few low clouds over the city.

Salt fell back on her rear, knees bent.

"And don't keep fuckin' shit up. Man ain't gone like none a' this," said Lil D, going back to the Buick. He laid rubber speeding off, the beater's exhaust fouling the air Salt gulped as she crawled to DeWare while watching the red taillights disappear down an abandoned construction access in the weedy field.

The grass stubble was prickly and sharp, the clouds above tinged with orange. She took her gun from DeWare's hand and put her fingers to his wrist. He opened his eyes as a sound escaped his chest.

"DeWare." Salt tried to rouse him.

". . . shoot . . ." he rasped.

"DeWare, you live or die, you want to be the only one to pay for killing those girls and their mother? Who asked you to kill them?"

DeWare's head fell to one side, eyelids half-closed, but as the last breath left his body he rasped, "Tall John, that white man, Spangler," his dying declaration, courtroom and testimonial gold.

A LIGHT flashed across her eyes.

". . . shot last year," Wills was saying.

All she could see through the one eye barely open was lights, strobing blues, ambulance floods, and some flashes. She knew the air was warm but she felt cold to the bone and tried to get up from the hard surface beneath her. Lights blacklit someone who covered her first with a sheet, then several blankets, tucking them all around her. Her throbbing left arm was taped to a hard plastic splint.

"Shoulder, arm, fingers, ribs, eye, head—but other than that she's runway ready." A paramedic held her head steady while another secured a stabilizing collar around her neck. "We put the oxygen tube on her mainly so you assholes will leave her alone, let her come to without you asking her a bunch of questions she probably won't be able to answer right now anyway."

Huff, Pepper, and Wills came into focus as they raised the gurney and rolled it toward the ambulance. "You two go to the Gradys. The Things, Gardner, and I will work the scene here," said her sergeant. They shielded their eyes against the debris of the helicopter as it lifted off. Techs were expanding the pole legs on portable lights. Blue lights flashed outside the back window of the ambulance after the doors closed. When the ambulance reached the end of the street and took the turn to go north, more blues reflected off the ceiling of the ambulance. On the short trip to the hospital blue lights flashed continuously through the back window.

THE GRADYS

Sitting up on the exam table in one of the ER rooms, Salt drew a breath between clenched teeth. "Ow!"

"Almost finished," said the nurse, running her fingers along Salt's lower chest. "The ribs will heal on their own, but if you begin to have more severe breathing problems, come back in. We can't have you getting pneumonia."

"Can you make her suffer a little more?" asked Pepper from the other side of the curtain circling the ER table.

"Some friends you've got," said the nurse.

"You have no idea what she just put us through," said Wills, also from outside the curtain.

"Do we have the entire force out there?" asked the nurse.

"Seems like I'm here at the hospital all the time just for her." The familiar voice belonging to the chief came from the direction of the ER room door.

"Sir," somebody said, accompanied by the sounds of feet shuffling.

"How is she?"

The nurse pulled the ties closed on the hospital gown. "I'm finishing up. She doesn't look so hot, but . . . ta-da!" She slid back the curtain.

The chief stood front and center in the room crowded with Pepper, Wills, Huff, supervisors, guys from her old shift and detectives. Nobody said anything. They stood there, mouths open.

"She looks way worse than she is," said the nurse. "Her vitals are good. She's got fourteen stitches over her eye and more in her arm, as you can see, but the swelling will go down soon."

Salt tilted her head so she could see. "Fanks, Chief. Fank you for coming." Her lips had swollen and wouldn't pull together properly.

"Maybe one of you could, like, say something instead of standing there staring at her," said the nurse, edging her way between them to the door.

The chief moved forward, as did Wills and Pepper. "Damn," said the chief. "I'd shake your hand or something, but I don't see anywhere on you that looks like it wouldn't hurt."

She lifted her right hand but winced at the resulting report from her ribs.

The nurse turned from the door. "Careful, though. No hugging. A couple of ribs are badly bruised. But other than that, she can go home if there's somebody there to monitor her."

"Have you got family at home? If not we'll assign somebody," said the chief.

"We'll make sure she's taken care of, Chief," said Huff, lifting his lip silently, snarling at her behind the chief's back.

"Once again, Salt—" The chief brought his hand to his brow and snapped to attention, causing the others to automatically attempt some sort of formal posture, feet together, straightened backs. He turned and left and they all slumped.

"DeWare," said Salt. "Nex' of kin?"

"The medical examiner is taking care of that," said Wills.

"No," she said. "Wills, do it. DeWare auntee."

"If there's something else that would help with the scene or the investigation, at this point I'd appreciate any direction you suggest." Huff looked at Pepper and Wills and shrugged. "I have to ask."

Salt closed her eye and saw Lil D back at the street, his face leaning toward her.

"Salt?" said Huff.

"Hey, Sarge." Pepper moved around so he stood at her back facing the sergeant.

"Who's taking her home?" asked Huff, taking a step back.

"I've already got her gear in my car," Wills said.

"You know the drill, Salt. You just went through this last year: chaplain, statement to Internal Affairs and one of our guys, mandatory three-day administrative leave." Huff looked tired, heavy on his feet as he came close. "I wish we'd been able to get to you sooner." He nodded to Wills and left the room.

"Wills, I'll stay while you go get your car. I'd like a minute with her alone," said Pepper.

"Be right back," said Wills. "I'll tell Gardner to keep everyone else out." He patted Pepper's back, then tucked a lock of Salt's hair behind her ear. "Be right back."

As the door closed Pepper came around and sat down beside her on the gurney. "Ann is coming to help you out tomorrow. She'll bring food and God knows what else. Somehow she's got it in her head that this is her fault; that it's because of something she said that you risked your life to save me back there in the club." He leaned his head to look into her one open eye. "She's wearing out my phone." He held up his phone, lit and vibrating.

"Answer, Pep. Don' let her worry. Here, I'll talk." She took the phone and answered. "'Lo."

"Salt?!" Ann was crying.

"I all righ', Ann. Ann?"

Ann drew an audible breath and sniffed. "I hope you like chili."

"Love chiree—with 'eans?"

"What's wrong with your voice? Oh, God."

"They let e go hoe so not ad. Cuh see, to-orrow."

She handed the phone back to Pepper, who put it to his ear. "I'm on my way. We'll talk. Love." He put the phone in his pocket. "It's like old times, on our beats." Her bare legs dangled off the side of the table. Pepper swung his legs back and forth beside hers.

"Ol' ties? A fonf?" She laughed. "We only 'een detectives a fonf. Ouch." They both laughed, then winced at the same time.

"Ow, stop. Seriously, I hurt just looking at you. I know we've been here before and I know it's what we do." He put his arms around her gently and spoke into her good shoulder. "For my boys and Ann." He lifted his head and stood up, wiping his cheeks. "Now I'm going home."

Wills was at the door when Pepper opened it. Pepper hugged him. "Ann'll be down tomorrow with food." Wills put his arm around Pepper's shoulder before they parted, then held the door for the nurse with a wheelchair.

WHAT IS REMEMBERED

The end of spring had always been signified for Salt when the wisteria lost its blooms. "Memory can be tricky. We unconsciously select what we recall," Wills said, picking petals from Salt's hair that had blown from the vine on the fence. "A couple of weeks ago you asked me if the cases ever, what? Change me?"

"Something like that. Yeah. You said not, if I remember right." She and Wills were sitting in the glider under the trees in the backyard. She held her face to the warmth of the sun as it shone between the sun-speckled leaves. Wonder, stretched out in the grass in the full sun, was dreaming, his eyelids flickering. It was the last day of Salt's mandated leave. Combined with her off days, she'd been away from the job for five days since the incident with DeWare. A warrant had been obtained for Spangler and he'd been arrested without incident at his home.

"Do you remember the family murdered in Adairsville?" Wills

bent down, pulled up some blades of grass, and wove them back and forth between his fingers.

"Five years ago? It was a whole family if I remember right," Salt answered.

"Seven victims. Women and children. My case."

"Oh, God, Wills."

"One of the guys said to me afterward, 'What's so different about seven bodies in one place? Same number of bodies as seven different cases, right?' The house was tiny. I was processing the scene, the bodies, for over eight hours, and there were things—blood dripping from the ceiling and other stuff that I never could explain. One toddler, alone in a corner of a bare room, was shot in the head and bleeding into an adult-sized sneaker. The girl's all-pink bedroom, pink ribbons on the tips of her braids. But I can't remember even one of their names or the perp's." Wills looked off as if the names might be written in the bright day.

"And are you changed because of Adairsville?" she asked.

Wonder lifted his head briefly when one of the sheep gave a baa.

Wills leaned back into the glider to better face her. "Yes. But it's not so simple as to say I was changed. Because how we are changed depends on who we are. Some people who come back from wars go on to lead heroic lives and some fall into the abyss. Most live somewhere in between."

Wonder finally got up and went over to the paddock to reassure himself that the sheep were all still grouped and safe.

Wills sat up. "There's no reason for me to document in the file or to mention to anyone how I knew to contact DeWare's auntie as his next of kin. And asking her about her knowledge of DeWare's involvement in the Solquist murders would have been standard procedure. Salt, you—we—are going to be okay. We will be changed in some ways, but there are some things that remain constant."

"Do you think she'll hold up in court?"

"I'd say yes, but we need Spangler to give up Solquist, admit Solquist initiated the murder contract on his wife. I interview Spangler tomorrow."

"Will you ask him about other crimes, Midas Prince, Curtis Stone, Mike Anderson, others?"

"We need to see how it plays. He may give up something, but it'll probably have to wait for sentencing. What time are you scheduled to make your statement on DeWare?"

"Hamm and Huff are doing it at ten a.m."

"I'm bringing Spangler from jail at noon."

ON MAY 10, 2015, *at approximately midnight, I was part of a team that served a search warrant on the Toy Dolls Club. We also had information that a subject of interest in several murders, DeWare Lovelace, might be hiding at the club.*

SWAT made entry and secured the occupants, employees, and customers. I had entered after SWAT with other detectives and we were beginning to question employees and patrons as SWAT and narcotics detectives continued to search and secure other areas in the back and basement of the building. I went to a hall closet to find the house lights for the main room, and when I was in the closet, some insulation fell from the ceiling, so I climbed up to check and came face-to-face with DeWare Lovelace, who then came down on me. As he came through the ceiling, a part of the metal shelving supports cut my arm, and he knocked me to the floor as he dropped down. There was no chance for me to get to my weapon before he stomped and kicked me and took my gun.

As he left the closet I tried to grab him to keep him from firing on officers that were in the hall. Then he put the gun to my head and forced me outside and into the SUV. I couldn't see out of my left eye. It was bleeding and swelling and two fingers on my left hand were broken. Also my ribs, shoulder, and collarbone were messed-up. I was shot last year, and when DeWare kicked me in the head—I don't know if there was damage, injury to the same area, but I got blurry. My vision was screwed up and I was hyperaware of some things and not aware of others.

He told me to drive to The Homes and then had me stop on a side street, Amal Place. He put the gun to my head and choked me. He snatched the Saint Michael from my neck.

I was in and out of consciousness. We were out of the car and he was shot. I had gotten a gun that wasn't mine from somewhere. I crawled to him, got my gun, and saw that his wound was to his chest and that he was dying. His breathing was ragged. I asked him who was involved in the Solquist murders. He said, "Tall John," then he quit breathing.

She hadn't told any lies and had kept Lil D out of it. They believed she'd found the gun in DeWare's SUV. Her reputation preceding her, they believed she'd been the one to shoot and kill DeWare. And she let them.

MAYBE THE BOUQUET was a little over the top, a bit more funeral-like than get-well, but Salt appreciated Rosie's welcome-back gift. And since she was restricted to desk and office duties, she would enjoy the blooms.

The bruises around her eyes had faded to yellow. The stitches over her eye and in her arm were coming out the next day. Her left hand was in a brace, the fingers splinted and taped. Her ribs were still slightly tender when she tried to draw a deep breath. Already there were moments of the incident with DeWare about which she had become uncertain, didn't know what she remembered or didn't want to remember. The statement she gave for the record that morning was followed by the usual Q and A conducted by Detective Hamm.

Hamm: *What was your level of consciousness when DeWare forced you to drive away from the club?*

Alt: I was, the best way to describe it, fuzzy, disconnected.

Q: *Do you remember driving to the street, Amal Place?*

A: Some of it.

Q: *Were you aware of where you stopped?*

A: My attention was on DeWare. He held the gun to my neck.

Q: *You were in fear for your life?*

It was the central question to every use-of-force incident—the one that established the legal use of deadly force.

A: Completely.

Q: *What happened when you stopped the SUV?*

A: He grabbed my throat to choke me and he ripped the Saint Michael from my neck.

Q: *And he still had the gun at your head?*

A: Yes, with his right hand. He pulled the hammer back and grabbed my neck with his left hand.

Q: *What happened then?*

A: My awareness became erratic. I'm uncertain of exactly what happened.

Q: *Do you remember finding a gun in the car?*

A: No.

Q: *Do you remember shooting DeWare?*

A: No. I was on the ground outside the driver's door and then I was beside him, and he made the dying declaration.

"Thou shalt not bear false witness" was the ninth commandment, and one she hadn't broken with this statement. Her parents had taught her not to lie, and how not to tell.

WILLS SLAPPED a fistful of papers on his desk, fell into the chair, and grabbed the computer keyboard. "This is happening," he said, staring at the monitor. "The feds found a paper trail."

Salt stood beside Gardner at his desk. Together they watched the Wills whirlwind.

"Arthur Solquist was helping Spangler launder his money. Laura Solquist's lawyer friend said she'd found a list of storage units that Arthur had rented—different locations in different parts of the city."

"And the lawyer failed to bring this to us why?" Gardner rolled his chair around to face Wills.

"Laura'd asked him not to mention her concerns to anyone. Apparently she was still hoping to get her husband to quit his nefarious dealings. And since the press had reported Arthur having an alibi and us as having no suspects, Overmeyer, the lawyer, had kept Laura's confidence, even though it'd been informal.

"Oh, and by the way, Salt." He turned to her and Gardner. "Looks like Spangler was also donating tons of cash to Big Calling Church. Prince might have been washing away more than people's sins."

WILLS CONDUCTS
THE INTERVIEW

Wills led Spangler through the outer door of the office holding his elbow, lifting it when he wanted him to go forward and pressing it down for him to stop. Spangler's wrists were cuffed behind his back, his ankles shackled. He was dressed in a tan prison jumpsuit that he wore with aplomb, collar turned up just so. His light hair was buzz-cut, sharp and close. As he entered he looked around the office as if assessing a hotel suite for its suitability. His small, black eyes briefly acknowledged Salt, seated in a corner chair of the waiting area, then passed over Rosie as if she were part of the furniture.

After Wills had escorted Spangler through the inner door, Rosie looked at Salt. "That is one creepy fellow. He looked like he was thinking of buying the building."

"That's exactly what I was thinking," Salt said. "I'm going to go watch Wills change that. Word is he does great interrogations."

After giving them time to get Spangler settled, she went on back, passing Huff, Wills, Gardner, and the district attorney as they stood in the hall outside the interview room. She entered the observation room adjacent to the room where Spangler now sat facing the two-way mirror. His arms were extended on the small office table in front of him, relaxed, legs stretched beneath the table. He bent his elbows and waggled his fingers at the mirror. Huff, the DA, and Gardner joined her in the small room.

Spangler remained in his unconcerned posture, chin jutting, literally looking down his nose at Wills as he came in the room. Wills plopped a fat file on top of the table. "Your lawyer is on the way. He called to say he'll be here shortly and not to question you before he gets here. I wouldn't do that anyway."

Spangler nodded at Wills, then at the mirror. "Bit of a cliché this room, don't you think?"

"Oh, you mean the mirror?" Wills said. "Well, yeah. Some folks don't notice or think about it at all. You'd be surprised. It's not like we try to hide it. But just so you know and all our cards are on the table, on the other side of that mirror today are some of my colleagues, my boss, and the district attorney. Oh, and there are speakers in there. This room is wired." Wills pointed up at the ceiling. "And now that you ask, I'll tell you—not asking questions, mind you, just telling you, Mr. John Spangler—that today—" Wills leaned halfway across the table. "Today and today only, we, my colleagues and I, will be offering you a onetime, once-in-a-lifetime deal."

Spangler turned and lifted his head toward the blank wall.

"I see you're not interested, Mr. Spangler. And perhaps your lawyer will advise you otherwise, but between just us—" Wills smiled and swept his arm toward the mirror. "Between us, today we're going to give you this one opportunity to avoid having to deal with that pesky death penalty thing. Your lawyer may or may not concur."

"I'll wait to speak to you when he gets here," Spangler said.

"Don't blame you one bit. That's the smartest way to go," said Wills. "But here's our offer, and don't worry, I'll repeat this for your esteemed attorney. I'm sure he'll be here soon, and I'll repeat the offer, but here's the deal." Wills removed a series of photos from the file and laid them out in rows covering the desktop. "Here's what we have." Wills walked behind Spangler, looking over and reaching across his shoulder, spreading the display of photos with his fingers. He cleared his throat and continued. "Now, I'm a hardened homicide detective, Mr. Spangler, but you being a psychopath and all are able to detect and mimic emotions even if you don't experience them. So you know that these photos of these little dead girls and their mother cause me to anguish and want justice for them. These photos make me want you dead." His voice had changed. It came through the speakers of the observation room tight and straining, pinching his words. The men standing in the room with Salt looked down from the window and away from each other. Wills slapped the wall behind him, loud enough to rattle the window.

"I want my lawyer," said Spangler, sitting up.

"And have him you will," said Wills. "But I'm going to continue just a bit, not questioning, mind you. Have I asked you even one question, Mr. Spangler? No, I haven't. That was rhetorical, by the way.

"So to continue with this once-in-a-lifetime deal, we also have what's called the 'dying declaration.' Dying declaration. Isn't that a powerful phrase, 'dying declaration'? The alliteration is wonderful, don't you think? I love saying it in court—'dying declaration,' 'dying declaration.'" Wills bowed to an imaginary jury. "Anyway, we have the dying declaration of one Mr. DeWare Lovelace, and he says in his dying declaration that you were responsible for these little girls' deaths." Once again Wills waved his hand toward the photos. "He said that you were responsible for their deaths by arranging for him to kill these children and their mother. We believe that you arranged their deaths at the behest of Arthur Solquist, their father and husband. And in that behest may lie your once-in-a-lifetime, one-day-only chance to avoid the sure-as-shit Georgia death penalty." Wills aggressively swept the photos into a pile and closed them into the murder book. "Those two beautiful little girls were supposed to be at their grandmother's that night.

"Still haven't asked you a question, have I? That was again rhetorical," said Wills, taking a paper towel from his pocket and blowing his nose. "But, Mr. Spangler, that's not all. You know these narcotics charges that we're holding you on from the club? They won't stick, even though it was your club and your dope. But the war on drugs is a joke and we know it. So we'll not even talk about that, but you should know that we have another individual that will bear witness to your involvement in arranging the deaths of the Solquist children. But more important, we're going to interview Arthur Solquist next, and he may get the deal we're offering you today. He may say he only confided his concerns about his wife's knowledge of the shady dealings between you and him, and that you, without his knowledge, initiated the contract with DeWare Lovelace. That you felt your business was threatened by Mrs. Solquist, and therefore *you* should be the one the jury should seek the death penalty for. Someone, after all, should pay. He'll say he never meant for you to, well, do what you did." Wills picked up the file, tucked it under his arm, and turned to go out of the room. At the door he paused and looked back at Spangler. "Oh, and there's all those now-empty storage units and the paper trail of your dirty money leading us right to Counselor Solquist."

Spangler didn't move as the door closed. He leaned back very slightly in the chair, his arms once again resting on the table, chin raised, staring in the direction of the two-way mirror. Then his eyes narrowed as if he were trying to focus on some distant point.

THE LAWYER wasn't pleased that Wills had spoken to John Spangler before he got there but readily made the deal. Spangler was going to prison for life and Arthur Solquist would go to trial to try to avoid the death penalty. In the presence of his lawyer, John Spangler signed a full and detailed confession.

WILLS AND SISTER

Every surface, even the exposed crossbeams, held glowing candles that blurred the in-progress construction of Wills' dining-kitchen area. Three white candles in Mason jars sat in the middle of the table, and beside each were sprigs of white jasmine. The Rotties were in the backyard with new marrowbones. They were celebrating Wills' closure of the Solquist case and Salt's healed injuries; bruises gone, stitches out, her hand and arm freed from the brace.

"I've never seen you in a dress," said Wills.

"I was in the thrift store on Moreland getting some things for Pearl, and I found it." She looked down, smoothing the bodice of the cream-and-white cotton-lace shift, the small unravelings hardly noticeable.

"Well I've got just the accessory." He got up and left the room. Salt took a sip of the white wine that had accompanied one of Wills' best-ever meals, Vegan Divan. They'd had dark chocolate squares for dessert with the last of the bottle of white wine. She licked her thumb and finger.

Wills came back and stood behind her, once again lowering the

Saint Michael and chain around her neck. "I hope this continues to have power and that it gives you positive memories rather than ones of DeWare."

She turned to him, holding the medallion to her chest. "I thought it had to be kept in evidence. And you've gotten it repaired and cleaned." She lifted the gold Saint Michael and threaded the chain through her fingers.

Wills knelt down beside her. "The photos will be good enough evidence—and your testimony. I cleaned and fixed it. You look so beautiful."

"WHERE DID you get those blue eyes?" her father asked like always.

"From you, Daddy," she answered like always.

They were standing in a large church walking up the center aisle. "Are you giving me away?" she asked.

"Never," said her father. "Never."

SALT WOKE with a start. Down the street somewhere a dog barked, too far away to be Pansy or Violet on the back porch in their dog beds. Wills was asleep beside her, his hand on the pillow next to her face, on his fingers a slight fragrance of chocolate.

The dog in the distance barked in threes, *Aruff, aruff . . . aruff!* Then he'd be silent for half a minute. *Aruff, aruff . . . aruff!*

"BLACK FOLKS used to say that white people smell like wet dogs," said Sister Connelly.

"I've heard that before," said Salt. Pepper had told her that one night in their rookie days. "I have been dreaming about a dog."

She and the old woman stood looking out at the downpour from under the portico at the front of Sister's small church. Salt always noted Wednesday nights, because when this had been her beat she'd try to come by to sit in the patrol car and listen to the weekly choir practice. Knowing that Sister always walked, Salt had come and for the first time gone inside and sat listening to the old hymns and gospel music, her uniform no longer a distraction.

"Legba always has a dog with him. Someone trying to get a message to you from the unseen world?" The old woman's smile was sideways.

Salt thought about it. "Maybe," she said. "Maybe."

"Some a' that ol' voodoo true. You carrying Legba around your neck—oh, I know high church say that's Saint Michael. But it's all the same big thing. We get messages from another place, call it the dream world, call it your unconscious."

Salt opened the umbrella, took Sister's hand, and wrapped it through her own arm for support going down the steps. In the car Sister shook rain off a collapsible plastic rain bonnet. "I don't mind the rain, 'specially these spring showers."

They both sat watching the distant lightning and clouds moving. The windows of the old stone church were still lit from within, each window depicting one of Jesus' disciples. "Your choir was in top form tonight," said Salt.

"We were, weren't we? You got a favorite?"

"That was a rockin' 'Roll Back Old Jordan,'" Salt said. "I love the old stuff."

"So does everybody if they admit it. We got these old songs in our head from way back. It's like in movies—they play in the background of our lives, white and black. We got the same music going on in our heads."

"The big new churches don't seem to do much of the old music, do they?" Salt asked.

"That's a symptom. The problem is that people try to forget the past. Now don't get me wrong, I'm all for progress and creating new music, art, computers, all that. But you can't do it without honoring the ones who've gone before and how hard it was, the good and the bad. It's what brought you to here." Sister patted the seat between her and Salt. "Like in the Bible they saw fit, thought it was important to include all those 'begats.' Cain and Abel begat their sons and Noah and Moses begat theirs. It's important to know your begats. Slaves and convicts begat the roads and the tracks that begat the railroads, and the railroads begat the buildings and banks, and they begat this city."

"And the work begat the music," Salt added, humming as she turned on the ignition. They worked out a little harmony for "Roll Back Old Jordan" on the short drive to Sister's place.

"You still smell like a wet dog." Sister grinned and got out of the car, leaving Salt laughing, and went through the gate and up the walk of her lush yard.

CALLED TO CHURCH

The Homicide office was all but deserted. Rosie had left for the day. During these last hours before the end of the shift, knowing people would be out, most of the evening-watch detectives were taking advantage of the first summer-like night of the season to work the streets. So all around Salt the cubicles and gray-carpeted aisles were empty. One of the harsh fluorescent tube lights in the recessed ceiling flickered behind its plastic panel. Huff's presence in his office across the room, the only one of the wall offices lit, the rest all dark windows and closed doors along the wall, somehow made the unit seem even more desolate. The silence of the space distracted Salt—silence punctuated by the occasional muted rumble from the elevator on the other side of the offices or the pings and pops of pipes expanding and contracting behind the walls of the old building. Salt was used to the funky rhythms of the street, a backbeat to her days and nights, not these lonely Homicide sounds.

She stared at the notes she'd just added to the e-form on the monitor. *Call to Melissa Primrose, 8:47 p.m. this date—In response to my query, Primrose recalled that there were two children at Michael Anderson's house the night before his death. She said that both the children were African-American boys, approximately eleven or twelve years old, one dark and one light-complexioned. She hadn't seen how the boys arrived, if they were with anyone. She just recalled them being there for a brief period of time and hadn't even seen them interact with anyone.* Salt felt sure she knew who those boys were. She printed the notes and added them to the file. She checked her e-mail, browsed the Internet, straightened the already neat desktop, and finally sat still for a minute, then looked down the aisle. She got up and headed to Huff's lit office.

He was behind his desk and just reaching for his Handie-Talkie when she got to the door. "Sarge, sorry, Huff, I just got off the phone with—"

He held up his hand to indicate he was monitoring the radio and simultaneously turning up the volume knob.

"Raise any negotiator," dispatch called.

"4144, go ahead," they heard Felton respond.

"4144, we have a hostage situation, man with a knife at 2199 East Avenue, Southwest."

"4144, copies," acknowledged Felton.

"I didn't know Felton was a negotiator," Salt said to Sarge.

"He just completed his certification right before you came to the—"

"Wait, Sarge, that address, it's Big Calling."

"I'll drive," he said, grabbing his fedora from a wall hook.

Salt ran to her cubicle, picked up the Handie-Talkie, and grabbed her coat, shrugging it on as she followed Huff into the stairwell and out to the parking deck. "Warm for the coat, doncha think?" he said.

"Maybe." She shut the car door.

Waiting for a break in traffic before turning out of the driveway, Huff cleared his throat, then cleared it again. "I'm not into all this touchy-feely stuff."

She waited, then asked, "You mean the negotiator training, de-escalation?"

"Nonverbal communication, yeah, yeah." He turned onto North Avenue. "Don't make me say it—come on."

"What?"

"You, the coat—I know it was your dad's. I know. And the thing with Stone—I shouldn't have been such an asshole. My wife says it's good for me to say it."

"Please don't. Don't and we'll say you did."

"I'm sorry." He made a bereft-like sob, then grinned at her, his teeth brightened by the passing lights.

LANDSCAPE LIGHTING on the grounds glared off the edifice of Big Calling Church, making a deep, sharp darkness of the surrounding areas. Other than the two patrol vehicles and Felton's Taurus parked beside the side door of the church, there was only a lone dull sedan parked beneath one of the pole lights in the vast asphalt lot. Sergeant Huff parked near the patrol cars, next to the same door that Salt had previously used when she'd been to the church the first time. A uniform officer stood at the door, and as they approached he held his hand out. "Sergeant Fellows said to let her know when anybody—chiefs, commanders—got here, and she'll come out." The tall, young black officer had a military bearing, but there were streams of sweat running down the sides of his cheeks. The night was warm but not that warm. He stuck his head in the door, silently raised two fingers, and nodded into the sanctuary.

Fellows, the new sergeant Salt had talked to across from the shelter, came outside. She was pale and serious. "This is what we got. Your negotiator, Felton, is in there now talking to the subject. The first officer here"—she nodded at the officer in the doorway, who swiped sweat from his face with one finger while he both listened to his sergeant and monitored the inside of the church—"was dispatched to a silent alarm call at this address.

"When he got here, he found this door unlocked and partially open, so he called for backup and entered because he heard voices, specifically a kid crying." She looked over at the officer, who nodded his confirmation of her account. "I arrived just minutes after he notified radio, and when I went in, he was trying to talk to the man who had the kid at knifepoint. Salt, it's Twiggs, the guy I pointed out to you at the shelter, Devarious Twiggs. When Twiggs first saw my officer, he jumped up like he'd been shot from the pew where they were sitting, and both he and the boy had their pants unzipped. Then Twiggs pulled the knife." Sergeant Fellows released a long breath. "SWAT has an ETA of fifteen."

"How's Felton doing?" Salt asked. "He establish rapport?"

"Twiggs is crying and shaking. I'm worried." Fellows looked toward the dark interior of the sanctuary.

Sergeant Huff took out his notepad. "What's the guy's name again?"

"Sarge, I'm going in—give Felton some backup. I've had the de-escalation training."

Huff nodded his head and continued to get the details from Fellows.

Inside, the cathedral-like space was dark except for the red exit signs, some spotlights on the dais, and wavy aqua reflections that floated around the walls. Behind the pulpit and between the choir lofts on either side, a waist-high crimson curtain had been retracted along a brass rail, revealing the full-immersion, glass-sided baptismal tank. The water in the tank was lit so that congregants could view the preacher submerging the newly saved. Salt moved quietly along one wall, positioning herself close enough so she could hear without being a distraction.

"I was just comforting him—just comforting him," Twiggs repeated over and over, crying and wiping his face on the inner sleeve of the arm that held the knife to the boy's throat, then using his other fist to swipe the top of his upper lip. The boy in the crook of Twiggs' arm was wide-eyed and trembling. "Be still, Thomas," D.V. said to him. "I don't want this knife to cut you."

Felton, standing twenty feet in front of Twiggs and the boy, in the center aisle, picked up the cue. "We know you don't want to hurt him. Put the knife down. Let's work this out."

Salt thought Twiggs might have glanced at her. He took a breath, then dropped the arm he'd had around the child. The boy ran to Felton as Twiggs put the point of the knife into his own neck. Salt stepped up as Felton led the boy out. "I know about Midas, D.V. I think you've been hurt."

Blood dribbled from his neck where the knifepoint had punctured the skin near his jugular. The knife was large, with a curved point. "No one will believe that I was keeping Thomas away from Midas." He raised his eyes to the ceiling, a supplicant expression on his face. The wavy light gave the place a submerged feel.

"Isn't it time to let someone help . . . to let someone help you?" Salt stepped into the aisle.

"No, you don't understand." Twiggs closed his eyes briefly, then popped them open. "I want to be Midas' right hand. I always wanted him, to be what he wants. Now he wants to get rid of me. I'm not stupid. Midas has chosen Thomas now."

"Thomas? The boy with you tonight?" Salt slid the coat off her shoulders and down her arms, taking several more steps toward D.V.

"Don't come any closer," he said.

"What about your faith, D.V.? Isn't the Bible all about salvation and how it's never too late to acknowledge our sins, the past, and how we got from there to here? I just talked to Melissa Primrose tonight, you remember, Mike Anderson's girlfriend. She remembered you and DeWare from the night before Mike died. You were just a kid, not much older than Thomas."

D.V. sighed and shrugged, some of his energy draining.

"Put down the knife, D.V.," she said.

He lowered his arm so that the point of the knife still punctured the skin but was no longer pulling at his vein. "I was twelve when Midas took me into his program. 'Program.' More like a family for us. Most of us didn't have any kind of family. My mother was a full-time junkie."

Salt folded the coat over her right forearm.

The sound of heavy vehicles arriving came from the parking lot. Blue lights bounced off the side door mingling with the aqua waves. Twiggs' eyes darted to the door, where a helmeted SWAT sergeant peered around the doorframe from the outside. "Oh, my God," he said. "Tell them to go away." He lifted his elbow again, straightening the angle of the knife.

"D.V.," Salt said, "you can control this, how it goes. You do have some say. Those officers cannot leave. By law and the police department rules they have to stay until we resolve this. But you, by what you decide, right here and right now, can determine what happens. You can put down the knife and let me walk you out. I'll stay by your side."

"I'm going to jail?"

"I think that what happened tonight will be evaluated by the court in terms of your lack of a criminal record and your history. You've never been charged with any crime. You've been victimized and, for now, yes, you'll have to go to jail until a judge makes a preliminary determination."

"I can't go to jail."

"D.V." She stepped to an arm's reach of him. "You can. My sergeant can call the corrections supervisor to make sure you'll be in a safe section, the medical ward of the jail."

There were footsteps, a lot of heavy bodies moving, some clanking of gear against the marble walls behind and to the side of where Salt and D.V. stood. From the corner of her eyes Salt saw shapes along the sides of the sanctuary. D.V.'s eyes widened. Salt stepped to him and without hurry or haste laid her coat over his arm, hand, and the knife, which she pressed downward and away from his neck. She took the knife from his fingers. "Walk with me."

SERGEANT HUFF had made the call to the jail, and Devarious Twiggs was admitted to the medical unit on suicide watch. Felton stayed with Thomas until Child Protective Services arrived—he had the experience not to interview or let anyone else interview the boy, leaving that to the medical specialists and the forensic interviewers. Felton did have his suspicions, however. He said that without prompting, the boy kept saying, over and over, that Reverend Prince loves him.

MITIGATING CIRCUMSTANCES

I am Detective Sarah Alt of the Atlanta Police Department Homicide Unit. With me is Sergeant Charles Huff. We are conducting this interview at Georgia Regional Hospital's prison unit. Please state your name for the record."

A: Curtis Dwayne Stone

Q: *Are you on any medications that would affect your memory or ability to reason?*

A: I take medicine for my nerves but it don't make no difference in how or what I remember. They just help me be calm.

Q: *You previously gave a statement to the FBI regarding crimes that you knew about, including the death of Michael Anderson, who you refer to as the bluesman. Is that correct?*

A: Yeah.

Q: *We now have reason to believe that a young man, a juvenile at the time, delivered uncut heroin to Michael Anderson. Do you have knowledge of that transaction?*

A: Tall John use kids in his business all the time back then. He use me to take heroin to people lots of times. And, yeah, that night the preacher had two kids with him, one dark-skinned and one real bright-skinned. Tall John give the bright-skinned one the hot H to take to the bluesman.

Q: *The preacher? Are you referring to Midas Prince?*

A: Yeah.

Q: *Do you know the names of the two boys?*

A: I know one—DeWare, he always 'round The Homes. I don't know the bright kid real name. His mama was a junkie lived in The Homes—they call him 'D.V.'"

Q: *How long was it between the time John gave the kid the heroin and Michael Anderson's death?*

A: I heard he was dead the next day.

Q: *How did you find out? How do you remember the day?*

A: That kid D.V. was a sissy, but just as raggedy as the rest of us. So I remember it was the next day he had on some brand-new Air Jordans. He say the preacher give him them shoes for doin' God's work.

Q: *Why didn't you tell the FBI about those boys the first time they interviewed you?*

A: Them was just kids back then.

HUFF HAD called in some favors—having Stone transferred from the jail in the city out to the state-run hospital located in the nearby county.

"I've got friends in the state prison system. Some of them good ol' boys owe me favors," he said. "Saved their asses couple of times finding escapees."

He'd also made sure that Stone would be transferred, as soon as he was stabilized, directly to the state prison hospital down in the most southern part of the state.

"YOU'RE CLOSE, KID." Huff stood beside her desk holding some old blue report forms, their edges dried and flaking. "Special Victims was holding these until they finished their search. I called and asked the sarge for what they had so far." He laid one of the reports on her desk. She leaned over to look at it. "This one"—he tapped the report—"was made fifteen or more years ago, reporting that Midas Prince had fondled a kid. The report was classified as 'unfounded' when the victim and his mother disappeared—grandmother said they moved to another state. Detective never could find them."

Salt slid the report into the light under the desk's overhead.

"But this is the one." Huff held two blue forms that were stapled together, their corners frayed to dusty bits. "Three days before the death of your bluesman he, Michael Anderson, was named as a witness to the initial outcry of a sexual assault on Devarious Twiggs. The kid's mother brought him in to the SVU. The report was also classified as 'unfounded' when the kid later recanted.

"Because of you we got SVU to dig these out." Huff slapped her on the back creating enough force to send her rolling chair, with her in it, into the desk edge. The partition wall shook. "Sorry." He grabbed her shoulders and pulled her back. "I think you're close to clearing this old cold case."

THERE WASN'T much difference between the medical unit and the other units in the jail—same riveted-down tables, bolted-to-the-floor metal stools, lidless, seatless toilets. But the tiny cells were single-bed, the inmates under close supervision, and they all wore tie-back hospital gowns.

At the request of the commander of the detective division, the supervising physician had signed permission for Salt to interview Devarious Twiggs. The law allowed her to question him about crimes for which he was not charged.

Salt was shown to a wide-windowed room that had no door and was open to the center of the two-tiered ward. Corrections and medical personnel came and went from the central station immediately next to the room. Twiggs shuffled in, not because he was shackled, he wasn't, but because he was wearing loose-fitting disposable slippers. "PROPERTY OF DOC" was stenciled on the sides and back of the gown, laundered to a pale beige. His eyes were already brimming, his nose running. He sat down on the metal stool opposite Salt at the table and extended his arms, lowered his face to them, and sobbed. "I can't do this. Please get me out of here."

"Devarious, you're probably safer right now than you've ever been in your entire life."

Twiggs raised his head, blinking. "What do you mean? Look at where I am."

Salt reached down into the briefcase she'd been allowed to carry into the ward, handed him some tissues, and put a digital recorder on the table between them. "Has anyone assaulted or hurt you here?"

"No." He wiped his eyes and nose.

"Have you had medical care? Have you been asked about your stress? Had regular meals? I know it's not the best food, but . . ."

"Yes."

"D.V., nobody wants to be in jail. And I'm not pretending it's easy. I know it's scary and that you're terrified. But you're not in general population and you're not going to be. No one wants to see you hurt."

"What about Thomas?" He sighed and raised his eyes upward.

"The district attorney is still evaluating the boy's forensic interview, so I can't say. But I believe that your lawyer will be able to provide the judge with enough testimony regarding mitigating circumstances so that you'll never be put in a jeopardizing situation."

He lowered his head to his chest then back up. "Is that recorder on?" he asked.

"No. I'd need your permission. I'm not here to ask you anything about the charges against you. I'm here to ask you about Michael Anderson." Salt was wearing her coat but still felt the cellblock chill. She rubbed her arms for warmth. "You must be cold," she said to D.V.

"I asked for a sweater or something and they said they would give me one, but I haven't gotten it yet."

She got up and went out to the nurses station, asked for a blanket and waited until they gave her one. D.V. settled it around his shoulders. "Thank you."

"Like I told you the other night, Melissa Primrose remembered seeing you and DeWare at the party the night before Michael Anderson died."

"She didn't know me."

"Not your name, but she saw two kids that fit the descriptions of you and DeWare."

D.V. sniffed and tucked his chin.

"I also found the report you and Michael made three days before his death."

"No. No. No. I told them I lied. I took it back." He rapidly shook his head side to side.

"It's not unusual for kids to recant. It's usually because somebody pressured them. I don't know who it was that made you recant. Your mother? Midas? But it's more common than you might believe. Kids have so little power."

Salt leaned across the table. "Midas' control of you, your dependency on him, all are mitigating circumstances for everything that followed. And you were too young. You won't be charged with murder. We also have Curtis Stone on record saying he saw you that night being given the heroin."

Devarious Twiggs shrugged and, as if a switch had been flipped, picked up the recorder. Salt put her palm up, gesturing for him to hand it back, but he pulled it farther from her reach. "I know what I'm doing." He looked closely at the front of the recorder, depressed the red-rimmed record button, and laid the recorder back down on the table between him and Salt.

"That night Midas drove us to Spangler's, one of the houses Spangler used to cut heroin. Oh, I do know about heroin, my mama was a junkie back then. He was furious with Michael for taking me to make the report. He kept saying Mike was a junkie and that it would be God's will if he died from an overdose—that it would set an example. I knew somehow that the stuff in the packet was hot and that Michael didn't have the habit. But I wanted Midas' forgiveness for talking to the police and to be the one he chose to carry out God's will, to take the packet to Mike Anderson. He's held me with that secret ever since, telling me I'd go to prison because I chose, I volunteered to take Michael the heroin."

Salt established her identity on the recording, as well as the time and place and Devarious' identity. "Do you stand by your previously recorded statement?"

"I do," he said.

PEACE

As Salt expected they would be, the Andersons were dressed in their Sunday church clothes, Mrs. Anderson in a cream brocade suit and Mr. Anderson in an immaculate navy pinstripe with razor-sharp creases. They were arm in arm as they came up the sidewalk from behind the new sanctuary of Ebenezer Baptist Church, the church Dr. King had led.

Salt met them halfway. "Mr. Anderson, Mrs. Anderson, thank you for coming." This time she didn't presume to offer her hand. "It's a beautiful day. Could we sit for a bit?" She indicated a nearby bench, to which Mr. Anderson led his wife. He then he continued to stand.

"Has your investigation progressed? Do you have any further knowledge of the circumstances of our son's death?" he asked.

"I do, Mr. Anderson. The nature of that information is why I wanted to meet with you today, here," she said.

The space where they'd stopped was a small green vale, below and alongside Auburn Avenue and directly across from the old historic

Ebenezer sanctuary, its flat, unpretentious redbrick façade towering over the street.

"I wanted you to hear this from me before it hits the media," she said.

"The media?" Both Andersons expressed their alarm with furrowed brows and stiffened backs.

"Tomorrow the Atlanta Police Department and the FBI will be serving search warrants on both Big Calling Church and the homes of Midas Prince."

Mr. Anderson sat down beside his wife as if buckled by what Salt was saying. "What?" he exclaimed.

"Our investigation has led us to a number of individuals who have independently provided information that Midas Prince has been engaging in crimes involving underage sexual activity as well as diverting church money to support and cover up his illegal pursuits."

Mrs. Anderson turned her head and kept it turned, looking out into the distance while Salt was talking. Mr. Anderson narrowed his eyes in a pained expression. "Is there some possibility these individuals have reason to lie? What does this have to do with our son? Oh, God." He leaned back as far as the bench would allow.

"Please bear with me," Salt said. "It's complicated, but I think you may find some ultimate comfort in what we found out. We do not believe Michael committed suicide."

Mrs. Anderson fumbled at the clasp on her handbag in her lap, her previously regal posture folding into a protective curve, her head coming to rest over her bag and soft middle. Mr. Anderson put one arm around her, then reached with his other hand to help her with opening the clasp. Though she made no sounds, her body shook and her hands trembled as she removed a packet of tissue. "Michael?" she asked.

"I believe he was murdered both because he resisted Prince and because he was trying to help some of the younger people who were Prince's targets."

"How? Who?" asked Mr. Anderson.

"One of Midas' other victims, a child at the time, twelve years old and under Prince's influence, gave Michael a dose of pure heroin that Prince and his associate knew would kill Michael. It's likely we can't prove a murder charge against Reverend Prince. The boy, at the time, was a victim himself and is one of the witnesses who will testify against Prince on child abuse charges. That boy, now a man, is also charged with child molestation. We probably can't rely on him as the sole witness to Michael's murder, even though we're certain about the manner of Michael's death. But we're accumulating a lot of evidence to charge Midas Prince with multiple counts of child molestation."

"This is horrible. This is a nightmare. How could you think—"

"Malachi. No." Mrs. Anderson cut her husband off. "No. It is not. My nightmare was not knowing the truth and wondering if he killed himself because he didn't think we, I, loved him." Mike's mother stood and walked a few yards away, her back turned toward them.

Salt waited, then walked to her. Mrs. Anderson was trying to straighten out a tissue that was shredding in pieces. "I'm so sorry, but I believed it was better for you to hear this from me, better to know than not."

"You're right. Even if we did send Michael to Rever—to Midas Prince. Maybe I can forgive myself for that, for sending him to the wrong person for help. Maybe in time I will be able to understand that we were victims, taken in by a wolf in sheep's clothing. Eventually I can get to that point, I hope. But not knowing—" She shook her bowed head. "You're right. That was hell, wondering if he didn't love us or if he didn't know he was loved."

Salt closed her eyes and waited, feeling the tide of grief. "There was another reason I wanted to meet you here. Please. Can you wait right here for a few minutes. I'll be right back." She led Mrs. Anderson back to her husband. "There's someone I want you to meet."

Salt hurried down a block and around the corner to the supportive living facility where Pearl was living. She was waiting in the lobby, also dressed in her Sunday all-white—shirt, jacket, a pair of white gloves—and wearing only one hat that Salt could see. "Wow, Pearl, you look terrific," Salt said.

"Yes, I do. Thank you for these." Pearl looked down at her outfit, then touched the brim of her white chiffon-layered hat.

"Are you sure you want to do this? Meet Mike's parents? I have to warn you they're having a hard time just now. I told them about Prince and the charges."

Pearl took Salt's arm and walked with her through the main door and out into the warm spring day. "My medications are workin' right now and I've always been good with people when the hallucinations are under control. It'll make me feel better."

They crossed Auburn Avenue and found the Andersons sitting together on the bench. Mr. Anderson stood as Salt and Pearl came down to meet them. Before Salt could begin the introductions, Pearl extended her gloved hand to Mr. Anderson, who responded on cue by grasping Pearl's hand. Then Pearl trapped his hand with her other hand. "How do you do? My name is Pearl. I have schizophrenia, and your son, Mike, was a good friend to me." She went from holding Mr. Anderson's hands to picking up Mrs. Anderson's hands and holding them, repeating word for word the same salutation.

"Pearl was close to Mike because of their love of the blues. Pearl is a singer," Salt explained.

Mrs. Anderson leaned back. "And you knew our son?"

Mr. Anderson bent slightly at the waist, head lowered, hands clasped at the end of straightened arms in a rigid posture.

Pearl was undeterred. She drew closer to the couple. "Mike tried to help me when nobody else cared. I was starting to get sick and Midas Prince had got me. But Mike, he wanted to hear me sing. He said I knew the old blues and that I had to teach him. He made me feel like I was special and that I had to save myself and the music, my music."

"You're a blues singer?" asked Mrs. Anderson, still with a tone of doubt.

"I can and do sing anything, gospel, some jazz, old blues, new blues, but I come out of Mississippi with hearin' them real ol' work songs and field hollers. Mike he knew some professor a' the university who was interested in that ol' stuff, the tunes my mama do."

"Did Michael say who the professor was? Dr. Clark White?" Mr. Anderson loosened his arms.

"That be the name Mike said." Pearl nodded. "Yep, I remembered 'cause my real last name is White."

"They call him Deacon Bluz," added Mrs. Anderson.

Mr. Anderson turned to his wife, brows lifted in surprise.

"He's on the college radio station," she said, as if she needed to justify her knowledge of Atlanta's "deacon of blues."

"Would you like some coffee? I live just around the corner. Salt"—Pearl reached and pulled Salt to her side—"has given me some CDs of Mike's, and on some you can hear me sing."

"Marissa?" Mr. Anderson looked at his wife.

"Now, there's crazy people live in my building, I'll warn you, most are like me and are stabilized, but some look awful," said Pearl.

"We've been misled for a long time by how somebody looked, by a man dressed like a king," Mrs. Anderson said. "Malachi. I'd like to hear our son on those CDs." She took her husband's arm.

"I'll catch up with you later, Pearl," Salt said. "Mr. Anderson,

Mrs. Anderson, you have my mobile number. Call me if you have questions."

Pearl turned up the path. "Mike had a voice like a angel . . ."

"He got that from my side . . ." Mrs. Anderson was saying as they walked out of range.

From the back of Pearl's white hat, just barely sticking out, was what looked like the brim of the Braves baseball cap. Salt could just make out a few of Pearl's words as the three reached Auburn.

"Wolf . . ." Pearl was saying.

WELCOME TO HOMICIDE
PART II

For Bring Your Pet to Work Day it was remarkably quiet in the Homicide office. Some animal-loving corporate tycoon had enough pull with city hall to demand the city's participation in bringing awareness to the bonds between people and their pets, and to encourage adoption from the local animal shelters. So the mayor ordered as many photo ops as possible throughout the city departments, no exceptions, including the PD. They especially wanted photos of the "hard-bitten" homicide detectives and their beloved pets. Rosie volunteered to keep order and had designated which interview rooms would be time-out for dogs in case they misbehaved or in the event of a callout on a fresh body. Majority ruled that only dogs would be allowed in Homicide—they'd let the robbery boys bring in their kitty cats.

Huff's wife had read about the program and had been relentless in insisting that their Foo Foo, a Shih Tzu–Pomeranian mix, accompany the sergeant for their special "father-daughter" day, as he quoted her calling it. Huff had locked himself in his office. The detectives had seen only a glimpse of pink-tinted fur under his arm when he arrived.

Homicide did seem to be a unit for dog lovers, Rosie being the only one of the team that didn't own a pet. "Too busy petting myself," she said, looking up from under improbably long lashes. Pansy and Violet were being perfect ladies, reclining in the aisle at Wills' desk. The Things both owned cats so were exempt from the festivities. Gardner's hound was too elderly. They were all surprised when Felton showed up with a pit bull rescue named Roscoe. "What? You expected a coiffed, bejeweled poodle?" Roscoe went about his business of charming everyone, presenting his belly and back to each of them for scratches and rubs—not taking no for an answer. He'd stare at his targets, tail wagging his hind end, until they gave in.

And while Wonder was his usual standoffish self, he impressed the crew with his attention to Salt's every move and command. He arrived at her side off-leash and stayed at her heels. Actually he just wanted her, was dogging her, to take him home to his sheep. He barely acknowledged Pansy and Violet when they enthusiastically greeted him. They slumped back to the floor depleted by his rejection.

The Public Affairs photographer had set up a backdrop and lighting in the conference room. It was like some Wegman shoot, props, lanyards with badges for the dogs, and little fedoras. Salt didn't mind them putting Wonder in her father's trench coat. They took a lot of photos of the two of them taking turns wearing the coat.

Wills stood watching from the door as the last shots were finished. "You two look amazing, intense," he said. "I hope they can capture that beautiful weirdness you and Wonder share."

"What?" Salt said, dropping the coat over her arm.

"I don't know how to describe it. It's like an otherworldliness," he said, shrugging as they walked back to her desk. "We're having a meeting, break room." He tapped his watch. "Five minutes."

As the detectives came in the break room and gathered around a fresh pot of coffee, Wonder and Wills' pooches finally fell into their usual play-and-lay, rolling around, jaws opening to gently chew on each other. Thing One and Thing Two, Wills, Gardner, and a few detectives from day shift, Hamm and her partner, took chairs around the room. Felton saluted Salt with a raised mug. Rosie stood leaning against the doorsill holding Huff's little silvery-pink lapdog.

"Take a seat, gentlemen and ladies," Huff said. "Thank you, Rosie."

"Oh, Charlie, don't you mention it." Rosie glowed and scratched the top of the little pooch with a sparkled fingernail.

"Since our office has been conscripted for the edification of the public as to our canine orientations—"

Yap, yip, yap! snapped the soprano in Rosie's grip.

Huff raised part of his upper lip, Elvis-like, sneering at his "daughter." "As I was saying, normally we'd hold this small ceremony in our glorious conference room, but here we are." He lifted his arms, indicating the break room. "Mr. Felton, the floor is yours."

Felton stood and retrieved a large, round, brown-paper-wrapped box from one of the cabinets. Crime scene tape had been used as ribbon and bow. "As some of us know, not everyone"—he lifted his eyes to Huff—"was enthusiastic when it was learned that a brand-new detective, Sarah Alt"—Felton inclined his head to Salt—"was being assigned to our esteemed and lofty ranks."

"Hear! Hear!" marked the chorus of men and Rosie.

"But here she is. Her first day with us she single-handedly tracked and took into custody a child murderer." He smiled. There was more applause, and Hamm put her fingers to her lips in a loud whistle. Salt backed up to the wall. Her face felt hot. Heat spreading down her neck, she lowered her head.

"DNA came back." Hamm stood, letting her statement hang for a moment. "Positive for The Baby, Jesus!" She pumped the air in a touchdown gesture.

More whistles and applause.

Felton carried on. "She has since, in little more than one month, contributed to solving one of the highest profile cases this city has seen. Detective Wills thanks you."

Wills nodded and bowed to her while the crew pounded the tables in applause.

"And at great risk and incurring serious bodily harm, she closed not only Detective Wills' case but also the murder of Dan Pyne"—he straightened his shoulders and cleared his throat—"by hastening the demise of one DeWare Lovelace." The dogs barked and the men hurrahed. Salt dug her fingers into Wonder's fur, averting her red-blotched face. "Information you gathered has led to a large-scale child abuse investigation. And, most important for our team, you cleared the first case you were assigned, the murder of Michael Anderson, making your clear-up rate one hundred percent so far.

"And now, Detective Wills, if you'll do the honors, we can quickly relieve the distaff member of our gang of her torture." Felton moved aside and Wills stood, beckoning Salt to his side in front of the room. "Come on. Don't act like we're trying to murder you." He pulled her to his side, then pointed to the box. "Open it."

Salt opened the lid. Inside was a hat, a beautiful fedora, the same color as her father's coat. Her coat. Wills took it from her hands. "You are now officially the murder police. You speak for the dead. You stand at the gates of heaven and hell and listen and bring justice to those unnaturally parted from this world—"

"All right, all right, blah, blah. People we've got work to do," said Huff. "Put the hat on her head."

"Bow your head, Detective," said Wills as he fitted the crown, then turned the brim just so. The crew once more shouted and clapped.

Salt bent over and took a quick peek at her reflection in the microwave door. She got just a glimpse of her silhouette with the hat. She touched the soft felt brim, moved up to the crown, where the creases seemed to fit her hand perfectly. She tipped the hat to the room. "Thank you, gentlemen. Thank you."

"Who's she talking to? 'Gentlemen.'" The Things stood to get coffee. Rosie came up and kissed her cheek, the little dog yapping at Huff. Wills and Felton patted her back. Gardner saluted her from the door.

Hamm took her by the arm and walked with her out of the room and down the aisle. "Well, girl, you made it." Hamm had on her usual comfortable shoes, her feet spilling from the tops, shoes for walking crime scenes. They came to Salt's desk, where Salt had two books open, Dan Pyne's green one and the old manila one, Mike Anderson's, faded and frayed, soon to be an official murder book. Another brown file was beginning to fatten, her copies of the reports to SVU, accumulating reports from victims of Midas Prince. "This is harder than people think," she confided to Hamm. "And I don't mean the physical part or danger."

"I been doin' this awhile. I know what you mean. But you can't let them—" She tipped her head toward the center of the office. "You can't let them see you cry."

"Maybe it won't always be that way, Hamm. By the way, can't I call you by your first name?"

"Nope," said Hamm, smiling. She sighed, sniffed, hugged Salt, and walked away.

Salt held the hat out, turning it around, feeling the ribbon-trimmed edge, the silk lining. Then she held it beside her coat, confirming the color as an exact match.

———————

"AND IN the category of 'no good deed going unpunished' . . ." Wills stood beside her desk.

"Uh-oh," said Salt, clearing Dan Pyne's autopsy report off the chair.

Wills sat down and leaned on his elbows. He had his jacket on. "I just had dinner with a buddy from Internal Affairs who thought you should hear this first."

Salt's heart raced, thinking of Lil D.

"They're opening a large-scale investigation of extra jobs, hours, and possible conflicts of interest. The chief is also asking that the rules and regulations regarding the off-hour jobs be tightened. And Sandy Madison has been busted out of SWAT. He's going around saying it's your fault about the EJs."

"Damn," Salt said. "I can't seem to keep out of one thing or another."

"Yeah, but Sarah," he whispered her name, "there's a lot of good people who've got your back." He looked around and, not seeing anyone, tapped the back of her hand. "Homicide got your back."

STRING LIGHTS
AND TRAIN WHISTLES

There was a new neon sign outside the Blue Room, "BLUES," and a new door replacing the corrugated tin contraption that had previously been there. Salt went to the front take-out window and told Sam that she wanted to go over the crime scene one more time. When Sam let her in and turned on the lights, the room lit up with multicolored stringed bulbs crisscrossing the ceiling and giving the room an old-fashioned county fair feel. "Like the changes?" he asked.

"I do," she answered, coming on in, turning around in the center of the room.

Sam went back to the kitchen between the take-out business and Blue Room. The overhead speakers popped and Bailey Brown's muddy voice picked up mid-tune.

Good Lord, good Lord, send me an angel down
Can't spare you no angel, but I'll swear I'll send you a
  teasin' brown.

Probably recorded more than ten or twenty years ago, his voice sounded even then like he'd swallowed a '57 Ford pickup truck. The room, music, and party lights created a dream-like feel. She listened closely for the licks of a rhythm guitar while standing on the approximate spot where Dan had been shot.

"I dig the hat," Man said coming in, going behind the counter like he owned the joint. He bent down and the music fell to a low volume.

Salt reached up with a now practiced move, lifted the fedora, and ran her fingers through her hair. "That was Bailey Brown doing Blind Willie's 'Talking to Myself.' Blind Willie McTell lived in Atlanta, you know."

"How you know so much about black folks' ol' music?" Man asked.

"My dad liked blues, gospel, and old jazz, the sixties and seventies. You know, blues is not just for black people anymore," she said, grinning.

He waved his hand at the lights overhead and at the new door. He pointed at the neon. "What do you think?"

"I like it, the door and the sign, lights. I hope that means there will still be blues here."

"Yep, I'm keepin' it ol' school."

"So you got at least one club, huh, Man?"

"Not just this place but I'm gonna be runnin' both the others, Toy Dolls, and someday, Magic Girls." Man came out from behind the bar, sat down on a barstool, and crossed his arms in a self-satisfied posture.

Salt turned the fedora in her hands.

"You kept your deal with Stone, Miss Dee Tec Tive. He got his time reduced. They gone transfer him to Jackson for treatment, and soon as he gets well they're going to let him out."

"You think you're going to be able to keep him out of trouble, out of harm's way?" Salt asked.

Man laughed and shook his head. "What's with you? You worried 'bout Stone, 'bout me? You best be concerned les' you cross paths with him again."

"He's likely to be more your problem than mine. He'll want to be back with you, Man. He'll be your next of kin and asshole sidekick. It's hard to go legit when you've got a full-time psychopath on your payroll. And you know he and Lil D aren't fond of each other at all."

Man looked off as if considering her words. His eyes came back to the room and Salt, then he raised his chin, nodding at her. "Lil D gonna go legit with me." There was little change in Man's expression, no different tone of voice, nothing that would give more import to this information than any other.

Walking to the new door, she wondered if it would or already had come full circle—her and Man, Lil D. Man came along behind her. She really did like the new little neon sign "BLUES" blinking off and on, on and off.

"I want to show you something," Man said. When they were outside, he pointed to the familiar rise a half mile or so to the north. "See that ridge? You know what that is, right?"

"You mean the railroad track?"

"Sure," Man answered, "but it ain't just any old track now."

She turned toward Man, top man of one of the tightest gangs to operate in an Atlanta ghetto, "Let me guess—the BeltLine?"

"Yes, Lord." Man walked toward the ridge on the horizon.

The BeltLine was a project that the city expected would do more for its economy than any other undertaking since the airport. The plan called for using existing rails that had in the past been used for both passenger and freight, that had once supplied industrial sites, some of which had been discovered to be toxic, and rails that had become defunct, currently in use but only infrequently for light industry. Routes had been designated to create an approximate thirty-three-mile transit and green space that would encircle the central city, spurring business and housing and linking neighborhoods.

"Yes, Lord," Man repeated. "My business sittin' right up against the BeltLine." He turned to her, spreading his arms, smiling. "'Legit,' that's what I say. 'Legit.'"

SALT DROVE the half mile and parked in a liquor store parking lot, as close as she could get to the tracks, then climbed a rutted path to the top. From the looks of the trail, weeds beaten back and freshly strewn trash, people had been trespassing on the railroad easement for decades or maybe even a century. She'd always known that gangs, as well as others, used the tracks as an escape way, a meeting place, somewhere to stash stolen goods. It was gang territory.

She keyed the mic on the Handie-Talkie. "Radio, hold me out on the tracks at Pryor and McDonough." She listened for responses, in particular from Wills, but only dispatch acknowledged, then the frequency was quiet.

From time to time she and Wills had taken the dogs on walks along parts of the BeltLine already reclaimed for recreational use. Tracks had been removed, walkways had been installed and paved, and muralists had enhanced bridges and tunnels. There had been BeltLine-sponsored events, footraces, bike tours, art celebrations, and parades. New parks were being dedicated. Developers were buying up properties along the proposed route, the feds offering a lot of money for development and toxic site cleanups.

There were other stretches like this one she was walking, right-of-ways that were still active and still owned by the railroads. But now the railroad tracks that had created, then divided, the city would provide a means by which its residents could travel easily from neighborhood to neighborhood without impediment. Tracks that had once

been barriers were going to unite communities—paths that had first
been cleared by slaves and convicts building the railroad that ended
at the place that would become Atlanta.

From the top of the ridge she turned and faced south in the direction of The Homes, the housing project she'd spent ten years policing.

Man and Lil D might make it out, might be able to move from the
ghetto and transition to the paths of legitimacy. She hoped so. But
then there was Stone.

THANKS TO:

My agent, Nat Sobel, and the folks at Sobel/Weber, who have supported this project. Big thanks to my editor, Sara Minnich Blackburn.

I also thank Carol Lee Lorenzo and the Callanwolde Fine Arts Center's fiction writers.

I am grateful to Bill Thomas, Deputy Chief Lou Arcangeli, Doug Monroe, Lorna Gentry, and Carol Beavers.

I am so very appreciative of the support of my family. Noah, Viki, Gabriel, and Sadira have been cheering at every turn. And to my husband, Rick Saylor, who is my music man, partner, and "joy-in-every-samich."